I0788131

BELVIDERE.

V

X

Sans Nom

Verso: Copyright & Particulars

Copyright © 2006 by Belvideredot, LLC

ISBN: 978-1-950804-28-3

Title: **Belvidere.**

Summary: *A mysterious man is sent to a dead-end town; to do what, and to whom, he simply doesn't know. It's all part of a game he neither understands, nor controls. He befriends those he will likely betray; there will certainly be trouble if he does not. A fantastical, mysterious journey; an ephemeral olla podrida of raw erotica, graphic violence, racism, heathenism, bigotry and vulgarity, all buoyed by the providence of friendship, love and kindred souls.*

1.   Fiction-General.   2. Fiction-Fantasy.
17 18 19 20 21   j i h g f e d c b a
First Edition - American

A Special Note To The Reader Who Is A Self-Appointed Observant Orthographer:

To this special group, the spelling and grammar police, please put your pencil down; I will save you the suspense.

This novel may be a grammar and sentence structure nightmare to people who obsess about such things. The pages that follow are vaguely, or not so, reminiscent of Beat literature, which can be described, by some, as a rejection of standard narrative and linguistic values, including, but not necessarily limited to, syntax, punctuation, sentence structure and morphology. The writing style is idiosyncratic; it is how the author thinks, and how the author believes this fictional account should be told. And just as important, it's how real people speak and communicate in the real world, which is rarely textbook or *correct*. It is real, or at least how this author perceives reality, which is all that matters between these end-papers.

In any event, there **will** be mistakes. And all the mistakes in this book were purposeful, and will be defended as such, even if they weren't. After two long years of editing, this writer simply got tired of re-reading and proofing. So what you see is what you get, whether it's *right* or not.

My suggestion is to take the broader view: simply enjoy the characters and enjoy the ride they take you on. Along the way, if you feel the need to get enraged, do so at the abject violence, the graphic sex, the racism, the bigotry, the coarse language, the heathenism....but for God's sake, don't get enraged at punctuation....leave the poor periods alone.

TABLE OF CONTENTS - V

Chapter	Title	Page
Chapter 160	As She Lightly Rubbed, The Conte Began	1447
Chapter 161	Inside Her Panties, Cupping Her Crotch	1451
Chapter 162	Landing, Waiting, But Not For Long	1462
Chapter 163	She Never Came, And He Didn't Seem To Care	1466
Chapter 164	He Dried His Balls With Earl's Towel	1469
Chapter 165	Walked Out, Turned Left And Disappeared	1472
Chapter 166	It Was Time To Catch A Cannonball	1481
Chapter 167	Slipping Out, So He Could Strip Down	1488
Chapter 168	Smooth, Like A Baby's Bottom	1496
Chapter 169	She'd Carry That Present Around For Awhile	1503
Chapter 170	For You, Mom?	1510
Chapter 171	Shake Her Head And Whisper Aloud. *Shit*	1522
Chapter 172	Hey, What Fucking Time Is Dinner?!	1534
Chapter 173	No One Could Possibly Know, But Earl Was Dying	1543
Chapter 174	Left Standing In The Street, All Alone	1554
Chapter 175	Finally, Face-To-Face, It Was The Puppet	1564
Chapter 176	….Death	1566
Chapter 177	Take A Taste Of Anything You Like	1572
Chapter 178	Lost In Thoughts Of Herring Feathers And Hand Holds	1580
Chapter 179	Can I Please Have Another Cookie?	1590
Chapter 180	*Sante*	1598
Chapter 181	Ground Into The Gravel, Face Down	1600
Chapter 182	A Rumpus And A Howl, So It Is. And So It Was	1605
Chapter 183	A Shiver Shot His Spine	1616
Chapter 184	A Scary Couch Rock, High Above The Foul Rift	1629
Chapter 185	She Quietly Swallowed And Earned Her Money	1634

Chapter 186	She Felt His Tongue And Tried Not To Flinch	1646
Chapter 187	Be Good Brother	1650
Chapter 188	Sack-Squeeze; Lip-Lick; Bull-Charge	1658
Chapter 189	In Reckless Script, A Single Word: *Help*	1664
Chapter 190	A Half-Finger Too Far	1669
Chapter 191	Slow And Lonely	1681
Chapter 192	*Bugs Bunny, Mother-Fucker....Bugs Bunny!*	1685
Chapter 193	The Old Woman Was Gone	1687
Chapter 194	I'm Pregnant	1692
Chapter 195	As She Cried, He Raped Her	1697
Chapter 196	What Note?	1704
Chapter 197	Both Sad....And Both So Very Happy	1713
Chapter 198	This Is So Not Good	1715
Chapter 199	Southside Down, Yelling *Holy Shit!*	1721
Chapter 200	Get Ready; Two And One Second And I'm Gone	1739
Chapter 201	She Flew Straight. *Shit*	1745
Chapter 202	Disgusted, Dumbfounded, Sandbagged	1754
Chapter 203	Knee-Deep In A Nose Kiss And Neck Rub	1757
Chapter 204	Head Down, He Just Kept Plugging Away	1764
Chapter 205	She Meandered In Fields Of Gold	1766
Chapter 206	He Would Have Been Up For A Nice Hog-Tie	1770
Chapter 207	Best Friends Do Treat Best Friends Like Shit...Sometimes	1773
Chapter 208	All Alone In A Sea Of Ugly Faces	1778
Chapter 209	Pleading Not To Be Made, Yet Again, The Fool	1781
Chapter 210	A Whore He *Definitely* Was	1792

CHAPTER 160 – AS SHE LIGHTLY RUBBED, THE CONTE BEGAN

"Where is it? Where are we going?! When are we going?!"

Lilly sat up, grabbed C's arm and squeezed it, excited about the next adventure; and this one was for real, the one she was *really* going to - no more excuses, no more delays.

"Again, whenever you want; we can book flights tomorrow, if you want, first thing."

"Okay, that'll be my job; I can't wait! Is it expensive?"

Lilly was like a little kid, Christmas Eve.

"Don't worry about it."

C said, matter-of-fact.

"Are you gonna break out the aluminum foil money; is it *that* expensive?"

"Maybe I'll go back in your underwear drawer."

"Are you still sticking money in there? I thought I looked; if anything's in there, it's mine!"

"Relax, I'm out of your underwear, for now anyway."

And C smiled at her, and she smiled back.

"How bad do you want to go in there, my *underwear....drawer?*"

Lilly teased.

"You know the answer to that."

C said deadpan.

"We'll see; tell me a *really* good story, and we'll see if I let you open that drawer."

Holy shit! That's what immediately popped into C's head; *holy shit* was all he could think. Did she just really say that? Did she just say that getting in her pants was elevated to the *we'll see* category?

He had been dreaming of that little pussy, and this moment, since he first saw her through Sam's front door, wearing Frank's smock; that seemed a lifetime ago. And now, he was so close; he wanted to pull back the blanket and rip her pants off right there, and he knew she wouldn't resist if he did it, right here and now. He knew she would just let him do it; he was sure of it.

But for some reason, he decided to wait; the anticipation felt too good. The fish was hooked, and he figured he'd let it run on the line for a bit, enjoy the feel of the catch, before he reeled her in. And, under the camouflage of the blanket, his cock began to get hard.

Lilly looked at him, his eyes glazed over....far away.

"Hey, did you hear me?"

C snapped out.

"Trust me, I heard you. A challenge? Okay, here it goes."

"Make it good, C, *real* good; you got a lot riding on this story - don't get distracted."

And with that, Lilly purposely took her hand, slid it under the blanket and pushed firm on her pussy, giving it a squeeze and a hard rub, closing her eyes in the process. She had to do it for her own sake, and seeing him watch her do it made it feel that much better. Man, she was wet, she could feel it.…*real* wet. She had been waiting for cock a long time, too long, and tonight, she was getting it; of that, she was certain.

"Are you fucking kidding me? Don't do that anymore, please?!"

C said, his cock now straining his shorts, distracting him; what was the story again?

"We'll then, you better start talking. And you can't stop, no matter what I do, above, or *below,* the blanket. Start telling me a *good* story, or I might get bored and have to go downstairs and take care of things myself; what a shame that would be.….for you."

And with that, Lilly slowly pulled the blanket to the side, exposing her clothed crotch. She put her hand back on her pussy, on the outside of her clothes, cupped her vagina, and slowly started to rub a line in the fabric below which laid her pussy lips. Up and down her finger traced the vertical line, over and over, slowly moving her hips in time, while she stared at him. She extended the very tip of her tongue and barely licked her upper lip as her hips continued to slowly piston. No doubt about it; she was getting cock, real cock, tonight; the long wait was over. She smiled at the thought of opening up and finally letting him in. C didn't know it, but she did; regardless of his story, the decision was made – she was finally going to let him do her. Now it was just a matter of how long she wanted to tease him, torture him. Her head was still light and fuzzy from the booze, but the overall feel could only be described as way better than good.

Even though she had barely begun, C already couldn't take the tease. He was ready to abandon the story, and began to lean toward her, to reach for her cunt, to push her hand out of the way and take over the pussy grind.

"Eh, eh, eh…."

She scolded, pushing his advancing hand to the side.

"Story first; *if* I like it, you can take over. Deal?"

C could feel the throb in his cock and made a desperate plea.

"Fuck, Lilly, come on….the story can wait."

She sat up a bit and kissed him on the neck, a long sensual kiss, her tongue lightly touching his skin.

"Come on, have some willpower; be a good boy and tell me a *good* story, and then I'll be a good girl, or a bad girl, whichever you want, for the rest of the night, *all night long*….promise. Okay?"

C looked as if he was in a trance; he couldn't take his eyes off her pussy.

"Okay."

He said, directly to her crotch. And, as she lightly rubbed, the conte began.

CHAPTER 161 – INSIDE HER PANTIES, CUPPING HER CROTCH

C cleared his throat and turned to Lilly.

"Okay, you ready to go?"

"You know, she really likes you."

"Who?"

"You know who."

"No I really don't, who?"

"Margery; she thinks you're kinda cute. She asked me if I was gonna date you?"

"Really?"

"Yeah, really."

"So, what'd you tell her?"

Lilly was still rubbing her pussy lightly, she closed her eyes as she talked.

"I told her you already had a girlfriend."

"You did! Who?"

"The wrinkly old lady, at Brookfield."

"Mae! You told her Mae was my girlfriend!?"

"Isn't she?"

"NO!"

"Well you fuck her an awful lot for being a non-girlfriend."

Lilly opened her eyes and looked at C with a mix of wonder and disgust. Then she followed herself.

"How do you fuck an old lady like that? That's gross; isn't she all wrinkly and gray and loose skin and stuff down there, and everywhere....yuck."

"She's not all wrinkly; she's in great shape for someone…."

C didn't finish the sentence. How the fuck did this conversation start and the trip to get into Lilly's pants sideways into *this*?

"For someone what? How old is she anyway?"

"I don't know."

That was Lie No. 1.

"Come on, you know."

Lilly said condescending.

"I think she's in her fifties, mid-fifties."

And there went Lie No. 2.

"*Liar!* I know she's sixty-six! ***Sixty-six!* Eww, that is beyond gross!** Your boyfriend Earl spilled those beans awhile ago, by the way. You're such a liar. Yuck."

Lilly gloated.

C just frowned.

"She's not my girlfriend."

"Really? If I asked her that, would that be *her* answer? Are you gonna tell her I was up at your apartment, drunk, under a blanket with you, while you kissed my neck, holding my hand, while I was kissing your neck, and licking my lips, rubbing my pussy and thrusting my hips in anticipation of fucking, while you watched, with a hard-on, ready to jump me if I gave the okay? My guess is a big fat no. That's boyfriend/girlfriend, my friend."

That's it, C had to end it with Mae, *he had to!* Lilly was spot on; he could keep saying *no they weren't dating*, but to Mae, it was a definite *yes, they were.* And he certainly kept going back to the till, even knowing she was in deep. It was never going to get better; it was a bomb waiting to blow.

"Well, that's ending anyway."

"Yeah right, that's only because you *think* you're finally getting in *here.*"

Lilly said sarcastic, as she kept working her pussy in front of C. Her hand was now buried in her pants, under her panties, her fingers wet from her juiced pussy, as she slowly thrust her hips off the floor, toward C.

C didn't answer.

"Do you want to get in? It's awful wet down there; shame to see all that lubrication go to waste."

Lilly rubbed her finger harder, letting it slide in-between her lips. C could hear it; that's how wet she was. Jesus, she could have come right then, just a bit more friction, and she would have been over the top.

C grabbed his cock and squeezed it; it was rock hard. He turned toward her, with a ready-to-mount look in his eyes. She saw the tempest, and tamped him down.

"Eh, eh, eh, not yet; you still have a story to tell me."

"Well stop interrupting me!"

Lilly retracted the arch and removed her hand from her pants, to let the throb subside; she didn't want to come, not yet. She held up her slender middle finger, the entire length glistening, a show and tell for C, before she slid it slow and sexy in her mouth, to clean it off, sucking it, working it with her tongue, like it was a cock. *His* cock. C didn't know what to do, but he had to do something, fast.

Lilly spoke soft.

"Relax, I didn't tell her about your wrinkly old girlfriend; I said you were fucking the fat one, with the spindly legs."

"Mrs. Ackerman?! Are you fucking kidding me? Why did you say that?"

"To make you sound pathetic, since you *are!* Fucking that old lady, it's gross."

"Lilly, please, tell me your lying; please tell me you didn't tell her that; that's disgusting."

"Tell me about it! That's what I've been saying all along!"

"I mean Mrs. Ackerman."

"The other one too! Trust me, *everyone* thinks it's gross."

"Everyone? Who's everyone?"

"Everyone I tell about it."

"Who's everyone? Jesus, stop talking about it, to *anyone*!"

"Why don't you just stop doing it?"

"Why don't you give me a reason to stop? If she ever found out I slept with you, she'd never speak to me again."

"Really?"

Lilly liked that.

"Yeah, really; she asks me all the time, convinced I'm already sleeping with you.   She's threatened by you….crazy jealous."

"Cool."

"It's *not* cool; it's a pain in the ass. I get shit for fucking you, and I'm not even doing it. Same for Carol, and for Selena."

Shit! C said to himself; *shit, shit, shit!*

"Who's Selena?"

C just looked at her, his mouth agape. He had no quick answer; he had no answer at all.   Shit; fucking alcohol….he's gotta stop rambling!

"The black girl!   Hah, now I know her name! *Selena….Selena;* beautiful, the house of cards will soon fall my friend!   Selena, what kind of stupid name is that? She must be an immigrant; is she from Belize?"

C didn't validate the taunt with a response. He was still fuming that he let the name slip to begin with.   He switched the subject, to steer clear of Selena.

"And more than any of you, *way more*, she's threatened by Margery….crazy."

Lilly's mood changed like lightning, clearly annoyed by that last tidbit. *That* bit was a problem.

"*Margery?* Why would she care about Margery more than me? Are you kidding me? Clearly between Margery and me it's not even a contest; she's not even close to being in my league. So what's so special about her?"

The more Lilly thought about it, the more annoyed she became. Please, Margery more than her? What kind of joke was that?

"I don't know, but she was vicious about it, saying I better never sleep with Margery, more than anybody else. She said they had some business deal gone bad in the past. But man, she's fucking wired about Margie, I don't really get it, but who knows, I stopped trying to figure this stuff out....none of it makes sense."

Lilly was beside herself; she didn't take these kind of challenges lightly.

"*Margie?* Now you're calling her Margie? When did that start?"

Lilly barked, annoyed. The mood in the room was starting to frost, quick. C was fumbling, even though he had no reason to.

"When? About thirty seconds ago; I'm drunk, I never called her that before *[forgetting he first called her Margie in front of Lilly in the gym, three days ago]*. I'm not sure why I just said it now....I'm drunk, I guess."

At first, Lilly seemed to buy the explanation; she was drunk too and apparently also forgot the *Margie* slip by C in the gym as well. But as C stared at Lillian, he saw the wheels slowly turning in that drunk little brain of hers, and he knew he was in trouble.

And just like that, Lilly snapped.

"Maybe you should be sitting under a blanket with *her*, telling her stories to get in her pants! Do you want to fuck her? Huh? *More than me?* Is that what this is about? Is that why she is so crazy about *Margie*, because she knows you want to tag her, **bad**?

"No!"

C exclaimed, seeing the path to Lilly's pussy slowly slip away.

"Well, forget about the old lady; I'm telling you, point blank, you **better** not sleep with Margery, or *Margie! Ever!* Or you'll *never*, ever see any of this, I promise you that!"

Lilly grabbed her crotch, and said it again, for emphasis.

"That's for *sure....****never!***"

C's head was spinning; he didn't know if he should duck left or right, punches were fling in all directions.

"Now why the hell do *you* care about Margery; because Mae does? What's so special about Margery? I'm not interested in her; plus, she has a fiancé, doesn't she?"

C tried to act calm, dismissive. But Lilly wasn't buying it.

"I couldn't give a shit about that old hag, or what she thinks, but I work with Margie, for her, *with* her. She might think she's the boss at work, but we aren't even in the same league, on the same fucking planet, in any other way, especially in looks and guys. I don't compete with, or share with, Margery....*understand*? She's JV, junior varsity; strictly JV....bush league."

"Jesus, yeah, I understand, Margery is so off-limits, she's...."

C couldn't think of anything witty to end the sentence.

"….just off."

Lilly just looked at him and then spoke.

"Listen, if anything happens between you and me, and that's still a big *IF*, then there's no more Grandma – you're cut off, and no black girl – immigrant *Selena* from Belize, no *Margie [Lilly shook her head in disgust that someone thought they were actually in the same league as her]* and no, you know who; God help you C if you *ever* did that, with *her*."

Lilly wouldn't even say Carol's name.

"Okay, what about you?   *IF* anything happens, what about Button, what about him?   Are you gonna tell him to take a hike too?"

Lilly just looked at him, and didn't answer at first.

"Are you kidding me? You have to think about it? You tell me no *anybody*, you rattle off a whole *no-fly-list* of women I'm actually **not** sleeping with, by the way, except Mae, but the same rule doesn't apply to you, and one guy?"

"He's not coming back."

"*That's* your fucking answer? Nice, real nice. And what if he does? Then what?"

"Listen, I told you the rules; if you can't live with it, then maybe I'll just go back downstairs, to bed, and finish things on my own."

C huffed, exasperated.

"I *heard* the rules, and I didn't say I wouldn't live with them, I will. I already told you I'm not fucking anybody but Mae, and I'll stop fucking her; I told you I would. But it was *you* we were talking about; do the rules apply to you, or just me?"

Lilly looked at C hard, then looked away, at the gray wall, and sighed.

"*If* something happens with us, and if he ever comes back, then I guess I should stop....with him."

"Wow! Really?! That sounded *so* convincing."

Lilly just shrugged her shoulders; that was as good an answer as he was going to get, and his dick deflated.

"I don't get it Lilly, I really don't. This guy leaves, just leaves, for three fucking years! No word, no nothing, right? You haven't heard from him, have you? Not a word?"

Lilly just stared at the wall, silent.

"I thought so; no word, for three fucking years! And it's not the first time he's run away I'm told, like the little fucking girl he is. And he hates Earl, and Earl doesn't like him. And you're *still* stuck on him? Talk about pathetic."

Lilly turned away from C, and gave him a very cold shoulder. And just that quick, whatever chemistry built over the last few hours was just about snuffed, crushed by that asshole, yet again. This Button prick wasn't even around, and he constantly got in the way. If he ever *did* come back....Christ.

C saw the opportunity, the night, quickly slipping away; it might already be lost; with Lilly, moods changed like the flip of a switch. So he dove into salvage mode, lowering his voice to a whisper, and gently putting his hand on her shoulder, to turn her back toward him. She resisted, but after a prolonged tug, she relented, and turned to face him, but her eyes were still down, scanning the floor.

"What's so great Lilly; what's so great?"

She didn't say anything at first, still looking into the blanket.

"*Howdy Darlin.*"

She said, deadpan.

"What?"

"Whenever he said that, it meant he wanted sex; no foreplay, just rough, down and dirty, no holds barred fucking, and he would say it in the most sexy Texas drawl. I don't know where he learned it; he's from White Township, fucking Jersey for Christ's sake. He must have picked it up from his buddies in the Service. But whenever he said that, my heart would melt; don't know why, just did. If I could figure that out, I could figure out what's so great, because it really isn't, or wasn't, most of the time."

"*Howdy Darling*; that's all I gotta say?"

"That's all *he* had to say."

"*Howdy Darling.*"

C said, in a ridiculous comical drawl; any true Texan would cringe.

Lilly recoiled.

"Yikes, that's certainly not it; that will make me *shut* my legs. Listen, it's *Howdy Darlin.*"

Lilly gave him a sweet Texas debutante drawl.

"Howdy Darlin."

C's second attempt was a little better, but a Texan, he wasn't.

She smiled, more at him than with him, but at least it was a smile. And he began the slow, Sisyphean climb back up the hill.

"Better, but I wouldn't be betting money on *that* getting into my pants; needs a bit more work."

"I'm willing to keep trying."

C said as he leaned into her, kissing her neck again.

"I'm willing to keep listening."

She said, and her hand resumed its position, slowing sliding back inside her panties, cupping her crotch.

CHAPTER 162 – LANDING, WAITING, BUT NOT FOR LONG

C was kissing her neck, and Lilly was rubbing her pussy, sliding her middle finger in deep, then pulling it slowly out, rubbing the length of her lips, before again diving in deep, buried to the third knuckle.

Then it hit him, like it usually did; a delayed reaction to the accumulation of booze. From nowhere, his eyelids felt like lead, and he immediately got dead-tired. Oh shit, he said to himself, and tried to indiscreetly shake his head, to clear the cobwebs; not now, for Christ sake, don't fade now.

Lilly was rubbing her pussy with purpose, and lowly moaning. She had long since unbuttoned and partially unzipped her pants, to afford better access to her panties. C could easily hear when her finger slid in deep and moved in a slow circle; she was that wet.

Lilly could have come multiple times by now, but she was purposely holding out, it always felt better, that first one, when she prolonged it as long as possible. So she would rub her clit, stop right at the door, let the tingle pass, and begin the cycle again. She had the routine down; years of practice.

C couldn't wait any longer.

He reached over and put his hand on her belly, and slipped it under her shirt, touching, for the first time, her belly. It was muscular, but relaxed, the skin smooth, and warm. He started to run his fingers south, alongside her hand, to take over. He got to the unhooked button and the top of the zipper, barely touching the top of her panties, when she gently grabbed his wrist.

"Stop."

And before he could protest, she added.

"I gotta go downstairs for a minute. You keep practicing your *Howdy Darlin*; I'll be back up, just give me a minute."

Now C didn't know what that minute was for, but he assumed it was birth-control related. He certainly didn't have any rubbers; he didn't need them – snipped and fixed years ago."

"Lilly, I'm fixed; my dick's snipped - years ago....promise."

She just kissed him on the neck....a long, slow kiss.

"That doesn't sound fun. Relax, it's not about that. I'll be back in a minute, promise, sit tight, have another drink....keep practicing."

"Howdy Darlin...."

"Better, you're getting better."

She said, smiling as she attempted to stand. And like someone drunk, who is fine and safe sitting still on the bar stool, once she went upright, her legs failed her, and she stumbled and crashed into the wall, face first, and slid down into a comic heap on the carpet.

"Ouch."

Was all she said, laughing uncontrollably at herself.

"Here."

C stood up, held out his hand, and quickly righted her, his hands on her hips, steadying her like a kid – her first time on a two-wheeler. She was just as shaky.

"You want me to walk you down? What do you need? I'll go get it."

“You can’t help me with this, trust me.”

He looked at her, puzzled.

“Jesus, I have to go the bathroom okay, *bad*, and I don’t wanna go up here, if you know what I mean. Stop asking me about it; it's embarrassing. I don’t go that often, and all the alcohol must have helped loosen me up. I'll be back, just give me a bit, trust me. God, I must be drunk; I can’t believe I’m having *this* discussion with you.”

“Okay, okay; do you want me to at least walk you to the door? Make sure you don't fall down the stairs, drown in the toilet?”

“No, I’ll get it; I’m okay now, and potty-trained years ago. All's good.”

She giggled, as she walked down the hall, hands planted firm on the wall for support.

“You’re gonna fall down the fucking steps, Lilly.”

“No I won’t; *don’t help me!*”

She barked, as she straggled to the door, him in tow, with her waving her hand behind her, keeping him at bay. She opened the door, grabbed the handrail hard, and made her way, slowly, in the darkened hall, to the second floor landing, about twenty steps south.

She got to the door, grabbed the handle, and the door swung open. She looked up at him, waved, smiled and said.

“Keep practicing.…*Howdy Darlin;* I’ll be back. Who knows what's in store if you can just get *just right.*”

And she giggled to herself as the second floor apartment door clicked shut; he stood on the third floor landing, waiting, but not for long.

CHAPTER 163 – SHE NEVER CAME, AND HE DIDN'T SEEM TO CARE

He couldn't wait any longer.

After tapping lightly on the door, he slowly turned the handle and peaked into the hall. The table lamp was on in the front room, and Earl was still scrunched in a heap on the floor, in a drunken stupor; he hadn't moved an inch.

Just then, he heard the toilet flush, and the water running in the sink; and he smiled. His cock was rock hard; he had waited *way* too long for this day, and was done waiting.

He snuck-up to the bathroom door, which was slightly ajar, letting a wedge of amber light escape. He pushed it gently open, and saw her standing, hunched over the sink, holding on to steady herself; even in the state she was in, she was beautiful. She saw the door swing out of the corner of her eye, looked to the left and gasped, startled at the company. She went to stand up, got dizzy, and nearly fell back into the shower.

He just smiled, winked sly at her, and drizzled:

"Howdy Darlin."

And it was the best Texas drawl she'd ever heard; it was next-to-perfect. She smiled, her eyes lit, and her whole body tingled in drunken anticipation.

The words had the intended effect.

She leaned forward, and fell into his arms, as if to acknowledge the long wait was finally over. He squeezed her tight and hugged her long, and hard. Then he scooped her off her feet, into his arms, and walked her down the hall, like a bride, her head resting quietly on his neck and shoulder, a custom fit. He nudged her bedroom door open with his right foot, quietly, so as not to wake Earl, and placed her gently on the bed. He turned and shut the door, just as quiet, turning the handle, so the lock engaged in the lightest of clicks.

She laid on the bed, in a half daze, unsure if this was really happening; she was sure it must be a dream. She kept blinking her eyes, and he was still there, standing in front of her, methodically taking off his clothes. She couldn't take her eyes off his body, off him, off his swollen cock. My God, she couldn't believe she was really seeing that cock; no more dreams, no more fantasies.

And then, standing naked in front of Lilly, he leaned forward, and proceeded to rip off hers, like an animal, all of them, her blouse was torn to shreds, as were her panties. And she just stood there, eyes closed, head leaning back, and let him ravage her.

Neither said a word, not one.

He pushed her on the bed, doggie-style, and in one thrust, shoved his cock deep into her pussy, right to his balls; no warning, no nothing.

"*Damn,* you are fucking wet, girl! Sopping; fucking great!

Was all he said as he pounded her hard; she didn't respond, other than a low steady moan. Neither said another word for hours.

They just fucked, non-stop.

And he fucked her hard, vicious and wild, slamming her over and over, doggie, legs on his shoulders, t-square, her belly flat on the bed, stag, thunderbolt, side-by-side, and a half dozen other positions, gyrations all night long, pumping in her pussy, in her mouth, and in her ass; the best was in her ass.

And the more he fucked, the more he wanted; he couldn't get enough….it felt too good. They'd bang, he'd come, they'd sleep, only to wake twenty minutes later and bang again. He came in her cunt first, then later in her mouth, and finally, in her ass.

That was always the order he liked.

She tried her best to be quiet, knowing she was drunk and trying nonetheless to be in control, to dampen his slamming and creaking of the bed, to be discrete, to not wake Earl, but her head was still spinning, and she wasn't sure what was really happening, and what she was thinking might be happening; it was all blurred by the alcohol….too much alcohol. She wondered if she'd even remember thinking such things, as he pounded away, like she was a rag doll.

It all felt like a dream.

She remembered his cock feeling so good, so right, like it belonged, like it always did, like her pussy was made just for his cock. She didn't want him to take it out, ever; three years without cock was too long, way too long; it would never be three years again, she promised herself. She remembered moaning and sighing with each stroke; it felt like she moaned all night long.

But despite it all, all that fucking, she never came, and he didn't seem to care.

CHAPTER 164 – HE DRIED HIS BALLS WITH EARL'S TOWEL

Early Friday morning; July 14th; day eighty-six - opening day of the *Blobfest*.

Earl rolled over, his head still full of webs. He was awakened by something; what, he wasn't sure. He raised his head a bit, his neck ached from the crick in it, and strained to listen. And that's when he heard the familiar noise, and he cracked a wide grin.

He picked himself off the floor and tiptoed down the hall. It was till dark out, but the sky had the beginnings of a wash of light; painting the hall a blush of rose. As he got closer to Lilly's room, the moans got louder, and it sounded like her head was hitting the headboard. He giggled to himself, picturing C on top of her, knocking her into the headboard, like a cartoon character.

The door was shut; he put his ear to the wood and listened, but couldn't hear anything but the squeak of the bed, and Lilly gasping and sighing. Every now and then he heard Cord grunt, and he snickered some more. *Man, C was working hard!* Earl thought to himself; he won't be up for a run after work today, for sure….too pooped. He snuck back to the front room, laid on the floor and pretended to be asleep, waiting, like a dog, for the door to open. He was so excited; he had waited for this day, it seemed, like forever. Now, maybe C would move in; maybe Lilly and C would get married, and Earl could be his real, *for real*, brother.

Earl rubbed his hands together in fast circles and ran his tongue back and forth along his lips in a herky-jerk way, like he did whenever he was too happy, and too excited. He couldn't wash the smile off his face; he was beaming, laying on the floor and looking up at the ceiling, thinking about Lilly and Cord, Lilly and Cord….Lilly and Cord.

It seemed like the moaning and creaking went on forever; after ten more minutes of it, he was getting bored. At some point, he fell back asleep; he wasn't sure for how long, but when he cracked his eyes again, it was light out and he knew one thing, C was gonna be late for work, for sure!

He sat up and listened again, and realized the moaning stopped. The bedroom door was slightly ajar, and he heard the shower running. He leapt up and ran down the hall, pushed open the bedroom door and saw Lilly fast asleep, laying on her belly, under a tangle of blankets, like a whirlwind blew through.

C was in the shower.

Earl galloped around the hallway corner and was upon the bathroom door in four giant steps. He was still giggling to himself, thinking about Lilly's head hitting the headboard, when he cracked open the door and saw Cord standing in the shower, behind the plastic curtain. His big meaty paw grabbed the end of the plastic and gave it a pull, while he exclaimed.

"Come on, you're gonna be late for work, and I heard...."

And Earl stopped, mid-sentence....dead in his tracks.

"Get the fuck out of the bathroom, you stupid fucking nigger! What are you, a fucking queer? Wanna join me? Suck my dick?"

Earl was too stunned to move; he barely heard the words. Button stood there, staring intensely at Earl; neither one moved, it seemed like forever. And then, just like that, Button's face morphed and he started to laugh at Earl, as he shut the faucet and grabbed the big green towel, hanging over the shower rod.

"What's that you heard, retard? You hear me banging your big sister's head into the headboard? Or did you hear her moaning, with my cock in her wet cunt."

"Shut up! *Shut up!* **Shut up!**"

Earl closed his eyes, put his hands over his ears, turned and ran down the hall, out of the apartment, and up the stairs, to find C.

And Button laughed, as he dried his balls with Earl's towel.

CHAPTER 165 – WALKED OUT, TURNED LEFT AND DISAPPEARED

Friday morning, July 14th, the first day of the *Blobfest*.

Sam's opened just fifteen minutes earlier, and the store was still empty, except for a lone, tired-looking middle-aged woman, overweight and dressed in baggy, wrinkled clothing, who had just made her way to the deli counter, and was perusing the meats behind the glass.

C never saw her before, new customer, and other than a quick hello and offer to assist, he left her alone to roam, like he normally did, while he redistributed fruits that had been mixed in some of the baskets the previous day. His head was still fogged, and he felt off. The front door opened, and C caught a peripheral glimpse of Earl heading smack at him, at a quicker pace than normal.

"Dude, I *so* overslept; I don't even remember what happened last night. Where's your sister? She fucking baled on me; I was so close dude, she was up at my place, after you passed out, then she left to go the bathroom, and the next thing I know, it's morning and I'm *so* late for fucking work – didn't even shower. Had the weirdest fucking dream; creepy. So what the hell….."

C didn't finish the sentence, he just stared at Earl, who was positively pale.

"What? What's the matter? What happened? Is Lilly okay? She never fucking came back upstairs, and I must have passed out; did she fall down the steps or something? **Is she hurt**? **What**?"

And Earl's eyes teared up. C's heart dropped; something bad happened to Lilly.

He threw down the basket of fruit and made a beeline for the front door. He was just passing through the checkout lane, when the tinny bell rang, and C found himself face to face with a taller, angular man, who was not in any particular hurry, wearing old cowboy boots, snug, worn jeans, and a tight black tee-shirt, which creased along the hard lines in his muscular chest and torso.

A thoroughbred.

Earl gasped, and C knew *exactly* who he was looking at, finally, face to face. And now he knew why Lilly never came back last night, and he felt his face flush with blood, heat, anger, and shame.

"Whoa, slow down cowboy; I think I know where you're heading, but the little darling's asleep, plumb worn out."

Button brushed past C and took a good gander about the place. He yelled toward the deli counter, but didn't see anyone.

"Sambo! What the hell you do to this place! Looks like a bunch of fucking queers got at it!"

Frank, who had been bent over and out of sight, stood erect and laughed aloud, a real bark, the first out-loud guttural laugh he let out, he dared to let out, in months. He felt the slave-chains fall away, a free man at last.

"Frankie! How you doing buddy?! Man, it's good to see you, good to see the *whole* family. Your little niece is looking fine, *mighty fine*, as always."

Frank threw down his knife and scurried around the counter, the biggest shit-eating grin on his face you could imagine, a man happy to finally see reinforcements crest the hill. He stuck out his hand toward Button, but Button walked right through it and gave the sloppy drunk a big bear hug.

"They treating you okay Frankie? What's up with this fucking place?"

Frank couldn't wipe the smile from his face; he pulled away from Button and nodded in mock toward C, and then they both laughed at Cord.

C's heart was racing; his mind was fucking screaming….he didn't know what to do. Less than thirty seconds ago, he was breakneck to save Lilly. He was completely unprepared for this, completely; he couldn't focus….for what seemed forever, he stood frozen, a deer in headlights.

Button broke the trance; he took an aggressive, alpha step toward C, purposely kicking a piece of fruit that Cord had just dropped across the aisle. He grabbed whatever he could from the closest basket - a handful of outsized muscadine grapes; he held the mass to his mouth, bit off a few of the closest grapes and chewed the purple quid with his mouth open, gnawing the leathery skin and smiling at Cord like a mother-fucker. He spit the skins on the floor. A couple loose grapes fell off the vine in his hand, and rolled around the aisle.

That's all it took.

The blackness began its creep, as it always did in situations such as this. A black crescent ring formed on the periphery of his field of vision; it quickly grew and morphed, blotting from the outside in, a collapsing tunnel of light, on its way to a pin dot in front of his eyes, and then, after that, when it extinguished, and all vision was gone, his body would gorge on a cocktail of adrenaline and hate. The eclipse usually happened quick, twenty seconds or so, and then whatever was going to happen, would happen, and C really didn't have much control over it. In fact, Cord would rarely, if ever, remember anything that happened after the lights went out. For the person at the other end of the pin-dot, the outcome was never safe, and rarely good.

Button was in for a surprise, the likes he had surely never experienced before. The showdown C had dreaded, had arrived, and it had quickly become dangerous in Sam's Market.

And after the damage was done, and Cord *returned* from where he strayed, exits frequently occurred, without Jenny, on the run. These were the exceptions C tried to avoid; you never really wanted a Jenny-pass – that came with its own set of problems down the road. But it looked like there would be no avoiding this one; this black-creep was coming on strong, and would soon engulf him. There wasn't much time.

One thing was certain; C was pretty sure-as-shit his stint in Belvidere was over, as of right about now. C took in a last deep breath, as his ken quickly faded; he could feel the blood pulse in his forehead, his cheeks, his ears. He remembered clenching his fists.

This was gonna be a real bad one; it had that feel.

Suddenly, the tinny bell rang again, as the front door slammed open, and Lilly bolted in, breathless, wearing baggy sweatpants sans panties that were half-falling off and a plain white oversized tee-shirt she grabbed from the dresser top running out the door. They were Button's sweats, and it was his tee-shirt. She was barefoot, and it was clear to everyone who happened to look, that she wore no bra.

"*Stop!*"

She yelled, at no one in particular.

And for some odd reason, the likes of which C had never seen, his blackness began to recede; that had *never* happened before – **ever.** Once the black came, it was a one-way street, with no take-backs, no turns. But this time, somehow, it receded, as if on auto, like the slow disappear of a shadow, till it was simply gone. And the immediate danger that loomed, departed in tandem.

Strange. But then again, maybe not-so.

And Cord, to his chagrin, took his eyes off Button, and tracked the whirlwind that just came through the door. He took in an unfortunate full frontal of Lilly; the bare feet, the tee-shirt she wore, which he knew wasn't hers, and the lack of bra, and the assumed absence of panties under the hastily thrown-on *his-sized* sweatpants. The loosely tied sweats were slipping off her hips, revealing that smooth, golden, forbidden spread of skin below her navel and above her crotch; he couldn't tell in the awkward instant his eyes focused below the belt, but he was sure the top strands of brownish pubic hair were showing above the drawstring knot.

He was sure, moments earlier, she was naked, laying in her bed, the bed Button had just gotten out of. And C was right, on all counts.

His stomach, suddenly ill at the thought, dropped into his shoes. He slowly half-shook his head, exposing the utter disgust at having to witness her, standing in front of him, showing off the evidence of carnal acts that occurred last night, into this morning, until just moments ago. Part of it simply didn't seem real; part of him was waiting to wake up from a very bad dream.

And, to his dismay, his eyes involuntarily cast upward, and met hers, just for an instant, but it was enough for her to see the disgust, the loathing, in his face; you could cut it.

But what was worse, much worse, than the outfit she wore, *his* outfit, were her eyes. He didn't see *anything* in her eyes, no regret, no sorrow, no apology; no recognition of anything special about him….he might just as well been a store display. They felt like stranger's eyes, like they had never met before, and he felt like a fool.

Her eyes quickly left his and took in the rest of the scene, hoping she wasn't too late, hoping that Button hadn't hurt Earl. She gave Cord no credit for being able to protect Earl. If Button wanted to hurt either one of them, he would; that is what she thought. C was simply no match for Button; Lillian was convinced of that.

"What the hell's going on?!"

Sam roared, as he came out through the back room door, to see the back of Button in the aisle, still staring at Cord.

"Button?"

Button didn't even give Sam the courtesy of turning around.

"Hey Sambo, what's doing?"

Sam didn't answer.

"What the fuck did you do to this place? It's like a fucking freak show."

Sam walked from behind the counter, toward Button.

"Button, not here."

"Shut up, fat man; you're out of your league, trust me."

Button kept his feet planted, and slowly turned at the waist to glare at Sam as he raised him hand in a stop sign. And even though Sam was more than twice his size, he stopped, just as Button ordered him to do.

"Just stand back; I have some *issues* to settle up with your employee here. He's been running his mouth, and….trespassing….where *no one* is allowed to trespass, and I don't like it….I don't like it at all. And something needs to be done about it, Sambo, so that's what I'm here to do."

"Frank, call Marty….*now!*"

Sam barked, to which Button mocked a laugh.

"Marty? Is that fucking Barnie still playing sheriff? My God, some things never change. Frank, you just stay where you are, don't move; no one's calling anyone."

Frank didn't even give the matter a second thought; he ignored Sam, and he obeyed Button.

Earl put his head down and looked at his shoes, in a submissive pose, as he backed up against the shelves of fruit. Button looked at Earl and laughed aloud, as he shook his head, as one does when he knows he owns a scene.

"Same old cast of characters, same old. Except for one *very lost* newbie; but nothing changes in Belvidere, my little friend….nothing."

C took an ominous step toward Button, and Lilly saw the move. She quickly ran past Cord and stood in front of Button, her back to C, and quickly whispered to him, which made him chuckle.

"Really? Again? Sweet; okay, okay."

And he slapped her hard on the ass, then gave it a good squeeze, one that says I *own* it, and will be taking it again, in a few minutes.

"Saved by a girl, who's begging for more."

Button said, as he shouldered by Cord, just missing body contact. Lilly was in tow, hanging on Button's arm, and didn't make eye contact with C, looking down and away.

C just stood there, emasculated, de-balled. In less than five minutes, way less, C handed Button the keys to the store; all the work he did, the ownership he felt, melted away, gone. Button owned the place, the people in it, the Town....and him.

Billy Bones pulled open the market door, forcefully, and didn't bother to turn back toward Cord as he lectured him, for all to hear.

"I live by one rule, there are none. Got to go tag some more of that *thang*, but we're not done, jerk-off, not by a long shot."

Lilly pushed him out the door, and he laughed at her, cinched his arm tight around her tiny waist, and tugged her into him, as the two walked away together, back to her apartment, to fuck again. When it was clear the confrontation passed, and Button made his way up the apartment staircase, casually unbuttoning his pants on the way, to save time, she quickly slid away, swung back in and cracked Sam's front door half-way, yelling as the door swung open and the bell jingled hollow.

"Cord."

She didn't even call him C, she called him Cord, and her tone was that of calling someone who dropped something in the street; a complete stranger would get a warmer greeting. It was as if she had simply written him off.

He was simply, once again, a no-name grocery boy.

Ay was in the process of picking up the loose muscadines he dropped; he didn't touch the skins Button spat on the floor, and didn't turn or even acknowledge her voice. He continued crouching, staring at the floor, pretending to be busy; in another moment, he heard the door swing quietly shut, the same stupid bell marking the act. He waited a second more, looked up and saw nothing but an empty sidewalk in front of the store. And just like that, the confrontation was over, and his defeat was utterly complete.

Sam started to talk to Cord, but C put his hand up to stop him, and Sam went quiet, and redirected his glare to Frank, who clearly disobeyed.

"Go home Frank, *now*; just go home."

The bellow was ominous, uncharacteristic of Sam, and Frank wasn't sure if it meant he was to *ever* to come back. The words echoed in Frank's ears, as Sam lowered his head and slipped back into the obscurity of the back room. The drunk looked around, unsure what to do; was he fired? He got nervous; no job means no booze money. So Frank quietly crept back behind the counter, picked up his knife and continued to trim the meat he was displaying in the deli case, trying to be as quiet as possible, hoping Sam would forget what he just said.

C just stared through the plate glass, at the sunlit street, blew out a force of air from his nose and didn't say a word.

Earl whispered to C, head down.

"I guess were not going to the *Blobfest,* are we?"

C just looked at Earl, frowned, and didn't answer. And with that, C quietly walked out, turned left, and disappeared.

CHAPTER 166 – IT WAS TIME TO CATCH A CANNONBALL

C wandered aimless.

It was nothing more than a slow shuffle, starting and stopping for no particular reason, as he made his way east on Water Street, away from Sam's, walking with his hands in his pockets, then out, then back in; neither position felt right.

As he walked away, he couldn't escape the thought that right then, *right now*, as he scuffled around like a mope, Lilly was getting fucked yet again – plugged with another round of cock, drilled hard, *at her request*. He tried to block the visions in his head, but he simply couldn't, wondering how she was being done *right now* - in the ass, the mouth, the cunt – all the above - and knowing whatever way it was, she was surely moaning loud, telling him she simply couldn't get enough of his prick, no matter where he shoved it. He was feeling sorry for himself, and beyond pissed that he was even in such a dickless situation. It wasn't as if he could just go and kick in the apartment door and *save* her – save her from what? She **wanted** it! Practically begged for more of it right in front of him! He was furious at himself - caring about a girl? *That* girl? *That* cunt? He *never* fucking cared, not really, about *any* of them; except this time, this one, he fucking *did*.

What a fucking chump.

He found himself less than two blocks from Sam's, in front of the old two-story brick *Good Will Firehouse*. Woodie told him last week the *Good Will* used to double as the *Town Hall*; it was a cool, old historic building, and it might be going up for sale - two out-of-towners bought it to open an antique shop years ago - their business never went anywhere, they had some sort of falling out and were looking to unload it, cheap, according to W, making the sales pitch to Cord.

Now what the fuck would C do with an old firehouse in Belvidere? He told W from day one he could be in Town days, maybe weeks, a year at most. But Woodie, the consummate salesman, always *on*, threw out ideas, to anyone who would listen, figuring something might stick…someone knows someone who might want an old firehouse; *has a cool elevated band stand and a huge honey-maple dance floor in the back*, W said.

And what Woodie knew about C was that he didn't know much about C; that alone was reason enough for the wild pitch. And it didn't cost him a cent for the toss. Classic Woodie.

And funny enough, a week ago, C actually considered it, as crazy an idea as it was. But what a difference a single week can make; what a different world existed in Belvidere for Ay a week ago....hell, how about less than twelve hours ago.

Ay stuck his nose against the closest glass panel in the large front bay door; it was mostly soaped up, but he could see the faint outline of some reclaimed wood flooring, stacked high, and piles of antique furniture, most of it in pretty beat-up shape, strewn haphazard, fading into the blackness, deep into the building bowels.

He wiped his nose of grit and kept walking; his mind still dazed from what happened at Sam's. He found himself involuntarily shaking his head in disbelief, as his mind kept replaying the unexpected confrontation. *How in the world did last night become this morning?* C didn't hear it, but the puppet was quietly laughing, snapping his teeth. Ay blew an extended sigh; at least he was temporarily off the Lilly/Button *fucking* video that had been torturing him, endlessing looping his head.

Small improvements.

He hooked a right on Hardwick, over the Pequest Bridge, watching the summer water lazily pass below the road. For a moment, it brought him back to that first day in Halifax, watching the moon jellies float around the bulkhead, down in the harbor of *Olde L'Acadie*. And for a moment, he wished he was there.

But in the end, after quiet time with the jellies, there were problems there too; there always ended up being problems wherever he went. It was the gum forever stuck to his shoe.

He ambled, not in any particular hurry, up past the Courthouse and County Library, and found himself in the Park. It felt a bit like a safe haven, being close to Carol's house; a short, safe stay on *Free Parking* in *Monopoly*, between risky rolls of the dice. Now he *really* knew why Carol stayed close to home; it was a different Town up here. Belvidere had a decidedly different feel between Water Street – downtown – Lilly's home turf, and the Courthouse Park. A mere four blocks, but a whole world away.

He shuffled his feet along one of the gravel spoke paths and ended up in the middle of the Park, sitting on Earl's bench, like he knew he would. The Park was quiet, empty, but he wondered if he was really alone. He figured Carol hung around there quite a bit – the dead one. It was beautiful summer morning and already hot, on its way to hotter. This day didn't deserve to be nice; it should be raining, he thought.

He cracked his knuckles and let out another exaggerated, extended exhale. What a night, and what a morning; what a fucking trip….never had one quite like this. And that was saying something. He wiped his mouth and let his head fall back, looking skyward, but with closed eyes, and rubbed his head, just like that first day, when he got off the bus, at *Luigi's Rancho*.

Why did he even get *on* that bus?

But it was a stupid question; he knew why, he had to. Those were the rules. But this place seemed to be bending rules, and maybe he was ready to do some bending himself.

That caught the puppet's attention.

C turned his thoughts to Carol; he was convinced she was nearby....for all he knew she was sitting next to him, or standing in front of him, arms folded, smiling, as if she was in on some sort of sick gag, with him the butt. So he began the conversation.

"You know, somehow, I think this whole trip is one big fucking joke, some sort of strange payback for a mess of a life, an accumulation of bad decisions, bad deeds, lost lives, whatever, and you're somehow the ringleader. I'm not sure how, or why, why you, how you got elected, how you somehow joined the team, but the more I think about it, the more I think you are....and you're laughing your ass off.

But you know what? It isn't really funny, not at all. You're not just hurting me, it's Earl too, and Lilly, although I don't give too much of a shit about her right now, if ever again. To think that I was running out of the Market to save her [Cord snorted a laugh to himself]! What a fucking joke that was; what has she ever done to deserve that, to deserve me even caring, even giving two-shits, about her? I never will again, I can assure you that....guaranteed. Is that the outcome you were looking for? If so, congratulations....you win.

*Everybody keeps asking me, so, maybe I'll ask you; maybe you have a better answer, because I sure as hell don't. Why the fuck am I really hear, in this bum-fuck, shit-ass nowhere Town, hanging out with your fucked-up kids, sucked into all their problems? For real....why?! I didn't want **any** of this, none of it! I'm ready for a fucking take-back, that's what I think."*

C sat there shaking his head, as he continued the one-way harangue in his melon. Outwardly, he just stared blankly across the Park, with pursed lips, eyeing Carol's front porch, his fist was methodically pounding his right thigh, which he didn't even realize.

*Are you the voice in my head? Have you **always** been that voice? How long have you known me, and what **exactly** do you know about me, everything? Everything....now that's a **lot** to know, isn't it? That's a lot of hurt, a lot of bad, and **lots** of dead, and you know what? I don't regret any of it....**none!** You get that? **None!** Do you know the puppet? Are **you** the puppet? Do you keep moving the bullet? Did you throw the fucking dart in the river? Why? An angel for Lilly and Earl? Well, I got news for you; Earl doesn't need an angel, not like me anyway, and Lilly doesn't deserve one. And you know what else, your stupid game is over; I'm breaking the rules. I'm not waiting for Jenny, or you, or anyone else in my head telling me what to do, and when to do it. The box is going, unopened, to anywhere but here, and **I'm** picking the place, not some drunken dart. And I'm not waiting to get pissed off and black out, and do something stupid. I'm done! I'm so fucking done; so congratulations again, you win. I'm outta here."*

C was fucking angry, his voice screaming at Carol in his head as he sat in silence, both fists clenched, his nails digging into his palms. He was sure she heard everything he said, even though he didn't think she really even existed. And somehow, in his mind squirming, that contradictory statement made sense; she was just another phantom stalking him, living between his ears – join the fucking club. And he was convinced she knew the puppet; somehow, they were connected, he just felt it, like he always felt the puppet.

A forty-three-year old man, who felt much older, arguing with himself on a park bench, talking about imaginary puppets being real to invisible dead people sitting next to him.

He shook his head, mocking himself; God, he was truly pathetic.

The carnal thoughts wended their way back into his brain. Despite his utter disdain for her, and his supposed write-off of her forever, in spite of himself, he just couldn't get the thought of Lillian out of his mind. Once again, he was imagining her getting pounded, fucked in every position, non-stop sucking and fucking by that jerk-off, all night long; he still couldn't even believe it really happened. How did he not hear anything? Was he *that* plastered? That out of it? He was passed out on the floor in the front room; that must be why he didn't hear anything. If he was in his bed, he would have heard it; he would have heard everything, because they would have been only ten feet below him. *Fucking A, could you imagine that, less than ten feet below his bed, him pounding her, all night, all morning! God, ten feet away, straight down, right below him!*

And what if he had followed her downstairs, and walked in on them? He couldn't imagine what would have happened.

He had to stop obsessing.

Yet every time he tried to think of something else, he would immediately boomerang right back to Lilly, legs spread, getting pumped, sucking his cock, him unloading in her mouth, her moaning, he knew she must have, the fucking whore, over and over and over, all night long.

And everything she said to him up in his apartment, just *minutes* before, the innuendo and flirting, he can't even believe she said all that? Why? It was all just a big bag of horseshit. She couldn't have written him off faster if she tried. It was breakneck.

He shook his head in disgust, disgust that he bought it, hook and all, when she was just waiting for that jerk-off to show up again. She couldn't spread her legs fast enough, and then come prancing in the store, with his tee-shirt on, no bra, no panties, walking around full of his fucking cum….*Jesus*! And they are fucking again right now, again! She practically begged him for more.

Shaking his head did no good, he simply couldn't jar the repulsive visions. He just needed to divert his attention somehow, to go to bed, for about a year. He couldn't forget her fast enough; he couldn't think of a punishment good enough.

Nah, he had to do what he said earlier; he had to go, and go now. He'd move on and forget her soon enough, like he forgot all the rest. New place, fresh start, on *his* terms; game be damned. Three months here was three months too long; Lilly and her boyfriend could have each other and this God-forsaken dump till the end of time. Good riddance.

It was time to catch a cannonball.

CHAPTER 167 – SLIPPING OUT, SO HE COULD STRIP DOWN

C rose slowly from the bench and looked around the Park; it was too quiet, too pretty, too calm. The world had no idea what just happened downtown at Sam's, and didn't care; it simply went about its usual business.

He sighed; he wasn't going to skulk back downtown and pack; he certainly couldn't do that now, with them likely in the building, probably still fucking….no way. If he never saw Lilly's face again, for the rest of his life, it would still be too soon.

And Carol wasn't there yet; she didn't come into Town till early evening on Friday's. Plus, he didn't want to see her anyway; she wouldn't understand – in fact, she'd be pissed at him for caring so much about Lilly….he was supposed to be on *her team.*

And he wasn't going back to work; he was done with that job anyway, as of an hour ago, he quit – he just hadn't told anyone yet.

What to do? How was he going to kill time, till he could sneak into the apartment, grab the essentials: the herring gull feather, the box, the aluminum foil packs….maybe a *DeMuth*, if he had any left, and get the fuck out. He'd arrange for the rest to be packed up and shipped somewhere later; W would do it, or Smillie, no big deal; he had done it before when he had to make a hasty exit.

What to do, what to do….what to do?

He could go to the Cemetery, but he already said his peace with Carol, no use sitting by her shitty grave marker and rehashing it again. He was done with her too; she could find some other schmuck to do whatever bidding she had in mind.

How did he get sucked into this whole sticky mess? C shook his head as if to reset, his mind groping for a quick solution.

Boat ramp? Al was long gone, and on a Friday in July, it would be teeming with jet-skiers and fisherman; not in the mood to deal with that crowd, with any crowd.

What to do?

He looked north, out toward the library, just staring into space, when it hit him. He'll go over to the gym; as long as Margie's boyfriend or his goons weren't lifting, that weight room would be empty. The more he thought about it, the better that felt….a refuge. It should be quiet, he could go push some weights, expend pent-up frustration, be alone, not bothered, and then he would figure out where to hole up till he could get out of Town, quietly, and never look back. C was good that way; the Belvidere chapter was already closed in his mind, compartmentalized, hermetically sealed, and packed away, never to be opened again. A strange little nightmare was about to end; not the worst, not by far, but the strangest….*absolutely*. Lilly who? He was already feeling better about dropping her, and the rest of the motley lot, like a bad habit. He said *good riddance* in his head again, for good measure.

Then he remembered a small matter, overlooked in all his anger; a kindred spirit named Earl. And he frowned. Why did an Earl have to be part of this fucked-up place? Earl was the only good thing about this hole, the *only* thing, but C was pumped so full of hate right now, he hadn't thought about Earl, until now.

C resigned himself to deal with Earl later. He'd stay in touch, probably through W, invite him to Panama someday; he promised him Panama, and he wouldn't renege on that. He would miss Earl, terribly, and C didn't miss anybody, ever, except for regret; regret for Kristine.

Then it hit him; why wait?

That's it; from Belvidere, a one-way, long-overdue trip to *Bocas Del Toro*! He smiled thinking about swinging in his hammock, the first good thought he had since Sam's. And he'd invite Earl to come along; a Panamanian tag-team.

That cheered him enough as he shuffled down the gravel path, heading to the gym. Hopefully, Margaret wasn't there; he wasn't in the mood to talk to anyone. She didn't seem the type to pry anyway. Suddenly, Margie seemed the most normal person he knew, and somehow, he felt close to her, even though he didn't even really know her, not at all. She had no baggage, no agenda, no issues, no nothing….just a nice girl.

He quickened his pace, to get out of sight before he had to deal with talking to anyone; he was in no mood for that, for sure. Not once in the whole mind-wander did he think of Mae; and he never even realized the slight later; she wasn't even an afterthought.

And that was a bit sad.

He crossed the diagonal between Second Street and Hardwick, making his way past the Library. A smattering of people were entering and exiting the side door of the Courthouse; two older women, both overweight with toadstool hips, stood outside, sucking long drags on cigarettes and chatting away, oblivious to anything else. A young frazzled mom, with two toddlers clinging to her legs like chimps, made her way down the library steps, again, in her own little world. C didn't know any of them, nor them him, and none of them noticed him at all.

Good.

He crossed over Front Street, past the oversized community clock, the same type you see in all small towns; aluminum, painted green with the town name cresting the top, made to look antique, donated by some organization trying to do good.   For this one, in Belvidere, it was the Rotary.   And along the base were a bunch of donor names from people long forgotten, names that no one ever read nor gave two-shits about.

He shook his head in disgust at the community spectacle, why he didn't really know, and scampered down a grass knoll, barely twenty-five feet from the old mill building door.

That's when he spied that goofball Jim-Bob in the distance, just coming over the Pequest Bridge, a half-block away, his both-hands-in-pockets and penguin-waddle a dead give-away. The comb-over was glued to his head, and the outfit was same-old, blue maintenance pants, floods above his ankles, showing stained white socks, with a paunch overhanging his belt, clad in a gray tee-shirt.

Jesus, if *that* moron sees him, the whole fucking Town will know he's at Margery's in less than five minutes.

He quickly darted from the penguin's view, snuck along the front of the old mill, and ducked in the front door. He waited at the entrance, peeking out to see the little man waddle by, oblivious. He let out a deep breath; good God, he felt like he was in grade school, hiding from the hall monitor.

He slowly turned around, just now realizing that whole juvenile act was played out in Margery's foyer. He expected to be the butt of a whole lot of jokes, but to his pleasant surprise, the foyer, and the hall, were dead….empty. A small bit of luck on an up-to-now for-shit day.

He wandered down the hall and stuck his head around the corner of Margery's office, as he simultaneously rapped lightly on the door jam.

"Hello?"

The light was on, and papers spread about the desk; busy-work in progress, but no Margery.

He walked down the hall, toward the gym, when he noticed the closed bathroom door; the fan was running, and he heard Margery's voice muffled in the whirl. Christ, he probably just walked in on her taking a quiet dump. He looked to get out of the hall and quick, lest he hear toilet noises he'd rather not.

But it was immediately evident she wasn't on the john; instead, she sounded agitated. Pauses of silence, followed by accusatory rants screamed into the phone, directed to what had to be her fiancé; C couldn't hear the substance, and honestly, didn't want to.

He turned around and went back down the hall, to her office, ducked in, and sat in her sole guest chair. After staying for fifteen uncomfortable seconds or so, he figured now wasn't a good time to be here; she apparently had her own set of problems. He quickly rose and leaned against her office doorjamb, just to say a quick hi and bye down the hall, in clear view when she emerged from the bathroom.

But even from this distance, he heard her voice raise, shouting something or another, muffled and incoherent. It seemed to be getting worse. And it was crystal clear it was time to fucking leave, *right now*; he didn't need to be headlong in another mess....someone else's problems.

He turned and started to quick-step-it down the hall, toward the front door. He got a half-dozen paces, in no-man's land, too far from the door, and too far from her office, when the bathroom door suddenly, loudly, jarred open; it was stuck, so she shoved it hard, and half-fell into the corridor. Margery spilled into the hallway, cellphone still glued to her ear; her face was flush.

1492

"And what am I *supposed* to think?"

Then she saw him.

C was embarrassed, inadvertently eavesdropping on her, and waved his hand in a combined gesture of apology and goodbye, as he mouthed *Sorry*.

She immediately put her hand up for him to stop, to wait.

"Listen, I gotta go, I got stuff to do; I'll talk to you later."

She said, blatantly annoyed, holding the phone away from her ear, with a killer look on her face, apparently listening to some bullshit line.

"Yeah whatever, I gotta go! I'll talk to you later....***whatever!***"

And she flipped the phone shut, surely cutting whomever off mid-sentence. She quickly opened it and held the *End* button down, till the phone went dead. She walked toward C, smiled weakly and stopped at her office door; she took the phone and looked as if she was going to toss it gently onto her desk. But out of nowhere, she wound up major league and whipped it through the door; he heard it slam against the far wall, and break into pieces.

She just stood there, in the hall, looking at the carnage in her office, in removed silence. They Margie turned to him, and spoke calmly, as if nothing violent just happened.

"Maybe I should have just dropped it in the toilet."

Was all she said.

"I know the feeling."

C responded in sympathy.

And she smiled again, and then studied him hard.

"Aren't you supposed to be at work?"

C didn't answer; he just snorted a bit of air and frowned.

"Hey, sorry to bother you in the middle of the day."

"It's the morning."

She answered, deadpan.

"Yeah *[C frowned at himself for the mistake; a bit out of sort]*. I just was wondering if I could take you up on that offer to use the gym. I'm kind of in the mood to lift; crummy morning, *really* crummy - actually, crummy doesn't come close to describing it. Anyway, need to take my mind off....stuff. I'm kind of in the mood for a good, mindless workout."

"What stuff? Lilly stuff?"

He didn't answer.

"Uh, huh; Lilly can do that."

"Is your boyfriend, fiancé, going to be using it in the next hour or so; I know it's for him."

Margery snorted a bit of her own air and added her own frown.

"Hardly. He's got his own workout going on, down in Atlantic City, at a *conference*....so he says."

They both shared a look of annoyance, directed at others.

"Go ahead, you know where it is, stay as long as you like. This place is dead for another couple hours, till my

Pilates class starts at noon. I'm just gonna do some paperwork till then; it should be quiet, no one will bother you down there. Lilly doesn't have any classes today, so you're safe....if that's what you're avoiding."

"Hey, thanks, I really appreciate it."

C said, sincere.

"No problem."

Margery answered, in an even tone, as if the rage she just harbored had already slipped down the drain.

"Hey, listen, I'm not trying to freak you out, but I wasn't planning on lifting, kind of a last minute thing; so I didn't bring a change of clothes. I was gonna lift in my boxers; they're just like gym shorts, and my tee-shirt, and barefoot. Is that okay? Don't want to scare you, or give you the wrong idea."

Margery laughed.

"As long as you're not naked, I'm sure I can handle it; but thanks for the warning!"

C smiled; she was so nice and laid back, he thought....she just kinda rolled with it. He didn't even know her, and he figured she was someone he would miss – a shame he didn't get to know her, because he was sure they would get along fine. He felt comfortable around her, and he felt she felt the same.

"Thanks."

C hit the jam lightly with his hand to signal his appreciation, slipping out, so he could strip down.

CHAPTER 168 – SMOOTH, LIKE A BABY'S BOTTOM

The first hour flew.

Just lifting and not thinking, the radio playing softly, background classical, Tchaikovsky, Mozart, Haydn; it helped his head. And he started to feel a bit better. He knew it wouldn't last, but he would take it, for now; a welcome respite.

He worked up to heavy sets, cranking a lot of reps, and found himself out of breath and sweaty. But he felt good.

He had finished benching first, and was now squatting; he always liked to squat, it was his favorite lift.

He un-racked three-hundred-twenty pounds, a relatively easy rep weight, but heavy enough to get in a good work. He typically decided on a rep count before he un-racked the weight, but today, he was just looking to occupy his mind, so he would just sink as many reps as he felt, then rack it, and go again. This was his third set at three-twenty, and he settled under the bar, lifted it off, and took two half-steps back, settled his feet, and was ready to sink, when he saw Margery's reflection in the mirror before him, as she slipped quietly into the room.

She had changed her outfit. Before, outside her office, she had been wearing tight, not skin-tight, but tight, faded jeans and an un-tucked white Oxford; now she sported black spandex bottoms, which extended halfway down her sculpted thigh, and a black jog-bra, which pancaked her breasts against her chest. She had a washboard stomach, china white.

C stepped forward and re-racked the weight.

"My God, is it noon already?!"

C said, through a deep exhale. He thought he got there around 8:30 am, maybe a bit earlier; no way he was there three-plus hours already - time couldn't have gone that fast.

"No, no, it's only 10 am; actually ten-of; I just figured I would take you up on your offer."

"My offer?"

"Yeah, you told me to come down and lift with you, get under the bar, remember?"

"Oh, yeah, good."

She walked over to the rack, and gently placed her hands on the supports.

"I thought your boyfriend, fiancé, tried to get you to squat?"

"He did, but lifting with them is just too much testosterone for me; it hangs pretty thick."

"Great thanks; so you want to lift with me because....there's *no* testosterone? Just estrogen? Just what I need."

C let out a huff and shook his head in a self-mock.

"I didn't mean it that way; I have been watching for a bit, out in the hall, and you seem to be very intense, but without all the yelling and banging, you know, *guy-noise*."

"Yeah, I know what you mean. I've lifted with guys like that; I like to lift, but not with all the histrionics."

She smiled.

"So you gonna show me what to do?"

"Didn't you ever watch your boyfriend, you know, the guy-guys?"

He smiled, and she returned her own. She had a great smile.

"Not really, if you're not driving, you don't really pay attention, if you know what I mean."

"True; we'll come on in."

C motioned her to join him in the power rack.

"Am I gonna get in trouble? Get *you* in trouble? I don't know your boyfriend."

Margaret ignored the comment; he guessed the answer was no.

"Let me watch you up-close first; I pick stuff up pretty quick."

"Okay."

And with that, C turned back toward the mirror on the wall, reset, took in a big gulp of air and held his breath as he lifted the weight off the pins. It felt a lot lighter with her standing so close behind him; the wonders of adrenaline.

He raised his head, looked toward the upper part of the mirror before him, and began the set. He punched out about five before he decided to rack the weight.

"Okay, easy enough? Did I do enough for you to get the gist of it?"

"I think so; might have to take a bit of the weight off though."

They both creased smiles at the joke and began to strip the plates.

"Bring it down to the bare bar, that's forty-five pounds. We'll start there, if that's okay."

"You're the boss."

Is all she said.

"Hardly; how many bosses have you had that go around barefoot and in their underwear?"

Was his retort.

She eyed him up and down, and again.

"I have to say, you're the first, not that it's a bad thing. Shorts are a little baggy though, in the seat; need to size down."

"Yeah, lost some weight, have to order some new ones. At least you didn't say they were baggy in the crotch; thanks for that."

"Don't mention it."

The empty bar sat on the pins, and she gingerly approached it, ducked under and rubbed the steel on her back, trying to find a spot that felt right, but none did.

Seeing her fidget, C saddled up behind her and gently grabbed her shoulders.

"Here, let it lay right along this line."

He ran his fingertip across the width of her upper back, just below her shoulders. He didn't see it, but she closed her eyes, just for a second, while he drew the line on her back.

"Okay, got it! Let me give her a rip!"

"Rip away."

C said as he stepped back. She set the bar across her back and stood up. Even though it was just the bar, she was a little wobbly; not from the weight, just the general unfamiliarity of the position, and the motion.

"Wow, never know I was good on my feet; this feels really awkward!"

So C stood behind her, and gently mirrored her from behind, and extended his hands along her sides, palms up, by her breasts.

"Okay, just slowly squat down, but be sure to keep your chest up, and sit back, into me, on your heels, not your toes. Don't let your knees go forward, and be sure…."

Before C could finish, Margie figured she'd heard enough, time to give it a whirl, and down she started. And just like C said *not* to do, her knees went forward, and up on her toes she went, her back rounded over, head looking down at the floor. She wobbled down, and wobbled back up, like a sot. She concentrated all the way down, and laughed all the way up.

She stood and looked straight ahead in the mirror, and her eyes caught his in the reflection; and he was smiling and much as she was.

"That had to be the absolutely *worst* squat I have *ever* seen in my…."

She cut him off, by bursting out laughing, at herself. And he joined in.

"That's hard to do!"

She yelped, in self-defense.

"I know it is, trust me! I've been doing it for years, and sometimes I still can't get in the groove. People think it's so easy, just down and up, but it's not, not if you do it right."

Margery had been standing there with the bar resting on her back. She got a determined look on her face, and was ready to go again.

"Okay, this one will be better; chest up, back on my heels, back on my heels….okay."

And she took a deep breath and exaggerated her posture, sitting back too far as she went down too quick. It all caught C by surprise, and soon, since he was standing so close behind her to spot, found that she was running her ass down his front-side, pushing into him. She was so far back, that her center of gravity failed her, and she fell back into C like a domino, and the two of them went down like a sack of potatoes, on their asses. The bar fell off her shoulders and landed on the safety pins, but she kept going, like an avalanche, right to the floor, landing on top of him, wedged in his lap.

And she couldn't stop laughing, nor could he.

"Margery, you are, by far, the *worst* squatter in the whole world."

C squeezed out as he laughed. She was cracking herself up and couldn't get any words out in retort. She just sat between his legs, him wedged up behind her.

It felt good to laugh.

And that's when, for reasons he didn't know, he certainly didn't plan it, he just leaned forward, and wrapped his hand around her waist, and kissed her on the neck.

The power rack had become a fleshpot.

And just like that, her laughing stopped, and she found herself pushing back into him, her head tilted away, giving him as much neck as he wanted.

But he didn't want just the neck.

And as quickly as that happened, he cinched his right hand around her waist in a fillip and pulled her closer to him, so he could feel her body against his cock, which was already hard, and his left hand went to her stomach, and in one motion, slid under her spandex pants and right down to her crotch, looking for the patch of hair.

But there was none to be found.

She was shaved clean and smooth, like a baby's bottom.

CHAPTER 169 – SHE'D CARRY THAT PRESENT AROUND FOR AWHILE

She did nothing to stop him from exploring, completely compliant.

He held her tight against his crotch, and slowly rubbed his cock against the back of her spandex, dry-humping her, while he kissed her neck. His lips never left her skin; he just kissed somewhat hard, then somewhat gentle, and moved his lips and kissed again, not sloppy, mostly dry, with a touch of his tongue here and there….controlling.

And she liked it.

His fingers, two of them, had found their way inside her pussy and he was sliding them in and out together, not rough, but not gentle either, hooking and grabbing her pubic bone, rubbing her clit with each cycle. She was so lubed that his fingers clicked wet as they worked inside her, loud enough for both of them to hear. Then, just as she was arching into his routine, for more friction, he abruptly pulled his fingers clear out; she let a little gasp at the change, the void. But he didn't make the limbo long; C simply moved to her clit, rubbing gently along its left side; her body language made it clear he found a spot she liked, and she shifted a bit, and pushed her body harder into his finger.

In less than thirty seconds, she squirmed in-between his legs as she came on his hand. It sounded like the *end-of-a-long-dry-spell.*

She didn't want it to end, so she extended the orgasm as long as she could, arching back into him, her long black hair falling around his shoulders. He liked the feel of her hair, and its smell. He was still kissing her neck, but he had worked his way down to her collarbone area, around the base. Her skin was almost too perfect, not a blemish, a spot, or a mark, and smooth as silk. He forcefully grabbed her chin and pulled her head away from him, making her give him maximum access to her neck.

She struggled a bit against his bind on her, but it was more for show than anything; he could tell she liked the constraint. She tried to move from between his legs, but he cinched her tighter.

"You want to go again?"

He whispered in her ear, as he kissed around her lobe. Before she answered, and he knew the answer was yes anyway, he started to rub her clit again, in the same way as before.

She responded by going limp, giving in to him, falling back between his legs and slowly rubbing her ass on his cock, while he worked her clit.

And she quickly came again.

"God, shit."

Was all she came up with, as she exhaled heavy. And he let her lay there and relax, enjoying a post-orgasm tingle and tire.

After a bit, she gracefully rose from between his legs. She stood and half-spun to face him, then slowly pulled up and off her jog-bra - not in a slutty striptease, but in a matter-of-fact *you can do whatever you want to me, and I'll let you* way.

C just relaxed against the steel power rack and enjoyed the show. He loved little tits, and small, hard, erect nipples; it is what he imagined she had all along, and he was spot-on. He wasn't really a breast sort of guy, but hers, he liked; to him, they were perfect.

She smiled, knowing he liked what he saw. Then she grabbed her spandex bottoms and underwear and deliberately peeled them off, together, in one continuous motion, right down to her ankles. And that's when he first laid eyes on that bald pussy he had been playing with.

He liked hair; a trimmed bush, a neat, triangle, that was his favorite. Strangely enough, he had never been with a girl *truly* clean-shaven, with not a single hair to be found; this was a first. And although he didn't like it, he was a bit surprised at how attracted he was to it, or at least hers, right now. He figured rejection works on you that way.

Her lower lips stood out, puckered a bit, no doubt a bit swollen from his fondling, but they were also naturally puffy; that was just the look she had. He couldn't take his eyes off that pouty, bare pussy, staring at her a bit goofy, like a little kid.

She kicked off her shoes, she had no socks, and stepped out of her clothes, standing before him, completely naked, and china-white. Her stomach was washboard, and she had an elongated oval innie. He couldn't decide, but figured that stomach was probably her best attribute; that flat stomach, and those tiny, perky tits....they both were real good to look at.

She gave him a pirate smile.

"You look like a little kid, smiling like that; I'm glad."

She said, low.

"I've always loved ballerinas, had a thing for them since I was a kid, but never been with one."

"Never's about to end."

She whispered. And with that, she quietly knelt down between his legs and tugged on his boxers, which were hung up on his cock. She yanked a little harder, unhooked the jam, and pulled them down clear to his ankles, then, in another quick tug, right off, tossing them behind her, somewhere.

"Did you lock the door? What if someone comes in?"

He said.

"Do you care?"

"I don't; thought you might."

"Does it look like I care?"

Margery whispered as she got on her knees, between his legs, and slowly took the head of his cock into her mouth. Nothing touched his dick except the tip of her tongue, which she ran lightly around the rim and center, licking whatever he leaked.

My God, he thought. He's been chasing Lillian around this stupid fucking Town and this was waiting here at the gym the whole time? That jerk-off could have her. He closed his eyes, leaned back against the power rack and let her blow him. Quick enough, she took his shaft into her mouth, slowly bobbing up and down, head to balls, taking it out and licking his cock along its length. She wasn't too fast or slow; again, it was calm and deliberate. Christ, she was fucking good, *really good*, that is all C kept thinking. Mae was a good cock-sucker....real good; but Margery was better. That was his first, and last, thought about Mae.

And then, abruptly, she stopped. Margery smiled, and rose up before him, looking down like a girl in charge. She straddled his hips and slowly squatted down, perfect form.

"How's this?"

She said, as her pussy inched ever-closer to his cock.

"Getting better."

He said.

Her lips were just above the tip of his cock. He grabbed it and held it straight, and she slowly dropped till his head, still wet from her mouth, barely pierced her lips. Then, in one slow motion, she slid down his pole, till it disappeared inside her, one smooth stroke.

"I think I like squatting."

She said.

"You're the best squatter *ever.*"

C said, and smiled at her.

And with that, she started to rock back and forth on his lap, as she bent over and kissed his neck, her arms resting gently on his shoulders. She was *so* relaxed, it was like she had done this a thousand times, rehearsed. It was that smooth, that natural. It felt like she belonged there, his dick snug inside her. It just felt right.

Face-to-face, in silence she slowly ground on his lap, lost in herself. But she kept her eyes open, staring into his, but they were kind eyes, fun eyes….happy eyes. He could have stayed there all day; it felt that good.

She closed her lids and seemed to go into concentration mode, fucking him harder and harder, while he simply held on for the ride, pinned against the rack. It didn't take her long; she sped up to a frenzy as she got close, and whimpered when she came, holding the moan in, but not quite, which turned him on even more.

"Jesus, that feels good."

She said as she continued to grind, trying to elongate her third come. She never stopped pumping, right through the end of the orgasm and beyond, and soon found herself speeding up again, picking up the pace. Christ, she was going for four.

But this time he was taking the reins. He was ready to unload; it felt too good to keep holding out just for the sake of holding out. Plus, she had finished a couple times already, his typical prerequisite met, and then some.

He cinched her hips, and for the first time, humped along with her, as opposed to her solo ride. And because of it, he was thrusting harder, and going deeper, and she clearly approved.

"Come on, come on, come on, let me hear you come like a bad girl, come on, come on!"

He whispered, egging her on, and she responded by pumping faster, and breathing hyper-fast.

"You ready? You gonna come with me?"

C urged her on.

"Yeah, yeah, yeah, yeah…."

She kept repeating, one chant for each hip thrust.

"Okay, come on, *now*….come on my cock *now!*"

And that little commentary was the over-the-edge she needed; no further help necessary.

And the two finished together, hers lasting a bit longer than his. He couldn't always tell, but it felt like a heavy dose from him; pent up, no doubt. And it felt good unloading deep in her pussy.

He figured she'd carry that present around for awhile.

She just sat there, on his lap, while his dick shrank inside her. She was kissing his neck gently, and he did the same to her. Not once did he think about any repercussions up to, during, or after, the act.

Till now.

And the thought was not Lilly, who told him to *never* fuck Margery, not that he gave two shits about her at all, ever again. Somehow, she didn't seem to matter at all any more, and he liked that feeling; he liked not giving a shit about her. Not that Lillian would ever care anyway, certainly not now. But the defiance of, the total disregard to, her *Margie ultimatum*, made him feel better nonetheless. Fuck her.

No, his thoughts instead suddenly focused on Mae; good God, she *just* told him on Monday *not* to even see Margery, the last time he was with her, fucking her hard, just eighty-odd hours ago! And here he was, sitting with his cock in Margery's pussy, right here, right now. He looked down as if to confirm the fact.

Yep, still there, and he didn't want to ever take it out. A train derailed once again; how does this shit always happen to him? How?

"We both needed that."

Margie whispered.

"Agreed."

C said, trying to shove Mae out of his brain.

"Felt good, thanks; can't remember the last time I came four times at once, if ever. Four times, wow; I usually have to rush one in before Walt finishes. He doesn't give a shit, not like you."

She said nonchalantly, C's dick still tucked inside her pussy, getting smaller, about to fall out.

C looked at her, and answered, even though it wasn't a question.

"I can't remember the last time I came first with a girl; I'm a one and done kind of guy, even when I was younger, and I've always wanted the girl to come at least once first, the more the better; kind of a validation, I guess, that the sex was good for her, and she enjoyed being with me. Her orgasms matter much more to me than mine; mine's easy."

She pecked him smack on the lips, with a closed mouth….a goofy kiss.

"Well, safe to say the sex was good for me; mission accomplished. How bout you?"

"It's weird looking down and seeing no hair; I expect to look up and see you wearing braces and pigtails. But fucking you was good, real good, even better because it was not something I ever expected to happen, not today, not ever, not really. Don't know why; figured you were tied up with your boyfriend, and I've got too many irons in the fire already, and a heap of trouble tied to all of them….story of my life."

"Regrets?"

She said.

"No way."

He said, even though a small piece of him did, but just a small piece. Mae would never forgive him for this little dip, *ever*. But she wouldn't find out; it was a one-off, likely, and therapy for both of them. Margery said so, right? No harm, no foul; Mae and Margery never talked anyway; Mae despised her. And they had no common friends, as best he could tell, so his secret was safe. As long as he didn't keep coming back for more, if there was ever even any more to come back to.

"Hey, you never asked, not really time, but just to let you know, kinda late I guess, but anyway, I'm fixed, you know – snipped, so no worries about that, I mean, if you were worried."

She smiled.

"Thanks for that tidbit. Actually, I had it covered, but hey, thanks for the *snip*."

"You're welcome.

C smiled sarcastic. Then he continued.

"You know, I've never had a one-nighter, you know, a one-off like this, hookers excluded."

C said, as he slowly traced a circle around her left nipple with his pointer, barely touching her skin.

She giggled.

"That tickles. You've been with hookers? Really? I wouldn't have guessed it; nah, maybe I would....not sure."

"Well just one, actually, and it didn't really happen, thank God. I was in my early twenties and I couldn't get a hard-on. Christ, at that age, the wind blew and I got a hard-on; but she was some fat, hairy-bellied blow-pig from Missouri, an orangutan. Actually it was a foursome; my brother was with me, both drunk off our asses. He had another slut with a gold tooth; God, what a fiasco that was - took years to get that monkey memory out of my head."

C shook his head to wipe the thought.

"How bout you?"

"Male hookers? No, can't say I have."

She chuckled.

"No, I mean one-offs, like this?"

"This is the....second, no, I think it's the third *[Margery looked up at the ceiling, pondering]*. Yeah, the third; but the first one where I've been sober! So congratulations!"

"Wow, I feel *extra*-special."

C chuckled.

"I like you Cord, you're mellow, not dramatic....nothing like what Lilly describes; and trust me, she describes you a lot, over and over."

C didn't want to talk about Lilly, not now, not ever again.

"I assume that was him on the phone, your boyfriend?"

She nodded yes, and kissed C's neck again.

"Guess we should get up."

She mouthed lightly.

"I'm in no rush."

C said.

"Good, me neither."

And with that, she placed her head lightly on his shoulder, her nipples pressed against his tee-shirt.

"So what happened with Lilly? Or don't you want to talk about it?"

He really didn't, but he did.

"Her boyfriend's back; had a little run-in with him and her at Sam's this morning, kind of caught me off guard. I thought something might be happening with her….and….me, but, I guess not."

*"Button's back?! **When?**"*

"Last night; apparently."

"Wow, that sucks; sorry about that. He's been gone a long time; wonder why he came back?"

"Apparently people have been telling him, wherever he was, that Lilly was seeing me, or something like that; I don't know if that's why he's really back, seems to be, but who the fuck knows. That's a closed chapter anyway; time to move on."

"You know, I asked her why she wasn't going out with you; she likes you, she really does, it's so easy to tell. But I know she's had this thing for, and with, that guy for a long time, a lifetime, I guess. Besides, she said you have some girlfriend, anyway."

"*Please,* I know what she told you; that I'm fucking some senior citizen, and that I'm pathetic, and all that. Do you know Mrs. Ackerman? Good Lord, she's almost a seventy-year old marshmallow body stuck on popsicle stick legs. Lilly said that just to get a rise out of you, and annoy me. And of course it worked, like it usually does with Lilly. She's going around telling everyone about me fucking Mrs. A; no wonder she's always so nice to me lately in the store, buying up all the star fruit.

Margery smiled.

"Mrs. A?"

"Yeah, that's what I call her. She really *is* a nice woman, not to fuck for Christ sake, but just to talk to. You know, there's a whole group of them that hang out together; a bunch of Bergen County transplants, that's what they call themselves."

"So you're not fucking Mrs. A?"

C chuckled.

"No, afraid not. Thank God."

"Who then? Anyone? Ever get in Lilly's pants?"

And C was gonna say no, and change the subject. But for a second, he got the urge to just tell the truth for once, to stop lying to everyone about just about everything; Margery, for some reason, felt like a safe haven.

"Not Lilly, no. Believe it or not, it almost happened last night, but then she ran down to her apartment for something, I passed out, and the next thing I know that jerk-off showed up and slept with her last night. Pretty impeccable timing, by him; not so good for me *[C shook his head negative, and chuckled pathetic]*. So that was the end of that, before it even started. So, with Lilly? No. But Lilly was *partly* right....mainly wrong, but a string, a thread, of truth, is weaved in somehow, about the older woman. Anyway, there *is* one women, much older than me, that I have fucked a couple times; okay, maybe more than a couple, but she's no marshmallow, that's for sure; great body for an older woman, but man, kind of a basket case, clingy, possessive....a *real* problem. Sex with her comes with *lots* of strings."

Margery just smiled.

"There's nothing wrong having sex with an older woman; who cares? I hope someone wants to have sex with me when I get older."

"Trust me, they will."

C said, as his limp dick finally couldn't hold on any longer, and slipped out of her pussy.
She smiled at the timing, feeling it hit her inner thigh.

"But they might be thinking about someone else."

She looked at him odd, with head cocked, waiting for an explanation.

"I swear I'm not making this up, and I *did* come here to lift, promise; I had no ulterior motive. But when I banged her, this older woman I'm talking about, on Monday night, this past Monday, three and a half days ago, it was right after I first met you, here, you know, at the kick-boxing class. So when I was banging her, later that same night, Monday, I was banging her doggie - she can't get enough on all-fours - loves it, I fantasized about banging *you* on the gym bench, cause I figured your boyfriend must of shagged you there a bunch of times."

"You thought of fucking me while having sex with an old lady? How sweet!"

Margery said mockingly, and kissed him on the tip of the nose.

"Was it better sex with me when it was her, or when it was me? Know what I mean?"

"Trust me, she gives good sex, no doubt, but this impromptu was pretty fucking good; I'd say this one wins."

"I bet you say that to all the girls, but thanks."

And she pecked him on the nose a second time.

"And to answer your question, no, never fucked Walt in this gym. He's always here with his buddies; we've never done it in here."

"Really?"

C was surprised, and happy, that he did her first in her gym; she was a gym-virgin.

"Really; we did it a bunch of times in the bathroom and bent over my desk, on top of my desk, yeah, but never in the gym."

"Anyway, when I thought of fucking you on the flat bench, my dick got rock hard. So when I was fucking my friend, I was really fucking you. But your legs were up on my shoulders, not how we fucked just now, and I figured, hoped, you had a nice hairy pussy, trimmed neat, but full, you know, that I could look down on; I figured you had one of those thin landing strips; never expected shaved-clean."

Margery shook her head in regret, as she looked down at her crotch.

"Me neither, that was simply for him; actually just shaved her clean this morning, because he was *supposed* to be coming over, and told me to *get her ready*. And like a jerk I did. But he changed his plans at the last minute; apparently got a better offer. He's fucking a twenty-something he works with, I know it; I think he's with her now. Don't know her, but I've seen pictures; she's pierced all over, with tattoos, and of course, she's shaved clean. The idiot tells me this, and when I ask how *that* topic possibly came up in casual office conversation, he said he heard her talking to a girlfriend about it. Then couple days later, he pretends the idea turned him on, you know, *he likes the look*, so he asked me to shave, and like a jerk, I did, and have been for the past couple months or so. Never again though….*never*. Can't wait for it to grow back in, but I know it's gonna itch like crazy. [*Margery looked down at her crotch as she spoke, pulling and poking on her puffy lips and pushing her skin around].* And I feel like I'm ten years old; Christ I even had hair back then. I don't like how she looks; do you?"

C shook his head a slow no.

"Listen, I liked *her*, a lot, as you know, but sorry, I feel like I should be in jail."

She chuckled. And Cord continued.

"Anyway, I came thinking of fucking you, while I fucked her, on Monday; isn't that kinda strange?"

Margie shook her head yes.

"So, who did you think of just now, your apparently nameless senior citizen fuck-buddy, or Lilly?"

C cocked his head.

"Actually, no one, which, for me, is unusual; I just enjoyed the ride with you."

"Me too; look at all we have in common."

Margery poked him playfully in the shoulder and smirked at him.

"Anyway, after I banged my *older* friend on her kitchen floor, I told her, casually, that I met you at the gym, this gym; nothing about the sex fantasy, obviously, just that I met you when I was working out with Lilly and…."

C was interrupted by a loud banging, coming from down the hall.

Like teenagers, they both instinctively shot up.

"What the hell is that?"

C said.

"Obviously someone's banging on the front door."

Margery said, matter-of-fact.

"Why don't they just come in?"

"Because I locked it."

"You *locked* it? I thought you didn't care."

C said, incredulous.

"I don't, but I still locked it."

"And why did you lock it? Did you plan this?"

C looked at her, both puzzled, and impressed.

"No I didn't plan this, not exactly; but yeah, I was thinking something *might* happen, and it did. Lucky me."

Margery said deadpan, as she slipped on her clothes super-quick, like she had plenty of practice. C fumbled getting his feet in his boxers, falling over into the power rack like an old man, cursing.

The banging was getting louder.

"Jesus!"

Margery exhaled, already annoyed at the intruder.

Margie was at the gym door, fully dressed, with C close behind, bare-foot, clad only in his baggy black boxers and tee-shirt. She ambled down the hall, him skulking behind. They made it to the corner, and peeked around to see who was at the door, at the end of the long hallway.

Fear gripped C; his feet and fingers tingled pins and needles.

"Holy shit, it's Mae!"

He whispered, not so softly.

"*Mae?* You know her?"

Margery said, in a surprised tone.

"Yeah, she's the doggie-lady I fuck! The nutty one I was just telling you about; she told me to stay away from you though - *big trouble* - some business deal with you went bad, lent you money or something....she said she used to tan here. She was fucking adamant, steer clear of you and this place, which I said I would....I guess."

Margery just looked at him, with a blank expression, and said, sarcastically.

"Guess you didn't keep your word."

"Well, unlike you, it's not like I planned it."

C said, in a weak defense.

"Margie open up, I know you're in there; I just want to ask you a quick question."

Mae was slamming the door louder, with an open hand.

"*Jesus!*"

C yelped like a little girl.

"This should be interesting; well, I guess I should go let her in, see what she wants."

"Why the fuck is she *here*? I thought she hated you? Don't let her in! Well, if you do, don't tell her *I'm* here, for Christ's sake, she'll fucking stab me!"

"No worries; your little secret's safe with me."

And with that, Margery kissed C on the forehead, a peck coupled with a devilish, crooked smile. C didn't like the look of that.

She slowly ambled down the hall, deliberately going slower than her normal gait, and C continued to peek around the corner, a voyeur, watching the horror scene unfold. Margery reached the end of the hall, twisted the thumb-lock and swung open the door to greet Mae, who looked frantic and much older than she did on Monday night, standing, meek, in the threshold.

And then Margery said it, C heard it, and his legs went numb.

"What can I do for you, mom?"

CHAPTER 171 – SHAKE HER HEAD AND WHISPERED ALOUD. *SHIT*

"Why was the door locked?"

"Why are you down here?"

"What, I'm not allowed down here?"

Margery sighed, knowing how conversations with her mom always progressed….from bad to worse.

"Mom, why are you here?"

"Did you send your payment? I didn't get it?"

"*Really,* maybe because it's due August 1st, and it's July 14th, and the mail takes what, one day? *Why* are you here?"

Mae huffed in annoyance, and Margery didn't even flinch, one of ten thousand huffs she endured in a lifetime. Margery just stood, arms crossed her chest, waiting for an answer she knew would never come, not directly, anyway. Such was the game they played, and they were both very good at it.

Margery was a grounded, secure woman. But when it came to her mother, and the forty-seven years of baggage she carried around, it sometimes, more-often-than-not, got a bit ugly. And Margery didn't like that, she didn't like who she sometimes became. She didn't want to be mean, or sarcastic, or nasty, but her mother had a knack for quickly, and effectively, dragging her right into the mud. She was forty-seven, yet her mother treated her as if she was forever stuck at twelve.

"I was supposed to get a grocery delivery, and the delivery man didn't show up."

Margery raised her eyebrows and said, indignantly.

"So?"

"So, I thought he might be here! They said he left in a huff from the store, and I really need the groceries, for a party, and I thought, maybe, he stopped here. I looked everywhere else; this is the last stop."

"Why in the world would he stop *here*, mom, with *your* groceries? That makes absolutely no sense."

"I don't know, that was what I was going to ask *him*. I think you know him, his name is…"

"I know his name."

"Really? Are you two friends?"

"Best."

Margery wasn't sure why she said that, it just came out – life of its own.

"*Best?* Really? Funny, he told me he just met you on Monday, this past Monday. How can you be best friends in four days? Is he lying? Does he know you longer than that? When did you *really* meet? Can I come inside? Or do I have to stand in the doorway?"

Margery stared at her long and hard, and begrudgingly stepped to the side, arms still folded across her chest, and let her mother barely squeeze past. Letting her in would just escalate the rhetoric, she knew it. This was an old drill.

Mae immediately assumed search mode, antennae up.

"Why was the door locked? You never lock the door."

"How do you know what I do here, mom?"

"Do you normally lock the door, in Belvidere?"

"No, not normally."

"Well?"

"Seems like a lot of interest in a grocery delivery, mom; why can't someone else just deliver the order?"

"I'm very particular about how things are done, young lady *[Mae scowled at Margie, knowing she knew that, without saying]*, and this young man has the procedure down. I don't want to have to go through it all over again with someone else, damaged fruit, and such."

"Word is, about Town, he has more than the fruit procedure down."

Margery knew she shouldn't have gone there, but it too snuck out, and there was no take-back.

"What's *that* supposed to mean?"

Mae snipped.

"Well, you know Belvidere; why don't you tell me?"

"What kind of *best* friend is he? What does that exactly mean? How well do you *really* know Cord? Is he lying to me, saying you two just met?"

Mae barked.

"No he's not lying. And, well, right about now, I guess I know him just about as well as you do, I guess."

"What does *that* mean? Why can't you just answer a question, straight?"

"Because I learned from you. How's dad?"

"Don't you talk to him?"

"I talk to dad every day; I was asking *you* how dad was."

"Your father and I don't talk as much as we used to."

"Well, you never used to talk, and now it's less; that's not much talking, mom, not much at all."

"Please, Margie, stop playing the hurt daughter; it's a bit old, don't you think? Anyway, your dad and I got over all that."

"Really, he did? He's over it? Funny, I didn't know that; I don't think *he* knows that."

Margery took a long, deep breath and reset; this was degrading quicker than normal.

"Mom, he's not here; why don't you just leave, please, so we don't end up shouting at each other over stupid things, like we always do, like we're doing now.....please. I was in a good mood; I want to stay in a good mood."

Mae completely ignored Margery's plea, and started to wander down the hall, past the Pilates room, toward Margie's office.

"Done some renovations, huh? Looks nice."

"No, I haven't done any renovations, actually, but thanks for noticing. And fine, if you don't believe me, *big surprise*, and want to snoop around, go right ahead; maybe Cord's hiding under my desk, with the groceries, and all that damaged fruit."

"Don't make fun of me, young lady."

Mae talked, half-distracted, as she traveled down the hall, till she came upon Margery's office, then she ducked in, out of sight. Margery didn't even have to look; she knew Mae was around her desk, bent over, looking under, for Cord, and the groceries.

She yelled from inside the office, out to Margery in the hall.

"Do you know *anything* about that young man? Why is your phone broken on the floor? Cord has a shadowy past; you need to be very careful around him, trust me....I think he's a bad seed."

Just then, Margery felt a glob of C's cum drip from her pussy; it soaked into the Spandex crotch, and smeared against her upper thigh. The irony.

"You're right, maybe I should just stay away from him, *bad seed.* Plus, you know, I have a fiancé; you remember him, Walt?"

Mae emerged from her office, frazzled at not finding her quarry.

"How's Walt; is he good?"

Mae didn't even look toward Margie as she answered automaton, she just crossed the hall and tried the bathroom knob. She jiggled it; it was locked.

"He's a jerk mom, you know it, and so do I. But I do love having sex with him; I keep him around just for the sex, you know, a boy-toy."

That finally got Mae's attention.

"That's not something I want to hear about my daughter; please don't talk to me about stuff like that!"

"Sorry, I thought I learned that from you too; haven't you always had a toy, or two, or three, around, pretty much your whole life? Do you have one now?"

Margery's heart was racing; she was getting upset, protecting her dad, as was the usual drill. Mae ignored her.

"Why is this door locked?"

Mae asked a second time, yanking harder on the knob, to no avail.

"Well, do have a new *friend*? Or is it getting harder? Not as easy as it used to be, is it? Getting old, that must kinda suck, for you."

She knew it was mean, a low blow; but Margery unleashed it anyway.

"That's none of your business, and no I don't; sex isn't really that important, you know."

"Really, that's not what I hear. In fact, I hear your having sex with the grocery boy!"

"*What!* Who told you that? Did C tell you that? Why would he say such a hurtful thing? That bastard."

Cord sat on the toilet, still punch-drunk from the mother-daughter surprise. But he was quickly turning incensed, listening to this fucking nonsense, and the endless insults from Mae: *bad seed? bastard*?; never mind it was all true, and he had done his own fair share of insulting. But despite the indignation, he didn't move off the toilet; he was being a pussy, hiding in the john.

"I didn't say he told me; it seems a lot of people know, including my employees."

"And you believe that little blonde bitch!"

Mae snapped venom.

"I didn't say it was Lilly, and why is she a little blonde bitch? What has she ever done to you, mom?"

"Have you ever seen how she treats C? It's disgusting; I feel bad for him, is all. He doesn't understand she doesn't love him, and it's kind of pathetic, for him; he should move on."

"Yeah, pathetic….it certainly is."

"Well it is; **why** *is this door locked*?"

Mae said, yanking on the bathroom knob harder still, shaking the whole door frame.

"Mom, please don't break the door! The bathroom is out of order; the toilet leaks."

Another bit of cum dripped from her pussy, soaking into her spandex crotch.

"What are you smiling about?"

"Just thinking about the leak."

"You're strange Margery, you really are."

Mae went down the hall further, around the corner, toward the gym.

"Did you just meet C or not, Margery?"

"Funny, he went from the *delivery man to young man to Cord to C* in what, less than five minutes?"

"Well?"

"Yep, just met him on Monday."

"Then why did you say you're *best* friends, just to annoy me?"

"Why would that annoy you, mom? He's just a grocery boy, right? What is he to you? Is that nasty, nasty rumor all about Town really true? Please say it isn't so."

"He's just a *good* friend, is all."

Mae said, as she rounded the corner and stuck her head in the gym, which was empty.

"He's *your* good friend, but someone *I* should avoid, since he's a *bad seed,* with a *shadowy past*?"

Mae answered with her own question.

"What is he to you?"

"He's just a *good* friend, is all."

Mae didn't appreciate the mimic, and frowned at her daughter, as she stood in the doorway to the gym.

"Please, honey, did he stop by here? Please stop playing games; this is important, and you know it isn't easy for me to be here. Was he here, today, to see you? Just tell me the truth."

"Just because it's important to you, mother, doesn't mean I give a shit….truthfully."

And Margery sighed, regretting the biting insult just as the words left her lips; she wished she could rewind.

She stepped back, in her mind, and saw past her anger, and she saw the utter hurt in Mae's face. And she realized, as bad as her mom had been to her, and especially her dad, over the years, that she was still her mom, and the good feeling a daughter usually has about her mom, when the relationship works, wormed its way through the anger, and somehow broke the surface, at least a tiny bit.

And suddenly, Margery felt like shit.

Before her, she didn't see a manipulative, controlling woman, who tried to dominate her all her life; she saw a tiny frail woman, who was sad, and lonely, not dealing terribly well with getting older, trying to communicate with a daughter that she knew really didn't like her.

And her mom apparently had genuine feelings for Cord; Margery could clearly see it. This was different; this wasn't another mindless fling to satisfy her mother's ego and libido….both larger than life.

And like a flash, Margery got a double-shot of apprehension and dread, realizing how important it was to get her mom out of the building, past the bathroom, past any hint of Cord, and onto the street….*now*. It was no longer funny, nor oddly satisfying, knowing C was there anymore; it just felt wrong, and manipulative, and hurtful….and it had disaster written all over it.

"Sorry, mom, I didn't mean that. Look, it's been a busy morning; guys have been in and out all day."

Mae looked at Margie with sad blue eyes, like a lost doe, with nowhere to go, not a real friend in the world. She shook her head in resignation and disappointment, knowing Margery was never going to be honest with her.

"Then why was the front door locked?"

Mae said, in a halting voice which rose just above a whisper, displaying the face of a woman being lied to, a woman worn down; more of a plea, than an accusation.

She had heard of the blowup at Sam's less than an hour ago; she got the scoop from Mrs. Ackerman, who heard it all from Frank, who was only too happy to tell all within earshot. And Frank's rendition was less than flattering to Cord, for sure, and the true story was bad enough.

And Mae was torn. Although she felt bad for C, it was a golden opportunity for her, a solid stroke of good fortune, the one she had been waiting for, to finally extract Lillian from the picture and secure C all to herself. She thought for sure he would have shown up at her door, in less than a flash, for consolation, and sympathy sex, both of which she was more than ready to dish. But he didn't show up. And she was worried sick as to the why.

So right now, Mae just wanted to find C, to be sure he was okay, to comfort him, and to be sure he wasn't leaving Town.

Where could he be? He doesn't drive, and she had been to his apartment, to the *Palace*, to the boat ramp, to the Park, to the Cemetery, she even knocked on Carol's door – and Ji Sue answered. She knew he wasn't with Lilly, that was a given, so where else could he be?

Did he get on a bus? Was he already gone, for good? He wouldn't do that, would he? Without saying goodbye? Without saying *anything*?

Margery's was the last stop in Town; if not here, then where?

She desperately wanted to find him at Margery's, and she desperately didn't; she wasn't sure which outcome was better.

Didn't was better.

Mae's mind was racing the whole way over. Lilly was bad enough, but Margery with C? That couldn't happen; nothing, *nothing* could be worse than that....***nothing***. The thought looped in her head, him seeking comfort with Margery, and not her? It drowned all else.

"Mom, I'm sorry you can't find him, really. If I see him, I'll be sure to send him to your house, with the groceries.

I'm sure it will all work out, it'll be fine, I'm sure he's fine, and he'll be along….he's a good guy."

And Mae looked at her daughter, and in her words, she felt comfort, and relief, and care. That's what she needed right then and there. And in that moment, she loved Margery just about as much as she ever had.

"Okay, thanks honey."

And with that, Mae shrugged her shoulders at dropping a heavy weight, and ducked into the gym. She sat down in a heavy thud on the flat bench and sighed, deflated, one big heap of mixed emotions wearing her down.

And Margery, for the first time in a long time, touched her mom, placing her hand lightly on Mae's shoulder, in comfort. It felt strange, for both of them.

And Mae looked up at Margery and smiled weakly in recognition of the act, which was significant, and they both knew it.

Then Mae's gaze fell downward, toward the wall of mirrors across the room, next to the power rack, and in the reflection across the way, she saw her daughter standing beside her, her hand lightly resting on her shoulder, in comfort. And Margery actually wore a face of compassion, and Mae smiled again at her, a faint smile, but a smile just the same. A good smile.

So rare was this scene.

And Mae's eyes casually drifted to Margery's left; and there, tucked quietly under a bench, she spied the neatly folded set of jeans and an adjacent pair of slip-on, polished, black Kiltie loafers, set against the wall, perfectly placed, perfectly neat. Mae knew those shoes, and she knew those jeans, deposited more than once beside her bed.

And as her eyes grew to the size of saucers, Margery followed the line of sight, and saw the same evidence, right at her feet.

Evidence of a bad seed.

And the first thing Margie did was hurriedly look back at her mother, across the room, through the reflection in the mirror, and she saw the tidal wave of hurt; she knew that hurt, and she wouldn't wish it upon anyone, not even her mother.

And as Mae abruptly rose, brushed by her and ran down the hall, as she heard the front door swing open and slam shut, all she could do was shake her head and whisper aloud.

"*Shit.*"

CHAPTER 172 – HEY, WHAT FUCKING TIME IS DINNER?!

"What?!"

Button was a mix, partly annoyed at her for caring, and partly amused at the fortunate turn of events....mostly amused.

"I said, looks like the bird flew the coop."

He said a second time, with devilish delight.

Lilly sprung from her bed, naked, and ran down the hall, elbowed past his grin and saw the spray of evidence: opened drawers and half-pulled, mussed clothes; a general *in-a-hurry* mess, which blanketed the room. She quickly scanned the scene, processing, her mind racing.

And that's when she saw the worst part.

The armoire doors were swung open, with the lower drawer half-drawn and cocked, off its glide. She ran over and stuffed her hands blind into the back, past the never-worn shirts, under the stack of 1980's *Penthouse, Swank* and *Oui*, groping frantically, looking like a blind man for Earl's most important possession.

But it was gone, and she knew how serious this was; this was no joke. The *Kama Sutra* was gone.

Button ambled over, half-can of warm beer in hand; he was parched from all the pussy-pumping, barely making the effort to look like he cared, and spied the *Swank*. He swiped it from the drawer and splayed it to a random page, with one hand, the magazine flopped open.

"Whoa! Maybe he isn't gay after all!"

Lilly grabbed it, but he held on and it ripped the corner off the page he was holding.

"Let it go!"

She yelled.

"Jesus, don't be a fucking bitch!"

"It's my brother's!"

"I *know* who's it is; what do you think I am?"

A moron was implied. She didn't answer.

He glared at her and tossed the small triangular piece of magazine corner left in his hand onto the floor. She closed the vintage magazine, neatly pressed the pages, and placed it carefully back in place, along with the rest.

"Don't fucking grab shit out of my hand, *ever again*, you understand me?"

He said pointing at her, but she didn't pay attention, still sizing the room with her eyes, her heart beating hard in her chest. She walked over and opened the top drawer of his nightstand, the one nearest where he laid his head every night. And she frowned, knowing it too would be gone.

And it was.

Jonesy, that stupid dried-up lizard that C gave him, that he kept in a box by his bed that she wasn't supposed to know about. She knew that was a close second to the *Kama Sutra*.

She sidestepped Button, since he wouldn't move out of the way, and walked down the hall, into the bathroom, knowing what she would see.

His toothbrush was gone; nothing else, just his toothbrush.

And that's when she started to get upset.

She walked with purpose back to her bedroom, to get dressed. Button was sitting on the bed, naked, dick at attention yet again, ready for another go, with the quarter-can of warmish beer still in hand. He looked at her, and didn't like what he saw.

"Hey, I was just getting a drink; were not done yet."

"I'm *sore;* we've fucked for, what, six God-damn hours straight, take a break for Christ sake."

"I got three years to catch up on."

"That's not my fault."

She dished, dismissive.

"What's sore?"

"My ass, my pussy, *everything.*"

She spit, exasperated at the stupid question.

"Doesn't sound like your mouth's sore."

He stood up and placed his swill on the dresser, took her by the hand, and led her beside the bed. Then he looked lovingly into her eyes, and she saw a look of compassion, and believed it, even though she knew better. He placed his hand on her hair, and gently ran his fingers through the strands, just the way Lilly loved, just the way Button used to do to her mother, right before he would fuck her.

And Button kissed her forehead, and he was kissing Carol.

"Hey, come on, I'll help you find your brother. I'm sure he's just upset, but it'll be okay, we'll find him….just, in a minute."

And as he spoke, he placed his hands on her shoulders, and gently, then firmly, pushed down, till she bent her knees in compliance, and found herself eye level with his hard cock, still glistening from her cunt.

And, like a good girl, she didn't protest. She simply closed her eyes, opened her mouth and took him in, running his shaft in and out of her mouth. He sat on the bed, put his hands on the sides of her head, and pumped his dick in her open orifice. She didn't move, nor make a sound, she just kneeled, mouth open, a receptacle for him to use. Button knew he wasn't going to get much more for now, and he was unsure how long she'd stay still, so he pumped quick and hard, gagging her, hoping to unload down her throat quick.

And while he pumped, he thought of Carol, and how much he used to love when she blew him, just like this. And Lilly, with Button pumping piston in her mouth, was gone, in another place. She couldn't get Earl off her mind, wanting Button to finish quick, and just be done with it. She faked a long, low moan to move the process along.

And soon enough, he unloaded, groaning while he held her head firm, his cock buried deep in her mouth, letting it run warm down her throat. She began to gag, but he wouldn't let her move an inch until he was done, holding her head tight, in a vise, making sure she didn't let a taste escape - every last drop was going into her belly.

Then he freed his grip on her head, pushing it away from him, with a tinge of disgust, and fell back lazy on the bed, his dick drained. She quickly stood up, ran her fingers down the sides of her mouth to wipe away the wet; the action was emotionless, rote. Without a word, she turned and rifled through her drawer, looking for something to throw on.

"Maybe he's just upstairs, or at Sam's; can you go check the *Palace*? Ask around...."

"Upstairs? What's upstairs?"

"Cord's upstairs."

Button sat up, his attention piqued.

"Are you kidding me? You gotta be shitting me?! You mean that guy was *upstairs* when we were fucking all night? *Fucking golden!*"

Button nearly screamed the last two words.

Lilly didn't say a word; she was disgusted with herself, and that reminder just made it worse. She never told Button she was up there, *with him*, until five minutes before he showed up, and would have surely spread her legs for C if he hadn't shown up. Her *wet* was C's wet; Button simply stole it, and tagged it hard, all night.

But she didn't want to think about that anymore; that seemed like another life, years ago. And that chapter was closed, with Cord, of that she was certain. Cord was simply a casualty she would learn to live with. But she *wasn't* giving up her brother; Cord *wasn't* keeping her brother as spoils in the break-up of a relationship that never really got started.

"Are you getting dressed? *Come on!*"

She pleaded.

"Hey, what's the rush? It's not like Earl's leaving Town, or anything. I gotta shower and eat; I haven't eaten yet. Then we can go. What are you making, to eat?"

Button said nonchalant, playing with his half-hard dick as he spoke. His prick refused to deflate completely, wanting just another taste of whatever hole Button selected next.

She just looked at him, incredulous at being played yet again.

"What? I can't eat?"

He said, in mock annoyance, but that didn't work.

"Please will you make me breakfast? Please?"

He was sure that, especially the last *please*, would do the trick. It usually did, said in the right, apologetic tone, which he had down, pat.

"Whatever, eat; I'll see you later….make it yourself."

"Hey, I have some rounds to make, catch up with some people, you know; this trip is not just a social call. So I'll hook up with you later today, around dinner; what are we having?"

She slammed the dresser drawer shut in response.

"So you're not helping me, at all? To find my brother? *Fine!*"

"I'll help you *after* dinner; I'm sure he'll show up by then anyway, guys get hungry, you know."

Button said, talking to his dick, as he flailed it around, with one hand. It was finally giving up, for now, shrinking to sleep. She watched him pull on his pecker with disgust. Then she asked the question, trying to force him to get dressed, get moving and get out, so he would be gone before she found and brought Earl home.

"Where are you gonna stay?"

"You're looking at it."

He said, lightly patting the mattress next to him with his dick-free hand.

"You've got to be joking; you can't stay *here!* Not with Earl, *no way.* Not with C, Cord, upstairs, no way."

"Lilly, I'm staying *here*; your brother is gonna to have to get used to me, is all. Times have changed, I've changed, it's a brand new day. Hey, I'll try, give it my best, you know that, but your brother, he has to try a little too, you know. Two-way street, right? Only fair. And hey, remember, I'm not the one that went running away, you know; I want to try and make it work, for all of us. And as far as the other jerk-off, that's a non-issue; I don't think he's gonna be around much longer."

Button was preoccupied with the piss-hole at the head of his dick, opening and shutting the slit like a ventriloquist, smiling at the process.

"What's that supposed to mean? What are you going to do? To Cord?"

"Nothing. I just think, if he thinks about it, *really* thinks about it, he'll probably figure this just isn't the place for him, you know? I have no grudge with him, just tried to scare him, is all, having a little fun. *I* live here, *not* him; this is my Town - he's just passing through, right? Right. That's what I hear, anyway, on the street; so now, it's just about time for him to pack up and pass on through."

She didn't have time for this nonsense exchange, she had to find Earl; she'd deal with Button later.

She jumped into her *Capris*, sans underwear, a cotton top, sans bra, slip-on sandals and headed for the hallway, thinking about her brother, hoping he was okay, and wondering how she was going to apologize to C, or if she should even bother, not wanting to give him the satisfaction of throwing it back in her face. Any hope of salvaging a friendship with C was simply impossible. She rationalized that what she did last night to him was simply chalked up to being drunk – which was all Cord's doing, by the way. If it wasn't for him plying her with booze, and selling her his stupid travel fantasies, she wouldn't have gotten drunk and he wouldn't have been able to take advantage of her. Plus, Button *was* her boyfriend, had been for years, since they were little kids, in case Cord forgot. Cord Brin, or whatever his *real name* was, was actually the intruder, the trouble-maker in *her* relationship with Button. The story sounded good to her; she was convinced. Case closed. But the problem at hand was how to get her brother back. She knew Earl went running to Cord; where else would he go? She had to settle up with Cord Brin in some cordial fashion, or she would lose Earl, for sure. And she needed Mr. Brin to stay in Belvidere; if he left, Earl would certainly be in tow; and she wasn't letting that happen....*no way.*

And as Lillian ran out of the room, her mind racing a mile a minute, Button slowly laid back on the bed, content, alpha dog. He smiled, clutching and pulling on his cock like a sock-puppet, as it finished it travels to flaccid, resigned to rest a bit, for now.

And as he laid, and stared at the ceiling, smiling, his mind began to plot, figuring how to best keep the big stupid, fucking nigger out of the house, and Lilly's life, once and for all – for good, until he could kill him. If he could only get him, somehow, into a Black Dog barbecue pit, that would be fucking *awesome,* watching that retard rotisserie in a slow burn, as he stuck marshmallows on a stick. He thought about Black Dog, and how stupid-easy that was; Earl would be even easier. But more importantly, how, *specifically* how, to best finish the jerk-off intruder upstairs; now that would be a little harder. Although, given his pussy reaction at Sam's, maybe he was a chump, a coward, and would be easy too. It's not what he heard about this guy around Town, but people aren't always what they are played up to be. Either way, all he knew was the game had to be better than Mr. Chills; that process was not *nearly* satisfying enough. This one had to be slower, more painful, the more utterly unbearable, unwatchable, the better. He smiled wider at the thoughts; that was a very cool two-item to-do list and two new entries in his little black book; a retard-nigger and a queer-coward.

Then another thought popped into his head, pushing the retard and queer to the side. It was a very important, unanswered question, just as Lilly was slamming the apartment door. He yelled out to her, hoping she would hear, hoping for an answer, so he could plan his day accordingly. This was too important to wait, and he was already hungry.

"Hey, what fucking time is dinner?!"

CHAPTER 173 – NO ONE COULD POSSIBLY KNOW, BUT EARL WAS DYING

She heard Button yell something, but didn't hear what. She knew it certainly didn't have to do with Earl, so it wasn't important.

She ran up the steps, stopped at Cord's door and took a deep breath. Lillian knew he wouldn't be home, no way, but her stomach felt queasy just the same. It was as if she was intruding on a stranger. She felt further from him now than from the first day they met, if that was even possible.

Now he *was* truly a stranger.

But she had to go in, to see if there was any evidence of Earl hiding, or sulking, or moving his stuff in, or....she didn't know what. She grabbed the knob and turned it, to thrust open the door, just to get the anticipation over. But the knob didn't turn; the door was locked! That door was *never* locked, not once since the day he moved in....*never*.

Holy shit, maybe C *was* in there! She lightly rapped on the door.

"Hello, Cord, Earl....hello."

She said it so low, even if they were there, they would've never heard it.

She jiggled the knob some more, just to be sure it was really locked, and craned on her tippy-toes to look through the glass diamond panels in the door, which C left exposed – no curtains. The lights were out, and from what she could see, nothing was amiss. She spied Chicken sitting on the kitchen counter, staring at her with saucer-eyes. Chick didn't move, not a muscle, just stared scared at Lilly, like she was some sort of monster, trying to get in.

Lilllian gave the door one last shot, a good turn and shoulder shove. Nothing. That was enough to send Chicken scurrying; in a flash she was down the hall, and disappeared.

That was a bad, bad sign.

That door was locked for her, and her alone, but by who? Did C come back? Or did *Earl* lock it? She banked on the latter.

Earl had blown up about Button in the past, many times, but they were boomlets, really, and passed quickly; that was Earl's nature. It was what she banked on, to help balance, to manage, the Button/Earl dynamic, to avoid tipping into uncontrollable territory.

But he had never packed and left before....*never*. She had Cord and that bitch Carol to thank for that, for emboldening Earl, giving him an option other than coming back home, back to her. Fucking asshole Cord; fucking bitch Carol.

This was heading toward uncontrollable, and her stomach-churn reflected the concern.

She hurried, quietly, down the stairs, past her apartment, lest Button hear her and want to start another fuck-marathon. She heard the faint din of the television through the door; Button must be eating and watching the tube. She shook her head in disgust at this whole situation; everything that seemed to be going so well, fell apart so fast....*everything*. And the thing she wanted most of all for the past three years, at least what she thought she wanted, pined for, was propped up on a Friday morning couch, no doubt drinking the always-next beer and watching cartoon re-runs.

But she didn't have time to think about that.

In a flash, Lilly was on the street, and began to tick off the usual suspects in her head: the *Palace,* Sam's, the boat ramp, the Park, Uncle Franks, Marty's, the DSM plant – although that was a long shot, the Cemetery, Mae's - no, he was too afraid of her – the wing-nut she was, the gym – with Margery? Possibly.

Of course she ticked off every conceivable stop except where she knew he probably was, where he probably bee-lined, to Carol's….the one place strictly off limits, to Lilly.

She vowed to try that one last, as she cracked open the front door of *Nonpareil,* which was packed; Patsy Kline crooned *Back In Baby's Arms,* which she barely heard above the din. She quickly scanned the room, searching for Earl.

Earl was sitting quietly, trying not to move too quickly. He took a careful sip of his *Vernors,* with Earl lying beside him, purring like an engine, his funny white nose, with the crease in it, a third of the way down, buried in Earl's arm.

Earl turned to Ji-Sue, with a surprised look on his face.

"Did you just call him Earl? That's *my* name! Why'd you call him Earl? His name is Wasabi."

"No anymore; Mrs. C doesn't call him Wasabi anymore, she calls him Earl, so do I, for the last month, maybe more. He like it too, he purrs all the time, even more than he used to; Mrs. C told me I could tell you his new name."

"Wow, his name's *really* Earl?"

Ji-Sue just shook her head yes, and smiled at the two of them.

"Hi Earl."

Earl whispered to the warm ball beside him.

"He's so shy and sweet, just like you; that's why she call him Earl."

Ji-Sue whispered, as she knelt down, and gingerly rubbed Earl's jaw, which he jutted out, to get maximum rub. Earl ran his finger gently along Earl's nose, from the tip back toward the top. Earl closed his eyes and kneed his paws into the couch beside Earl's leg.

"Now I got blue fish and black cats and *everything* named after me!"

Ji-Sue kept smiling as she stroked his jaw; she really liked Earl, *both* of them.

"He's really shy; he *never* comes out. When anybody shows up, he runs and hides, so it's real big deal that he likes you so much; you're really lucky Earl."

Earl just smiled.

Ji-Sue got up and grabbed a shoelace off the floor.

"Play string with him for a bit; I have to feed the rest of them and do the litter boxes."

"I'll do it, I'll help! I'm suppose to help you! Plus, I like doing it, but I'm not gonna lie, I don't really like the smell of cat poop, just cow poop; cow poop smells good."

Earl said matter-of-fact; Ji-Sue laughed.

"Nope, play with Earl; he's happy, and we always want him to be happy."

Earl looked down, and Earl was still purring in a low loud rumble, from the pit of his belly; he *was* a happy boy. Earl grabbed the big pouch of extra skin on Earl's furry underside and rubbed it lightly between his fingers, then he stroked his little round belly good; it was warm, and he was content.

The first of several heavy knocks on the front door sent Earl vertical. In a shot, he scurried off the couch, out of the front parlor, bounding up the steps, to hide in points unknown on the second floor.

The large doors swung open and Marty stepped in, with Cord in tow.

"Yo, Earl, you in here!"

Marty yelled into the empty hall.

Earl jumped up and greeted the two of them in the foyer.

"Told you not to worry, Earl, I'd find him! He was heading out of Town! I tracked him down, *brought him in!*"

Marty said, chest puffed; Martin Brewer – *Bounty Hunter*.

"I wasn't heading out of Town you idiot; why the fuck are you saying stuff like that?"

C said, annoyed at Marty.

"Are you going….*away?*"

Earl said sullenly, head suddenly down.

"No, I wasn't leaving; I was just walking around, trying to figure a new place to live."

Theoretically, that wasn't a lie. C *was* walking around, thinking, trying to find a new place to live, just not within a thousand miles of Belvidere.

C had left the gym and had been walking the streets, trying to figure how to get his stuff out of the apartment, and how to best get out of Town, quickly, and preferably site unseen, and that prospect was getting ever harder. Now, he had to avoid Lilly *and* Mae. Holy shit, he still couldn't believe *that* bombshell; he popped mom and daughter in the same week; that was new territory for him. Well, maybe not, but it had been awhile.

He shook his head; he couldn't even think about Mae. C could only imagine how horrible, betrayed, she felt, par for the course with him. Her never talking to him again was pretty much assured.

Margery, believe it or not, was actually pretty cool about the whole thing, not that they talked about it. He just kind-of-left, and they just kind-of-said *bye,* with no drama. C wasn't sure if he would ever see Margie again either, for that matter. This Town simply wasn't big enough to avoid that many people in the ring. Plus, technically, he quit, so he really couldn't, or wouldn't, be going to Sam's anymore. Maybe he would join Carol and live on an island by the Park, in exile. That was the fate of the misfit toys.

Nah, he had to go; this trip had run its course. It felt over, and he didn't need a voice, he didn't need Jenny, to tell him that. He'd have to buck the rules and endure the consequences, if any were to come. Maybe he'd be given a pass; that happened on occasion, in a pinch, and this certainly seemed to meet the definition of *pinch.* He would just have to take that chance. But he still hadn't figured how to tell Earl; that was going to be the hardest part. Unless Earl wanted to hitch along; he knew he would, in a heartbeat, but he wouldn't want him to, or let him; his place was with Carol. They both needed each other. Maybe he'd just bring Earl to Panama for a stretch; after all, he *did* promise, and C kept some promises, not many, but a few, and one to a kindred spirit should most certainly be kept.

Earl interrupted C's mind wander, and he accused Cord of something he never had before, something serious.

"You're lying."

Earl said, looking straight at him, dead in the eyes. And C knew that wasn't just Earl speaking; his mom was standing beside him, for sure, shoulder-to-shoulder.

C didn't say anything, he just frowned....busted. They both could see right through the bullshit. Then came the fess-up.

"Earl, I can't stay, not with your sister and that jerk-off, and...."

He was about to say what just happened with Mae and Margery, but caught himself. And Marty cut in.

"Lilly has called me three times already, in the last half-hour, frantic, looking for Earl, and I let them go to voice-mail. She knows I *always* pick up when she calls, *always*, so she knows I know *exactly* where Earl is, and that I'm covering for him. That alone is gonna get my *ass* handed to me, by the way, but Earl said don't pick up; if she calls, so I didn't. So you're welcome Earl, and it was nice knowing you all, by the way. Say nice things at my funeral."

Martin let out a long huff, stopped for a moment, thinking, then began a rant.

"I knew it wouldn't last; three quiet years, great years, no problems, then that asshole has to show up again. And that mother-fucker went *back* down at Sam's C, making fun of the whole store, telling everyone you were some sort of fag, and a coward, and that you were already gone, ran away, like a little girl. Of course, Frank was laughing and loving it, all the shit-talk and stuff about you. I told Button to shut his mouth, and he got right up in my face, daring me to do something.

Then he made fun of me for taking Lilly to the *Ball* and not even getting a kiss out of it; he said the whole Town thought I was some sort of gay dry-hump, or something like that. I can't believe Lilly told him that; I thought she had a good time at the party, kind-of, anyway. Geez, I wonder what else she told him."

"So what did you do? Did you just fucking take it from that cock-sucker?"

C yelled at Martin.

Marty looked at him and said calmly.

"I did what you did, stood there and did nothing; then I left, just like *you* did."

C just looked at him and went numb; Marty was mocking him, and he wasn't even trying to; he was just telling it like it was, and he was fucking right. Dead-on right.

"But at least *I'm* not leaving Town."

Marty added, and a pang shot through C, sliced by the words, by the truth.

Marty was right, C was acting like a fucking pussy. And as much as he couldn't get in trouble, not here, there was too much at stake, too much to risk, he found himself backed into a corner, and really had no choice. Familiar ground.

Ji-Sue came back in the room, cell phone stuck to her ear.

"Okay, okay, you're welcome Mrs. C, you're welcome, okay; here Earl."

Earl just looked at Ji-Sue odd, and gingerly grabbed the cellphone.

"Hello?"

He said, hesitantly.

And then Earl stood there, head cocked, and listened, and listened, and then listened some more, interjecting with a repeating string of *okay, really,* and *I promise,* each accompanied by an ever-widening grin.

C, Marty and Ji-Sue stood in silence, waiting for the word as to whatever was going on.

C was steaming inside, his mind racing; why couldn't it be fucking yesterday? Better yet, why couldn't it be March? But then again, March wasn't any better; just a different set of problems, going from bad to worse. He sighed.

"Okay, I'll tell him."

Earl flipped the phone shut and smiled at C, but didn't say a word, he just kept smiling.

But C wasn't in the mood for games.

"What! What'd she say?"

C huffed.

"She said to tell something to you and me, to both of us."

And then Earl stopped, and kept on grinning.

"Well, what?!"

Earl stepped forward, bear-hugged C, lifting him clear off the floor, and, in a line right out of their favorite movie, *Neighbors,* he proclaimed:

"What do you say....neighba?"

"What's that supposed to mean?"

C said, in a halted breath; Earl was bear-squeezing a bit too tight, the excitement got the better of him.

"It means we're moving in next door! Right next to Carol, in the house next door, the one you found Chicken *Chimichanga* under, you and me, *like brothers!* For free! No rules! No Lilly! No Jerk-Face! All the music videos I want, and I don't have to wear headphones, and I can read the mail with my Gregson-glasses on and take all the time in the world, and I get to live with Chicken, and I get to see Earl and Big Banana *every day,* right across the yard! This is the best ever C, the best!"

Earl took a big breath, since he hadn't taken one in that whole excited string. And then he quietly said it again, with a head-tilt, in a whisper to his best friend in the whole wide world.

"The best."

C just stared at him.…speechless.

His mind continued to race, figuring how this would work, and why it wouldn't; what was good, and what was bad, what was the angle, and how could he possibly stay in this Town, and how, now, could he possibly leave? He just stood there, motionless, mouth slightly ajar. His own version of a codfish. And although he hadn't fully realized it, not just yet, it was inevitable, there was no other acceptable outcome.

He was staying in Belvidere.

And with that, he closed his mouth, didn't say a word, and just smiled his trademark uptick smile, and held out his hand to shake that of his new roommate. Earl walked right through it and gave his best friend a hug; Marty smiled, and so did Ji-Sue.

And as he hugged him, Earl whispered in C's ear, so no one else could hear.

"C, can I tell you something, really important, but I don't want you to get mad at me."

"Sure, go head."

C whispered back.

"Is it okay to say it, you know, to another guy, to your best friend….ever?"

"Sure it is; say whatever you want, doesn't matter."

"I love you."

No one had said that to Cord in years, in decades, not in a way that meant anything. And the tears began to well in C's eyes.

"I love you too Earl, and I'll never leave, not without you, never, you got my word on that, okay? Never."

And Earl smiled and hugged him tighter.

And while neither one knew it, and neither could certainly feel it, it had already begun, months before, maybe years before; but now, it would soon be upon them.

No one knew, no one could possibly know, but Earl was dying.

CHAPTER 174 – LEFT STANDING IN THE STREET, ALL ALONE

Carol didn't realize, but she had the Spider up to one-hundred-eight miles per hour; she rarely let it top ninety, and then it was just a dip over and back. Never, until now, had she passed a hundred on the dial.

And her mind sped just as fast.

She was worried; worried for Earl, worried for Cord, worried for herself. The last time she saw Button, she had just stuck a black dildo up his ass, not something that a *man's man* is likely to *forget*; then sprinkle a psychopath in the recipe and you have a disaster.

The last words he said to her: *we'll see,* as he left the house, with a maniacal smirk, rang in her head.

She quickly became scared of him, and was more so now. To this day, she couldn't believe she did to him what she did, and got away with it. Maybe she wouldn't in the end; maybe now *was* the end.

Adrenaline coursed her body; she pressed on the accelerator, and the needle inched toward one-hundred-fifteen; she was three miles from Exit 12, and about ten minutes from the house - much less at that speed.

Brick was dead, car accident, just three months prior, and the crew was his; she hadn't any idea how to reach them…she didn't even remember their names. She had frantically gone through her contacts, trying to find replacements, but realized she had better get on the road; she needed to be in Belvidere. She was shit-scared, yet excited at the same time, curiously drawn to the train wreck in progress.

She had to be there, and soon wasn't quick enough. These developments were game-changers, for sure; a whole new hand was being dealt.

Besides, Cord and Earl could handle that nut-case, she was sure they could....right? And they'd be next door; if she had her way, they'd have sleeping bags at the foot of her bed, or maybe *in* her bed, maybe she'd let C watch. She smiled at the thought of Earl beside her, naked, a short respite from Button-worry.

Lilly was on her bike, riding through Town like a mad-woman. Fucking Marty wasn't picking up the phone, so she knew Earl must have gotten to him first. She'd deal with *that* issue later, sticking a fork in Marty's fucking chest, for sure! Who was he to listen to Earl over her; take Earl's side over hers? Marty was a dead man. She had to talk to no more than three people in her two-wheel travels before she knew, for certain, that C was seen coming out of the gym, solo, and that Earl was driving around Town with Marty in his squad car, lights flashing, looking for Cord. But where they ended up, she didn't know, no one had that real-time tidbit except the dispatcher, and she fucking *hated* Lilly, and would never give her reliable information. But she had a pretty good guess, and despite reservations, that was right where she was headed.

"Well?"

"Well what?"

Button said, lazily, the bottle-bottom tipping lazy toward the ceiling.

"Did you tell your girl she's gonna dump your ass hard once she gets a taste of my cock; once they go black, they don't go back."

Dr. Pool laughed hard into the phone.

"Calm down, it ain't happening that fast cowboy. And I've seen that cock of yours nigger; you certainly aren't the *Mandingo* poster boy *[Button listened a bit, then exhaled, instantly annoyed]*. Dog, take a fucking breath,

I haven't even laid the groundwork yet; I had some catching up of my own to do! Heavy pounding, and that pussy is as good as ever, man....gold; still tight, clamped shut for three years, just waiting for my cock. Nah, she's out looking for that retard nigger brother of hers."

"Is she gonna buy in, bro?"

Dr. Pool asked anxious.

"She'll do *exactly* what I tell her to do, trust me; she always does in the end. Hey, the troops still okay? Anybody out of line?"

Button switched subjects.

"None, mother-fucker, none! I believe they've bought into the white man; you were right, can't fucking believe it! It's like Black Dog and Mr. Chills *who*? They bought the whole bullshit story hook and line bro, and moved the fuck on; the promise of fucking lots of women, free pussy, and easy cash goes a long way; fucking *Drin*, it's really gonna happen dog!"

Dr. Pool exclaimed, a kid on Christmas.

"Fucking-A it will. I shouldn't be here too long, maybe a week, maybe more. This is the last stumbling block dude; get my tribe, up here, on board and move her down there, set up shop, and watch the fucking cash pour in! *Drin* baby....*Drin*."

"*Drin*! Yo, later."

And with that, Button heard the Dr. switch to another call, and the phone went dead. He tossed the phone lazy on the couch, and turned up the volume, lit a cigarette, and dead-stared the tube, as two guys in cammies fired automatics on the *Outdoor Channel – Shooting Gallery*. He inhaled the last swig of beer, finishing off the sixth bottle, which he clumsily leaned against the base of the couch. It fell over, joining the rest on the beer-stained carpet.

Marty's pick-up, his dad's actually, inched along the curb, west of the sidewalk door, in front of the pet shop.

"Okay, we just need to pick up Chicken and get a few things, one trip for each of us, and were outta here, for now; we'll get the rest later. I don't want any confrontation with Lilly or him now, not now; plenty of time for that later. I'll deal with him later, solo. I don't wanna see either one of them, not now. Understood?"

C said stern to the duo.

"Me neither!"

Earl whispered.

"He says anything to me, or any of us, and I'm gonna shoot him, I swear; I've wanted to shoot that dick since I was five years old."

 C looked at Martin, with the officer's jaw set hard, and actually believed him.

"Take it easy Marty, we'll deal with him, *I'll* deal with him, later; let's just get this done."

The three men exited the truck cab and quickly made their way up the long flight of stairs, C in the lead. Cord took out the key and had it ready, before he hit the second floor landing. As they passed, they all heard the loud drone of the television, but no one said a word.

"Your stuff all together in my hall, Earl?"

"*Yep!*"

Earl whispered, excited at being part of a secret mission.

"Okay, you grab that, and get Chick; I'll grab the couple things I need. Marty, stay here by my door and just keep an eye out, to be sure neither one of them try to get in the apartment, or get in our way."

"You think they're gonna do that?"

Marty asked, suddenly apprehensive. And as quick as that, C didn't think Marty had to balls to shoot anything, or anybody, ever. He answered dismissive.

"I don't know *what* they're gonna do, and I don't give a fuck; I just want out of here quick, before I do something stupid."

And with that C and Earl disappeared into the apartment. Martin stood at the door, adrenaline pumping, his insides swirling like a scared kid, as the two boys rushed around the rooms, gathering supplies. Marty wasn't sure how long he was standing there, still hearing Lillian's television all the way up on the third floor hall landing, his mind racing, when he suddenly realized he didn't hear the television anymore, just silence from behind the door on floor number two. And Marty got another shot of juice through his veins, and immediately started to sweat. He stuck his head in C's apartment door, and half-whispered, half-yelled down the hall, as the boys scurried around.

"Guys, we gotta go, now!"

Marty's chest was heaving as he started to hyperventilate.

Lilly cut quick through the Park diagonal, kicking gravel beneath her bike tires. She was twenty yards from the intersection of Hardwick and Third, when she first spied the candy apple roadster in the driveway; that bitch *never* came out this early on a Friday....*never!* So Lilly knew Carol must already know the whole fucking scoop, and that whore couldn't wait to come out and stick her nose in.

"Fuck!"

Lilly cursed aloud.

She crossed the sidewalk and pedaled her bike into the road, past the corner, and headed down Third Street; no sign of Earl outside. She got to the alley and looped back, slowly riding past the Third Street side of Carol's house, scoping for any sign that Earl was holed up....nothing.

She tried, nonchalant, to turn the corner and look at the house in the periphery, out of the corner of her eye, but in doing so, she rode too close to the curbline, and her bike tire nosed into the storm grate slats. Before she knew what happened, she arced, slow motion, right over the handlebars and landed hard on her rump, in the street, alongside the curb.

And it hurt like a mother. But not nearly as much as the shriek of a laugh from the porch did.

Lily shot up like a bullet, left her bike in the street, and ran down the sidewalk to confront Carol, her face already crimson, and her blood a-boil.

"Where's my brother? He better not be in there!"

She screamed hysterical.

Carol just laughed, arms crossed nonchalant over her chest and didn't say a word, didn't even give Lilly the dignity of a response. Ji-Sue stood beside her, but a step back, and she wasn't laughing; she was scared shitless of Lilly.

"Earl! *Earl!* **Earl!**"

Lilly screeched, each one louder than the last; by the third chant, she was nearly apoplectic.

"My God, you really *are* white trash, you know that….pathetic."

"If he doesn't come out here, right now! I swear, I will fucking…."

"You'll what? Sick your boyfriend after me? Last time I checked, he was naked in my house, busy with a big-ol black dick up his ass, and *liking* it."

Lilly was rabid; she figured if she just charged the porch, she could take the bitch out once and for all; the little fucking Asian would run scared, for sure.

She was just about to launch into a full sprint, and would be on top of Carol in less than five seconds, kicking her perfect fucking teeth in, but the cannonball coming down Hardwick sidetracked the offensive charge.

Marty laid on the horn and kept it down for a good quarter-block, till he finally got Lillian's attention. She turned to see Marty behind the wheel, with Earl co-pilot; it was just the two of them.

It was the palliative she needed.

Lilly's shoulders, arched and stiff in attack stance, loosened and fell limp at the wonderful sight of her brother. She ran over in front of the truck, to make Marty stop, and quickly dipped around to the passenger window, which was rolled up tight. Earl looked straight ahead, even as she lightly rapped on the glass.

"Earl, Earl…."

She whispered sweet, lightly tapping on the glass.

But he wouldn't look at her, eyes still arrow-ahead.

"I'm sorry."

She said treacly, but he still wouldn't look. So Lillian abandoned door number one, and immediately moved to door number two, without skipping a beat.

"**Hey**! Open the *fucking* window; I'm tired of playing games!"

Earl still wouldn't look.

"I'll break it Marty! Tell him to open the fucking window, or I'll break it with my fist, *right now!* ***You know I will!***"

Earl swung his head and glared at her, as he rolled down the window, cranking it manually.

"What, *What **What***! I don't wanna talk to you!"

"Where's your stuff; when are you coming home?"

Lillian said, in a serene, calm-as-can-be voice, turning off the vicious like a light.

"I'm not! I don't live there anymore; I moved in with C."

"You're living upstairs?"

"NO!"

"Then where?"

"I'm not telling; I don't have to tell you! You're not in charge of me! I don't have to do anything you say anymore, *ever*!"

"Who told you to say that, Cord?"

Lilly said, in as calm a voice as she could muster, although she wanted to scream it, considering she was about to explode. Cord Brin, that fucking, ***fucking*** asshole, pitting Earl against her.

"NO! Nobody told me to say that; I figured that out all by myself! Why don't you just go back to Jerk-Face!"

"Don't call him that Earl; that's not very nice."

"Yeah, well what about what he calls *me*? What about that?"

"I'm sure whatever he said he doesn't really mean."

Lilly said serene, not believing a word of what she just uttered.

"Oh yeah, he doesn't mean it? He doesn't mean it when he tells me to: *Get the fuck out of the bathroom, you stupid fucking nigger! What are you, a fucking queer? Wanna join me? Suck my dick?* He didn't mean that? He didn't mean it when he said: *What's that you heard, retard? You hear me banging your big sister's head into the headboard? Or did you hear her moaning, with my cock in her cunt.* He didn't mean to say that either? Those are the first things he said to me Lilly, after three years….the very first things! And you left C *all alone* upstairs to be with him, and you hurt him really bad, and he's always good to me and you, and C was gonna leave today! Leave forever! Go away and *never* come back! And I'm his best friend, he even said so, and mom likes him and thinks he's an angel, she even told me! And I don't care that you don't believe in her….***she's real!*** And you made C sad, and made him feel bad, and he was gonna go away forever and leave me, because of you and Jerk-Face! So I don't like you anymore, and I don't want to see you anymore, and I just want you to ***go away, forever!***"

Earl was screaming and crying hysterical at the same time; he put his arm over his eyes to hide the tears.

Marty just looked at Earl, mouth open, then he looked at Lilly, who was too shocked to say a thing. She just stepped away from the window and dropped her arms to her sides, like they were lead weights.

Marty pulled away in silence.

Carol slowly shook her head, turned and walked into the house, without saying a word, with Ji-Sue close behind.

Lilly was left standing in the street, all alone.

CHAPTER 175 – FINALLY, FACE-TO-FACE, IT WAS THE PUPPET

C waited till the two of them, with Chicken resting safely on Earl's shoulders, to spill onto the street and duck out of sight, telling them he would be along, in a bit.

He slowly descended the stairs, stopping at the second floor landing, set his jaw and turned the knob.

Button was standing in the kitchen, back to the hallway, when he heard the apartment door quietly click open.

"I was expecting you."

Billy Bones slowly turned, still liquored-up, and revealed the knife he stole from Mr. Chills after he gutted and cooked him in the fire pit next to Black Dog; a black-handled, five and a half-inch double-edged Bowie that Mr. Chills himself stole, years ago.

"Just stole this from a monkey; was gonna slice his throat, but decided to gut and barbecue him instead. Thinking about the same for you, or worse, *much* worse."

Button said stoic, as he turned the Bowie blade slowly back and forth, so it caught the glint of the overhead kitchen light, looking at it like admiring a child.

C didn't say a word, and didn't react, just an icy stare.

"Ever smell cooked monkey meat? Oily."

Button said, almost in a whisper, and then he laughed, loud, with his mouth open, almost *too* open, showing his teeth. And as he first began to laugh, C heard it, and he saw it, just for a split second. But C *knew* he saw it; he swore he wasn't dreaming.

It wasn't a regular laugh; it just didn't seem real, or right, coming out of Billy's mouth....and Button didn't make a regular face afterward; something was odd about it, the way he swiveled his head upward and gazed at Cord, mouth now closed in a creepy smile, with blue eyes that looked dead. Again, it only lasted a flash, and as fast as C saw it, it was gone....vanished.

Like a quick peak around a curtain.

And when Cord realized what he heard, and what he saw, a chill shot his spine. And he realized this wasn't going to be the typical conflict, the typical confrontation, the typical hate that so often filled his insides; *this* was going to be different.

And suddenly Belvidere made sense; it made all the sense in the world. Belvidere must be its home.

It had been thirty-one long years since they last met, face-to-face; thirty-one years since they last spoke. But he knew, somehow, this day would come.

Finally, face-to-face, it was the puppet.

"Are you gonna get me?"

C asked the puppet, directly, eye on eye, without emotion, without inflection.

"What?"

Button said, cocking his head, thrown by the strange question.

C was disappointed in the answer. For now, the puppet was hiding.

C mouthed the rest of his soliloquy in a calm, quiet tone, the sentence strung like Ay was tired, and ready for a nap. Cord pointed to his own face as he spoke, to the same spot that Button knew well. It had all but disappeared, as they always quickly did. But this one was deep, and a fault line, barely visible, ever-remained on Billy's facade, to mark the important event, his own fence spikes, so to speak.

"Nasty, nasty scar....*knife*? That's what you tell everyone, but I don't think so. Nah, looks more like someone threw you through a fucking wall, like a little girl, a little pussy. Must have been a nasty fucking nail in the wall to rip your face up like that; nasty....*nasty.*"

C said slow, as he shook his head negative. Button, smile long gone, cocked his head again and squinted, staring at Cord; this time, he stepped forward, thrown off-guard. And C smiled at him, a dead smile....and Button didn't like that look, not at all.

Billy Bones cocked his head a third time, staring hard at Cord, trying to rack his squirming brain, trying to figure out how this guy could *possibly* ask that question, how he could possibly know that fact, since no one, *no one* saw him pull his dead head out of that wall so many years ago, and rip open the right side of his face on that jagged nail. He knew for sure Earl ran out of the house; he found that out later, *for sure*, that Earl knew nothing of what happened inside that wall, to Billy's face. And Button never told a soul the truth; a knife fight was the answer he came up with, and it stuck. Earl didn't know, couldn't know, no one could know; so how could this fucking nobody from nowhere know? Billy mumbled and stumbled his answer.

"There was no….what the fuck are you talking about? Who told you that?"

C just kept smiling, but now *his* was the face that was corrupt, malignant, threatening. And now it was *his* dead eyes that spoke, and they were wild, and they looked dangerous, and Button noticed; that stuff, he noticed, because *that stuff* mattered.

"Maybe *I'm* the puppet, mother-fucker, ever think of that? All these years, waiting, and maybe it's been me all along! Maybe this shit-hole is where *I* live! *Ormia Ochracea,* crickets and flies, and they're following with *me*."

All of that nonsense talk made absolutely no sense to Billy Bones, but it sounded fucking creepy, from a man possessed, and for the first time in a long time, Button felt vulnerable, and unsafe, in front of this stranger. But that tinge lasted just a second.

And then Button did what he always did when he felt that way, the fail-safe mechanism to buy time, to figure a plan, to cope with a potential risk, a potential danger.

He laughed, and then spoke through it, making light.

"I don't know what the fuck you're talking about, you fucking mo, but it don't much matter, soon enough."

And with that, Button ran the flat blade slowly across his jeans.

"You have no idea, do you, what I'm talking about? You really have no idea."

Cord said, as he looked deep into the eyes at the other end of the hall, and saw no recognition, no trickery, no cleverness, no nothing but glassy from drunk. C shook his head, disappointed in who Billy Bones wasn't. It looked like Button Pierce was gonna turn out to be just another jerk-off, another in a endless line, over the years; C long ago lost count. He was hoping for more, hoping for the puppet to finally show, then maybe all that happened here, in this stupid fucking Town, would finally make some sense. No luck.

Cord sighed and returned to a common theme, how he typically dealt with white trash like that which stood before him. And so he continued, in the same tired voice, knowing the drill, and knowing the ultimate outcome.

"Okay then, let's see what you got, one shot, one free shot, then you're done; you don't get a second chance. And I always get up, trust me....*always*. And then *you're* done, for good."

C stood, and raised his arms up, palms to the ceiling, shoulder height, nailed to the cross. And with that, Button let out a small laugh.

"I don't need a free shot; I'll gut you when I'm good and ready, which will be soon enough, trust me. You ***and*** your retarded nigger boyfriend; you like black cock?"

"Apparently not as much as you, ass-boy; fucking homo."

Button knew that was Carol's dildo talking; he stepped right into that one - he knew it once the words *black cock* left his lips. And he was pissed at the easy grapefruit he served up.

"Yeah, well, that bitch is…."

Button didn't finish the thought, interrupted by the slow creak of the apartment door.

C didn't even turn; he just curled his lips in utter disgust. He knew who it was, and was immediately angry, even being in her apartment was bad enough, but now having to share the same air with her, having to endure standing anywhere near that fucking whore, that fucking cunt, was unbearable.

Lilly didn't say a word, startled at coming upon C in her apartment, the last person she expected to find….there….here.

She instinctively took a step back, away from C, and just stood there, looking at the two of them, who were staring each other down, without saying a word, each barely breathing. And although, outwardly to anyone else, Button seemed calm, and assured, he wasn't; Lilly could see in Button's eyes, tell by his crooked smile, detect in the way he took his stand, the way he leaned against the counter, the way he held the knife, that he *wasn't* in control of this situation, and that was scary, because Button was *always* in control. But now, somehow, he wasn't. A cornered dog is a dangerous dog….and Button was cornered.

"That bitch is….*what?*"

C said, so Button could finish the sentence in front of his girlfriend.

Lilly, not knowing the context, figured being the bitch, but didn't say a word. She was scared shit-less, afraid to move; this was a *serious* situation, about to become violent.

1569

Button stared hard at Cord, then looked at Lilly, and posed a question to the room, to move the subject, and buy some time, to think.

"What's that smell?"

C ignored the bait and egged an attack.

"You gonna do something with that knife, or just stand there, ass-boy?"

Button's eyes darted, Cord-to-Lilly-to-Cord, his mind racing, deciding what to do, how to control a situation he didn't control.

"You know, you got a big fucking mouth, and…."

C cut him off, and his mock continued.

"Talk, talk, talk, talk, talk; you gonna talk me to death….*homo*?"

Lilly was scared to death, and started to tremble uncontrollably; no one talked to Button that way….*no one*. She never heard a single person talk him down, *ever*.

Button's face flushed red as he raised the knife, waved the point of the blade at Cord's face and screamed.

"Who the fuck you think you are, mother-fucker?! ***You're dead!***"

C didn't flinch, not a muscle; he stared at Button with lifeless, Stygian eyes and answered simply.

"You're right, I am."

And then, without sensation, Cord Brin spoke the same words that had traveled beside him, long distances, for years. And as he spoke, it was clear Ay wasn't angry anymore, and he wasn't sarcastic, he was simply factual, mouthing the same rote answer to the same oral exam. And a strange calm engulfed him, and the room, like a blanket on a grave.

Behold a pale horse;
and his name,
that sat on him,
was...."

He didn't finish the verse. Cord simply, quietly, turned away from Button; he never once laid eyes on Lillian, and just like that, the door quietly clicked shut behind him, and he was gone.

Lillian stared at the shut door, mouth open, still trembling, the hair on her arms at attention.

"What the fuck did *that* mean? What are you staring at? *Who's* name?"

Button yelled down the hall.

Lilly slowly turned to look at Button, and her face was ashen, as she finished C's sentence.

"....Death."

CHAPTER 177 – TAKE A TASTE OF ANYTHING YOU LIKE

Button stared icily at the closed apartment door, tense, waiting for something else to happen. Only then did he realize his forearm was burning; his grip on the knife had frozen in a tight squeeze, lactic acid frothing in his arm.

He released his muscles, and gently laid the blade on the counter, shook the lactic from his muscles, summarily dismissing the danger that just swept out the door. His bravado back, he moved onto more pressing topics.

"What's for dinner?"

Lilly ignored him.

She was still processing the prophetic words she just heard, words she knew well, a verse long ago committed to memory: *Revelation 6:8*.

They weren't religious, not by a long shot, not by *any* shot; they went to church exactly zero times. Lilly wasn't even sure what religion they were, or weren't....they were *nothing*, no religion at all. But for some reason, her mother knew that one, single biblical verse; where she learned it, and why she committed it to memory, Lilly never asked, and her mother never told.

But Carol she would recite it ominous, in a fateful whisper, at the beginning of every scary story-time, without fail. Every time she, her and Earl would sit and tell spooky ghost stories, her mother would turn out all the lights, set some scattered candles afire, and utter those fateful words, telling Earl and Lillian to be careful of the spooks hiding under the bed, in the bedroom closet, lying in the basement, or lurking in the attic. And she would warn them to be *especially* careful of the monsters in disguise, the ones that don't look like monsters at all, on the outside; because those are the scariest and most dangerous monsters of all.

With C's words, Lilly was transported to the age of ten in an instant, and she was scared, standing in her apartment, at the age of forty-one, hearing that fateful verse.

But like most frights, after a few moments of calm, doubt about what you heard, or what you saw, sets in; questions fade, and you chalk the events to happenstance. And then you quietly dismiss, and then you ultimately forget. It's how you cope.

Such is what happened to Lilly, and as the hair on her arms returned to normal, she assumed Cord's comments were nothing more than sheer coincidence; that was the clean, easy answer. And she moved on.

Lillian turned to Button, and clearly had questions of her own.

"Why was *he* here?"

"How the fuck should I know? Trying to start trouble, I guess."

Button responded with disinterest. Lilly looked at him in utter disbelief.

"What did you say to my brother, this morning?"

"*You found him*? Good; I told you he wouldn't go far."

"What did you say to him, when you saw him this morning, the very first thing you said?"

"I don't remember."

"He does; *every* word."

"He walked in on me when I was in the shower! He thought I was the jerk-off upstairs! It was like he was ready to get in the shower with me or something, so he startled me, and I got pissed and maybe said some things I didn't mean….*sorry!* Why did he think it was *him*, in *our* shower anyway, are you fucking that queer upstairs?"

Lilly took note of the *our shower* reference, but didn't respond. And she didn't want to think any more about what he said to Earl; she knew he probably said it, *of course* he said it, Earl certainly didn't make it up, he couldn't make *that* up, no way would he ever utter those words, even think those words, on his own. And in the end, Button would never admit he said it – no matter what proof she offered, and he would never change, so what was the point. So she gave up, which is exactly what Button knew she would do.

"No, I didn't fuck him, did *you* fuck anybody?"

"Yeah, *you!* All night long, and all morning too; pretty fucking amazing, wasn't it?"

It actually wasn't, so she didn't respond. Since he arrived, Button fucking her was not sex, it was more of an assault, a rape. *He* had sex; she was simply a recipient, an orifice, for him to mount and maul.

"Anybody else?"

He looked at her blankly, and after a few moments of awkward silence, she answered her own question, since he had answered it already.

"Forget it, I don't want to know."

And then Button heard the magic words, the ones he didn't know how he would ever coax out of her, the ones she never said in her life, and really meant, anyway. But this time, she did, at least she thought she did.

"I need to get out of here."

Button wasn't going to let this golden opportunity pass. His demeanor immediately changed, chameleon, his specialty; in a blink, she met the Button she remembered, or at least thought she remembered, the one she longed for. She found that man standing in front of her, face-to-face, his arms gently on her hips, his eyes gazing lovingly into hers. His transformation was complete.

"Then let's go, *for real;* I have a great place in Philly for both of us to live."

"Is that where you've been?"

"Yeah, most of the time. Do you remember the Dr? From the service?"

She greeted him with a blank stare.

"Tyrone! My buddy Tyrone Jones from the Corp, remember? The black dude?"

Lilly could never figure how Button had a black friend, it had to be some sort of joke, some sort of scam. Button with a *real* black friend? No way, it made **no** sense. He hated blacks, more than just about anything.

"Yeah, I heard you talk about him. Wasn't he in jail? Wasn't he into drugs, or something?"

"No! Well, I don't know what he does. But anyway, he and I are in business, and we started this thing...."

"You're in business with him and you don't know what he does?"

Button got flustered; he hadn't really thought-out how he was actually gonna pitch this idea to Lilly. He figured he had plenty of time, working on getting her to leave

Town was the heavy lifting, he thought, but now, with the ball on the one-yard line, he was fumbling."

"I'm just saying, I have a place, I have a job, and it looks like *now* is the time for you to finally kiss this place off; you don't need this....you're miserable."

He was right, she was. But she forgot, conveniently or otherwise, that the misery started about twelve-plus hours prior, when *he* showed up; before that, she was pretty happy, at least more happy than not, and getting happier.

Button gently kissed her on the forehead; it was the first tender kiss, the first tender anything, he gave her since he got back, the kind she missed, the kind she kept coming back to him for. And she started feeling nostalgic, and receptive. She smiled, and he saw it.

Golden.

"Hey, remember when we use to dye Easter eggs? You, me and your mom, mixing up all the colors, newspapers and paper towels laid out all over the dining room table, a dozen little dishes of color, with the spoons and those little metal things you used to dip the eggs, remember? We used to put tape on the eggs, and wax, to make all those cool designs, and use those markers, making all sorts of faces and stuff on them; wasn't that the best? Your mom always made the best faces; I miss those times."

Billy kissed Lilly again, gently on the forehead.

What Button really missed, was Carol. It was one of the few things just the three of them did together. For some reason, Earl got it in his mind early on that he didn't like to dye Easter eggs, just didn't like it, and would never do it, so it was always, every year, just Lillian, Button and Carol. It was the one the best memories Button had of what family *should* be, what he wanted his family to be:

him, Carol and Lillian, dyeing eggs around the dining room table....no Earl.

He smiled at the memory, and kissed her again.

"Earl doesn't want me around."

Lilly said, deflated, her head buried in Button's chest.

Oh my God, can this get any better? Button smiled wide inside.

"He doesn't mean it, darling, but you know what, it would be good for *both* of you to take a break. I mean, forty years is a long fucking time to be joined at the hip, brother and sister to boot; it's just not right. There's a lot of cool stuff beyond Town limits, trust me; Philly's a cool place, all sorts of stuff to do, shopping....and stuff."

Lilly kept her head tight against his muscular chest, absorbing his warmth, and stirring the possibility in the glass.

Earl was mad at her, like he *never* was before, and wanted her to *go away.* Maybe Button was right, maybe she and Earl really did need a break from each other. Anyway, Earl had Cord to look after him, and *her* too; but Lillian didn't want to think about how Carol would glom onto Earl; that was a big downside to leaving. That was happening anyway, but her walking away would give that bitch free reign, and a huge *win.* But it would only be temporary, right? When she came back to Belvidere, because she was only leaving Town for a little while, right? Earl would be all over her, sprinting back to her, asking, begging her, for forgiveness. And as for Cord Brin, or whatever his real name was, well that was over, stone dead. At least nothing ever *really* happened, thank God for that. Thank God she didn't give it up for Cord; she would never be able to live that down, knowing he got in her pants. In the end, he never got a taste or even a peek of her, and he wanted it, *real bad.* That made Lilly happy, in hindsight, that he wanted her so bad, and she shut him out, and just gave it all to Button, as much as he wanted. And boy did he take it....all night long. Served Cord right for trying to poison her relationship with Button. Button *was* her boyfriend, had been for years, not Cord, so it wasn't like he didn't know that she was just in waiting mode, a holding pattern, till Button came back for her. And Cord would get over it soon enough; he had his wrinkly senior citizen to go back to anyway – that's what he deserved. Disgusting. And she really just liked him as a friend anyway, right? Last night was just a drunken-induced almost mistake – and Cord's the one that tried to get her drunk to sleep with her anyway – what kind of guy does that? A creep does; tries to get into a girl's pants only if she's drunk! Thankfully last night got nipped in the bud; it was a miracle that Button came back and saved her; thank God for Button. Her pussy, her body, all of it, the whole package, was Button's, *not* Cord's. And it wasn't like Cord Brin already wasn't over her and the little mishap last night – he ignored her completely in Sam's when she tried to explain and he ignored her again in the apartment just now; *fuck him....asshole!* And what happened last night really wasn't so bad for him, she thought; he got a little taste of foreplay; she was sure he'd jerk off to that little taste more months....you're welcome, Mr. Brin, and you're lucky you even got that. She shouldn't have to apologize to anyone for having sex with her boyfriend, right? And even Marty was mad at her, not that he really mattered one bit, it was just another notch in the *time to leave Town* column.

She processed the jumbled mess in her brain, turning it over and over, tossed salad, trying to convince herself. And when she was done, she looked up at Button and smiled weakly.

And Billy Bones figured that smile was ultimately going to morph into a yes; it may take a bit more massaging, but he was banking on a definite yes.

Then Lilly kissed him gently on the neck, but it wasn't a regular kiss. It was a kiss that said she was putting all her chips in with him. A kiss that said they were banging again, all night, as much as he wanted, any way he wanted it. She would do whatever he asked; her body was his for the taking.

And when she said the words that followed, in a silky bedroom voice, he knew the hook was set, and set deep. It was her and him again, just like old times, but even better. And Philly was close on the horizon.

Sweet music to his ears.

"So what do you want me to make you for dinner sweetie, *anything* you want. And after, for *dessert,* you can take a taste of anything you like."

CHAPTER 178 – LOST IN THOUGHTS OF HERRING FEATHERS AND HAND HOLDS

"But *why* would he do that? I don't understand why."

Earl asked, with a worried mind.

"I told you why, because the fox was scared, and selfish, so he betrayed his best friend to save himself."

"What did he do again?"

Now Earl remembered the story verbatim the very first time he heard it, just like every story C told him, but he would ask over and again for it to be retold, hoping the ending would change, just like with his friend Fred, the pig. C knew this, and would patiently explain the story again and again, never getting mad, but always sad at seeing the distress in Earl's face, waiting for the happy ending he hoped would come. It never did.

"The lion had caught the fox, and was going to eat him. So the fox made a deal with the lion; if the lion promised to let him go, he would agree to trick the donkey, the ass, who was his best friend, and lead him over to the hidden hunting pit and push him in, so the lion could eat his best friend instead of him.

And the lion agreed.

So the fox tricked his very best friend in the whole world, and traded the donkey's life for his own, letting him fall in the pit.

But once the lion saw the ass was trapped and helpless, he quickly turned and tore the fox apart; he ate him right then and there, while the donkey watched his best friend die, helpless and scared, never knowing he was betrayed. Then, later on, after he napped, he jumped in the pit and killed the donkey, who had nowhere to run or hide. The fox and the ass both got eaten alive, and the lion just laughed."

Earl put his head down, and closed *Aesop's Fables*.

"I would *never* do that to my best friend."

Earl whispered, on the verge of tears.

"I know you wouldn't."

C whispered back.

Earl looked up at C with sad eyes, and didn't ask the question he never asked every time he heard the story, so C answered, like he did every time.

"No, I wouldn't do that either, not to my best friend."

Earl pushed the book to the side, and rubbed his finger under Chicken's chin. Then he ran his hand down the length of her tail, till he got to the little bent nub at the end, bent to the right. He smiled as he ran his finger over it.

"You know, Chicken is kind of like a lion, just a real *little* one, but I don't think she'd trick the fox, or eat the donkey, do you?"

"Why would she? She gets all the food she wants served to her, like a princess, by a much bigger ass, *me,* every day in her own special bowl. No need for her to the trick the fox and donkey, she's got me."

"I'll feed her from now on!"

Earl exclaimed.

"*Great,* just one more reason for her to abandon the guy who saved her life with a rake from under the porch, in a rainstorm, in the mud, with gunked-up eyes to boot; ungrateful little bitch. Go ahead, have at it."

Earl looked down at Chick and smiled, and she purred, like she always did for Earl.

"Bitch."

C shook his head. The front door of their new digs, next door to Carol's house, cracked opened, and Marty stuck his head in.

"Hey, are we done bringing stuff in? Carol just got the Chinese delivered; she's warming it up and said it's time to eat. She's got it all set up on the porch....smells really good!"

"Okay, we'll be there in a minute."

C said, and Marty pulled the door shut. Ay looked over at Earl.

"You happy?"

"Yeah!"

Earl yelped, but the enthusiasm immediately drained from his face, remembering what he did.

"I yelled at Bibby; I was mean to her. I didn't mean to be, but she got me mad, about you, what she did to you last night, and Jerk-Face got me mad; I don't know why she keeps going back and...."

"Enough."

C said, putting up his hand to stop the commentary. He didn't want to hear any more Button and Lilly stories, the last twenty-four hours already felt like years. Less than twenty-four hours ago, he Earl and Lilly were planning out the *Blobfest*, which is where they would be, *should be*, right now. And later, he was snuggled up under a blanket with her, ready to get lucky, with her more than willing and able. He pushed the thought out of his mind with an exhale of utter disgust.

"She's a big girl, and she still loves you, but apparently she knows what she wants, and it's that guy, for whatever reason, so be it, no big deal. She'll be fine; he'll take care of her, I guess, and we'll take care of each other."

"Yeah, but…."

"No buts…..*done*. If were gonna live together, it's gotta be you and me, and moving forward; I don't wanna think about those two anymore, or talk about 'em, okay?"

"Okay."

Earl mouthed, weakly.

"Good, let's eat; Carol got all vegetarian Chinese food. She got it shipped out here all the way from some town called Montclair; she's something else."

Earl smiled, thinking about living right next door to Carol; he was nervous and excited, all rolled in a ball.

"You know, I think she smells…."

C cut in.

"….like flowers, I know, and you like the cleft in her chin and the space in-between her two front teeth and her teeth are so white, and you like the smell of cow manure."

"Hey! I don't like cow manure and all those things at the *same time*, you know! Cow poop is separate from flowers!"

Earl said in defense of Carol, as they both lifted themselves off the couch and headed for the door. Then Earl hunched his shoulders, in a submissive posture.

"Hey C, can I ask you just one more question, you know, about what we're not supposed to talk about anymore?"

C knew this was never going to be just the last question about Lilly. He sighed and let out a long breath.

"Yeah, go 'head."

"I kinda told Lilly something."

"Like what?"

"I kinda said that my mom likes you and thinks you're an angel, or something, and that she told me so, and I didn't care that Lilly didn't believe in her."

C looked at him, surprised, but was happy he told her, to her face.

"There's nothing wrong with that, Earl, it's the truth, right? So be it."

Earl wore a look of worry.

"Yeah, but, she doesn't believe me, she doesn't believe I *really* talk to my mom, I know it."

"I wouldn't be so sure Earl; I think Lilly believes a lot more than you think. Besides, who cares if she believes you?"

"I do, because if she believes, *really* believes, then maybe my mom will talk to her too."

"It's not that easy; wish it was."

"Hey C?"

"Yeah."

"How come no one else can talk to their mom, like I do, like I can? I don't understand."

"Me neither; ever ask her?"

"Kinda, but she never really answers me."

"Maybe she doesn't know either."

"Hey C?"

"Yeah."

"Is there an explanation, you know, *for everything*?"

C smiled at Earl as bullet-thoughts raced through his head: puppets, crickets and flies; getting un-stuck on a fence; 1:13 am; and, of course, dead is dead, unless it's not. And in this strange place: kindred spirits, fourth darts, angels, not-so-dead mothers and *Open When Ready*. None of it really made any sense; there was no *logical* explanation. Yet all of it somehow seemed to be linked to this backwater; that was the feel. It seemed to be a lock with a misplaced key. That was about all he figured out, which meant he really had *nothing* figured out. Then he answered Earl.

"No, there isn't, not yet anyway. But that doesn't mean there never will be; it just means you don't know how, or why....*yet*. And maybe you never will."

"What's *that* mean?"

Earl asked, perplexed.

"I have no idea."

C said matter-of-fact, as he let out a quiet laugh. The duo made their way down the sidewalk, walking around Carol's house, the long way, to the front porch.

"We're just a speck, Earl, *way* smaller than a speck. We don't matter much; in fact, we don't matter at all, not in the big picture, anyway. And *you* don't know other people can't talk to their moms; I mean, you don't know everybody, right? There are over six billion fucking people stumbling around this planet; although there may not be many, you certainly are *not* the only one who talks to his mom that way, Earl, trust me. I just wish I was one of them."

"You think other people do too?"

"Sure. Indians, Native Americans, you know, like cowboys and Indians-type Indians, and Eskimos – Inuit and Yupiks, they have special people in their tribes, sometimes they're called shamans, or sometimes they go by other names; they are *real* special people, just like you. They can communicate with spirits, *any* spirit, not just people-spirits, but *anything* in nature; they believe *everything* had a spirit: the trees, animals - like Aloysius….*everything*."

"Eskimos! Eskimos can speak to their moms like me, and even Aloysius?! I like Eskimos! I've seen them in cartoons and everything; they are *always* nice, and they wear big furry hats! I wish I had a hat like that! I like Eskimos a lot; maybe I can even meet one someday! That would be the coolest, ever!"

Earl yelped. C smiled and continued.

If you just figured out *how* to talk to them, the spirits in people, animals, trees, whatever….they'd talk back. And these special Indians, and special Eskimos, the shamans, they somehow figured it out. They'd use all sorts of tricks to help them talk, like those three scary wooden masks in Carol's coat closet. Those masks happen to be African, not Indian or Eskimo, but it's the same idea, and people in Africa can talk to spirits too. Like that one in the middle of Carol's closet, with the red light behind it, that's the *River Goddess,* the one that protects people from drowning; the shamans would use those masks to help them talk to spirits, and to the dead. Or sometimes they'd use other things, like pendants − you know, good luck charms, or feathers, rattles….whatever helped."

"I don't *like* that *River*-mask, that one scares me, the red-light one! I don't like going by that closet!"

"I know you don't, Carol told me."

C laughed.

"Do you know what *your* good luck charm is?"

Earl just shrugged no.

"What do you do with your mom? How do you talk to your mom? You told me a thousand times."

Earl furrowed his brow, then he shrugged again.

"Earl, you hold her hand, and she's holds yours; that's *your* good luck charm, holding hands, at least I think so….seems to work for you."

"Then why don't you just hold *your* mom's hand?"

Earl said to C.

"Just because it's easy for you, doesn't mean it's that easy; being a shaman is not easy − only special people can do it - you happen to be one of them. I don't think that would work for me."

"Well then maybe you can get a rattle to talk to your mom?"

C smiled.

"For me, I think it's gonna take a bit more than a rattle."

"Hey! You said a feather works! What about *the* feather, your white and gray feather, from the special seagull."

Cord shut his eyes and thought about the herring gull feather; to him, it always meant an end, and with that, a new beginning. A new beginning that was finally going to turn out well. It meant both, always did. But he was still waiting for that good ending to come; it never seemed to show.

He looked over at Earl.

"Maybe, but it takes more than a *thing*, like a feather, to help; it takes whatever *you* got: hope, trust, belief, innocence, goodness, love, all of it, I guess, in the right mix, along with a hand-hold, or a feather….those are the set of keys that open the lock, the things that kind of put you over the top, I guess."

"I wish I could tell you how it works C; it just does, for me."

Earl said, shrugging his shoulders again.

"I know it does, and I know you'd tell me, if you could. The hard part is figuring out the recipe on your own. I think everyone's got a different one, and most never figure it out, most never even try, but that's the only way I think it really works. And until I met you, I would have never even had a conversation like this, thinking it's all a bunch of crap, till I met you, and then thinking maybe it's not, maybe it's not at all."

"Hey, come on, dinner's getting cold!"

Carol called inside the house, as the two shuffled up the front porch steps, lost in thoughts of herring feathers and hand holds.

CHAPTER 179 – CAN I PLEASE HAVE ANOTHER COOKIE?

All four were stuffed to the gills, sprawled lazy across the south side of the porch. Earl and Marty sat on the loveseat; Carol in her master chair….C leaned on the porch rail, back to the Park. Summertime on Carol's porch, you couldn't beat it with a stick. Ji-Sue had a well-deserved, and rare, day off, so Carol played hostess.

Carol passed the third round of *Southsides,* her favorite event drink. C had been busting her for awhile to make a round, and she finally obliged, times three.

Earl chewed on the sprig of mint, and tried to take a gulp while dodging the chunks of crushed ice and floating wedge of lime.

"This is good!"

Earl declared aloud, on his way to another drunk.

"She could give you a tub of piss and you'd say it was good."

Marty mocked.

"Would not!"

Earl said, as he downed the third gin concoction.

"I'm getting drunk!"

Earl proclaimed, stating the obvious.

"What a surprise."

C said wry, as he nursed his drink.

Carol stepped onto the porch with a small tazza in hand, set on a silver tray. Within the shallow cup sat four pristine fortune cookies.

"Okay, everybody gets one, but don't open them, not yet."

The cookies were quickly fingered and snatched from the tazza, each guy holding their own present, like Christmas; the last one standing was taken de facto by Carol.

"Okay, Carol, you go first."

C ordered.

"Why me?"

She protested, mainly because C ordered her to go first.

"Because I asked you to, that's why."

C said.

"But I don't want to go first."

"Who wants Carol to go first? Raise of hands."

The three boys shot up their arms and laughed; she just frowned.

"That's a stupid way to choose."

"Democracy, yeah, that's dumb."

C said sarcastic, as he grabbed a *DeMuth* from his jacket pocket, bit off the end and lit it.

Carol cracked the cookie and discarded it daintily in the tazza. She grabbed the little white note with blue lettering, looked past the *Lucky Numbers* and read the fortune aloud:

Keep your feet on the ground even though friends flatter
you

"That's the best fortune ever! What's it mean?"

Earl shouted, louder than necessary; alcohol induced. C smirked.

"How appropriate; it means don't have a big head."

"Does not!"

Carol whined.

"Of course it does! What the hell else do you think it means?"

C snapped. Carol ignored him, and spoke directly to Earl.

"Earl, it means good friends can say nice things about you, to make you feel better; they don't have to make fun of you all the time *[she shot a friendly glare at Cord]*. And when they do, you should understand they say those things because they love you, and you should say nice things back, because you love them too."

Both Marty and C looked at each other, and busted laughing.

"What the hell was *that*? How did you even come up with that bullshit answer? That wasn't even close!"

C snorted.

"Was to me."

Was all she said smugly, as she smiled at Earl and took another sip of her drink. Earl just put his head down, his cheeks flush, embarrassed. C just laughed again.

"Whatever; you're so gay. Okay Earl, go ahead."

"No! Stop ordering everyone around; you go next!"

Carol yelled.

"Fine, no big egos around here."

Carol frowned.

C cracked open the shell and threw the halves in the tazza. He read the inscription:

Red....Hong Se

"That's not it, the other side; read the other side!"

C looked at Carol incredulous, and said sarcastically.

"*Really?* Thanks."

He flipped over the note, and above his own *Lucky Numbers*, it read:

God of Fortune is beckoning you

"What's that mean C?"

Earl shouted, again, louder than he needed to.

"Well, I think it means the God of Fortune, like the *pile-of-cash* kind of God, is beckoning me, ready to hand me a wad of money and put Mrs. Big Head over there in her place; bring it on, Fortune God!"

C took a long toke of the *DeMuth*, and blew it forceful toward Carol.
"Really? You're gonna have a lot of money C? Can I have some? Can you buy me an Eskimo hat?"

Earl was excited at their new-found wealth; thank God for the fortune cookie.

"Sure, you can have it all; it is written, and it is so."

C preached. Carol harrumphed.

"That's *not* what it means; it means you're going to have some good luck, as in good fortune."

C looked at her incredulously.

"So now you know what both your *and* my fortune means?"

"It's common sense! You should be happy; good luck is on its way to your door."

Carol exclaimed.

"Well, that can't be too fucking hard, since I've had nothing but shit-burger luck up to now."

C said, matter-of-fact.

"But we have *good* luck! We get to live together, and we're right next to Earl and Big B, and...."

Earl's voice trailed off.

"....and *what*? You're *extra-special-favorite*, neighbor, right next door?"

C nudged him, and Earl clammed.

"Leave him alone."

Carol whispered.

"Okay, I'll give the living together as a turn in luck, as long as you keep the place clean and cook all my meals….and rub my feet."

"Deal!"

Earl yelled, before Carol could protest.

"I'm only kidding, he doesn't have to keep the place clean, I'll do that."

C whispered sly toward Carol.

"Earl, you don't have to rub his feet, or cook for him, or anything! Don't let him boss you around!"

"What, like you're doing right now?"

She ignored him.

"Okay, Earl, you go next; can I *request* that Earl go next?"

Carol asked faux-timid, looking to C for the mock okay.

He slowly nodded approval.

"Thank you. Okay Earl, you're up."

Earl cracked the cookie open and immediately shoved the two crunch halves in his mouth, chewing loud while he fiddled with the paper, too excited to even read it. He loved to eat fortune cookies, almost as much as *Animal Crackers*.

"Here, you read it."

Earl said to C, mouth full and still crunching.

If you continually give, you will continually have

C looked up at Carol, eyes wide open.

"*What?*"

She said.

"Well, you have an opinion on everything else, and apparently know what *all* the fortunes *really* mean. So, what does it mean?"

She turned lovingly to Earl, gazed into his eyes and softly said.

"It means the fortune cookie *knew* it was yours, *it found you*, because no fortune in the whole wide world could be more right for you than that one. You do continually give, Earl, without reservation or condition, more than any person I have ever known. And for that, you will continually have friends who love you and need you and would do just about anything for you, like the three friends you have right here."

C smiled, held his glass to the sky, and motioned the others to follow.

"Well at least you didn't fuck that one up. *Touche, Sante;* to Earl, the best egg ever!"

"*Sante!*"

The chorus rose, and Earl smiled, and emptied Southside number three into his gullet and looked out blankly, staring into nothingness, into the Park, a slight smile on his face and a drunken glaze in his eyes.

"Well, anything to say, Earl?"

C said.

His face changed, and he sheepishly looked at Carol, barely breathing a whisper.

"Can I please have another cookie?"

Marty was just about to crack his fortune, until he heard Earl.

"Sure Earl, you can have mine; you don't like yours?"

"Thanks, Marty."

Earl said, as he turned and was about to leave.

"Whoa, whoa, what are you doing?"

C said, grabbing Earl's shirt.

"Carol said that cookie *knew* it was mine; maybe this cookie knows it's Bibby's."

"Earl, that's Marty's cookie, and your sister is probably at home with her boyfriend; don't go back there, not now."

Carol said.

"She's not with him, and she's sad, I just know it, and I think she needs a cookie, I think that would help; cookies *always* help when you're sad. And I yelled at her, and that wasn't nice."

C looked at his friend.

"Okay, okay, you want to give her the cookie, fine, but do it later, do it tomorrow; I don't want you running around Town looking to give her a cookie."

"I don't have to run around Town, I'll just bring it right to her."

"Okay, where?"

C said.

"There."

Earl said, pointing to the Park, pointing to his bench, his and his mom's bench, the one that Lillian was sitting on, all alone, in the fading summer light, shoulders slumped, staring at her shoes.

The three looked, and Earl quietly skipped down the porch and trotted to the center of the Park.

"If you continually give, you will continually have."

Marty said, rereading Earl's fortune.

"Why doesn't she just go away."

Carol said, in disgust; then she continued.

"She tortures him, plays with his head and tortures him."

C looked at Carol and put his hand gently on her shoulder.

"She needs him much more than he needs her, but neither one knows it. And as much as I dislike her, the reason we just saluted Earl is because he is the only one who would have done that out of all of us, without question, without hesitation, because he loves his sister unconditional, despite her faults, and her bad judgment....despite it all."

C raised his glass again, pointing it toward Earl.

He whispered toward his best friend, with Martin and Carol following, in unison.

"Sante."

CHAPTER 181 – GROUND INTO THE GRAVEL, FACE DOWN

Earl walked the last couple steps to the bench; she never looked up. He sat down quietly next to her, and put his hand on hers, which was resting on her thigh. The fortune cookie was sandwiched between their hands. She felt it, and turned her hand, which turned his, revealing the light tan treat.

"It's for you."

"No it's not, it's for your friends."

She breathed, dejected.

"It was Marty's; he said I could give it to you."

Lillian frowned and grabbed the cookie, rolling it around her fingers.

"Are you coming home?"

She had bags under her eyes; she looked dead tired, and sad.

Earl leaned over and kissed his sister on the cheek.

"Open the cookie; mine was meant just for me….maybe this one was meant *just* for you."

"Who told you that, mom?"

Lilly said, with no air of sarcasm or derision; it was more hope than anything else.

"No, sometimes fortune cookies just know."

Lillian cracked the cookie in two, the effort seemed monstrous, and held the halves in her palm; the blue printed note stuck out, waiting to be pulled. But Lilly was defeated, and just let it sit.

So Earl gingerly grabbed the note and pulled it out slowly, the paper scraped loud against the baked flour and sugar. He placed the note in her palm, and hoisted the two halves.

"I'm eating the cookie, just saying...."

He said, the halves already to his lips. He hesitated for a second, in case of a protest; hearing none, in they went.

He crunched as Lilly sat. looking at the back of the note, which was blank.

"I'm sorry about what he said to you Earl; it won't happen again."

"Yes it will."

Earl whispered.

"He's not nice to you Bibby, he isn't, and he's not your friend, he's not anybody's friend, and you look sad; I don't want you to be sad."

"It's not that easy, Earl, it just isn't."

"Yes it is! Just tell him you have new friends now, friends that really care about you."

"Like who? Cord? He *hates* me. And Carol? *Please.* Even Marty's mad at me; you're my only friend, and even you're mad at me, and don't want me around anymore."

"I'm not mad at you Lilly; I love you. You're the best sister anyone could ever have....*ever!*"

Earl put his fingers into her palm and flipped over the fortune; Lilly read it to herself, and began to quietly cry.

All the answers you need are right there in front of you!

"See! I told you!"

Earl was so excited - the cookie was right *again*! Those were some amazing cookies; the best fortune cookies ever!

"Button wants me to leave, to leave Town and go live with him, in Philadelphia."

"*What!* You can't leave! If you go with him, you'll never come back, *ever*. He'll never let you come back home Lilly, he won't! And he'll treat you worse than ever! He'll hurt you Lilly; he'll keep hurting you, like he used to, but worse; I just know it!"

Lilly was silent. Then she spoke, barely above a whisper.

"What does mom think I should do?"

"I don't know, she didn't tell me. How would she know you were going away; did you talk to her?"

Earl's voice raised in anticipation.

"No; she doesn't talk to me."

Lilly said, in deflated sarcasm.

"Are you coming home? I'll make him move out."

"He's not gonna leave Bibby, and he doesn't want me around. He wants you all to himself, so he can hurt you, and make you sad. Make him leave, make him go away;

you can do it Lilly, I know you can, but *you* have to do it....*you*."

"Hey Buddy!"

Came the chipper voice, approaching from the rear.

"Glad you're okay; your sister was worried about you pal."

A chill darted down Earl's spine as he jumped a bit, startled. But he didn't say a word in response.

It was the ugly sound of Button's voice.

Billy Bones smiled at Earl, an evil, cocky smile, walked around the front of the bench, placing himself between Earl and Lillian, and gave Earl his back. He squatted and put his finger under Lilly's chin, hoisting it a bit as he gently spoke to her, only to her. Button let out a small belch into her face, and Earl could smell the beer on his breath, even from behind.

"Hey, I was worried; when I woke up, you were gone. You gotta tell me where you're going from now on; no more leaving on your own, leaving without me knowing where you are, or where you're going. I need to keep an eye on you; take care of you. Remember, we're a team now, a team again, and *the team* stays together, at all times, right?"

She didn't answer.

"Come on, let's go home; we'll get you to bed. You look plumb worn out, too much *exercise*."

Button chuckled, as he hooked and squeezed her arm, a bit rough, and raised her off the bench; she was mostly dead weight. Earl stood by and watched, helpless.

"I'll talk to you later, Earl; say thanks to Marty for me."

"Thanks for *what*? Don't be talking to Marty."

Earl heard Button ask, and then scold, as the two walked away, her arm tightly cinched in his, down the diagonal gravel path, back toward downtown. Earl just watched in silence as the two disappeared into the darkness.

Earl hung his head.

And that's when he noticed Bibby's fortune, with Button's boot heel print on it, ground into the gravel, face down.

CHAPTER 182 – A RUMPUS AND A HOWL, SO IT IS. AND SO IT WAS

Friday, July 28, 2006; day one-hundred and two weeks, in the new digs.

"I knew we were really brothers, for real! We like the same movies, we know the same lines, and we even have the same favorite book! I *love* that book; my mom used to read it to me, and I even read it myself you know, sometimes, when she wasn't around. You know what my all-time favorite line was? Huh? Huh?"

"I'm sure you're gonna tell me."

C smirked.

"Let the wild rumpus start!"

Earl raised his arms over his head in triumph; Chick was on his shoulders, like always. Her ears folded back and eyes widened to saucers, in tune with Earl's crescendo.

"I forgot that one."

C said.

"How could you ever forget that one?! It's the best line *ever*! And then you know what I would do, after I yelled it? I would go chase down Lilly and tackle her! In the hall, on her bed, on the couch; it was the best! She would kick and scream and bite me, *hard,* but I didn't care; *let the wild rumpus start!* Whenever she heard me yell that line and start howling, like the *Wild Things* did, oh boy, she would start *running*!"

Earl scrunched his shoulders and giggled at the memory. Then he whispered, leaning into C, with Chicken digging her claws into Earl's shoulder to hold on, to which he paid no attention.

"She was *so fast and sneaky,* most times, I couldn't catch her, and I'm pretty fast too! And she's a *bad* biter, you know, *real bad;* she really chomps down, but it's worth it. But then I'd tickle her, and she was *so* done! Tickling is her downfall! But she'd always get revenge; Lilly always did, and it wasn't pretty, let me tell ya; *I got the scars to prove it.*"

Earl whispered the last part, letting C in on the big secret.

"But it was still worth it."

Earl said, through a toothy grin.

C smiled at Earl's story, because it was Earl's story, and for no other reason. He still had no use for Lillian. And he was glad she got tackled as a kid; the more, the better.

It had been two long weeks, and the two boys had settled into a bachelor's existence. C never went back to Sam's; that experiment was done, for now at least, since these types of decisions always seemed to vacillate for C. Sam begged him to come back, but he really didn't need Ay; the place by this time pretty much ran on its own. Besides, there was no way C was wearing a smock and dealing with that jerk-off coming in all the time, dumping fruit and making comments; that was just served-up trouble. And not seeing Frank, and Lilly, and Mae....simply a bonus.

Earl had seen and spoken to Lillian on and off, mostly off, especially as each new day passed, as Button tightened his grip. Cord, on the other hand, had not spoken nor even physically seen her in two weeks, and for that, he was grateful. She had apparently settled into a domestic life of bliss with her douchebag boyfriend.

Earl knew C didn't want to talk about Lilly, so he wouldn't really say what the two of them talked about, but Ay could tell Earl was constantly worried, and sad, about his sister. Earl said Lilly wasn't happy, but C didn't buy it; if she wasn't happy, why didn't she just leave?

Earl tried to hide his *Lilly-worry* around Ay, since he didn't want C to be sad and worried too. So he would constantly go off on his own, in the house or the yard, to pace and cry to himself; but then the feelings would slowly pass, till they came roaring back, and he paced and cried all over again. He looked to his mom for help, for comfort, but for some reason, these last two weeks, she was gone, nowhere to be found; maybe she was on vacation. But *no way* was Earl going on vacation; no way was he going to Panama now, not with his sister so sad. Panama and the hammock and the lobsters and little blue fish would all have to wait, he told C, and asked if that was okay; if they would all wait for him, till he was ready to see them. Cord said they'd all be waiting, they'd wait forever if they had to, until Earl was ready to go. Earl would sigh in relief every time Cord told him that, because Earl constantly asked the same question, just to be sure the answer didn't change.

Earl did tell Cord that Lilly was moving to Philadelphia, and he asked C where that was, and how far away she'd be, and was it as far as Panama. He thought there had to be some mystery about it, since both Panama and Philadelphia started with the capital letter *'P'*; but he couldn't figure it out; those kind of tough mysteries were best left to Ken and Sandy to solve, since they were way smarter than him about important stuff like that.

And although he never mentioned it again, after saying it at Sam's the day Button showed up, Earl was still sad he missed the 7th Annual *Blobfest*; he figured that was probably the best of them all, even though he missed the first six as well. But he was already laying the groundwork for the 8th Annual *Blobfest* next year. And this time he would be sure C bought the tickets, just in case Lilly forgot again. Then he got sad, wondering if Lilly would ever come home again, or would she be in Philadelphia forever, and never get to run out of the theater, 'scaping from the *Blob*.

Even though it annoyed him to no end, Cord still found his thoughts, more often than he wished to admit, drifting back to Lilly, and with it, obsessing about her getting dogged, non-stop, in every position imaginable, and loving every minute of it. And although Earl said the two of them were moving to Philly, as of today, Friday the 28th, they were apparently still living and fucking like rabbits in the apartment above the *Palace*, another place Cord hadn't stepped foot in since life changed in Belvidere.

In fact, all of downtown Belvidere was a quarantine zone, as far as Ay was concerned; no need to venture within blocks of it. God, he now knew how Carol felt, sequestered to her little island by the Park. And he didn't dare venture anywhere near Brookfield; Jesus, he hadn't seen Mae in two weeks; not a sighting nor a single word….*nothing*. He shook his head in regret at the thought of her running out of the gym that day, and with it, the lost, in-the-bag, sex on demand. Fuck, he missed that non-stop senior pussy.

Then he moved onto other carnal thoughts, as in Margery.

He hadn't been back to the gym either; no contact with her at all, although that was more awkward than anything else. Mother, daughter - bagged 'em both; he still smiled proud at that lottery thought. A small, silver lining in a general shit-storm that he found himself in. But that two-fer was a one-off for sure; no chance that was ever happening again.

He sighed.

In the end, he knew he would try to somehow find his way back to see Margery; he wanted to tag that pussy again, for sure. The question was, would she? That was a *big* question mark. For C's part, he really didn't think about the lingering Mae/Mom part of the equation getting in the way of fucking Margie; if he stopped tapping Mae, he figured that would be good enough for Margery. But that was just male logic, which usually amounted to nothing more than wishful thinking. He felt he had a pretty good shot at fucking Margery again, and hell, he'd do Mae too, on the sly, if he got half-a-chance. When it came to sex, Cord was good at making stupid mistakes over and again; he never learned….never. When he died, he was sure it would be asleep in bed, with a fork in his chest from her, whomever *her* happened to be at the time. It was inevitable.

Earl was distracted, playing with Chick; Cord turned his head and looked out the window, onto Third Street, beyond the front porch, and turned melancholy. He had molted into a male Carol, marooned on an island, adjacent to the Park.

Ay didn't have to work, of course; plenty of money nearby, with more available with a single call, no worries. And that didn't include his cut of the store revenue; Sam drove up and hand-delivered it to C each day over the past two weeks, padding the amount to boot, making a pitch for C's return upon the pass of the envelope. Ay told him to stop, to keep the money, but it was Sam's little bribe, and he couldn't help himself.

C wanted no part of it; he simply took the envelope, since Sam would drop it and run, and handed it to Earl, who handed the envelope to Carol to credit toward his half of Lilly's rent. Carol wouldn't take any money from Earl for anything, so she gave the sealed envelope to Ji-Sue, who would take it down to Sam and use it to buy the freshest fish from the market for the cats, and more cat-treats than she was supposed to feed them.

And the envelope would invariably be re-stuffed with cash and end up on C's porch, attached to Sam's outstretched hand….an endless circle of green.

And in the end, the winners were the cats, of course, all fat and happy, with bad fish breath.

Cord was a storm of stir-crazy, anxious and bored. He couldn't leave Town; no way would Earl be okay with that, fretting that C would never come back. Earl was worried enough about his sister; C didn't need to heap more on his *worry-pile*.

So Ay stayed put, and spent the past two weeks catching up on unread newspapers, delved into the first of the pile of classics he brought along, smoked too many cigars in the Park, drank port and whiskey, neat, on the porch – both his and Carol's, and ran, lots of running, to the point that he actually enjoyed it. He was now in the low one-hundred-eighties, and felt good, light on his feet. He still ran around the Park at night; but during the day, he went for longer jaunts, mostly out-of-Town a bit, three to six mile loops, that he would run one, or two times, alone, or with Earl. He smiled and thought about that first race around the Park, goaded by Carol, accompanied by the lilting rhythm of *Fat Bottom Girls*. A single lap, one-third mile, and he blacked out at the end, chest heaving and belly bloated. He looked down; that stomach had long left town.

It seemed a lifetime ago.

C looked over at the side table, at the neat stack of pro forma statements, dozens of adaptive reuse scenarios on Brownfield sites in and around New Jersey, ones he found online, in the newspaper, along with sites Woodie dug up, trying to help Carol fill a regional portfolio of sites for her Fund, which was near closed to new investors. Bud Wiseman liked the prospectus, and so did his friends, and Carol found herself with a Fund flush with cash, earmarked to the tune of *three-hundred-*

fifty million dollars in initial investor equity, including twenty-five million of her own. And she found herself talking more and more to C about it, more to him than anyone else, since he somehow seemed more knowledgeable about the topic than she did….much more, in fact. She still never figured that one out, and at some point, simply stopped trying.

And for C, the one site that always seemed to rise to the surface, the one to hit first, was Georgia-Pacific, right in Belvidere, right in their own backyard, the one Earl first pointed out on their quarry excursion. They hadn't been back to Georgia-Pacific, or the quarry for that matter, since that beautiful, lazy 4th of July. C thought about the crack in the quarry ledge, that ominous, dark crevice in the limestone; falling in there was a one-way, for sure. Why that came to mind, he wasn't sure.

C's mind-wander was interrupted by a poke in the shoulder.

"Hey, do you think the *Wild Things* live on Skeleton Island C? Do you think Ken and Sandy might find 'em, you know, rumpusing and stuff, when they go looking for the bad guys?"

C turned and smiled at Earl.

"I don't think so, Earl; I think the *Wild Things* live in a different special place, a secret, special place."

"Like Panama, with the lobsters and little-Earl, swimming around the coral under our hut?"

Earl asked excited.

"Yeah, more like Panama; maybe they live on a little island hidden somewhere in Panama….you never know."

"Then we'll meet 'em, when we go; we're still going right, once Lilly isn't so sad?"

"Absolutely; whenever you want to go; up to you."

C answered calm; then he continued, with a tease.

"….and I even know where we can get a little wooden boat to sail to that special island, where the *Wild Things* are hiding, just like Max did. But it's a secret, you can't tell *anyone*, not even Carol."

C leaned in and winked.

"Really? A real secret? Tell me!"

Earl was positively beside himself; he loved secret stories from C.

Ay looked at Earl, studied him, checked him out as he cocked his head a bit to the left, and then to the right; then he figured he could let Earl in.

"Okay, I'll tell you."

Earl let out a breath of relief; he was *in*!

"It's tethered to an old, worn tie-line, which runs up the beach, knotted off somewhere unseen, hidden in the thick dune grass. It's a little *Susan-Skiff,* an eleven-footer, flat-bottomed, with only three side planks, barely held together with copper nails. It used to be painted white, with a bright red bottom, but both have long-since peeled and faded, like an old woman, more bare wood than paint. It lies, all alone, on a little no-name spit of sand, near the mud flats just off Scarborough Beach, where the quahoggers rake endless for clams at low tide, and the herring gulls fly nearby, waiting for an easy meal. That's our boat Earl. It's a rowboat, not a sailboat, but she's fast, a good girl; that's the one we'll use to find the *Wild Things*."

Earl scrunched his shoulders and drank in Cord's tale, tall or not, it didn't matter. Earl loved when C told stories like this, about things he'd seen, places he'd been; it was like Earl was right there with him, that's how it felt, anyway, since Earl hadn't been anywhere, at least anywhere beyond the far stone row at Mr. Gill's farm.

"Really? We can just walk up and use it?"

"Well, we'll borrow it; I know the owner - he's a real nice guy. He rescued the boat himself; it was an orphan, he found it on Camden Beach, that's another stretch of sand a bit south, about fifteen years prior, she was left for dead. He nursed her back; she was a good little boat, still is."

"Wow, an orphan!"

"Yep, and she leaks a bit, just a bit, a slow drip from the left transom planks, lower left. When high tide comes in, and she's tied on the beach, she slowly fills with water, about quarter-way; it takes a couple hours for the water to trickle out, but that's the best part, watching the water run out of her. She's a good girl Earl; we'll just keep her bailed and take her to see the *Wild Things*….deal? That's if we don't sink her; she might not be able to hold both our fat asses, but we'll give it a shot."

Earl held his breath and rubbed his hands together quick and excited, like he was starting a fire, like he usually did when C told him about the adventures they were going to share. There were so many, he could hardly keep track. Actually, that wasn't true; Earl remembered every detail of every tale, every single one.

"Deal! Hey C, what's her name?"

C looked at him, curious.

"You know, I don't know. I don't think she has a real name; so go 'head, name her."

Earl didn't hesitate, not one second.

"Can we call her *Lilly*?   Then Lilly can meet the *Wild Things* too!"

Cord thought he would frown, but surprised himself and didn't. Instead he smiled wider at Earl, with Chicken sleeping sound on his shoulders.

"Sure we can."

Earl let out a *Wild Thing* moan and clapped his hands hard in excitement.

"I'm not telling her, not yet; it'll be a big surprise. But I'll tell my mom, when she shows up next; she's been on vacation for awhile, but has to be back soon, she *never* goes away this long. And my mom will be *real* happy; she likes when you're nice to Bibby."

"Your sister doesn't make it easy Earl, for sure."

C looked at Earl, and thought about Carol; he had been thinking about her a lot lately. He needed to go see her again; it was one of the few places in Town which wasn't *off limits*. He needed to lay on the grass and rub his arm across her marker, to talk to her, like he did his own mom. It felt right to do that, and to do it soon; maybe later today….maybe.

"Hey Earl."

"Yeah."

"When we die, when one of us dies, we should make a pact, you and me, to try and talk to each other."

"Are you dying?"

Earl's face sunk.

"No, and neither are you; but eventually, you know, it'll happen. And when it does, we should have some code word, kind of like Houdini had with his wife."

"Who's Houdini?"

"Some dead magician, doesn't matter; but we should pick a word, something, some phrase that *no else else* would ever use, to let you know it's really me, or let me know it's really you, our little secret. What do you think? But *whatever* we pick, we can't tell anyone, not Lilly, not Carol, not even Big B! Deal?"

Earl shook his head in excited agreement, and he didn't hesitate; he grabbed C around the neck and pulled him in tight, so he could whisper in his ear, so absolutely no one could hear, even though no one was around but Chick. But since Big B couldn't hear, then, Earl figured, neither could Chicken-Little. *Sorry Chick*, he whispered to her; but she didn't hear him, she was fast asleep.

"*Let the wild rumpus start*!   And then we'll howl at the moon, like the *Wild Things*, like this...."

And Earl let out another mournful howl, like a lone coyote. Chicken woke in a fright, her ears perked back and eyes saucered in horror. That was just about enough for Chick; she jumped off Earl's shoulders and ran into the other room, putting distance between herself and the coyote.

Earl grinned at his friend; C grinned in return, shook his head in tacit agreement and whispered.

"A *rumpus and a howl,* so it is."

And so it was.

Saturday, July 29th; day one-hundred-one turned the corner and there was still no word from any of the usual cast. It was 9:45 am; a sticky, summer day began to settle in.

C strolled down the front walk and grabbed the *New York Times* that just landed in a dull thud on the slate sidewalk. It was a precise ritual; the blue plastic jacket was hurled from the open window of a clunker - the newspaper girl never let up on the accelerator - yet that damn paper landed in the same square of stone every time she tossed it, a bullseye. It was a skill worth nothing, but she excelled nonetheless.

C ambled back onto the porch, in no particular hurry. Three minute eggs were cooking inside, and the rye jumped from the toaster as Carol descended the second-floor stairs; black coffee cooled in the mug she carried.

Carol was in a good mood; having the boys over her house always made her so, but having them next door – knowing they were sleeping next to her house all week when she was gone, just made her smile. And not sharing them with Lillian was the fucking cherry. She half thought about moving her office west, at least for part of the week, just to spend more time with the two of them.

Ji-Sue called out from the kitchen to the boys on the porch. Earl was playing rubber band with Earl, his favorite, as C sat in Carol's chair, already buried in today's paper. Chicken was sleeping on the ottoman.

A lazy unwind of the last Saturday morning in July.

Or was it.

"Hey C, what are we doing today?"

Earl chirped, as Earl lunged and bit the rubber band.

"Eating breakfast and reading the paper."

Ay said rote, never looking up from the *Times*.

"I mean after that!"

C didn't answer Earl's plea.

"Hey, ***pay attention!***"

And with that, Earl pulled back hard and shot C square in the chest with the rubber band; Earl leapt after it, jumping right through the newspaper, landing hard on C's lap, crumpling the news in a loud heap. Chicken woke and bolted in a hiss.

"Hey, hey! What are you doing?!"

C snapped, annoyed.

"That's what *I* asked!"

Earl whined.

"I don't know Earl; I wanna read the fucking paper, in peace!"

"That's all you ever do, read the stupid paper....read, read, read! That's boring! Let's do something, it's Saturday!"

C shook his head and sighed, knowing he wasn't reading again anytime soon.

"Okay, what do *you* want to do? I know you want to do something; this charade is all about *that* something, so just spill it."

"I wasn't thinking anything."

"*Liar*. You're a crummy liar Earl; what do you want to do?"

Earl spilled quick.

"Let's go lay on *Couch Rock*, at *Foul Rift*; today's a good day to lie on *Couch Rock*, probably the best day ever, that's what I think! And we never did that before, together!"

"What the fuck is a *Couch Rock*? And why do I want to do that, rather than sit here and read the paper in peace on the *front porch rock?*"

"***Because!*** It's kinda scary, and fun, and you get to stick your butt in the hole in the rock, and it's not a *Couch Rock*, it's **the** *Couch Rock*, the only one in the whole wide world, as far as I know, but I haven't been too far around the world, just to the Gill Farm, but I'm just guessing it's the only one, just saying, and even if it isn't, but I'm pretty sure it is, it's the coolest rock ever! But you gotta be careful of poison ivy – *leaflet three, let it be!* My mom told me that and I *never* forgot it; that stuff's itchy, especially between your fingers – that's the worst! But don't scratch it C – that will make it *even* worse!   I know, because I'm not so good at not scratching, especially when it's between my fingers – they get all sweaty thinking about not scratching, then I gotta scratch!   Just saying…. oh, and don't forget to check under the leaves first, that fall on top of the rock, 'cause sometimes salamanders are sleeping in there, nice and cozy, the skinny brown ones; sometimes I think they're worms at first, but they're not, because the salamanders have short, tiny legs, like Jonesy, and big brown eyes, and worms don't have legs, and they don't have eyes, and even if they did, they still wouldn't be salamanders, at least I don't think they would, but anyway, you gotta be careful about the salamanders because if they're there, we can't just go sticking our butts in the hole in the rock, 'cause we might sit on them, and hurt 'em, but if they're *not* there, then we *can* stick our butts in the hole, so we don't fall out, when we lean way over and sideways and almost upside down and watch the rapids *way* below us and hear the water and the trees and the birds, and see the moss on the rocks and the crunchy leaves are everywhere, and there are islands in the middle of the river, right near where *Couch Rock* is, but you can't get to them without swimming, and I can't swim, so I've never been on one, for real, but I wish I could, and I've pretended I've been on them, with Ken and Sandy, exploring and solving sneaky mysteries in the middle of the river, and ….and….*lots of other stuff*!"

Earl ran out of *stuff*, and wind. But he gulped in a huge gob of air, quickly recovered, and prattled on.

"And you can *only* get to Couch Rock if you go on the *Blue Trail,* not the *Red Trail* or the *Orange Trail*, or the *Yellow Trail, just* the *Blue* one! There's little blue squares nailed to some trees that you hafta follow, kind of like bread crumbs on a treasure hunt, like with Ken and Sandy, like you're looking for Skeleton Island, and it's tricky spotting those little blue squares on the trees, you gotta really concentrate and pay attention, and they're lots of sneaky rocks and roots hiding under the leaves that you can trip over, and it's kinda scary when you're deep in the woods, 'cause that's where the monsters and zombies are, and you hafta be *real* careful, or they'll get ya! And the chipmunks hiding in the rocks will be squeaking at you: *'look down, so you don't trip cause the monsters will get ya!'* And the blue-jays are squawking up in the trees saying: *'look up, cause the zombies could be hiding behind that tree up ahead!'.* So you gotta look up, for the monsters and zombies, but gotta look down so you don't trip on the roots and rocks hiding in the leaves, with the chipmunks and blue-jay both yelling at you, look up!/look down!/up!/down! It's *very* tricky business, just saying! I tripped last year and scraped my leg and it was all bloody, and it hurt real bad, but I didn't cry or nothing, I just got up real quick and started running as fast as I could go, and no monsters or zombies got me that time, but I'm real worried about you C; *you* might get lost and trip on some sneaky rock or root and if you do, for sure you're gonna get eaten by the zombies, get your brains sucked out, *for sure*, cause you're not that fast C; sorry, don't mean to hurt your feelings and all, but you're still kinda slow, and you'll be an easy lunch for a monster, just saying. So you gotta speed up and follow me *real close!* Remember, *always* listen to the chipmunks and blue-jays – they know best, and don't ever forget - stay on the *Blue Trail [Earl pointed serious at C, like Mrs. Gregson would do to Earl in class, when she wasn't sure he was listening]*!"

"Got it; what trail was it again?"

C said sarcastic.

"The *Blue Trail! Pay attention, this is important stuff!* And even if the monsters and zombies don't get you, and I think they will - I think you're a goner C, for sure - but if you get lucky, and somehow sneak away from the monsters and zombies, and don't get your brains sucked out, you still gotta get **way** faster, because the skeets will get ya, or the gnats, or *both*, if you're too slow. They'll swarm ya and eat you alive! They never get me, because I can outrun them, and then they don't bother you, but you, I'm not so sure – I think they're faster than you. Sorry C, but if the skeets and the gnats attack us, like *Godzilla* or the *Blob*, I'm gonna have to leave you behind, because if I wait for you, then they are gonna get me too, and I'm not getting eaten by the skeets! No way! They got Marty once; he was no match for 'em, took him down like hog-tied cattle, and I think he's faster than you C, sorry, don't mean to hurt your feelings, but I think he kinda really is *[Earl whispered the last part]*. Oh, and even if the skeets and gnats don't get you, you have to worry about all the spiders, because they build webs right across the trail, even the *Blue Trail*! And when you're running, you go right through them! I hate to bother the spiders; I feel bad, because, you know, they work real hard and everything to build them sticky webs and then I go and mess them up - but I don't do it on purpose, you can't see them till **bam!** Then they're stuck to your face like glue! Yuck! And then the spiders sometimes come along for the ride! But if I feel them on my face, or neck, I don't hurt them or nothing, - I just brush 'em off, so they can build another web, maybe somewhere else, safer, not near the trail. Oh, and I almost forgot about the pickers and the ticks! Lots of bramble-rose in the woods, that's not their real name, but that's what I call 'em – I just made it up one day and it stuck in my head ever since, and raspberry pickers too, they both pick your ankles when you're running on the trail – they can *really* hurt you know! I'm not a big baby, or anything, but they hurt! They really do! And they are *everywhere*! They're sneaky too; they just kind of swing into the path, all sneaky-like, to pick your ankles! Oh, I almost forgot about the ticks! They just sit around waiting all day for you to run by and **bam!** Once you touch the weed they're hiding on, they leap onto you and stick like spit! And ticks aren't very good-looking, you know; if you really look at them, they're kinda ugly – I wouldn't tell them that, don't want to hurt their feelings, but they are, just saying. And everybody I know that sees one kills 'em, **bam!** Just like that! But I don't – I just lift them off and gently put them on a leaf or something, you know, off the trail, so they don't get hurt, because some of them are even girls, you know, and I don't want to hurt anyone, but I especially don't want to hurt a girl, even if she's just a tick. And how can you tell if it's a girl-tick or boy-tick anyway? They all look the same to me - I can't even tell the difference! And you know, it's not the tick's fault that it's a tick, it's just trying to do the best it can, you know, with what its got, so I kind of have to give the ticks some credit, because being a tick can't be that easy or fun, just waiting around all day to bite someone, and then getting smooshed, just because you're a tick! I'm not doing that – I'm not a tick-smoosher, not me. But I don't want 'em sucking my blood either, like a vampire! So I just put 'em back in the woods, and maybe they'll be safe for awhile, I hope so, anyway, especially the girls; I like the girl ticks the best, just because."

Earl took a big half-breath, and surged onward before C could interrupt.

"But even if the monsters and zombies and skeets and gnats and spiders, and pickers and ticks don't get ya, and you make it all the way to *Couch Rock*, like Ken and Sandy would, for sure, because they're real smart, it's still pretty dangerous, even when you get there, right by the water and stuff since, you know, you're on a big cliff, and it's about four of me tall, above the water *[Earl held his arm straight up, pointing in the air]*. That's pretty high up C; you might be pretty scared 'cause it's so high! And all the rocks are covered with moss and leaves and there's a big white tree, like the one right on the side of Carol's house *[Earl pointed past the crytomaria]*, but this one is a real big-un, and it's leaning out over the water like it's gonna fall in; it's pretty spooky!"

Earl looked at C hard, to see if he was convinced yet, but he didn't *look* convinced. So Earl pressed on, with a fresh gulp of air.

"And it's only for guys; ***no girls allowed!*** Ever! That's the rule….no girls! And if you lay backward on *Couch Rock*, with your head down there *[Earl pointed to the left, though the point didn't really mean anything]*, it slopes down, the rock, like a hill, so your almost upside down, with your feet up there, and your head down here! And the sky is the water, and the water is the sky, and that's the coolest thing ever! The sky is full of waves, and there's water running by, right in the sky! And sometimes a duck floats by, you know, in the sky! How cool is that? And if you're not careful, you could slide right off *Couch Rock*, right off the cliff! And it's a long way down, let me tell ya! And when the river is running low, like in the summer, kinda like now, maybe not just yet, but maybe just yet, there's even a little sandy beach along the river bank, right below the *Couch*. I like that beach, but I've never really been on it, way too scary to climb down the cliff to get to it, but maybe I will some day, maybe I'll find a way to sit on that beach in the sun, with my toes dug in the sand, and watch the ducks float by; wouldn't that be the best day ever! And there's one of those white and brown trees right in front of the *Rock*, and a bunch of smaller ones growing down by the beach, right by the water, and if you fell off the *Couch*, and down the cliff, you'd probably get hurt *real bad,* 'cause it's pretty high above the water, pretty scary, even for someone like you, Mr. C!"

[Earl taunted C with a point at his face, pretty much at his nose]

"You already said it was scary about six times, *Mr. E.*"

[C returned the taunt with a finger of his own]

"I know! But you know what else? You know what I forgot to tell ya? Sometimes, when no one is looking, which is *never,* but I only go to the *Rock* alone, I spit in the river, or throw twigs and watch 'em float downstream, like they're little boats, and sometimes there's even a turtle on the trail, sticking his head out as far as he can, munching on grass, and you hafta move them out of the way so nobody steps on them, or a bike runs over them, and they hiss at you if you move them, cause they want keep munching the grass you know, and you're interrupting their lunch, or dinner, but you gotta just apologize and move 'em anyway, because they could get hurt, and it shouldn't hurt your feelings if they hiss at ya, because, you know, you're just trying to help them not get hurt, and you know what, there's also lots of deer in the woods and sometimes, even though you don't mean to, you can kinda sneak-up on them while they're munching the same grass as the turtles, or maybe even some leaves on a tree that the turtles can't reach, and then they get kinda scared, like I did when my mom used to tell me scary stories - maybe their moms tell them scary stories too, about bears and people and stuff!

Anyway, you can see 'em running away from you, maybe only ten feet away, maybe even closer, when you crunch all the leaves! They have big white fluffy tails, I saw one the last time I was there; it was so close I almost touched her tail, I almost did! Promise! It was a girl, I know because she didn't have antlers, and she had a very pretty tail; only a girl could have a tail that pretty. And there's *lots* of raspberries in the woods in the summer, right along the trail, that I eat, and no one can stop me, or even knows I'm eating 'em. You can eat as many as you want, for free! And you know what else, huh? There's a secret sign nailed to a crooked tree, right by the cliff, that says *[Earl sucked in a big breath and pointed in the air as he spoke the words, like following the bouncing ball]*:

Cliff Area
No Trespassing
Beyond This Point

All persons are hereby warned against trespassing hereon, under the penalties provided by Section 3503 of the Penna Crimes Code of 1972 #334

Pennsylvania Power & Light Company"

C was looking at Earl, with a smirk on his face; he always smirked whenever Earl recited stuff like that, stuff he read once and never, ever forgot, not a word.

"….or something like that."

Earl added, as his voice tailed off, sheepishly.

"Yeah, *or something like that.*"

C mimicked, knowing it was rote, right off the tree, down to the word.

"And I don't even know what a *Penna Crimes Code* is, but I bet it's some pretty serious stuff, we could get it big trouble! Go to jail, even!"

"I bet."

C said.

"But I don't listen to that stupid, secret sign anyway and go right next to the crooked tree anyway, right at the edge of the cliff; I don't pay attention to that sign *at all!* And when you lay on *Couch Rock* upside down, it's real hard to sit up again, *real hard,* you have to have real strong stomach muscles! You could probably do it C; I know you're not too fast, sorry, but you're not, but you're pretty strong, not world champion strong, you aren't gonna have groupies or panties or anything, but you did do five hundred pounds! And that's kinda a lot; way more than Billy, who has pretty skinny legs, and his shorts are too big. So I think you could probably sit up on *Couch Rock;* I'm not too worried about you doing that. And when you do, and you look up the River, at all the choppy water, that's called *Foul Rift,* but I really don't know why it's called that, it just is, always has, as long as I've been around, which is almost forty years, you know, I'm getting old, and the *Rift,* that's what we sometimes call it, when we're trying not to talk too much, it looks like a big long water slide, but it's *really* dangerous, and my mom always said it was the *most* dangerous part of the river, lots of people have drowned there, *lots,* because of the tricky, sneaky currents and trees and stuff hiding under the water that can snag you and pull you down, like a sea monster. Yep, lots of people have been eaten up by the river, even people that can swim real good! And I can't even swim at all, not one lick, and I wasn't allowed anywhere near it, but my mom doesn't know I lay on the *Couch Rock,* it's a secret; and she won't know you are either....and it's *really scary.*"

"Christ, take a breath Earl; take more than one."

1625

C said, as he tried to straighten out his newspaper, uncreasing the wrinkled mess both Earls made with the rubber band trick.

Earl took in a big lungful and rubbed his hands together, like he did whenever he got too excited. Then he saw C starting to try a sneak-read of his paper, so he smashed his hand down like swatting at a fly, and crinkled the paper all up again, like a little kid.

"Hey, pay attention! This is important stuff!"

Earl yelled.

"Jesus Earl!"

C whined, to no avail.

"You know it's really fun laying on *Couch Rock,* but we can't lay on it together, you know, it's big, but not *that* big, especially if there are salamanders on it….remember, you gotta be careful not to hurt the salamanders, cause they live there you know, did I already say that? *[Earl knew he did, but he knew C was having a hard time concentrating, so he figured he'd repeat, it, just to be safe, for the salamanders].* Anyway, we can tell scary stories right there, out in the woods; we haven't told stories in a long time C, can we tell scary stories? Can we? And you know what, when my mom told Bibby and me scary stories, she would always start by turning out the lights, and lighting spooky candles and stuff, and then she would whisper something to us, and then we knew, Bibby and me, that the most scariest scary stories of all were coming next! Oh boy, I always used to get *extra* scared when she whispered those spooky words. And you know what else? My mom said the monsters could be hiding anywhere in the house, *anywhere,* even under the bed, or in the closet, or basement, or the attic! But she always said the scariest of the scariest monsters of all were the ones that you don't see coming, 'cause they're good hiders, good fakers, and they could be right in front of you, even sitting right next to you, maybe even trying to be nice to you, and be your friend even, and you wouldn't even know it, that they're monsters, till it's too late, then **BAM**....they get ya!   Those are the worst monsters of all she said.   But I never believed it; a monster hiding in your closet, or under the bed, is *way* scarier to me; but I never told my mom that, just trying to be polite, just saying."

Earl got a chill down his spine just thinking about scary-story-time with his mom and Bibby, and his mom whispering those spooky words.   Earl shivered his shoulders to shake it, at the same time rubbing his hands together again, all excited and stuff.

"Earl, why all of a sudden do you want to go see this *Rock*?   You've *never* mentioned it ever before, ever....not once; why is so important to go *right now*?"

"I don't know why, it just popped in my head and I wanna do it.   Doesn't stuff ever pop in your head that you want to do right away?"

C thought of Margery, which meant he thought about tagging Margery, yet again, right now.

"Yeah, good point."

C said flat.   And Earl quickly started up again, forgetting the whisper part.

"I forgot to tell you the whisper!   So you know what my mom would say, right before the monster stories, huh? Whenever she said this *[which was every time]*, we knew a real scary one was coming, remember, the sneaky ones are the worst, and Lilly and me would pull on the blanket, trying to hide from the monsters under the blanket, but both of us wouldn't fit, and she always yanked the blanket right when the first word came out of my mom's mouth, before I could even think, and she would hog that blanket all up and then she was safe, and I had to stay outside the blanket and wait for the monster to come eat me! Lilly said I should just give up, because it would always get me first, because I was big and she was small; she always said that….is that true C? Is the monster gonna get me first 'cause there's more to eat? Anyway, you know what my mom would always say, C, do ya, right before the monster story started?"

"No Earl, I don't; but please, just tell me, my ears are starting to bleed."

[Earl got all serious and quiet, and held his hand up, in a pious stance. And with his pointer finger, he followed the invisible words in the air, looking up toward the porch ceiling, and far beyond it, into the deep blue summer sky]

Then Earl cast his heavenly gaze downward, and stared C straight in the eye, and whispered in an ominous tone.

"She'd whisper:

Behold a pale horse;
and his name,
that sat on him,
was Death.
And Hell followed with him. "

Isn't that really scary C? And it even has a curse word in it! And I don't even know what it all means!"

The hair on C's arms stood straight, and a shiver shot his spine.

CHAPTER 184 – A SCARY COUCH ROCK, HIGH ABOVE THE FOUL RIFT

Earl poked Cord in the shoulder; C's eyes had glassed over - he had left for somewhere else.

"Hey C, you okay? You're not supposed to get scared *yet;* we aren't even at *Couch Rock,* telling scary stories."

Cord shook his head and returned to the porch, with a confused, worried face.

"Yeah, I guess, just a strange, another strange...."

But Earl cut him off and poked him harder in the shoulder, more of a shove. No time for whatever C had to say.

"So, when are we going to *Couch Rock,* huh? Can we go right after breakfast? Can we? Can we go after breakfast? Huh?"

Now Earl was tugging on C's shirt, pulling him along with it.

"Can we go? Can we go? Can we go?"

"Forget him, I'll go with you."

Carol said, with two trays of warm breakfast in hand; it didn't look like either had C's name on it.

Earl answered her quickly and decisively; Rule Number One: there was clearly no room for girls at *Couch Rock*....ever.

"Okay, you can go."

And C snapped from his funk.

"Okay?! *Okay?!* I thought only *guys* could go to *Couch Rock?* You *just* told me *the* rule five minutes ago! You said *we can't break the no-girls rule!* What just happened to *that* rule?"

Earl answered just as quickly and decisively.

"Um."

"Don't listen to his stupid rules, Earl."

Carol said, condescending.

"It's not my stupid rule, it's **his!**"

C yelled, pointing at Earl.

"It's not my rule."

Earl said sheepishly.

"It's not *your* rule? Then whose rule is it? Where's the *Couch Rock Rule Book?* Does anyone in the whole fucking world even know the *Couch Rock* exists but you Earl?"

Earl just shrugged his shoulders; he had no idea who made up that stupid rule, but he sure wasn't admitting to it.

C huffed.

"Earl you are unbelievable, led around by the nose, and starting to lie and lie."

"Oh, listen to you talk; where do you think he learns it?"

Carol goaded. C shot her a wicked look.

"Two egg-on-toast? No really, I couldn't possibly eat two, but thanks anyway."

C said snide to Carol, pointing at the invisible third tray of breakfast she brought for him.

"I'm not your maid."

"You brought Earl's plate!"

"Because he doesn't expect it."

Earl went to hand C his breakfast.

"Earl!"

Carol yelled.

And he instinctively recoiled.

"Don't give him your breakfast, that's special, for you."

"Earl, it sure would be nice if you shared, you know, with your best friend, the one going to the *Couch Rock* with you, all scary and everything, with monsters, zombies, ticks, spiders and whatever else you said is hiding in the fucking woods, ready to eat me alive because I'm so slow, *just saying*."

C goaded him.

"Don't fall for that Earl."

Earl was conflicted, looking to Carol, then C, then back again; and he was getting upset, unsure what to do, and who not to disappoint, which was both of them.

Without Earl ever seeing the approach, so he had no chance to deflect, Carol slipped her hand on Earl's knee, gently, and give him a little rub and a little smile, showing off that tooth gap he loved so much.

"Please Earl, eat your breakfast, for me, then you can show *me* the *Couch Rock* and the river and the moss and the salamanders. I've never seen a *Couch Rock* before; I bet it's *really* scary! Maybe Ji and Marty could come too, if you want."

And she squeezed his leg, just a bit. And all Earl could do was smile goofy; he was done….cooked and ready to serve. C harrumphed in defeat.

"Christ, pathetic Earl. It's a slippery slope my friend; it always starts with a leg rub and a smile, trust me. And do I have to knock a gap in my teeth to get breakfast around here?"

And with that, C got up, whereby Carol slapped him hard in the ass.

"Good for ya; get your own breakfast!"

And Earl giggled, and half-heartedly pulled his leg away from Carol, even though he really didn't want to.

"Hey Ji, Carol forgot my tray; can you bring me out my breakfast?"

And C followed with the delayed, obligatory finish.

"Please."

And no sooner did the P-word leave his lips, when he heard the quick patter of tiny footsteps; Ji-Sue, with two trays in hand, hers and his.

"Thanks Sweetie, you're such a good girl."

And C squeezed her shoulder. Ji-Sue liked C, she always had, since she first met him.

"Oh brother, you are pathetic Ji."

Carol said in disgust, as C flashed a shit-eating grin.

And with that, the four of them, with Chick and Earl by their sides soaking in the morning sun, sat, talked, gorged and laughed about rocks and moss and rivers and leaves and newspapers and cats and salamanders and anything else that didn't mean much, yet were the only things that really did, in the end, mean anything.

A loud sneeze and congested cough broke the conversation.

And it was then that it truly became apparent to Carol, unspoken, yet clear, that Earl wasn't eating as much as he used to. And it became apparent, but not yet discussed, that Earl seemed to be a bit smaller, just a bit. And such things came to the fore with that hearty sneeze and stuffy nose that one doesn't normally see in July.

And below the surface, unbeknownst to them all, hid a virus, uncommon and cruel, which had taken hold and was swimming inside him, hitching a ride on his white blood cells, attacking, destroying, the very immune system meant to protect him.

And there was no particular reason it chose Earl, he did nothing wrong, nothing to deserve it; it was just luck....the wrong kind.

But this gorgeous summer morning, on Carol's porch, overlooking the myriad of lush greens in the public Square, a peak was all it gave, hiding behind a single sneeze. And with it, quickly slipped back behind the curtain, into the dark, and was forgotten, overridden by banter of ducks and beaches, trees and leaves, all beside the dangerous rapids and a scary *Couch Rock,* high above the *Foul Rift.*

CHAPTER 185 – SHE QUIETLY SWALLOWED AND EARNED HER MONEY

Still Saturday, July 29th; as a porch breakfast was enjoyed Parkside, the lazy, summer morning continued in downtown Belvidere.

"What?"

Lilly abruptly stopped sucking Button's cock and sat up, rigid, to reset, and confirm what she heard was indeed a mistake, a mishear….something.

"We'll talk about it later; finish what you're doing."

Button said with indifference through a puff of nicotine, roughly grabbing her hair and redirecting her head back to the task at hand, to brush the topic aside, at least for the next minute or so.

She pulled back in disgust, realizing that was *not* a mishear. She knew doing that would probably get her into yet another yelling match, or a slap, or worse, standard fare for the past two weeks, but belligerence was a lifelong reflex, and she couldn't take it back now.

Or just maybe it was a deliberate tweak, subconscious, or not so, knowing violence was always on its way, like waves rolling in, one after another, and the only safe time was between the crests breaking on the beach. Maybe, in her own way, she wanted the thunder now, to get the anxiety, the fear, of waiting out of the way. Just get hit and be done with it for awhile, since it seemed like it was about time.

It wasn't always that way.

She usually thought of it as a genie, in a bottle, the violence and rage in him. It made it easier, for her, to think of it in those terms. Button had it his whole life, and she was one of the few who could control it, and stay outside the fray, at least most of the time. No one was truly immune, but she was special when it came to the genie; that's how she felt, how she described herself, how she dealt with it, rationalized it. The bottle top would jiggle and rattle around, but she had the touch, the ability, to corral him, to calm the rage, walking it back into the bottle....safe, for now. Mostly, the key to the corral was sex....insatiable, marathon sex, which was really more like violence, more like domination, more like rape, but she didn't like to think of it in any of those ways; she simply called it *sex*. It sounded better, like it was mutual; but there was really nothing mutual about it.

In a strange way, she was proud of her ability to tame what most couldn't, and what most feared, which was Button himself. She thought of it as a kind of talent, something that made her special, extra special....like no one else. And her mother always loved Button, like a second son; if she liked him, he *had* to have good qualities, right? More good than bad, right? So she was just like her mom; they both understood him in ways that others simply didn't. And, in a small, strange way, she felt she controlled him as much as he controlled her; it was always part of the allure, her own version of a tiger by the tail. That was the rationalization, anyway.

But, truth was, since Button came back to Town, he was different, *way different*, more violent, more controlling, more mercurial than ever, and she simply couldn't control it, or him, anymore. The last two weeks were ample proof of that, and the direction was quickly going from bad to worse. Now, when the top came off, she couldn't get the genie back in. Now it was simply a wait for the assault, and the rape, usually in that order.

How did she end up *here*? How did Button coming back, so full of anticipation and hope for three long years, result in *this*, alone and abused, in a matter of fourteen long days, each getting longer. And she felt helpless to stop it, with no friends to turn to. Of course that wasn't true, but that was the feel, to her, being utterly alone. And because of that, she was tired of treading water in the deep-end, exhausted, about to go under. She wasn't thinking clearly, or rationally, and had gotten to the point where she just didn't care anymore. Or maybe the truth was, she didn't really know the reason, likely the sum of all the above.

So, as expected, the pullback from his cock got him pissed.

He went from zero to sixty, which is how it usually worked for Billy; there was no build-up, just eruption. He shook his head left to right as his anger grew; why didn't he open his stupid mouth about a minute later, after he blew and she swallowed his load? He had waited two fucking weeks to broach the issue, what was another minute? Now all it cost him was a wasted hard-on and frustration. She was getting more annoying by the minute.

He dropped his butt on the floor, and half-crushed it under his boot heel, grinding the ash with purpose into the wood grain. He slowly half-rose from the bed edge, and reached for his crumpled pack of cigarettes on the dresser, atop piles of already-worn, wrinkled clothes, knocked one out and looked for his lighter as he sat back down beside her.

"You gotta stop smoking in here."

"Says who, the fucking landlord?"

"Says me; I don't like the smell."

Lilly kept poking the beehive, taunting him, asking for trouble.

"Too bad; like I told you a hundred times before, too fucking bad. Now just shut your fucking trap and listen, for once, just shut up and listen to a good thing, without the wise-ass comments, *for once!*"

Button seethed as he lit up and took a big drag and half-blew the smoke away from Lilly's face, as a courtesy she didn't deserve. He let out a long sigh, like he was about to lecture a child, and began to speak.

"Okay, what the Dr. and I are doing has a lot of tentacles, kind of like an octopus, and most of that you don't have to know about, but...."

"It's all illegal, big surprise; like I couldn't guess that was...."

And that was the straw that got Lilly the wave, the genie, the tiger, the thunder and the bees, all rolled into one ugly mess. It was a bad straw too....a real sea change.

Her sarcasm was throttled short by his iron grip on her throat, which came fast, out of nowhere; she never saw it coming. And as he spoke, he squeezed harder, and she started to wheeze, her face turning red; but despite her distress, he wouldn't let up, not like the other times in the past two weeks that he choked her, his *new* specialty. This time, with the sound of her wheeze, he just squeezed harder still.

"I swear, you interrupt me again ...."

Billy held her, like a dog, till she was *this close* to passing out, staring at her with the vicious, wild eyes that always preceded a beating. Usually it was just one punch, or one backhand, or one grab and twist, but it always hurt, *always;* he made sure it did. And he didn't half-care anymore whether the bruises were visible or not; except he needed to be sure he didn't permanently damage the goods, for real. He was always sure to keep that in mind.

And although this certainly wasn't the first time he hurt her since he was back, usually as quickly as the assault happened, it would end, and he occasionally uttered something that wasn't quite an apology, more often than not, he usually was man enough to forgive her for whatever she did wrong. And then there would be calm, for awhile anyway. And she would pretend to accept whatever he said, to allow the waters to settle, till the next storm.

But this one was different.

For the first time, as he squeezed the last of the air from her, she realized this morning's Button was brand new, like he somehow shed his skin. He was always scary, getting scarier, but this was a new genie, and a very different type of tiger. And right now, for the first time, Lillian Liddell realized she had *no* control over Button Pierce, none at all. She felt her windpipe being crushed, and she wasn't sure if he would ever let go; she wasn't sure if this wasn't really the end, for her. Her field of vision started to shrink, darkness and flashing white stars closing in from the sides.

And Button saw it; he saw the terror, the abject fear, and he *drank* it. It was better than an orgasm....*way* better.

And just as quick as he snapped, when he saw utter compliance in her contorted face, in her bloodshot eyes, Billy knew for sure she would never interrupt him again.

He cracked the faintest hint of a smile and let go; her head dropped toward the floor as she coughed and gagged, trying desperately to do it as quietly as possible, to limit the upset, to avoid a repeat, to get back to the calm....and safe. She was trembling, and the more she tried to stop it, the worse it got. All she could think of was him choking her again, and what she could do to prevent it. Which would have been anything, anything he wanted. And strangely enough, her pussy was throbbing, pins and needles, pre-orgasm, like some sort of sick joke. It was raw adrenaline shooting through her system, not knowing what to do or where to go, so it somehow ended up there. She could feel it, was disgusted by it, and tried to shut it off, but couldn't. It simply throbbed, a dull electric pulse deep inside her vagina.

Button put his finger gently under her chin, and raised her head to meet his eyes. Her eyes watered, and choke tears ran down her flush cheeks.

"You're okay, I'm okay, everything's okay; now just breathe easy….that's it, good. Now hear me out."

Billy stared at her in silence, as she tried her best to regain composure and not upset him. He saw she was trying and he nodded in acknowledgment, gently wiping a streaming tear off her left cheek with the sweep of his thumb. Then he smiled at her, and continued his tale, uninterrupted. And as he spoke, she tried her best not to let him see her shaking; she placed her shoulder against the bed, to try and stop the trembling.

"This octopus has a name, it's called the *Drin,* and part of the *Drin,* a very important part, involves you. Do you know what a *Circuit Girl* is?"

Lilly sat frozen, shoulder glued to the bed, afraid to answer; she tried to move her eyeballs, to see his hands, to see if another choke was coming, but she couldn't, so she just nodded a no, hesitantly, and slowly, in silence.

Button smirked at the control.

"It's okay sweetie, if I ask you a question, you can answer, okay?"

The two stared at each other in silence, followed by a faint response.

"Okay."

Was all she said, her voice hoarse. Button could feel her whole body trembling through a single light fingertip which touched gently under her chin. And he smiled to himself some more, knowing, finally, that Lilly would do whatever he said. And once she was out of this fucking Town, there would never be another outburst, another retort. As she had gotten older, he realized Lilly had gotten a bit smarter. It only took one not-so-short choke-hold, and his bitch, like a dog, quickly remembered how to obey.

Button's thoughts turned to Carol, and obedience. It was something he never quite got to work on her mother; he was too young, too inexperienced. If only he was older, if only she would've lasted a bit longer, he would have had what he *really* wanted, her, all to himself. But that bitch denied him; twenty-five years later and he was still pissed she slipped between his fingers. Instead, he was stuck with second-helpings, which were trembling on the floor beside him, ready to piss the carpet.

He looked down at Lilly, but he was talking to Carol.

"Okay, all I'm saying is, you're still my girl, you'll always be my girl, and even at thirty-nine, forty, whatever, you are still one of the hottest girls I've ever met....*ever*! And you should use it, we should use it, to make ourselves some money, lots of money, easy money; it's not like it means anything."

Lilly just stared at Button and didn't emote a thing....dead still.

"Sweetie, a *Circuit Girl* is kind of like a high-end, chaperone, to high-end business people on the conference circuit; you know, like business events, conventions, you know, stuff like that. Philly and New York are full of that shit, and I'm talking *high-end:* two-thousand, four-thousand, even six-grand a night....*a night!* Sometimes more than ten grand a night for someone choice, like you! And that's just to keep them company, you know, arm-candy, at business functions, parties, whatever; old, and not-so-old overbites, white guys, with too much cash and ugly, fat-shit wives at home. In fact, you'd be in charge of a stable of girls – a woman typically runs these sorts of things; they would all work for *you*, under me of course, and they would do all the grunt work, but you, like champagne, would only be brought out for the *special occasions*. Ten thousand bucks per night Lilly….*per night*! Sometimes even more, *twenty grand* even, for real high rollers, or if they want some weird or kinky shit. But don't worry, they'll all be doctor-cleared for disease and shit like that; we don't want to put you on the sidelines or anything, not our star player! Think about it Lilly; think about all the fucking and weird tie-up shit you did your whole life for free, and now ten or twenty grand, *cash*, tax free per pop; can you *believe* it!"

And as those steely-blue eyes pierced hers, all Lilly could think was that Button didn't even know, or remember, how old she really was. She wasn't thirty-nine, or forty or *whatever;* she was five months away from forty-two. And he apparently thought she was, and had always been, some sort of whore who did it for free, and that the discussion went from her being a *chaperone* and *arm-candy* at business functions to a *fuck-whore* in the same sentence. And he didn't even realize it, or care.

The whole thing seemed like a bad dream.

And as she stared at his beautiful, hideous face, all at once, she had an overwhelming desire to jump up and run as fast as she could, as far away as she could, to be with Earl, and Cord, and feel safe, and talk about all the stupid things they always talked about, and laughed about….anything, to just laugh, and be safe.

But she was chained to the bed by a rapist, and now a pimp, held in check by a single, light fingertip, pushed gently up under her chin.

Button cocked his head and leaned a bit closer to her, looking at her glazed eyes which clearly were somewhere else. He grabbed her chin hard and jerked it to the right.

"Hey, are you listening?"

She shook her head and gave him a quick, forced smile. They both knew it was fake, but he really didn't care. Laid bare, she was now simply choice livestock, on the way to auction. And just like that, he let go of her chin and sat back in a relaxed mode, and took a long toke. He gave up any pretense of sugar-coating it any longer – no need; she was onboard, whether she was, or wasn't.

Didn't matter.

"Good, then were set. Hey, you remember that *kinbaku* stuff we used to do? That Jap rope-tying shit we did - *you loved that shit [Button took another long drag; this time, he blew it right in Lilly's face]*! Anyway, we gotta find that book and relearn that stuff; that was some good shit, worth money; people will definitely pay extra for it, fucking kinky old bastards *[Button chuckled at the thought of fat, old sweaty white men, premature jacking all over Lilly, paying and never getting a real taste of that tied-up bitch – no refunds!]*. Hey, just so you know, these girls you'll work with, some are homegrown white-bread, strays we round up, but most are foreign - Russian and Vietnamese, mostly, some African, some Pakistanis, Asian, Mexican, all stupid-shit immigrants who believe anything you tell 'em. But all of 'em are top-notch, lookers, young and thin, some *real young* – I'm talking like twelve, maybe younger; there's a big market for that fucked-up shit, huge, especially virgins. We can probably resell them a couple times, you know, fuck, stitch and resell....there's a *need to bleed*! I know, I know, it's fucked up, but I'll still take the sick pervert's money; green is green.   And we did the research, that fucked-up kid shit means big fucking numbers, and big bucks in that virgin shit too....*boku*. So you gotta get over the whole conscience thing, just gets in the way of doing your job. Hey, another thing, none of them speak much English, but we have work-arounds for that. And there's a whole rulebook we have on how to best manage the team. It's pretty easy; you'll pick it up real easy, Sweetie, you're smart about stuff like that. I got confidence in you, and told the Dr. that too; talked you up big-time. He's really excited to meet you, in the flesh, so to speak. With your stable of girls, you'll have them set up in a house or two at first, like a sorority house; you're kinda like a den mother, you know, keeping a tab on 'em, being a dorm monitor. The girl's houses, you know, they'll be in Jersey, you know, on the Jersey-side of Philly; I like being on our side of the river, you know, closer to home, Jersey is Jersey; who wants to live in Pennsylvania, the inbred fucks. Hey, just so you know, I'll be living elsewhere, but real close by, you know, in case there are any problems. And of course, you get visiting rights to my place as often as we can, don't want to play it all away; still want *my* share!"

Even after laying the whole prostitution plan bare, because, at this point, he didn't give a fuck whether she liked it or not, Button still didn't want to say the word *Camden* out loud, knowing that even Lilly, sheltered in bumfuck Belvidere, knew that Camden was a fucking drug, murder and nigger-infested sewer, and *that* fact, and her living there by force, more than spreading her legs for money, may make her go rabbit. Such was Button's thinking. And he didn't elaborate on the *management rulebook,* that would come later, once he got her sequestered down south. The *management rulebook* was a cocktail of narcotics, beatings, bondage, family threats, and even low-level humiliation to corral the girls. But in the end, for a scared bunch of young girls far away from home, it took surprisingly little violence to foster obedience, as Lilly knew all too well. Well timed, well placed, terror had a long shelf life.

"You're not gonna know what to do with all the cash!"

Button smiled at her and took another long drag, thinking *he* didn't know what he was going to do with all the cash, since Lilly would never see a penny of it, except what he decided to spend on her, an allowance he'd spend, *if* she earned it. He blew the next mouth of smoke vertical, as a courtesy; he wondered if she even appreciated the gesture.

Throughout his whole soliloquy, Lilly just stared at him with empty eyes and the same weak, plastic smile painted on her face, like a creepy doll.

He frowned.

"Now Lilly, you said two weeks ago that you were ready to go, to kiss this place off, but you've been making every excuse under the sun since then to delay. First I gotta do Earl-this, or Frank-that, or Sam-the-other-thing, and I've been okay with that, because I had to take care of some *Drin*-related business up here anyway. But I'm just about done with all that stuff, and the Dr., and my other partners, are getting impatient to get this train down the tracks; so it's time for us to go south. *Now.* You can come back and visit now and then, it's not like we'll be that far away; it's only two hours for Christ's sake. But you need to pack and tell that cunt you're outta this dump, or don't tell her, I could give a shit either way. Now if we get out of here in the next day or so, say all your goodbyes and shit, I promise I won't hurt your brother's little friend; I haven't yet, right? You know he deserves it, but I kept my word, and I will continue to, 'cause that's what I do. But seriously, we gotta go, kiss this fucking shitbox good-bye once and for all. It's really time to go, okay?"

Lilly was scared shitless; she didn't want to go anywhere.

"Okay?"

He said a second time, more forceful, as he leaned toward her.

She quickly answered in a hoarse whisper.

"Okay."

And Button smiled at her, bent over and crushed the cigarette end into the bedroom floor boards.

"Good, now be my little *Circuit Girl,* and show me what you got; don't let any get away, not a single drop. Let's see you make your first ten grand….on account, of course *[Button chuckled]*."

He grabbed the hair on the back of her head hard, like grabbing a dog by the scruff, and shoved her down on his cock in one slow steady motion. It quickly grew rock hard in her mouth.

And his bitch offered no resistance, none at all, and in less than a minute, without spilling a drop, she quietly swallowed and earned her money.

CHAPTER 186 – SHE FELT HIS TONGUE AND TRIED NOT TO FLINCH

Sunday, July 30th, 2006; day one-hundred-two.

Button held the phone away from his ear yet again; this shit was getting old. He yelled into the mouthpiece, loud and annoyed, a bit of spittle left his lips, sticking to the receiver.

"Mother-fucker, would you shut your fucking mouth for ONE minute! I already told you, I met with *my boys*, not *our* boys, **my boys**, a couple times, and they're up to speed, they like the package, they certainly don't need to meet you, or you them. I just need one more face with them, couple more guys need to hear it from me, direct, and then I'm cool, and we got some serious seed to get things rolling. That last meeting is happening today, then done, and I'm outta here. They all still can't believe I'm tied with a nigger....*me!* But I told 'em you're really a Cracker in shit-skin anyway, just a bad tan."

Button laughed as the expletives rang from the receiver.

"Yeah, yeah, a brother, right. Anyway, I cinched some more of my own boys up here too, old ties I didn't think were still around; got lucky. Good guys, guys I can trust, and who can trust me; some of these boys I knew back in the local Klavern, dude....*tight.*"

Button stopped and listened, then interrupted; this call, like most, was a running series of interruptions between the two. As he walked around the room, he took long drags from his cigarette and kicked the empty beer bottles on the carpet around, like kicking stones on the street.

"You heard right, the Klavern, the *Klan* dude; fuck yeah! Fucking-A right, up north, Jersey faction, real thing; *I'm serious,* I can't believe I never told you this. I don't know, about a dozen guys, next town over, back in '91;

shit, fifteen years ago already, can't believe that! I never told you this shit, really? Yeah, fuckin-A they do, still got hoods in the closet, robes, everything! No, I never wore one, jokers wore 'em; everyone knew where I stood, no need to hide behind a fucking sheet. Anyway, these guys know I'll break their fucking heads if they get out of line, and they'll gut and cook *you* on a spit, like a greasy pig, if anything ever happens to me, mother-fucker - keep that in mind. Let me tell ya, these are some dumb-ass angry white guys, dog-fuckers – all of them, trust me – you don't wanna fuck with 'em, Jersey Crackers for sure....scary-stupid, but loyal. They can't believe I'm hooked up with a nigger, either; I'm surprised they don't gut *me*."

Button said in a reflective tone; he took a long drag, then laughed again.

"Yeah, man, pretty cool; it's coming together, the *Drin,* it's just about set."

The Dr interrupted.

"Yo, it better be, it's like, it's rough chilling the boys down here, time to hustle, man, get off the dime, you know; lots of promises, money to be made. Where's the little lady stand?"

"She's cool, she's cool, all on board, no problems."

"Shit dog! When were you gonna spill that?! Shit, then bring her down and let me tap that shit raw! Like right now! Let her feel a real man, like, you know, real cock; don't think I forgot who gets to bottom out first on that tang."

Button laughed.

"Yeah, you wish; the only thing you're gonna do is ruin it for all the other niggers who want to pop her, once she sees that shrimp dick of...."

Button eyed Lilly down the hall, slowly opening the apartment door, trying to make a quiet exit; he dropped his hand to his side, mid-sentence.

"Hey, Hey! **Hey!** *Where are you going Princess?"*

Lilly didn't say anything; she just froze, a doe in high beams. Button stared hard at her, then picked up the phone and finished the call in a low tone.

"Listen man, chill the troops another day or so, I gotta go. Couple more days at most, one or two, and I'm outta here, business will be done, goods delivered, then ramp-up time, big-time."

Button half-listened for about ten more seconds, staring down Lilly, who was still frozen, hand glued to the knob. He couldn't tell if she was trembling.

"Yeah, trust me, worth the wait...."

Button said quietly, flipping the phone shut. He heard the Dr. still talking trash as the phone folded shut; the conversation was over.

"Hey little girl, where do you think you're going, without telling me? Are you trying to sneak out? I thought we talked about this darlin."

Button said in a condescending tone, like talking to a child, never taking his eyes off hers.

"You were on the phone; I just wanted to go for a walk is all, it's such a nice day."

She talked barely above a whisper, wondering if her eyes gave away the rabbit.

"Well I'll go with you; all you have to do is ask Sweetie. No need for you to be wandering around without your No. 1, right partner? Listen, we really gotta get out of here tomorrow, next day latest, no joke, no more delays, heat is really coming down, maybe sooner, maybe even tonight. I got a meeting today, and hopefully, that should be it."

And with that, Button dropped his cigarette on the wood floor and crushed it under his boot, snagged the crumpled pack off the table, piled haphazard with dishes, caked with streaks of dried food, and slowly sauntered down the hall, a trail of smoke encircled his head. He met her at the door; her hand was still frozen on the knob. She had that same weak, plasticine smile she wore since yesterday morning, but her face was paler, the bags beneath her eyes dark, half-moons.

"Christ, you're right, you do need some sun, and some sleep. You gotta stop whining for cock all night, plum wearing you out. You're looking bad, Sweetie."

Not good for business was running heavy through his head. He grabbed her awkwardly around the waist, in a crude attempt at affection, and kissed her sloppily on the neck, like a drunk.

Inhaling his stale cigarette breath, she felt his tongue and tried not to flinch.

CHAPTER 187 – BE GOOD BROTHER

C smiled at the thought, laying in the thin, dry grass, his arm sprawled lazy across the marker, looking up through the twisted, muscular branches of pin oak.

He whispered to Carol.

"Can you believe it? He had to call Marty, of course, and he made Ji-Sue and Buck go too, but he went! He really went, to the *Couch Rock* with Carol, even though no girls were allowed; unbelievable! I never saw him so nervous, and happy; he kept rubbing his hands together like he always does when he gets all excited....pretty funny. Good for him, he deserves it."

C smiled broadly.

"Oh sorry, you weren't supposed to know about the *Couch Rock* thing; cat is out of the bag, I guess. But something tells me you knew about it anyway, and kept an eye on him, on all those solo trips out there in the deep, dark woods, and just never told Earl; no way you would've let him out there alone. At least I don't think so. Just a guess, since you're not talking."

C rubbed his arm and felt the *bas relief* of her name run through the light brown hair on his forearm. For him, it was just like touching her, for real. And for some reason, that mattered. But the smile receded with the jump in thought, still staring overhead. He grabbed a handful of wispy grass, and slowly split a blade in two, and then another, as he spoke.

"*Behold a pale horse;* just a bit strange we've got that in common; then again, maybe not. But the news to me probably wasn't news to you; I'm sure you already knew all about that.   But let me tell ya, no joke, the hair rose on my arms when Earl spilled that little gem. You and I, we got some serious stuff going on, don't we? Wish you'd clue me in as to the how and why, and what else we share, but my guess is, you probably won't. Makes it more interesting that way, doesn't it, me talking and you just listening? Or maybe I'm just talking out loud to dirt, who knows. You know, I first saw that verse, those words, etched in a huge stone frieze, bigger than life-size, on a large war memorial, in Missouri....Kansas City, many, many years ago, when I was out on a long run. Strangest thing, for some reason I stopped at that Memorial, in the middle of my run, in the middle of a park, and looked up – didn't know why I stopped or looked up at the exact time – still don't. But the first thing I saw was *Death*, astride his horse – he was a skeleton carrying a scythe, carved in limestone, it looked like limestone, anyway, in *bas relief*. And I felt I'd been there before, although I never had.

And I read the first four words, high up on the wall, well over thirty feet above my head….just the first four:

Behold a pale horse;

And then closed my eyes, and the rest of the words fell off my tongue, as easy as pie, a stanza I didn't know – a verse I had never read or seen, from the fucking Bible no less. That alone is a joke. But for whatever reason, I recited those God-forsaken words, like it was a poem written *just* for me, like it was one I'd known my whole life:

and his name,
that sat on him,
was Death.
And Hell followed with him.

I almost didn't look up to see if I was right, like checking the answer on a test you know you aced. I knew it was right, to the word; I don't know how, but I did. And of course, I was. Spot on. Never figured that one out, just like never figuring out how I knew *Ormia Ochracea,* the orange-eyed fly, when there was no way I should have, could have, known that as a twelve-year old coming off a wicked dream, after being skewered on a fence. But somehow I did.

Strange stuff.

The whole thing is strange, and you're just the icing on top. And I'm laying in a cemetery, discussing it, rationally, in my mind anyway, with a dead person that I never met, who tells her son she knows me, and that I'm a kindred spirit, some sort of angel. *Christ!* Maybe I'm dead too; maybe we're dead together, which is why this relationship works *[C shook his head and snorted a half-laugh].*

Funny; fucked up, but funny.

You know, I've been on that horse a long time, too long, all the way back to the puppet, crickets and flies, and I never told anyone that *Death* story, till you, till now. And I only told you because I have the feeling you already knew, that you've somehow *always* known; and when I get those kinds of feelings, I'm usually right. I'm right, right? But, and sorry to belabor the point, but I just can't shake it, what I don't get is what does all of this have to do with *you*? How do *you* fit in, to the grand scheme? And why did it take forty-three years for you to finally show up? Another player in the game? For what? Why is this place any different from every other end-of-the-road shitbox I seem to end up in? Is that dart yours, the fourth one? It was, wasn't it? *But why?* I just don't get the *why*. Do I know you? Have we somehow met before? Did I know you, somewhere, somehow, and just don't remember? I can't imagine not remembering someone like you; if you looked like Lilly, or she looked like you, that's a look that's kinda hard to forget. You know, I've been having weird feelings about the puppet lately; he feels *real* close, too close....closer than he's been in a *long* time. And I don't like it, not one bit. Where is he hiding? Do you know him? He's kinda hard to forget too, and he doesn't let you forget, even if that's all you want to do. Is he lying on the grass beside your grave, right now, talking to you? Is he *me*? Has he always been me? Or is he *not* me? Or am I just fucked in the head? I'll pick Door No. 3. Do you even know what I'm talking about? The puppet? And why *am* I here? To finally meet him, in Belvidere, or simply in the mirror? I don't get it….do you? Do you play by the rules too? Rules you don't control, and don't understand, set by someone else, you've never met, or even spoken to? Are they the same rules as mine, or are yours different? Mine are fucking complicated, contradictory, and don't make much sense at all; but *fuck*, if you don't follow them, let me tell ya, there are *consequences*.

[C shook his head, like he many times did, to reset]

You know, bad things happen wherever I go.…people die, sometimes planned, sometimes not, but the end is *always* the same. But I think you already know that, and because of that, the *why* I'm here scares the shit out of me, because I don't know why; I rarely do. I don't want anything bad to happen here, not here, not to people I care about, anyway, and this place *actually* has a few, one, at least.…two, if I count you. I like you; I would love to talk to you, to simply hear your voice. How cool would that be, if you just talked to me, even just once. I think we might have been friends, for a little while, at least. You know I'm never friends with anyone for long, for keeps. Doesn't work that way, never has. Don't think it ever will. Those seem to be the rules. Good thing is, I'm not sure how I can hurt *you*; that's already been done, I guess. So maybe I get a pass on that one."

He had been rambling for awhile, whispering aloud to Carol, to himself. But just then it hit him, that maybe someone would walk by, within earshot, and hear him talking to himself, laying between graves in a cemetery. Christ, that had bad written all over it. C half-lifted his head and looked around for embarrassment's sake; thankfully, it was quiet, empty....no one, nothing in his ken.

He laid his head back softly in the dry July grass and stopped talking; thinking was as good as talking to Carol anyway. He was sure she was somewhere, hiding in the folds in his head. How she got in and out he didn't know, just like the rest of them, he guessed. So he just went on a mind-wander, letting whatever thought came to fore run, with no rhyme or reason, no logical progression, just a smash-up, like when he spoke with his mom, after a hard rap on the mausoleum wall.

So began the aimless wander.

Had another dream last night; I was an adult, but I was back home, my childhood home, visiting my parents. I don't usually have dreams like that, ones where they're alive; in fact, I never do....they're always already dead. But this time, for some odd reason, they weren't. And my childhood home had been converted to some kind of fun house, a spook house, with chintzy, cheesy props set up in all the rooms – witches and devils and goblins leaning out of closets and showers when doors were opened and curtains drawn - lots of doors and lots of monsters. But the whole display was idle, abandoned, like the circus had long left town. And my mom, she was apologizing for the mess, and telling me I simply couldn't stay, till they cleaned up, so I wandered around the house, looking at all the sad props - none of them worked - they just hung there....dead. And I wanted to stay, but I couldn't, I had to go, was told to go, and that was that....don't remember if I ever left, or want happened next. It just kind of dissolved, like dreams do.

I want to be, and sometimes I still am, but most times I'm not, mad at Lilly for what she did to me. We had a pretty good thing going, the three of us, and it just fell apart, just like that. Maybe that means it never really had legs to begin with, but I hope I'm wrong about that. But the truth is, most times I'm really just sad, for her, and Earl, and me....especially now.   C knew Carol already knew that, whether he admitted it aloud or in his head. It had been two weeks since that jerk-off came back and Belvidere changed, but it felt much longer....like a lifetime. It was like C never really knew Lilly at all; maybe he really didn't. The girl he knew was a place-set, just play-pretend, waiting for life to return to normal, for her anyway, when Button returned. And although he would never say it aloud, and he felt uncomfortable even thinking it, he knew he loved Lillian, still did, and was mad at himself for even admitting it, to himself. But falling in love doesn't mean it will work, in fact, it rarely does....the relationship part ruins it, gets in the way, always does. And for C, it never worked, never in the end; he had a long history proving that theory, one hundred percent.

Lozeta Fresca Nopizar....he just remembered that phrase was in his dream too, it must have been after the spook house dream, he wasn't sure, but that's how it felt. It was scratched sloppy, with a nail, into a marble tile floor in a bedroom for someone he didn't know, in a building he had never seen; the words were spelled wrong, but essentially meant 'fresh tile - don't step'. He had no idea what it meant, but the misspelled words, they were crystal in his mind....and it just popped in, from nowhere. It was strange he just remembered that, just now; do you know why? He waited, but Carol didn't say a word.

I don't do anything, with other people that is, for Christmas, haven't in many years; always spend the day, and the day before and after, alone. I like it that way. I wonder where I'll be this Christmas; I wonder if I can get out of it, you know, with Earl. I doubt it; he's been talking about what to buy Carol for Christmas since May, for Christ sake. I can't imagine getting away with a Christmas bypass with Earl around [C smiled and put his hands behind his head, blinking at the sky].   That assumes, of course, I'm still around this backwater; five *more months is a long slog for me, considering I got three in already. But you never know, do you? Do you? Will I still be here when the snow flies? You know, one of my favorites, probably my favorite Christmas of all time? I was in Ft. Lauderdale, on a beautiful, sunny Christmas day, running along the beach, right along Atlantic Boulevard. And I got a blister; man, it was a bad one, bleeding like hell in my sneaker, and my legs were cramped, and I felt like shit. So I decided to stop, to take a bit of a rest, and sat on this concrete ledge, right by a tall pillar on the beachside of the road, across from 9th Street, a real good seat, front row, looking out at the ocean. Anyway, the beach, and the sidewalk were packed with people, late morning, on Christmas Day! It was very cool; people were sunbathing, walking dogs, riding bikes, and there were plenty of other runners too, and I'm just drinking in the scene, sitting on this whitewashed concrete ledge, minding to myself, when I hear this annoyed snort beside me. And who is it? Son-of-a-bitch if it isn't Santa Claus! Well he looks like Santa Claus to me, if the big man was unemployed, and down on his luck. He was a grizzled street bum, with an unruly, peppered beard, wearing thread-worn black pants and a too-tight V-neck tee, grayed and stained, stretched hard over a cartoon paunch. Santa's stubby feet were shoved hard into found sneakers, a full size too small; so small that he couldn't lace them up. He dragged along a frayed backpack, a sad sack which held his possessions - all of them. And I realized the nasal snort had to do with his seat; Santa's seat on the beach, stolen by me, the same seat he probably warmed most of the year with no problem, but on Christmas day, the beach was packed, and seats were at a premium. And here I was, in his seat, Santa's seat, the one he had easy access to the other three-hundred-sixty-four days a year. As I realized my error, I shifted to stand up, but the big man was already over the slight, and instead, offered an observation.* **"Can't beat Christmas on the beach, can ya?"** *He said in the baritone of a sage, looking out over his beach, out past the anonymous crowd, and into the surf...his surf.* **'No you can't'** *I answered. And with* *that, I slowly stood up on my blistered, bloody feet and gave him a friendly pat, my open hand falling half on a bush of peppered gray chest-hair protruding from his V-neck, and half on the top of his pot belly, hard and tight as a drum.   'All yours, empty.' I said apologetic, as I relinquished his seat. He half-smiled and looked at me with crystal eyes, and, as I kept my hand gently on his chest, he spoke in a familial tone "Be good brother...." And you know what Carol, he really meant it; it wasn't a flippant saying, or an empty salutation in exchange for a concrete seat. They weren't lifeless words, I could see it in his eyes....this Santa meant it. I smiled back at him, genuine, my gift in return, and didn't say a word, and turned away to continue on my run along Atlantic Avenue. About two hours later, I passed back that way, and there he was, fast asleep on the seawall, prone, his lower belly exposed where his too-tight, too-small tee-shirt hiked-up, his backpack a pillow, in the middle of a Christmas day, tight sneakers still untied, all alone, surrounded by a hundred people swirling, walking, running, all moving somewhere else. And I remember it being a beautiful day, and I remember thinking that was one of the best Christmas presents I ever received, ever. "Be good brother...." ; that was more than enough; for me, he'll always be Santa Claus. I never told that story to anyone before, just you.*

Cord closed his eyes and let the dappled sun warm his face, as he whispered the words aloud.

'Be good brother.'

CHAPTER 188 – SACK-SQUEEZE; LIP-LICK;
BULL-CHARGE

Vinny's chest was heaving heavy from the two-wheel sprint down Oxford, leaving the Cemetery in his wake. He kept looking over his shoulder, nervous, but C never saw him.

Vinny thought he spied the duo walking slow on Front Street earlier, heading toward the Hotel, and he was right. He smiled at his good fortune; he'd make some more shit up about Brin and spill it to the psycho - a little stoke of the fire, poke of the bees nest, never hurt. Mother-fucker will hopefully get what he deserves.

Cord sat up, stretched good and long, cracked his knuckles, and lazily turned his head, left, then right, and left once again. Oxford Street was empty, except for the odd car that puttered by. He stretched again and thoughts turned to Margery, maybe he should go test those waters again. He was ready to fuck something; his hand was getting old and his dick deserved better.

Ponte Vedra, the wide swath of thick, broken shells, stretched for miles along the water line, cracking under foot. He remembered that one day, man that was *years* ago, sitting on the upper part of the beach, up by the spotty dune grass, watching a pod of dolphin swim by, about fifty yards off the surf, heading north, in no particular hurry, followed by a lone pelican, gliding low. He wasn't sure why such random memories stayed with him, but they did, like other pointless snippets from other places….minutia that really meant nothing, but somehow stuck. Maybe there was a reason, and nobody bothered to share it with him.

He closed his eyes and saw them again, the white-bread middle-aged and senior dog-walkers, shell-pickers and horizon-gazers ambling by on that same stretch of shells. It was a clean, safe beach, in a safe white community, no vagrants, no undesirables to be found, except maybe him. But he seemed to look the part, and the locales paid him no heed.

Then along comes the lone beauty on a bike, thin and lean....athletic; those were the ones he always remembered, riding on the hard-pack sand, below the scatter of shells, right at the water's edge. And he remembered that intense desire enveloped him, sprung from nowhere; an insatiable need to run her down, pull her from the bike, rip her shorts and panties off and violently fuck her, rape her right there, on the beach, in broad daylight, to violate her in the ass, in the cunt, in the mouth, over and again.

A predatory rape....brutal, overpowering.

God, it felt like yesterday; and, lying in the Cemetery beside Carol, he was embarrassed that his dick reacted with the slightest of swells. But, of course, it was never rape in your head; in the end, the villain always thinks he's the hero, and the girl inevitably wants it. In the end, they always acquiesce, humping and moaning hard and long. Such was the fantasy.

He looked down at Carol, self-aware of the continued hardening in his shorts, and was ashamed at the thought. Did she know what he was thinking, just now? Of course she did, didn't she? And he wondered again what she really knew about him, about his past; what did she *really* know?

Before he sat on that dune, before he watched the shell-pickers and dog-walkers, and the skinny girl on the bike, before all that, running down by the water's edge, he spied a piece of white paper slowly skipping across the upper part of the beach, headed toward the surf, pushed along by a choppy wind. When he first noticed it, the paper was a good ten yards ahead of him. And while the movement of the scrap across the surface of the sand caught his eye, C did nothing more to acknowledge or engage; he didn't speed nor slow his gait, he simply maintained a steady pace, as the paper followed its own path, an adagio on its way to oblivion in the salt surf.

But in nothing more than a fluke, right then, a healthier gust of *Boreas*, an unseasonable cold cough, strange, hit C's right cheek and the paper accelerated to a quick sprint across the silica to meet him. And just as his left shoe landed on the wet beach, the paper slipped under his sneaker and he snagged it, pinning it between his sole and the sand, and improbable catch....one in a million. He could never have timed trapping that quicksilver in full stride, the feat would have been impossible to replicate. But this time, somehow, by mistake, he did. That little shred didn't want to end in the drink, it somehow wanted to be found, by him....and it was.

Minutia, meant for some reason, some meaning, sometimes years in the offing. Decided by others, rarely revealed. Such was the game.

C stopped and peeled it off his sole, slid it in his tee-shirt, and paid it no more mind, as he resumed his run.

Once he sat, well after the dolphins and pelican and beautiful biker had passed, and it was quiet, and the beach was his alone, he reached into his breast pocket and examined the dirty white paper, about the size of a gum wrapper, an inch by two, somehow neatly folded in half. He spun it around in his hand, and only after inspecting it much more thoroughly than it deserved, did he slowly open the sheet, like some specially wrapped gift, expecting some providential phrase, a nugget of advice, since it clearly sought him out.

Whatever it was, it would be important, he had that gut.

And as the simple, succinct message, seemingly hastily scrawled, stared back at him, he remembered wondering the setting, the context, the absent author and the result, the ending, and if there was one, was it good or bad? He sat silent and processed. But no answers were revealed that day, or ever. He smiled sad at the memory, years ago and a thousand miles away, questions unresolved.

C opened his eyes and looked up through the tangle of oak branches, then slowly closed them again, slid his right hand down his shorts and cupped his ballsack, like he often did, for no reason other than it felt comfortable. His dick had gone limp again, nothing but a quick up and down nod to the memory of the skinny *Ponte Vedra* biker.

And he waited for Carol to speak. There are over two hundred billion stars in our galaxy, and fifty billion galaxies, and still counting; he wondered just where Carol might be....lots of places for her to hide. He directed his thoughts to wherever she was, still cupping his balls, his left hand resting behind his head.

'So, pull a Houdini and tell me what was on the paper. I remember it all these years, and never told anyone about it. It's long buried, filed somewhere, but I'm sure you can read it wherever it is; so, make me believe. Earl said I'd believe; here's your chance. I'll just lay here next to you and wait, patiently, for you to change the water in the bathroom cup to blue.'

And C waited, soaking in the July sunshine, wishing he knew what Carol really looked like, and how cool it would have been to know her. He did the math in his head, figuring out her age, today, in 2006. After a few seconds thought, he came up with the shock of sixty-one....*sixty-one for Christ's sake!* In his mind, when he talked to her, she was always Lillian's twin. He wasn't talking to a sixty-one year old, for sure. No, Carol, to him, would always be young and beautiful; that was the gift of dying young; you stay young, *forever*. He smiled at the thought of a young Carol, his Carol, then he thought of Lilly, and then Carol and Lillian together....a duo; my God, that must have been *some* pair.

And he thought of Carol some more, and he felt, or maybe he just wanted to feel, that she was, somehow, close by, and she really did hear him, hear all his ramblings and pointless stories, he just wished he could know for sure. He let out a long, relaxed exhale from his nostrils; a faint smile creased his face, hand in his pants, cupping his scrotum, soaking in the summer sun.

What a nice day, and a nice place, to relax.

He decided to practice *Amazing Grace* again; he had been practicing in the shower most mornings, and Earl was right, he was *awful*. He decided to sing aloud, but in a whisper; he didn't have the drone of the shower head to drown him out. Eyes still closed, he cleared his throat, and, in the faintest audible, just loud enough to hear himself, he began to sing. And to his surprise, it didn't sound half-bad, to him at least.

*"Amazing Grace, how sweet the sound
that saved a wretch....*

It was then, mid-verse, that the pain exploded in his right shoulder, like a gunshot.

"What the fuck!   What the fuck are you doing, mother-fucker?!"

Button's face was vermilion, spitting as he yelled rabid, seeing Cord lying by Carol's grave....*his* Carol, with his hand cupping his cock, singing *that* song.

"Why the fuck you laying there! Mumbling with your hand in your *fucking pants*? **Fuck! You fucking queer!"**

Button swung his foot back and was aiming a heavy steel-toed boot to the side of C's head; but Cord half-rolled across Carol's marker and was up on his feet before the follow-through; it wasn't till then that he saw Lillian standing by Billy's side, head down, in a submissive pose he didn't recognize, one he could never imagine her wearing. Her face seemed sunken, sallow, that of a beaten soul.

She didn't even look like Lilly; she was some hollow form.

Billy shook his head in anger, back and forth in the negative; he was so riled at the violation of Carol's space, his space, he didn't, or couldn't speak anymore, not knowing what to say, or what to do, or how to kill that mother-fucker, right then and there.

And when C saw the rage irrupt in Button's eyes; he did the one thing he knew, for sure, would send Billy Bones over the edge, would get him stupid, would get him to attack.

Cord didn't say a word; arms limp by his sides.

He simply, deliberately slow, moved his left hand and squeezed, pulling on his nutsack as he seductively licked his upper lip, like a fucking 'mo. Then, with his sack-squeezed, Cord half-smiled at Billy Bones, a queer smile, and licked his lips sexy, sticking out his tongue seductive. That was all the bait it took for the bull to charge.

Simple formula: sack-squeeze; lip-lick; bull-charge.

CHAPTER 189 – IN RECKLESS SCRIPT, A SINGLE WORD: *HELP*

It was a polite dance, in a strange sort of way.

Both stared into the others eyes, as they slowly two-stepped forward, then back, a weird, counter-clockwise, slow-motion promenade, careful and utterly quiet; not a word spoken, nary a hint of struggle. Neither was willing to acknowledge breathing any way other than normal.

But, as happens in any row, someone, at some point, realizes the beginning of an advantage, be it strength, or endurance, or will, or some combination thereof.

And Cord Brin felt it, and Billy Bones knew it.

And Button, rarely on this side of the coin, realized he couldn't match Cord for much longer; C's grip was tighter and his clench stronger, and Billy's arm quickly burned lactic.

Both had somehow shot and landed single-hand choke-holds on the other, stiff-armed, trying to squeeze shut the opposing windpipe and end blood flow to the brain in an ever tighter grip. Both faces were beet red, eyes bulging and bloodshot, but neither spoke, nor coughed, nor gave any outward utter of struggle or pain....this was a silent squeeze, to be kept up until one broke. Somehow they both knew the rules, and both abided, with nary a cheat.

Lilly stood to the side in a daze; she didn't make a sound, nor try to help one, or the other, or seek assistance elsewhere. She simply stared at the dance in a fog, seeming to fade toward the rear of the stage, toward her mother's grave, her marker.

Without warning, sensing his advantage, C jerked Button to the left and ran him toward the nearest oak, the one with the rusted, bent metal fence post half-absorbed into the trunk. Billy couldn't put up much of a struggle, he felt lightheaded, his legs starting to wobble. In a quick thrust and lunge, C pushed him up against the trunk, sensing the last of the fight was about out of his adversary.

Button put his left hand half-up in a surrender gesture, and shook his head, accepting defeat. It was only then that C smiled, just a tick, and let up his grip, acknowledging the matter had concluded. And for the first time, he again felt the sharp throb of pain in his shoulder, courtesy of Billy's earlier boot swing.

Button shook his head and attempted, multiple times, to clear his throat, head down toward the ground. He spit several times, hands on his knees, regaining air, and composure in as quiet and dignified a manner as he could.

C just stood and waited.

Finally, after a half-minute, Billy looked up at C, shook his head in the positive and half-smiled; the kind of look that acknowledges a fair-fight, the kind that says I can lose gracefully, and I can congratulate the victor, and not be less a man for it. C was surprised at the gesture; never expecting it from a guy like Billy Bones.

It was a pleasant surprise.

And, C thought, maybe this was an ever-so-slight defrost, the first small turn for the better in a dangerous relationship. Maybe, the two *could* co-exist in the same space without one killing the other. And if, in the end, Button kept Lillian, so be it, C would accept it, he decided right then, as long as he wasn't forced to do something he would regret.

C knew he wouldn't lose this fight, he never did in the end, not fights like this; it was never allowed. But he usually lost plenty else along the way, and had to carry that baggage called regret. And he was long-past-tired of carrying that load. Like powder off the moth's wing, at some point, you're done. He was at that point; he was tired....and he was done.

So C smiled back, and was the first to offer his hand in reconciliation.

Button looked at the extension of Cord's hand and then raised his head to look C in the eyes and saw they were calm and relaxed. And before Billy offered his own hand in return, in a hoarse voice, he felt the need to make a confession.

"Man, that was one serious choke; pretty impressive."

Cord responded to the kind words.

"Thank...."

But the sound of the letter *s* in *Thanks* never left Cord's lips.

Like lightening, Button had grabbed C's shirt with both hands, just below the collar, and delivered a seething head-butt, a loud, dull crack of skulls, a brutal, crushing blow which immediately whiplashed C's neck and buckled his knees. Ay never remembered going down. Complete darkness; out - cold sober.

The second time this trip.

Sometime later, how long he didn't know, maybe a few minutes or so, he blinked and awoke in a drunken spin, the leaves and branches blended and fuzzed into the background sky. For a second, he didn't remember where he was, or how he found himself prone, he simply continued to blink in silence, trying to register, to reset where the fuck he was, and what had happened. Pain pulsed behind his eyes, a knife driven deep into his skull. He opened his mouth to crack his eardrums, and, slowly, the haze began to recede. He felt the sensation of liquid pooling around his left eyelid, blurring his vision. He raised his hand to wipe the blood, and felt moisture on his lower cheek, too much moisture. He looked at his hand and focused his gaze on the mucous mix of chaw and saliva that dripped from the side of his palm.

The fuck had spat a wad of tobacco on his face.

C sat up and slowly tried to shake the cobwebs; the pain was intense, and he felt nauseous. He sat perfectly still for several minutes, breathing slowly, waiting for the throb to dull. His eyes were full of flashing stars; the specks of light you see when you sneeze too hard, or get smashed in the face.

He gingerly moved his head, looked about, and saw that the Cemetery, past the pulsing stars, was empty, as was Oxford Street before him. It was quiet, and calm, no Button, nor Lillian, nor anyone. He must have been out longer than a few minutes, he thought, much longer. He shifted slowly and leaned gently back against the oak, trying not to move, to soothe the residual pounding. He closed his eyes again, and felt his brain throb inside his skull; it wanted out, the pressure was *intense*.

He opened his eyes again, and after a bit, his vision began to clear at the edges, and the stars began to fade, one by one. He stared like a zombie at nothing in particular, until he noticed the last white speck, off to the right, just on the periphery of his vision. It seemed to dance there, atop Carol's marker. A star that wasn't pulsing, or fading; it just sat there.

A single white period.

He blinked a few times, and the pointillist morphed, ethereal, into a small scrap of bleached paper, about the size of a gum wrapper, sitting on the spelter, folded in a vee, like a fortune cookie. He crawled over on hands and knees, about fifteen feet; it felt forever. The

Cemetery was eerie-still; not even the leaves made a sound....nothing.

He grabbed the paper and could see it was folded over twice; a hastily ripped scrap, one by two, a bit dirty, about the size of a gum wrapper. He unfolded the first, and saw the black of pen hidden past the second fold.

He blinked his eyes, still in a fog, and unfolded the next, reading that which was clearly meant for him.

In reckless script, a single word:

Help

CHAPTER 190 - A HALF-FINGER TOO FAR

Cord didn't consider a backup; there was no need. The place to be, to go, *right now*, somehow lit in his head, more of a spike-jam into his brain, an urgent call of desperation, distress, and he hadn't been as sure about anything as he was about this.

And the adrenaline dispatched the violent throb in his head, and the misery in his shoulder; he felt no pain.

He must have been out for longer than he thought, for it took just under ten minutes to jog the length of Oxford, past the Belvidere Hotel, down Front Street, past the bank, and another three residential blocks, to the top of the ramp, and he didn't see either one of them along the road. And he suspected they took their time; he pictured a somewhat leisurely stroll.

And the whole half-run he thought about nothing but saving Lilly; what that actually meant, he wasn't yet sure. He couldn't shake seeing her sunken features, the look of utter despair, and that sole word, a *Mayday,* that she hastily wrote on that tiny scrap of paper.

Help

Ay stopped at the crest of the boat ramp, and as right as rain, about thirty yards away, the two were standing by the water, facing away; her stiff, him, half a foot taller, indifferent to her presence. Billy and Lilly weren't talking, holding hands or engaged in any manner; in fact, they weren't doing anything, simply statues. Both stared at the far shore, but there was nothing of note to see, just water, and a tangle of trees along the far muddy bank. Some geese and ducks floated and sunned on a temporary, long, narrow river islet closer to the far shore; it only emerged when the river ran low, like now.

Cord slowly walked toward them, and got within twenty yards before Billy spoke, as if the act took great effort.

"Thought it would take longer."

And with that, still looking at the far Pennsylvania shore, he quarter-turned his head and slackly spat a wet wad of tobacco and saliva into the sand by his own feet. He lazily tossed a rock he had cupped in his hand in a slow graceful arch, out toward the flock of mallards quickly swimming toward the duo; figuring there with a loaf nearby to feed them, usually a good bet at the boat ramp, no matter who was standing at the water's edge. When it comes to food, ducks aren't dumb.

"Lillian, go home."

C said loudly, without emotion.

But Lillian didn't move a muscle, nor acknowledge the call.

And with that, Button turned and smiled possessive at C, then spied the blackened knot on Cord's forehead and the trail of crusted blood that circled his eye, smirking at his handiwork. C had refused to wipe the blood away, letting it dry in place. Button still sported the remnant of a red bracelet around his neck, courtesy of C's chokehold. Both tattoos on both men would be gone soon, healing long before they normally should. Such was the case, an oddity the two strangely shared.

Then again, maybe not so odd.

Billy spat another wad of tobacco juice, this time in the direction of Cord. He took his finger and pointed at Ay as he spoke, like a bored professor, standing at a lectern, teaching the same tired tale.

"Now, see, here's the problem, and here's why you keep finding yourself in all sorts of trouble. You don't talk to

Lilly, *ever again;* you talk to *me,* and only when I tell you to, which will be *never.* Got it? Very simple rules that even a faggot like you can understand. Now get lost, forever, before you regret ever stepping foot in my sights again."

"Lilly."

Was all C said, never looking at Button; he just stared at the back of her head. She was perfectly still, and, again, didn't turn into his words.

Rather, she slowly dropped her leaden head, as if in defeat, from gazing at some unknown point, far beyond the Pennsylvania shore, far beyond the woods and fields, to places she had never been, to staring blank at the tops of her mud-speckled shoes, and the dark brown, moist, silty sand along the water's edge.

The three stood in tense silence, for what seemed like forever: Billy Bones staring hard at Cord, who gazed confused at Lilly, who simply fish-eyed her muddy shoes.

As she stood statue, a satisfied smile slowly creased Button's face, realizing the discipline of the dog, the bitch, at his side. And just then, as if C's words took that length of time to soak into wherever Lilly was, still spying her toes, she spun and began to slowly walk up the ramp, automaton, away from the water, away from Billy's side.

And the smirk melted from Button's face. But to his surprise, he didn't grab her, or erupt. Rather, he spoke in a calm, fatherly tone.

"That's right *darlin,* go on home and finish packing; we're leaving tonight, couple hours and were gone. No discussion, no delay; the Dr. calls."

Lilly didn't need to finish packing, she needed to *start.*

She walked by C slowly, a bit too close, as if to whisper something to him, or grab his arm for support, or hide behind him, for safety, *home base* in tag, to give him some clue, some sign, something more than *Help* quickly scrawled on a gum-wrapper. But instead, she was silent; there was nothing more to say than that single word; that apparently summed it all. And she soon passed him and disappeared over the crest of the gravel ramp, out of sight, while each man eyed the other in strained silence.

The ramp was empty; not a boat nor human in sight, up or downstream. It was just the two of them, all alone, and somehow, strangely, on a beautiful, summer day at the public boat ramp, would stay that way till this matter concluded. That somehow made sense; it made all the sense in the world.

C slowly closed the distance by half to Button, to ten yards, even less, never taking his eyes off him....a deliberate, careful stride. And witnessing C's new-found caution, Button simply laughed.

"Never expected you for that; stupid-shit, dumber than I thought. Everyone says you're so fucking smart; not really, I guess."

Button laughed again, staring at the knot he birthed on Cord's head, and spat sloppy toward Ay. Then he spoke again.

"Spare me the tough-guy look, pal; last time I checked, you were passed out on your ass with my chaw spat all over your pussy face. I could have gutted you right then and there, if I wanted to bother *[and in one quick motion, from a sheath in his boot, Button yanked and held aloft a slender ornate knife, with a slightly hooked blade – it looked Arabian – the kind that can slice you like butter]*."

"The only reason you're still alive is I haven't decided, yet, how I want to do it. All I know is, it's gonna be slow and lonely, for you."

"Lilly's not going anywhere."

C said in response; Button guffawed.

"Let me ask you something, you stupid shit….simple question."

And with that, Button slowly crouched down, never taking his eyes off Cord, and cupped a handful of saturated river silt, squeezing the grains into a soupy sphere, about the size of a golf ball, letting the turbid water run between his fingers and down his forearm, weaving between the hairs on his arm. He stood up and tossed the wet orb into the river, and rubbed the remnant grit between his fingers slowly, as he spoke. The ducks all swarmed the disturbance, looking for bread that wasn't there.

"Why? Why the fuck are you even *here*, in **my** Town; why am I even talking to you, wasting my breath *[Button spat again, this time angry]?* And why hang with a stupid fucking nigger, who ain't worth shit, and has the IQ of a fucking dog? *Less* than a dog – dogs are way smarter than that moron. What's in *that* for you? What's the upside to that retard? Think it will help get you into my bitch's pants? Really? I heard you were trying to bang her for what, three months? And there was nobody stopping you, *nobody,* and you got shit pal, *nada.*

And I come back, knock on her door, and in less than three minutes *[Button held three fingers high in the air, in mock]*, after just sitting in your apartment listening to a bunch of stupid fucking made-up stories that she can't stand, and makes fun of, she's swallowing my cock? You realize that dude? *Three fucking minutes, and she's already swallowing!* And she's a good cock-sucker

1673

dude, I mean *real* good, and she loves to swallow; never wastes a drop, *never*.   And I unloaded in her mouth, in her cunt, and in her ass, all night long, while you were upstairs, jerking off *[Button laughed out loud]*.

And the best, this is the best, is when the little bitch came running into Sam's to *save* your sorry ass, she had a whole load still dripping down her throat, and leaking out both fucking holes.   And she still wanted *more*, told me to come back to bed and give her more cock, so I nailed her *again* right after she left the store, she was begging for it, moaning like a fucking whore, wanting it any way she could get it, so I shot all over her face, just for the hell of it!   And the bitch wiped it all off and swallowed it….*all of it*!"

No reaction from Cord; he stood stone-faced.

"Don't believe me? Ask her, mother-fucker; she left a snail-trail in the crotch of my fucking sweatpants - it was disgusting.   She's gonna get fat swallowing so much, and she *still* can't get enough. When I'm done with you here, I'll be sticking my cock in her *again,* in her ass, while she's standing, pinned against the wall, that's her favorite do, by the way, spreading her ass-cheeks, bellied up against the wall. Bet you didn't know that, did ya? Why would you, you fucking hump."

Button looked down and ran his thumb along the curved steel blade.   C didn't utter a word; he took one quiet, slow-motion step toward Billy Bones, who didn't see the creep, entirely too impressed with himself, and his knife.

"Hanging with a fucking retard-nigger, on purpose; I still don't get it. You know, buddy of mine, his dad, used to have this wind-up toy that he and I played with, you know, when we were kids. It was German, a dancing *Angus.* Know what it was called? Fucking-A, swear I'm not making this shit up, the righteous shit you could get away with back then; it was an *Alabama Coon Jigger;* I swear to Christ, that's what it said on the box

[Billy laughed aloud], with the words *'Oh My'* *[Billy jawed it in a high-pitched black mock]* printed on the box, coming out of its big fat nigger lips. Can you believe it? 1920's they were selling dancing nigger toys and hanging shit-skins from trees; those were the fucking days. This stupid *Bantu*, you stuck it on a stick, up its ass, and wound it up, and it would dance, herky-jerk *[Button jerked his head around, mimicking the look]*, with a floppy straw hat, white bug eyes, banjo lips and one of those round, flat nigger noses, and a retard smile, full of big white teeth – pathetic - just like your nigger friend. And this thing used to jump around on that stick, wearing a suit jacket with red checkerboard suit pants and a yellow vest….yeah, I still remember it. We taped an M-80 to its ass and blew it to bits when it was dancing, *funny as shit*; Christ, my buddies dad whipped the *piss* out of us for that one, but still worth it, blowing up that fucking monkey. I used to call your nigger friend *Coon Jigger* for years, slap him in the head when we were alone and told him to dance like an *Alabama Coon Jigger,* like he always used to do with Lilly; the two of them practicing dancing all the time, I swear….fucking queer. You dance too? You dance with your little *Coon Jigger* friend?"

Cord remained motionless and silent, but now sported a slight, almost imperceptible body-lean toward Billy Bones. Button didn't register the tilt, he just laughed aloud at his own jokes, a fake, hearty laugh. But then the smile, and the mock, vanished from his face.

"And why were you laying in the fucking Cemetery, by her grave mother-fucker? More than anything else, *anything,* that bought you a bad fucking end."

Button crouched down, keeping his eye on Ay, and stayed in that position. But this time, he lowered his voice a bit, in keeping with a secret.

"You know, I was dogging that little filly last night, my eyes closed and balls slapping her ass *[Button thrust a clenched fist in a piston-motion, to heighten C's humiliation].* It reminded me of the good old days, and I called that bitch Carol, you know, by mistake….you get me *[Button smirked]*?"

That got C's attention, and Button slowly reeled him in.

"And you know what she did? She turned her head, on all fours like a dog, and just looked at me, with this hurt, dumb-ass puppy face, but she didn't say a fucking word, not one – she knows better – I'd have cracked her God-damn head. I told her to turn the fuck back around, and shut up, even though she hadn't said a word *[Button smiled].* I knew she wanted to, though. So I just finished pumping her, *hard,* for five full minutes dude, *total silence,* and I was laughing to myself the whole time, her on all fours, humiliated, while I dog her, thinking about pumping her mother but good, just like old times, same way. Doggie must run in the family. And Lilly, the stupid shit, thought I was talking about *your* bitch, up by the Park, because she never knew I was tasting mommy….and mommy tasted *so good.* Too funny, like I'd ever think about sticking my dick in that slut up at the Park. No, this fuck was all about mom; God, to the day I die, I'll never forget her tight little pussy - the shape, the cut, the lips, warm and *so* wet, always sopping, and it was *all mine,* anytime I wanted; I *owned* mommy's little pussy."

C just stared at him, incredulous; his mind raced.

The one person he thought would never, could *never,* be sucked in by this jerk-off, the one person who was off-limits, pure, blameless, innocent, the one he confided in, talked to, *believed in,* or at least started to….was Carol. She was the one he thought must have the answers, to why he was here, to why he was the way he was….to who he was; Christ, he was only in this for-shit Town because of her! And now this? Has this cock-sucker fucked every woman he seemed to care about?

He didn't know why he thought Carol should be any better than the rest; he really had no reason to think she was pious. He just wanted her to be that way, to be above the fray. He *needed* her to be above the fray; *he* had the connection to her, not *him*.

Not him. It was lie; it had to be.

"No fucking way asshole, no way….nice try."

But even Cord didn't believe the words leaving his lips. Button laughed, and still in a crouch, whispered.

"Fucking incredible, incredible dude. The two pussies, just like twins; but mom, she tasted *much* better."

And the grin ran ear to ear.

C just shook his head in the negative; he couldn't stop shaking his head no, refusing to believe what he was sure was true.

"Why don't you ask her? Lilly tells me you talk her; that's fucking sick, by the way, screwing with her head like that, to get in her pants, jerk-off. Go 'head, have a chat with mom; be sure to tell her I said hi. And be sure to tell her I miss *Pump Time;* that's what she called it, you know, when she wanted my cock, which was *all* the time. *'Ready for a little Pump Time'* she would say, as I pulled down mommy's panties, that is when she even bothered to wear them. She never called it fucking, it was just *Pump Time;* and, you know what dude, for her, it was **always** *Pump Time*."

"Shut the fuck up."

Button kept poking the hornet's nest.

"Better yet, why don't you ask her about that *real big secret,* that big black secret, the one that no one knows about, except her….and me. She spilled that one close to the end, when she checked out. Lilly's little retarded brother. Brother? Yeah, right, that's a good one."

C took another half-step toward Button, no camouflage, and Billy immediately stood tall, and held the curved blade at waist level.

Throughout the exchange, a small group of mallards, about a half-dozen, had congregated at the shore line, several brave ones spilling onto the wet silt, milling about Billy Bones in a half-circle, about a five-foot ring, waiting patiently for the bread scraps he didn't have. And as Billy talked, he swayed a bit, left to right, and back again. And as he swayed, they swayed, always maintaining the same distance; close enough for bread, far enough to dash, if necessary. They had the routine pat.

"What about Earl?"

"Ask her yourself, asshole, ask her who the *Coon Jigger's* daddy is; better yet, ask her who the mamma is."

C just stared at him; he didn't know what to say. Billy Bones responded with a snort of a laugh.

"This *is* funny; you really *are* a fucking joke, you know that? Can't fuck Lilly, can't fuck mommy, butt-buddies with a stupid-ass no-name nigger who ain't nobody, and what, you're some sort of faggot animal lover, who doesn't eat meat, and saves what? Worms? In Seattle? Are you for fucking real? Do you even have a dick? Or do you have a snatch? My bet is a snatch. And how about ducks? Can you hurt them?"

And like lightening, Button pivoted and collared the nearest mallard before it had a chance to react. The rest scattered like buckshot, in a cacophony of high-pitched quacks, flapping wings and loose feathers, scrambling for the safety of the river. The captured mallard struggled in Billy's grasp, trying to cry out, but Button clamped its bill shut, and held the curved blade along its long, slender neck.

"Gonna save it?"

C's whole body tensed.

"You hurt it, and you won't walk away; trust me, you *won't.*"

Button simply smiled at the threat.

"I'm not gonna hurt it. Lilly tells me you like some fag song called *Thunder Island,* that true? You like that fag song, *fag*?"

The mallard had a burst of struggle, but Billy clamped down, and subdued it.

C couldn't believe Lilly told him about all that stuff: Seattle, the song, being a vegetarian, his trips, *why*? Did she really want to hurt him that bad? What did he do to deserve that?

But that thought came and went in a flash; he lasered on the duck, just the duck, with the eyes of a cornered dog.

"Well?"

But C didn't answer; his body tensed, ready to spring, his eyes focused on the Arabian blade.

And Button sensed it, and stepped to the left a few steps, towards the edge of the wooded portion of the boat ramp, off to the side, a little more time to react to the charge he knew was coming, the one he wanted.

"Okay, okay, no more silly games; Jesus, can't take a joke. Just fuckin with ya."

And with that, Button threw down the knife; the blade stuck vertical in the wet sand, close by his foot, to buy some time.

"See, unarmed, safe….just like the duck."

And Button loosened the grip on the mallard, and bent to place him gently on the sand. And as the binding was released, the mallard opened his beak and let out a high pitched call to his peers, to anyone; it was scared, and needed help.

"Poor little guy is scared."

Billy Bones said, as he calmly slid his hand in between the bills of the mallard, wrapped his hand around the top bill, and in one quick twist of his wrist, broke the upper bill in half. The duck emitted an ungodly noise, writhing in pain on the sand. Button quickly grabbed the bird by the feet, and tossed it to his left, into the river, like a bag of trash, the bloody broken half-bill stuck in the sand by his boots. The whole process was quick, and Button immediately lunged for the Arabian, to slice Cord in two as he charged hard.

But Billy was a half-second too slow, and the blade was a half-finger too far.

CHAPTER 191 – SLOW AND LONELY

The blackout was typical.

When Cord regained consciousness, he didn't know how long he was *away;* he was still swinging, slowly, fists landing one after another in the same wet spot. A spray of blood followed each blow, like spittle, peppering C's face in a fine mist of very-cherry red.

Billy Bones offered no resistance, his face a swollen pulp, nose certainly broken, one side tooth gone….swallowed in the fray.

The burn in Cord's arm was killer; only now, conscious, did he feel the intense pain. But he couldn't stop swinging, straddling Billy's prone body, half on his side, facing upstream, away from the ramp, towards the wooded bank. Blood flowed from Button's his left ear and eye socket; his eyebrow was split open – a good quarter-inch vermilion gash had yawned wide. His eyes were full of spider veins….bloodshot.

Yet through the brutal beating, Button remained conscious, and, while taking everything Cord could dish, was, somehow, it seemed, still smiling. To Cord, it didn't feel quite real.

C finally stopped, and quiet set in; his chest stopped heaving, and his breathing returned to normal.

Button just lay there, still smiling plastic, breathing quietly. Then C heard a faint throaty exhale, more like a weird, ethereal chuckle, followed by the ever-so-faint whisper of the beginning of a sentence.

"Now, I'm gonna get…."

But C didn't let Billy Bones finish the thought; he started punching again; and the last blows seemed to finally drop the curtain….lights out.

C slowly stood up, lording over Button, assessing the scene, covered in a spray of blood and spit. He could hear the lap of the water on the sand, behind him, and the quiet hum of distant tires, rubber on steel decking, every twenty seconds or so, as another car crossed the upstream bridge, a hundred yards away.

To his amazement, no one was around, save the distant cars, who couldn't see the two of them, tucked along the edge of the woods. No witnesses, no nothing, in the middle of a sunny Sunday, in July. Strange, but certainly opportune. And somehow expected.

Cord gazed downward and watched Billy's chest slowly rise and fall; saliva ran from the corner of his mouth, and he could hear the sucking sound as he breathed through blood and saliva pooled between his lips. C saw the Arabian, still stuck vertical in the wet river sand, and quietly grabbed it, looking at the blade briefly, before launching it far into the river. All the mallards were gone, nowhere up or downstream to be seen, except the lone assaulted duck, which slowly swam in a tight circle and made a strange sound, like a bleat, with its head down, beak dipped in the water.

It was heart-breaking.

He was too far out for C to reach, and all Cord could do was watch, helplessly, as the duck agonized, flapping its grotesque beak open and shut in the water. He turned back to Button, whose eyes had now just about swollen shut, and kicked him onto his belly. His back pocket revealed the top of a black leather booklet, and C quickly realized the find.

He grabbed the top of the Bible and slid it out of Billy's pocket. It was smaller than C had imagined, the leather worn to light gray along the seams and stitched binding. He opened it and carefully flipped to the first page, seeing a yellowed newspaper article, folded neatly square. He opened it and saw the headline, and the first paragraph about Atlantic City, French fries and thirty-five seagulls slaughtered on the street. He shook his head, folded it and slid it back into the Bible.

He flipped back to Page 1; the story started with a child's concentrated script.

No. 1: Barn Cat - Age 6 - Slingshot

And the carnage continued from there, a never-ending queue that traversed years; a litany of animals shot, pierced, gutted, trapped, skinned and hung.

Notes in the margins described in detail observations of suffering and game kept alive for the simple sake of extending the torture, to prolong the agony, to enjoy the kill...to test the limits of pain. Stars denoted memorable bounty, with some having codes he couldn't follow, a language understood by none save the author.

Cord shook his head in disbelief at the butchery.

The killing ended forty-plus years later, with the second-to-last entry, just twenty-seven days ago, right before he came back to Town. It was the eighty-ninth documented kill.

No. 89: 2 Monkeys - Age 45 - Morning Star & Gut Hook

Surprisingly, this one had no detailed notes on the kill; no stars, no description, nothing – just the single line entry, silent on the page, quietly staring back at him.

And that's when C realized just how truly special these two monkeys were. And he understood that No. 89 for Button Pierce was a trophy unlike the prior eighty-eight; these monkeys helped Billy Bones cross a *very* special line in the sand, one Cord Brin knew all too well. And once a man crosses the Rubico River, he joins a very special club, that only other members can know, understand, and appreciate.

It is a very dangerous club indeed.

C looked at the piece of shit prone in the sand, who had curled fetal, and shook his head.

And Cord returned his gaze to the Bible, and focused on the last entry, written today, probably no more than minutes before Cord emerged at the top of the ramp.

And Cord Brin thought about Carol, and the dart, and the puppet, and he began to wonder if No. 90 was *really* why he was in this quiet backwater, the end of the road at the far end of nowhere. He had been trying for No. 90 for years, playing by the stupid, nonsensical rules he was compelled to follow, for reasons he didn't understand, and probably never would. Perhaps at the tail end of July, in 2006, a too-long journey would finally end; perhaps he was finally going to ace the game....free forever.

He looked at the neatly scripted Bible entry.

No. 90: 1 Faggot - Age 45 - Slow & Lonely

CHAPTER 192 – *BUGS BUNNY, MOTHER-FUCKER....BUGS BUNNY!*

Cord bent over and rapped the Bible on Billy's head, progressively harder, till his swollen left eye cracked.

Ay shook the book, and Billy tried, feebly to grab it. C kept shaking it, in the air, as he backed away from Button, toward the shoreline.

"No. 90."

Was all Cord Brin said, as he turned and hurled the Bible as far as he could into the river over the dying mallards head. Cord saw it hit the water, landing in a soft splash, and swiftly bob downstream on the current. In less than a minute, it was out of sight; sunk or not, it wasn't clear. But gone it was, for sure, and Ay smiled.

Billy scouted blind for his knife, feeling feebly around his body. No luck.

"I don't know why, but you get to live, for now. Not my choice, I'd just as soon kill you right here and now, with my bare hands – it always feels better that way, more satisfying. But, for some strange reason, it just doesn't feel *right*, killing you, today, so for that reason alone, I won't. It's as simple as that; those are the rules, not my rules, just the rules. Instead, you get to suffer a bit longer, till I do kill you. And trust me, in the end, I will. I always do."

And with that, Cord kicked Button in the side of the head, just behind his ear; a wicked blow that would have ended a lesser man. A fresh trail of blood trickled from Billy's left ear.

"If you go near Lilly, ever again, if you go near Earl, or Carol, or anyone else I can think of, ever again, you won't get up, ever, and it'll be slow, and it'll be *real lonely,* no matter how I feel that day."

Somehow, Button turned his head, ever so slowly, and opened one eye, staring at Cord.

And C swore, although his face was bloody and distorted, that the mother-fucker was still smiling. And a distant voice emerged from the pulp, stronger than one would expect.

"Of course, you realize, this means war."

Followed by a low, maniacal chuckle.

C shook his head, turned and walked away, searching the river for the wounded mallard as he headed from the wooded fringe, up the ramp incline.

But the mallard was nowhere to be seen.

And the last words he heard, as Billy Bones raised his head, coughed and laughed through the blood and spittle.

"Bugs Bunny, mother-fucker....Bugs Bunny!"

CHAPTER 193 – THE OLD WOMAN WAS GONE

The voices on the television were muted; the knob was locked. He didn't bother to knock. He took two steps back, and ran full force into the door, splintering the jam and half-burying the knob in the plaster wall.

Cord fell hard into the hallway wall, was up in an instant and yelled her name as he ran to the front room.

No Lillian.

The apartment was a shambles; the blinds were drawn dark, soiled laundry strewn over the couch, the table, the floor. Empty beer bottles were tossed in every corner; the smell of cigarettes and stale beer hung heavy.

C coursed the hall and stopped to look at her bed; the covers were crumpled and disheveled, like a restless sleep. But it wasn't sleep he was looking at. He dropped his head, frowned, and made his way to the bathroom.

The sink dripped steady; toothpaste residue was smeared and dried hard in the bowl, along with butt ashes. The toilet seat was up and ringed with piss splatter; the bowl full of dark yellow urine and more cigarette stubs, floating in the stew. The smell of urea was overpowering. Soaking wet towels were piled haphazard, surrounded by puddled water.

No Lillian.

He took a quick peak in the kitchen; a familiar plastic container, empty, sat atop a mound of dirty dishes in the sink, which spilled onto, and covered, the counter. The container had held Earl's special ravioli, the ones Lilly slaved over, and made for the two of them. He remembered the day she made them, and creased a sad smile.

They were long gone.

C stood silent, and took a long, last look, and was just about to turn, when he heard the rumble of heavy metal, and it jarred him to a freeze. Till he realized it was the ringtone of a cellphone. He followed the tune, and it led him to the bedroom; buried in the sex-stained sheets, the music blared. He found the phone and saw the Caller ID, which simply said:

Dr. P

He grabbed the vibrating phone and walked it down the hall; it was still vibrating as he tossed it into the pool of piss in the toilet.

Then C left.

He stood in the bathroom; at least it seemed like a bathroom, a dim light, from somewhere behind him, faintly illuminated the mirror. He leaned forward, over a sink, perhaps, to get a better look at his face.

It was ashen, a death mask, his eyes bloodshot and red spider veins, thin, like webbing, mapped his powdered cheeks. Billy Bones raised his hands to rub the veins, the ash, away; this can't be real. But it simply wouldn't concede; his dead, porcelain skin pushed back and forth beneath his fingers, like a rubber mask.

It continued that way for a minute or so, time wasn't the same here, in this place, till his image faded to black before him. He turned into the dim light at his back, and as he turned, the scene brightened, and there she was, striped, like a tiger, by bands of sunlight peeking through the partially closed blinds. She was sitting on the edge of the bed, naked, with a cotton top-sheet barely covering her crotch. The shade banded her face, and he couldn't see her lips, or her eyes, he couldn't read her expression, just a bright rectangle of light stretched diagonal, across her cheeks and nose. But he knew in an instant who it was.

It was *really* her.

She had never visited him, never once since she left, till now.

And he let out a little puff of air, like one does when surprised by an unexpected, an unbelievable, stroke of good fortune. And then he smiled, like he hadn't smiled in years, twenty-five long years.

He lifted his arm to reach for her, but as he did, she began to melt away, disappearing from bottom to top, like water down a drain. He quickly put his arm down, to somehow reset the stopper, and stop the drain-away, but it was no use. Like sand through an hourglass, she slowly poured away, and was soon gone.

And he found himself alone, laying in the sand at the boat ramp, a beaten, bloody pulp.

Cord hit the street and ran down Market, up Mill, down Mansfield for a block, and found himself at the perimeter of the Park. His white tee-shirt was tie-dyed in Billy's blood, but he paid it no mind, nor the stares he got from passers-by.

He could see the center of the Park, the benches, where he figured she'd be; he had a gut feeling, and his gut was usually right.

But the center benches were empty, save for what looked like an older woman, sitting alone.

He ran to the middle of the Green nonetheless, and only when he was just about to the center, did he see Lillian fetal on Earl's bench, on her mom's bench. And he breathed a sigh of relief, and let up to a walk for the last several steps.

She was an older attractive woman, thin, in her sixties perhaps. Tied upon her was a bright red headscarf, a fashionable kerchief. She sat alone on the bench opposite Lilly, quietly knitting. She raised her head and half-nodded a friendly smile at Cord, and he back. C had never seen her in Town before; he would have remembered the face. She had a dignified air with the most beautiful eyes, quietly intense, consuming, the kind you can't help but notice, can't help but remember. *Mournful*....that's what those eyes spoke, that was the feel, as she locked her gaze on Ay for what seemed like forever, but which really lasted but a second, maybe two.

"She's been sleeping, seems awful tired. I've been keeping an eye on her; she's a pretty young lady, don't you think?"

Cord smiled and nodded again, in return.

"Yeah, she sure is."

And Cord knelt beside Lilly, and gently pushed the hair that had fallen in front of her eyes, and lightly rubbed her brow.

"You're safe."

But she didn't open her eyes, she just gently breathed, in time with his stroke of her brow.

"I'm sorry you and Earl missed the *Blobfest*."

Were the first words she had uttered to him in over three weeks.

"That's okay, maybe we'll go next year; wanna come?"

"Maybe."

Was all she said.

"Come on, I'm gonna bring you home."

And Lilly sprung rigid, and her arms started to quiver.

"No, not there….*home*."

And he felt her go limp, and she began to quietly cry.

Cord gathered Lilly in his arms, and turned to the old woman and said.

"Thanks for keeping an eye on her."

But the old woman was gone.

CHAPTER 194 – I'M PREGNANT

It was a quasi-state, almost conscious, a bit more than not; it was only when a lone crow past by, silent, high overhead, that he recognized he must be lying on his back, looking at the sky. And then he recognized the clouds, and he tried to figure the shapes, for they must mean something.

But he couldn't focus.

From there, he somehow drifted to that familiar place, the one he visited many times, the spartan hotel room, his favorite. It was the same one they always used, month after month, halfway between the airport and Fourth Street.

But this time, for some reason, he traveled back to the very end....April 7, 1981.

He rewound it a thousand times; it had been twenty-five empty years, wishing he played it different, wishing he could somehow alter the end.

He remembered her face, sullen, sitting on the end of the bed, naked. He looked lovingly at her, and reached for her touch, but she leaned away, and pulled the cotton top-sheet over her crotch, as if in shame.

"I know I've said it before, but this time I mean it, *I mean it.*"

And he just smiled that cunning, seductive smile, and deliberately batted his too-long eyelashes, the ones women would die for, and tried to redirect, like he always did, since it always worked.

"Come on, you know it's not the end, it never is, never will be, not for you and me; together forever....that's what's meant to be. So, how long till round two? How long till *Pump-Time.*"

"Stop calling it that; just stop."

"You said it."

"I said it *once*, a long time ago, as a joke, by mistake, and I told you I don't like it, and not to say it, not to call it that, not to call it *anything*. It's just stupid, and, and…."

Her voice trailed off.

"And what?"

"Just don't say it anymore; it doesn't matter anyway."

She grabbed for her bra, laid neatly over the back of the beat-up desk chair, to get dressed, and Button knew there wasn't going to be an easy second round, or third, and he got angry, but kept it to a pout for now, since that usually worked. A pout meant more pussy, in the end.

"What did I do wrong? I take leave and fly all the way here and I get a one-fer; are you kidding me?"

Normally she would feel bad, put her bra down, and satisfy him, like a child; sometimes she would snap at him for being selfish, tell him she should never even be with him, or doing this, and a short argument would ensue, after which she would invariably feel bad, put her bra down, and satisfy him.

This time, she did neither; she didn't acknowledge the plea, nor make eye contact, she simply hooked her bra and slowly pulled up the straps, in silence.

And he knew this time was very different.

"I should have never told you about Earl."

She said looking at the floor, ashamed.

"Oh, is *that* what this is all about? I'm sorry I said what I said; it was a mistake. I'm sorry."

He said, as if the mystery was solved, and they could get back to the task at hand, fucking again.

"You're not sorry you said it; you *mean* it, every word. You're just sorry it slipped out, and I had to hear you say it. I know you don't like Earl, you never have. I don't know why, he's so sweet, and he's never done anything to hurt you, never."

Button responded in silence, since they both already knew the answer to that question.

Carol grabbed her white, light cable-knit sweater and quietly slid it on, the worn sheet still covering her crotch. She felt horrible talking about Earl to Button while she was half-naked, after just having regretful sex. She couldn't remember the last time she actually enjoyed it....when she didn't feel the burden of guilt, and the weight of her weakness for the handsome young Marine standing naked before her.

She felt the need to expand.

"He's *not* stupid, and he *is* my son."

He answered her with a blank expression, and more silence.

"And I love him more than anything, or anyone, *any man,* and that will *never* change...*never.*"

And that's when Button erupted.

"He's *not* your son! He never will be! He's some stupid stand-in, shoved in your lap as a big black joke, because you wouldn't get rid of his kid! You should have gotten rid of it, it's no big deal, people do it every fucking day, and taken the money, like he said; we could have used it!

God, that was a lot of fucking money! A lot! We'd have been set, for good, for life! And then it would have been just you and me right now, like it's *supposed* to be….no Earl, because he wouldn't even be here; he'd be with his *real* mamma, and she'd have to deal with him, and all his retardedness, not you, not us, and you wouldn't have some kid walking around who you'll never know, always wondering. All that shit would have been gone, neat and clean, but you had to go and have that stupid kid, and they took it away anyway, and gave you a, a….fucking throwback, a defect."

Carol just looked at him as he ranted, and she realized how ugly Button really was, and was more ashamed than ever at never seeing it, or failing to see it, or simply trying to wish it away.

She felt like a fool.

She spoke quiet and calm, detached, to counter his rage, which only enraged him more.

"There is no *you and me;* this, what we do, is disgusting and wrong, and I can't even believe I ever did it, and how I even look at myself anymore. It's over."

And Button huffed indignant.

"Well, you certainly took enough trips to the the buffet before you got disgusted, now didn't ya? What, got a new toy you wanna try? Something better come along? Maybe a little younger? How much younger you gonna go? Maybe the talk in Town is right after all; maybe you are…."

Carol didn't dignify the taunt; and she couldn't believe he even would say such a thing to her. And as the cocktail of hatred and hurt and hormones cycloned inside her, she uttered the words she promised she would never say to him, for it could only mean trouble.

But the words left her lips renegade, struck out on their own. And there were no take-backs, not for this bomb.

It was just above a whisper, and she immediately looked up, to see if the utterance passed unnoticed.

It didn't.

"I'm pregnant."

CHAPTER 195 – AS SHE CRIED, HE RAPED HER

That pretty much shut him up.

He just stood there and stared, drinking in her flawless, light skin, smooth as silk, her high curved eyebrows, framing dreamy eyes and slightly droopy eyelids; seductive was the only way to describe them. Carol had killer eyes.

He looked at her angular nose, and the tiny cleft in her chin, which was wider than you would think attractive, yet on her face, it was perfect.

Her head was slightly tilted to the right, and her wavy, blonde hair fell beside her face.

She was the most beautiful woman he had ever met, ever even seen, ever. There was no close second; for Button, Carol was always the one. Lillian was beautiful; Carol was in another league. Billy was obsessed with her, always had been. It didn't matter how old she was, her thirty-six, him almost twenty-one; since he was a kid, he knew she was the one, and one day he would have her.

And he did.

And now, she was going to have *his* child; he was gonna be a daddy, and they were going to be a family, a *real* family. And suddenly, it seemed the air got lighter and the room got brighter; everything was finally gonna be okay. And just like that, he forgot all the horrible, hurtful things he had just said, tossed aside as yesterday's news; this providence changed *everything;* life was about as good as it could possibly get.

And he smiled content. She didn't return the look.

He slowly walked toward her, to run his hand gently through her hair. And she recoiled.

He pulled back and scowled; and just like that, the *good-as-it-could-possibly-get* was gone.

"Oh that's right, only Earl gets to do that with your hair; *sorry*. Maybe we should just fuck again; can I use *that* word, *fuck?* Or should we just go back to *Pump Time?*"

Her pants were on the dresser, half across the room, and she didn't want to get up, and expose herself, her crotch, not now, not anymore. She felt uncomfortable standing next to him; it had all changed, like the flip of a light, right after the fateful words left her lips.

"Can you give me my pants, please."

"No, I can't; get 'em yourself. I'll get your underwear though; oh wait, that's right, you never wear underwear when you meet me here, right? Just an extra step."

"Why does it have to be this way? We both had fun, but it's over; just leave it at that....done."

"Sorry, am I missing something?"

He said, dripping sarcastic. She just looked at him.

"You're having a baby, right? *My* baby?"

And she said the next words, a lie, that she would forever regret.

"Maybe it's not yours."

And that was the first time, and the last time, she felt the sting of his open hand across her face, and a whole new world opened between them.

Button's first reaction, while the back of his hand still stung from the contact, was fear, fear at what she would do, at how she would react; abject fear at the prospect of her walking out, of him losing her forever. But the gut-wrench he felt was short-lived, for what he saw, in her face, was shock, which quickly morphed into something he had never seen on her face, ever.

Fear.

And he realized, for the first time, that *he* was in control. And it was a steroid shot, direct in the vein.

"What did you say?"

He spooled, in a taunt. She just buried her face in her hands; he could hear her whimper lightly.

"Is it mine?"

She shook her head in silence….*yes*.

He smiled satisfied, walked over to the dresser, grabbed her pants, and tossed them, dismissively, on her lap. Then he sat in a chair, still naked, legs open, dick limp, and spoke to her hands, hiding her face.

"You know, everything I've done, I've done for you….*everything*, since I was a kid. Always bringing out your trash, mowing the lawn, shoveling snow, getting the bees out of the attic, the bat out of the bedroom; I even gave up Sniper School for you *[Button's voice rose angry]*, because it would have taken me away! I sneak back to see you, use up all my leave, and have to play-pretend boyfriend to Lilly, to lie to your daughter, who wants to marry me, by the way, while I fuck you, her *mother*."

Carol sat silent.

"So now it's time for *you* to do what's right, to step up."

She removed her hands from her face, and looked at him, directly, as she spoke, the red blush of his backhand still tattooed on her cheek.

"You did all those things, an errand boy, just to have sex with me, which I unfortunately obliged, and to my disgust, enjoyed, in the beginning anyway, to the shame of myself and my children. How I ever did that to Lilly and *Earl....[Carol stopped, closed her eyes and just shook her head in regret]*."

She opened her eyes and stared directly at Button.

"And to my horror, I got pregnant; stupid, stupid, *stupid [her voice trailed off]*. But that will be fixed, and this will be done, for good, forever."

And Button's eyes got wide, and he stood up, in an aggressive pose.

"Fixed? Did you say *fixed*?"

"There's no other way."

"You go and have that guy's kid, and he told you to give it up *[Button was screaming]*! Was going to pay you all that money just to give it up, and you wouldn't! And he probably drown the thing in a fucking toilet anyway, and now, you'll give *mine* up, just like that! **Mine!** You think you're gonna flush my fucking kid down the toilet?!"

"Don't say that! Stop saying that!"

And Button became calm, and he spoke in an ugly tone, as he pointed ominously at Carol.

"Here's what's gonna happen, and this shoulda happened a long time ago. Earl's gonna live with Uncle Frank, the fucking drunk, immediately, and permanently – I'll talk to Frank – he'll take him in, and you'll allow it, so that's done with, for good....stupid fucking retard nigger. And I'm moving in, and you and I will get married, and you'll have *my* child, one of many you're gonna pump out, and we'll be one big happy family.

1700

And little-Lilly will just have to get over me, and move on. And I won't even make her call me *daddy*."

Carol looked at him, shaking her head in astonishment.

"You're dreaming."

"No, *your* dreaming, because here's the alternative. I'll tell Lilly I've been fucking her slut mother, that you've been swallowing my cock, for *years*, in a dump hotel room, barking like a dog, while Lilly writes me love letters, saying please come home, because I'm the one. Every letter with the dot on the 'i', in Lilly, in the shape of a heart, with a little smiley face in it. Can you fucking believe it? And now she's gonna have a little baby brother, or sister, who's gonna call her boyfriend *daddy*. No, that won't fuck-up Lilly's head for what, a lifetime? Gee, thanks mom.

And she's gonna love knowing mommie never wears underwear when she sees me; oh, and better yet, how 'bout telling her that mom fucked me that very first time before I got on the bus to boot camp, in the woods, when we were picking up all the stuff along the trail for Lilly's favorite present, hanging on her bedroom wall, above her head for Christ sake; what a joke! Should I tell her all about that one? Tell her that first fuck was the very best, when you took my cock up your ass doggie in the woods, moaning like the whore you are? That's a one-way ticket to therapy, what 'ya think?

Oh, let's not forget about the nigger, your favorite; he'll be real surprised about *his* little story, don't you think? Considering you never even adopted him, or anything, just took him, wonder what Child Welfare will think when I call 'em about that? Can you spell kidnapping? How 'bout *jail;* can you spell that?

And what do you think his real parents think happened to him, if they even care, because, you know, they gotta be what, stupid coons, at least one of 'em, right? He's got the retard gene, you know. And how about when I tell him you and I call him a stupid fucking nigger, and a retard, and laugh at him, behind his back, all the time, while we're fucking our brains out."

"Stop it! *Stop it!* I never said anything like! Ever! About Earl….*ever*! **Stop lying!**"

Carol pleaded.

"Stop lying? Why should I? You don't.   You never have; you've lied to them all your life. You're just one big fucking lie.

And whose gonna believe you? *Earl*? *Lilly*? When they find out all the rest, the truth about how real shitty you are as a mother, that you're nothing but a liar, and a high-priced whore, isn't that what you really are, anyway? So when I tell Earl all the nigger lies I make up about you, they'll just be icing, and I'll make up more shit too, some real good shit, after I have more time to think about it. And who are they gonna believe? I'm a fucking decorated Marine, and you're a fucking slut."

"Button, if you love me, if…."

"Don't give me that, too late; you're not worming out of this by talking or spreading your legs. The sad part is, I *do* love you, why, I have no fucking idea. I used to think you were too good for me; shit, I'm too good for *you!* You really are a lying, worthless piece of shit, aren't you? Lying all your life to those two kids you love so much *[Button shook his head in disgust]*.

But lucky for you, I'll still take you, charity case. I just can't help it, I guess. But I swear to God, if you don't do what I say, Earl and Lilly get an early Christmas present *tomorrow*. And you know me, I'm not bluffing, I don't do that….I *never* bluff. Oh, and I forgot, before I tell Lilly I've been fucking mommy for what, I can't count how many times, I'm gonna fuck her first, and good, since she said I'm gonna be *number one,* the first to spread her, first to pop her and make her bleed. And I'll unload in her mouth, then in her cunt and finally in the ass, in that order, just the way her mommy likes it....especially the ass-fuck. I'm sure she's just like mom and loves cock in her ass the best. Maybe I'll compare the two of you, tell her who's pussy and ass...."

Carol let out a guttural yell and leaped across the room, wildly beating him on the chest.

"Don't you *ever* touch Lilly! I swear, don't you ever touch her, *ever;* she's not for you!"

Button quickly tied up Carol's flailing arms, bear-hugged her from behind and pushed her across the room, to the end of the bed, and leaned in, falling atop her, Carol screaming. She could feel his cock against her ass; it was hard as rock.

"Let me show you *exactly* how I'm gonna *touch* your little Lilly."

As he pushed her screaming face hard into the bed, muffling the sound. And he grabbed his cock, and forced the head between her cheeks, till the tip was shoved against her asshole.

"Say hello Lilly."

He whispered in Carol's ear, as he thrust forward, hard, and buried himself dry in her ass, straight to his balls.

And as she cried, he raped her.

CHAPTER 196 - WHAT NOTE?

He gently laid her on the couch in their living room, opposite the fireplace.

She was curled fetal, facing out, but her eyes were closed. He fetched an afghan, and laid it lightly over her; even though it was July, she was shivering. And he knelt on the floor, by her head, and gently stroked her brow.

"Portum pettimus fessi."

He whispered, as much to himself, as to her.

"What's that mean?"

She breathed, eyes still closed.

"We weary ones seek port."

"Where's that from, what exotic place?"

"Staten Island."

Cord said, with a little laugh. Then C got serious.

"Lilly, if you didn't like my stories, you know, about places, why didn't you just tell me? No big deal; I promise I won't tell them to you anymore....I thought you liked them."

"I *do* like your stories, I do."

"He said you thought my stories were stupid."

"I said a lot of things I shouldn't have, but I never said that. I told him I loved your stories, so much that I was mad I wasn't there to see them with you; *big* mistake. That was day one, and it got me choked; that's his new favorite, by the way, choking. It used to be twisting my skin, or slapping me, or kicking me, now it's choking. Years ago, he used to do things to me that could be hidden, by clothes, or explained away, whatever; now he's just doesn't give a shit. Hard to *explain away* a red ring around your throat."

It was the first time Lillian had spoken aloud, admitted, to *anyone*, the abuse she had endured, for years, at the hands of her boyfriend. The violence had ramped over the years, a slow steady incline. But the uphill had gotten steep since Billy got back; it wasn't an incline any longer, it was a cliff.

"Anyway, after that, I never defended you, or even said a single good thing about you. I was scared, and I betrayed you."

Lilly started to quietly cry, and C's thoughts turned to Julia, and Winston. He always wanted to save Julia, and now was his chance. He ran his hand lightly across her hair, her cheek, cupping her face, feeling her warmth.

"No worries, none at all; water under the bridge. And I only tell you about the good trips, the good stories, the good parts; they're not all good Lilly, trust me."

"I don't care, they're good enough for me. Tell me one, a new one....it seems like forever since we shared stories."

Cord thought a bit, then bent down and kissed Lilly gently on the forehead, barely keeping his lips on her skin, as he whispered to her.

"It takes one hundred and nine seconds, not a second more or less, from when the Aruban sun first kisses the water, at the horizon, till it disappears, melting into the ocean. I sat there and counted, every second. I promise, you can count it with me when we go there and watch the sun set together, deal?"

She just shook her head yes; she had stopped crying, but the tears were still wet on her cheek. He thought he saw the faint shade of a smile, maybe; he hoped so.

"And after dark, we'll lay on our backs by the pool, and smoke a cigar and drink port, and look up at the blackness, and watch the night clouds race by the waning moon, heading north, on their way to Belvidere, two thousand miles away."

"If I ever go away from here, promise me it will be with you, okay?"

Lily whispered.

"Well, you'll probably change your mind, you always do, but if you don't....deal."

Ay whispered back. She closed her eyes hard, squeezing them shut, like a kid's birthday wish. Then, eyes still closed, her face seemed to change.

"C, I'm so sorry about what happened, what I did to you; there's no excuse, and I'm not trying to make one up. I can't imagine how much that hurt you....I just can't."

C didn't say a word; he just lightly stroked her hair, her face.

"And I know you don't want to hear about this, but I have to tell you; you're the only person I can really talk to, the only one I trust, who is my friend, a *real* friend. What we do, we did, it *isn't* sex; sex is two people. What he does is for control and humiliation, and it's non-stop, always on-demand. And he did that in the past too, but it was sprinkled with some tenderness, some good, sometimes, not often, but it happened, just often enough to keep me around, I guess. And when you remember, when someone's gone for a long time, you tend to remember, to focus on, the good stuff, even if it was crowded out by the really bad stuff....you tend to forget the bad part. Human nature I guess, or at least that's what I did, to make it make sense. But since he's been back, it's ten times worse, *hundred times;* it's just rape, really, hard, violent, horrible. And I have to make noises and pretend to enjoy it, so he will hopefully just finish and be done and not hurt me. It's violent having sex with him, it's just.....*wrong*. And last night, you know what he called me, when he was doing it? He called me *Carol*, just to humiliate me; I know she's your friend, but to call me *that*? And then he told me to shut up, and I didn't even say anything, I just let him continue to fuck me, humiliate me, when he was really fucking her, and I just took it, and continued to take it, and didn't say a word, because I was afraid he'd hit me, or choke me, or worse, if I did. I'm a coward."

C looked at her, and spoke softly.

"You're not a coward, you were just trying to survive. Don't apologize for any of it Lilly, to me or anyone else; it is what it is, and you did what you had to do....end of story. I'm just sorry you had to go through any of it. But you won't any longer, it's over; I can promise you that."

Lilly continued, eyes still closed.

"I said a *lot* of things about you, C, to him, stuff that supposed to be secret, that I shouldn't have. I'm sorry, but he's relentless with the questions if he feels threatened, and he'd never admit it to anyone, but you threaten him, like no one I've ever seen, ever. And it makes him dangerous, and crazy, even more so, and if I don't tell, and he knows it, I'm...."

"Enough about him; I know what you told him, no big deal, I'm a big boy."

C said, touching her lightly on the nose.

"And you didn't tell him *all* my secrets, just some; I didn't tell you the really good ones."

C smiled.

"What are the good ones?"

"Well, that's a secret."

"I know you don't trust me, I don't blame you."

"Lilly, the good ones aren't really good, they're actually the bad ones, and you'll never know that baggage, *ever;* I don't want you to, no need."

Lilly opened her eyes for the first time, and they widened to saucers, seeing Cord covered in blood, with the swollen black and red knot on his forehead.

"Oh my God, what happened?"

"What do you think happened?"

"Is Button?"

"He should be, but no, for some reason, today, I didn't. It just wasn't in the cards I was dealt….today, anyway, so I let him live."

"Would you?"

C didn't answer.

"Should I be afraid of *you*?"

But before Ay could answer, she did.

"I don't care whether I should or not, I think you're good, and Earl does too, and so does my mom *[Lilly's voice quivered and her eyes welled].*"

"I'm not good Lilly, I'm *not*, you have to remember that, but I'm better than him, at least I am now, here, in this place, with you and your brother. But no, not good."

"Why aren't you good?"

"Nothing to do with you, or this place, just a big bag of bricks."

"I'm so sorry about that night; that was horrible. Can you ever...."

C cut her off.

"It's okay, apology accepted; I don't wanna talk about it anymore, or ever, okay?"

"I've done lots of things I'm not proud of, and...."

C huffed.

"Jesus, *enough*; I already heard way too many details from *him,* and now from you; normally I'd would be curious, but not this time. I've played it enough times in my head, on my own, trust me, the flavor is *way* out of the gum."

"You're not mad?"

"Of course I'm mad, but I've got some secrets too."

"Really, like what?"

"Like Margery."

"*Margery*? You slept with Margery?"

"Yep."

Lilly just lay silent a bit, thinking.

"Was she any good?"

"Yep, *very* good; she's an amazing squatter."

C smirked at the memory.

"What's that mean? Never mind, don't wanna know. Well, I'm happy for you, she's a nice girl; I think you two would make a nice couple, really, I wish you the best."

And Lilly closed her eyes, and stopped talking. C chuckled.

"Well I'll remember you said that, because *you* certainly won't."

And Lillian just laid there, eyes closed, breathing lightly….breathing safe.

"Funny, when I was in the Cemetery, talking to your mom, well, *I* was talking – one-way conversation, maybe she was listening, probably not. Anyway, I was thinking of going over to see Margery, you know, before dickhead kicked me in the shoulder."

"Sorry I ruined your afternoon, certainly would have been a nicer time with her, squatting, or whatever."

C put his hand on her shoulder and shook her. She opened her eyes in a pout.

"Hey, I wouldn't trade what happened today for anything, *anything [C pulled on his bloody shirt].* You're safe, that's all that matters."

"I'm not safe. You don't know him, he's never gonna give up, *never;* he'll never stop pursuing. He doesn't lose, he *never* loses; the game never ends for him. He'll continue to pursue you, and me, till he gets what he wants, which is me, all to himself. Till he hurts Earl, and kills you, and takes me away and makes me a whore. He was never a good person, not in lots of ways, but I could control him, most of the time, mostly; that was part of the attraction, I guess. But now, he's way worse, he's changed, he's scary, scarier."

"We're two sides of the same coin, Lilly. But the difference is, he doesn't *want* to lose, but I'm not *allowed* to lose, ever. And I never do, even when I really should; I'm bulletproof, at least have been, to date, batting a thousand. Even though what I win, isn't necessarily what you would ever want."

"What does that even mean, you're not *allowed* to lose, by who?"

C just shook his head no, and didn't answer, as he heard the puppet quietly snicker behind a curtain in his head.

"You just rest, I need to rest too. I'm gonna lock the door and we'll just sit quiet for awhile, okay."

"Okay."

And with that, Chicken jumped on the couch, at Lilly's feet, and curled in a ball, half-asleep in no time. Lilly smiled; the first real smile C saw on her face. And she looked over at C, who had settled in a rocking chair across the room, facing her.

"You can bring the chair closer you know."

She said, so he dragged it across the living room, saddling up just a foot or two from her head. And she felt safe, or at least safer than him being all the way across the room. Cord eyed Chicken, already asleep, and whispered to Lilly.

"You know, cats add ten years to their owner's lives, and they lower your blood pressure, your heart rate, an instant calming effect."

"Really?"

"Assume so; your brother told me that, so I guess it's gotta be true. But nobody *owns* a cat; they *own* you....especially *that* one, the little bitch. But I love her to death anyway; just a sucker, I guess. And there's gotta be some sort of years subtraction when your cat crowds you off the bed every night."

And C stared at Chicken as he spoke, in mock anger. But her eyes were closed, and she paid Cord no attention, as usual. Lilly looked down at Chick and smiled; she knew Chicken owned Cord. Then she turned her gaze to Ay.

"Thanks C, thanks for everything. I know it hasn't been easy, I haven't made it very easy, but I want you to know something, okay?"

C just looked at her.

"Okay."

He said in return.

"You're my best friend."

"Really?"

C said, as he smiled, a genuine smile.

"Really. Thanks for everything, especially for....today."

"No problem, I'm just glad you dropped the note."

Lilly looked at C, puzzled.

"What note?"

CHAPTER 197 – BOTH SAD....AND BOTH SO VERY HAPPY

From nowhere, a storm broke through.

Earl was the first to fall through the front door, jabbering loud, non-stop, barely catching a breath between words, like a kid coming home from the best class trip ever. Buck, Ji-Sue, Marty and Carol soon piled through behind him, all laughing and jostling to out-talk the others.

"Mine *did too* go the farthest! Six skips Marty, six! You just did five, I counted 'em! And you were 'fraid to lay on *Couch Rock,* and....hey! C, you missed it! You shoulda seen Carol hang upside...."

And Earl stopped dead in his tracks, seeing Ay slumped in the rocker, covered in spattered, dried blood, painting his face, arms, shirt, pant-legs; the knot on his head was still the size of a large walnut, swollen and black.

C slowly opened his eyes and raised his finger to his lips, in a shush, trying not to disturb Lilly; Chicken had already startled and bolted to points unknown.

"What? What?"

Earl's lower lip was already quivering; he couldn't even finish the sentence, thinking his best friend was hurt. Carol, at the end of the conga line, just made it through the door, still laughing, pushing into the back of Marty.

"What's going on? Why's the line stopped!"

But she quickly fell silent, along with the rest, upon setting her eyes on Cord. Earl almost started to cry, and his voice quivered.

"What happened? Are you okay?"

C slowly nodded yes, and pointed to the afghan lump on the couch, which slowly opened its sleepy eyes.

And Earl saw the *best-present-ever* under the tree. He fell to his knees and hugged her, whispering something no one could hear. The room was deathly silent, except for the sound of Lillian quietly starting to cry.

Carol didn't find the scene so *Hallmark.*

'What is she doing here?!!'

She mouthed silently to Cord, in an exaggerated way, pointing toward the couch, more like jabbing the air in anger; she was turning crimson, incensed at the scene steal.

C slowly stood up; Chicken, seeing Earl, emerged from hiding and hopped back on the couch, at Lillian's feet, which only served to annoy Carol even more; manifested in a head-shake and loud huff.

Cord walked over to the three of them, and the ragged black knot on his forehead, and the blood spatter across his body, fell into focus as he approached.

"Are you okay? What the hell happened?"

Martin said, barely above a whisper.

"Leave them alone; let's go next door."

Ay said, and in a minute, the front door quietly clicked shut, and the room was empty, except for Chick, Lillian and Earl, the latter forehead to forehead, both sad....and both so very happy.

CHAPTER 198 - THIS IS SO NOT GOOD

"You threw his book in the river, *the book*? Did you tell Lilly?"

Martin gasped.

"No, I forgot."

"Damn, that's a *big* fucking deal, *real* big, trust me!"

Marty gasped again, and continued.

"Did he get it out of the water?"

"It's was *gone* Marty, downstream, downriver, disappeared….done."

C said matter-of-fact.

"That thing probably floated by when we were all at the *Couch Rock;* how weird is that?"

Buck waxed, with a curious face, like that fact must mean something, and he was creeped-out by the thought.

Marty just shook his head.

"This is bad; nothing matters more to that cock-sucker than that stupid book, except maybe for the *Gurkha.*"

"What's a fucking *Gurkha*?"

Cord snapped at Martin, annoyed.

"It's a curved knife; he carries it around in his boot. I'm surprised he didn't pull it out on you."

"He did."

C lazily belched a bit as he answered.

"He *did*? Then what the fuck happened? Did he stick ya?"

Martin, questioning the witness, gasped for the third time.

"No, he didn't *stick* me, you idiot; he tried to grab it after the duck, but he wasn't quick enough, and I jumped him, then I blacked out. Afterward, I tossed it in the drink, right before the book."

Martin stared at him, mouth agape.

"Holy shit!"

"What? Who the fuck cares?"

C said, dismissive, annoyed at the constant Button-worry.

"He does! Does he know?"

"I guess he's figured it out, by now."

Martin just shook his head. This was bad.

"Lilly's mom gave him that knife, on his sixteenth birthday; real big deal, to him, best present he said he ever got. She told him it was from Nepal, you know, India; supposed to mean, you know, give ya, courage and valor, you know, in battle. He cherished that thing, obsessed about it, always pulling it out, waving it in peoples faces....threatening to *stick 'em*."

Buck nodded his head in agreement; he had seen the Button blade-wave, many times. Then Billy added his own two cents.

"Yeah, shit, anybody touched that knife, and they were in for big trouble; nobody was allowed to touch that knife....*nobody*."

C just shrugged his shoulders de facto and said.

"Oh well, touched and gone."

"Lilly's right, C, Button's never gonna go away, this is a *problem*."

Buck said serious.

"So I've heard."

C replied, not particularly worried, and he cracked his knuckles, one at a time.

"Can't you just arrest him, put him away?"

Carol interjected, more of a plea.

"For what, animal cruelty? For breaking a duck's bill, a duck I can't even find? He got the living shit beat out of him; I should be arresting *him* for assault *[Marty pointed at C]*. Is that what you want?   Cord, did you beat that man?"

"No sir, I didn't."

"See, now I don't even have a suspect."

"Good work, officer."

Cord said, deadpan. Carol sat silent, dejected.

"Carol, you know, if I had something on him, anything real, I'd be the first to arrest that cock-sucker, you know that; he's humiliated me my whole life. But I'm better than him, and I have to do things right, or mostly right, and there's just not much I can do….not right now."

The end of Marty's sentence was punctuated by the deafening sound of a truck engine racing in neutral, the gas pedal pinned to the floor. The muffler percussion shook the front windows of the house. C jumped up and ran to the front door, followed closely by Marty. Buck stayed in the shadows, beside Carol, afraid to show his face. Ji-Sue brought up the rear, peaking from behind the shoulders in front of her.

As the big, black double doors swung open, they heard the window crash in the dining room. Both men instinctively ducked, and they heard Carol yelp.

"Bring her out!"

Button screamed from the cab of his truck. From that distance, a good fifty feet, C could see Billy cleaned himself up, but his face was swollen and distorted, so much that it was difficult to make out that it was actually him.

"Holy shit!"

Was all Marty said, whispered under his breath, looking at the pulpy face in the truck.

"It doesn't even look like him."

"Bring her out, mother-fucker!"

Billy screamed; C and Marty stood still, staring down the truck.

Button spun round and grabbed at his rifle on the gun rack, behind the cab seat.

And Marty immediately drew his gun, and pointed it at the pulp in the cab. It was the first time he had ever drawn his gun on someone, on a real person, with real bullets, and his hands, to his mild surprise, were rock steady.

"Stop right there, Button, right now!"

Button looked at Marty, both hands on the rifle, ready to unrack it, and then he eyed C, who hadn't moved an inch. He carefully returned his gaze to Martin, still assessing the situation, the risk, his hands glued to the rifle stock.

"You *know* I'll shoot, **you know it; please give me the go.**"

Was all Martin said; a lifetime of pent frustration was waiting patient in the barrel of his gun.

And with that, the three stood frozen, eying one another, for several seconds. Carol, Ji-Sue and Buck stood in the shadow of the foyer, out of sight, scared to death.

And Button broke the silence with a single word, meant for one, meant for all.

"*Dead.*"

He spun in his seat, jammed the truck into gear and floored the gas, screeching the tires, turning hard onto Third; in a moment, he was gone.

Once the commotion cleared, Buck walked out onto the porch, with a cellphone in his hand; the projectile Button tossed through the window.

"Guess he forgot this. Doesn't work; looks like it got wet."

C looked at him and spoke plain.

"I wouldn't be touching that if I was you."

Buck instantly dropped the phone, for what reason he wasn't quite sure, and immediately wiped his hands on is pants, and smelled his fingers, as if that was the thing to do.

"Nothing, doesn't smell like nothing."

Buck declared.

"Well it should, I threw it in a toilet full of piss."

"Oh, man."

Buck said, running for the kitchen sink to scrub, and when he sniffed his fingers, and sniffed them again, now he could smell nothing *but* piss; it filled his nostrils....he couldn't get away from it.

Marty just shook his head, looking at Cord.

"Man, this is so not good."

CHAPTER 199 – SOUTHSIDE DOWN, YELLING *HOLY SHIT!*

Saturday, August 5th, 2006; day one-hundred-eight. Quiet, and tense.

The six days that passed seemed like sixty, constantly watching the clock, the windows, the doors, the street, waiting for the storm to return. And they all anticipated a much bigger storm.

After the initial turmoil died down, a new, strained routine set in; someone always had an eye on Lilly, guard shifts. That someone being Earl, or Cord, with a Marty fill-in, as needed. Cord only trusted himself in this arena, dealing with the likes of Button, but unless he took Lillian away - something she didn't want to do, since she rightfully said it wouldn't solve the problem, the *problem* needed to be solved, taken care of, permanently - Cord needed help. And Earl and Martin were the only two he could really count on to act, and act quickly, if Lilly was *really* in trouble. Surprisingly enough, he had more confidence in Earl than Martin if things went south in a hurry; when it came to his sister's safety, Earl would do whatever it took to protect her, without thinking of consequences, he knew that for certain, and he pitied the person on the receiving end. In dealing with a Button, that is what you needed.

Carol was simply intolerable. She was annoyed at the non-stop attention Lilly garnered from anyone, *everyone*, in their circle, but especially from the two boys who were supposed to be on *her team*. Earl, she could forgive, but Cord – he had no excuse being so nice to that bitch, and Carol seized every opportunity she could to remind Ay of same, to his utter exhaustment. And she was annoyed at having to house the enemy, annoyed at how physically close she was, trespassing in *her* part of Town – the little corner by the Park she could truly call her own, annoyed at the disruption in the weekend routine she grew to love, and anticipate throughout the work week; annoyed, annoyed….annoyed.

Lilly fared no better; a trapped animal in Carol's cage. After six long days of doing nothing but waiting for the bang to happen, she was suffocating, claustrophobic….never out of sight, no alone time, stuck at *Boreas* with the two boys, watching, and waiting, for something bad to finally happen.

Button's return, in a strange way, would be welcome respite.

The taut mood persisted, settling thick over the beautiful beginnings of a Saturday morning.

Earl was working at Sam's, stocking shelves and bagging groceries, as he sometimes did, even after Cord left. Uncle Sam needed the help, and Earl could never say no to him. But Earl working meant Buck was helping out as well, filling the role of emcee: grocery-carrier, customer-greeter and overall produce-explainer, skills he learned from C. Buck enjoyed working with Earl, and Earl would only work if Buck was working too, so he didn't have to talk to people or answer any questions that got him nervous, which was just about any question. Sam had given up on Cord ever returning, and since it was clear he wouldn't be there, Mae had quietly found her way back to the market, along with her friends, as part of the weekly routine. But she was different now, quiet, reserved, never up for banter, jokes or small talk, as much as Sam tried to engage. She was polite and cordial, as a sociable stranger might engage. And she never asked about Cord, and she never spoke to Earl; she barely even looked his way, as if he knew all the sordid details. And Earl was still afraid of Mae, so the slight was welcome.

But, Mae and Cord aside, things had returned to some semblance of order at Sam's. Not so Park-side.

Carol sat on her front porch, in her favorite chair, alone, a pile of unread newspapers by her side, wasting a beautiful summer day, brooding; no one to share lunch with, except Ji-Sue. Why was Earl working anyway? And why did C have to babysit that bitch, sleeping in *her* house next door?

Why?

She shook her head left to right as the thoughts bounced around her brain, staring blankly out over the Park, her foot unconsciously tapping. She never even heard the front door open.

"Would you like another Southside?"

Ji-Sue asked.

"Sure, why not; it's a party, right?"

Carol answered, but Ji-Sue didn't get the joke, to which Carol huffed indignant.

She heard someone walking through the lawn off to her left, obscured behind the crytomeria, and instinctively jumped from her chair, thinking it may be Button. But it was just C, walking across the Third Street side lawn, up toward the porch. Carol was happy to see him, but wasn't going to let him off that easy.

"What, left the princess alone? God forbid."

"Please, for once, give it a break."

He said, exasperated.

"Sorry; testy?"

He didn't answer.

"How's Little-Earl doing?"

He whispered seriously, as he sat quietly on the loveseat, next to her.

Carol shrugged and spoke quiet, as the sadness sunk in.

"His blood work looks pretty good, he's a little anemic, but nothing crazy; they can't figure out the weight loss. He's eating, which is good, but his nose is still stuffy, and he's sneezing a lot. They think maybe it's the pistachios he sometimes eats, maybe they're toxic, but they don't know. I think they just said that because I suggested it; they're grasping….they have no fucking clue."

Carol just looked at him, with worried eyes.

"He's not as feisty, and this morning, he tried to jump up on the kitchen counter, like he always does, and he fell back down; he *never* did that before. He can jump on that counter with no effort, but now he can't….now he can't."

She choked up on the last part, so she stopped talking.

"I'm gonna go find him and spend a minute with him; keep an eye out for shithead's truck."

Carol didn't answer, and the frown on her face stayed put.

Cord searched the house, and found Earl on Carol's bed, sleeping in the sun. As long as he said his name, not too loud, the same way every time he approached:

Hey Earl

Little-Earl wouldn't run.

His nose was chapped, stuffy and running, and he was skinny, clearly around the hips and butt, by his tail; his bones were showing. But he purred at the first touch of his belly, like an engine, like he always did. And Cord laid beside him for a while, fetal, just the two of them, rubbing his belly, with Earl purring, eyes closed. He was such a good boy, and didn't deserve to be sick.

Carol finished her second Southside and was reaching for a third, the one Ji-Sue brought for Cord, when he came back on the porch.

"Thirsty?"

He said, seeing her go for the drink.

"Shut-up; this is yours, by the way....*was* yours."

And Carol swiped it off the table, and took a long gulp, emptying a third of it in one shot.

C just shook his head.

"How did you get off guard duty?"

"She's taking a nap."

"Oh, that's nice; does she want us to make her some lunch after, perhaps? Room service? Dial housekeeping? How long is this gonna last? Really, this is no solution."

"Wow, did you come up with that all by yourself? Of *course* it's not a fucking solution; no one figured this dipshit would wait a week to come back."

"Go find him!"

"Okay, good idea; where?"

"Figure it out! Jesus! She said it was somewhere down by Philly, right? Fine, I'll hire a detective, we'll find him; but this has gotta stop."

C closed his eyes and rubbed his forehead in angst.

"Marty already put out a restraining order, but he can't serve him with it, if he can't find him. He's already been in touch with the Philly police, and the Camden Police, but they never heard of a Button Pierce, and they don't know a Doctor something, but they'll *keep an eye out,* which essentially means they forgot his name before the phone hit the cradle; they are going to do nothing....they are *absolutely* no help, *none*. The only way to end this is to get him arrested, or kill him....seriously."

"I vote for the latter."

"Great, me too; now who gets to kill him?"

"Isn't that your department?"

"And why is that? You're the one who has all the money; hire someone."

"Okay, I'll hire you."

"I don't need your money."

"Well, I don't know anyone like that; Brick's dead. And don't even talk about stuff like that, me doing something like that."

"Oh, but it's okay to talk about *me* doing it."

"Somehow I thought you'd enjoy it."

"I would."

The double-door opened again and Ji-Sue came out with three more Southsides, lining them up, with no ones name on them.

"Good thinking; good girl."

C said, to which Ji-Sue smiled.

"You're so nice, Mr. Cord."

"Jesus, Ji, don't flatter him, his head's big enough."

"Thanks Ji; *don't listen to her*."

The last part he whispered, as he put his hand on her waist; she liked when Cord touched her. Ji smiled, blushed a bit and turned, disappearing into the house.

"Earl was purring good; he laid his head on my hand and closed his eyes; I love when he does that. He seemed happy, seems okay."

Carol smiled politely at the story, even though they both knew he wasn't okay. Cord grabbed one of the new drinks and took a slow draw.

"Seventy left; did you know today was number seventy?"

Carol looked at C, confused.

"It started at one-hundred-twelve, and *every* morning I hear the countdown, like brushing your teeth; it's part of the morning ritual."

Cord said, sarcastic.

"What are you talking about?"

Carol asked, annoyed at the riddle.

"Your *Bacchanalia,* on the fourteenth, of October. Jesus, I wish it would just get here so he would stop obsessing about it. I have to hear about the five pieces of paper you sent him, the royal reception at *L'antre du Lion* and the fact that I'm the *revered guest* he gets to bring. He asks me about all sorts of French words he can't pronounce, and he says he doesn't own a black tie. That's got him all crazy with what to do, and he's all excited about the movies, and making S'mores, and the sleepover – he thinks it's a giant slumber party."

Carol just smiled; it was the first good smile of the day, and it took her mind off Little-Earl for a bit.

"Maybe it will be; a slumber party just for him."

And Carol smirked at the implied sex, and continued.

"You know, I can't believe that whole thing, inviting him to the party, was *your* idea, a good one, by the way, for once. You come up with a redeeming idea every now and then."

Carol grabbed drink number four and tilted it toward C, in recognition. C tipped his in return.

"Thank you. Do you know he gave Ji-Sue the *RSVP* this past Tuesday, the 1st of the month, the last day it was due. He wouldn't tell me, but I think, Christ *I know*, he thought he had to wait till the 1st to answer. The anticipation was killing him, holding onto that damn thing for over a month."

Carol chuckled.

"I know. Ji said he ran around the house looking for her on Tuesday just to hand it to her, and asked if that counted, did it count as being *in.* When she said yes, he still didn't want to take any chances, so he asked Ji to pretty-please call me while he stood there, to tell me, just to be sure. Then he yelled in the background, while I'm on the phone with her:

'I'm coming! And bringing C as my revered guest, okay?'

It made my day. Christ, it made my year. I like him so much C; I really can't imagine my life without Earl, I really can't. And I still can't believe all the years I wasted, not getting to know him, coming up on my porch, every month, handing me that stupid envelope. Thank God we finally talked, for real."

"And you can thank *who* for that, again?"

"You *again*, Mr. Brin. I give credit where credit is due."

Carol tipped her drink toward Ay a second time, and he tipped back in return, ending in a light tink of the rims.

"You're welcome; my pleasure."

C said, smugly.

"You know, your shindig's the week after his surprise birthday party; the man is gonna die twice in one week, he'll be so happy."

Carol took a leisurely sip of her drink, looking out over the Park, and smiled at the thought of Earl.

"I hope Earl's still around."

Carol frowned at the thought.

"He will be; we'll find out the problem and fix it....we will. And if this vet can't figure it out, we'll find one who will."

And C put his hand on Carol's leg and squeezed a bit, and she smiled, hoping he was right.

"You know, he keeps a calendar under his pillow; no joke, he really does, and crosses off each day, first thing he does, before his feet even hit the floor, sticking his tongue out and licking his lips like an excited little kid as he puts a big red X on the day; he's too funny."

"I think he's sweet."

Carol said.

"I know you do. You know where he keeps the invite, so Lilly won't find it? Under his *Kama Sutra* book."

Cord smiled wryly.

"I still can't believe he has that book...*Earl*?"

Carol whispered.

"He does, and has most of it, maybe all of it, memorized. Knowing him, it's *all* of it. But he won't talk about it, even with me; too embarrassed."

C said, taking another sip.

"Well, I hope I get to find out, first hand, how much he knows."

"You really want to bang the big man, don't you?"

C said sly, and Carol *really* did. But then she fibbed.

"No, I just say that to tease you. Well, maybe I want to, a little."

"Yeah right, a little; you're thinking anything but *little* when you're thinking about Earl, and that *package* you think he has."

And Carol blushed....busted.

"How big is it, *really*?"

She leaned into C, still whispering.

"Well, you won't believe...."

C started to say, when Ji-Sue spilled onto the porch a third time, this trip with a green concoction in her hand, filling a tall glass.

"Okay, *okay;* enough about that!"

Carol chided, hastily sitting back in her chair, with the slight blush of a guilty face, shutting down all talk of Earl, and his *package*. But man, was she annoyed at Ji, so close to knowing how that sentence ended! And her frustration surfaced in her barbed comment.

"What is *that* Ji? And I'm not drinking it, whatever it is!"

Carol gave it the annoyed one-eye, with a nose wrinkle.

"Oh, it's not for you, it's for me, a spinach-orange juice drink; very, very good for you."

"That's right, good for *you.*"

Carol said, as she took another swig of her Southside.

"Wanna try?"

She held it up to C, who took it and held it aloft, toward the summer sun, revealing an ugly sea foam froth atop the concoction, with bits of chopped spinach floating in a sea of orange pulp. He studied it some more, then ventured a cautious swig, swirled it a bit in his mouth, and let it slide down the hatch.

He pondered a bit, and said, slowly, with a sour face.

"Wow, not very good Ji, not very good at all."

She just smiled politely, and answered.

"Thank you."

Not knowing what else to say, as C handed back the glass.

"Have a seat, join us."

Cord said to her, lightly patting the seat cushion beside him. He would bang Ji in a heartbeat, he thought to himself, without question. And he found himself staring at her crotch, which he figured was typical Asian, meaning more hair than not, just what he liked. He caught himself staring a bit too long, and discretely looked away.

Ji missed it, looking at Carol, for approval to join.

"Well go 'head and sit; you don't listen to me whenever *he* tells you to do something anyway."

Ji-Sue smiled broadly and sat on the loveseat, next to Cord, thighs almost touching, pretty bold, for her. And Cord smiled devilish at Carol, and she frowned, knowing where Ji's loyalty lay. He gently squeezed Ji's thigh and raised his glass to her. She raised the spinach sea foam concoction in return.

Yeah, he would definitely take her; he wondered if that was in the cards. If he wanted to, he was sure she would go for it, but that would be a royal mess, on so many levels, if he got caught....*royal*. More mess C didn't need, but the aftermath was always an afterthought when it came to sex decisions, invariably bad sex decisions, that Ay ultimately made. Or, rather, his dick made.

An overhead bark, more like a nasal grunt, refocused attention on the porch.

All three looked up to see a fat, gray, white-bellied squirrel, upside-down, clinging to the cryptomeria, leering at them, with great suspicion. He grunted a second time, as his tail whipped frantically in a circle. He barked some more, letting them, and anyone in earshot, know that he saw them; there was no fooling him. He was half-hidden behind the tree, big black eyes peeking around the trunk, barking.

The three laughed at the spectacle, which shifted talk to the cryptomeria, and how simply beautiful a tree it was….regal, right beside the porch. It was a fairy-tale beanstalk, it's branches curving graceful into the porch space, making one feel as if sitting in a fanciful tree house, and could climb it, straight to the sky.

After a bit, the squirrel's chatter died down, and it got to work, ripping long ribbons of red bark from the tree, stuffing the shreds in its mouth, parts of a nest-in-progress, hidden high in the tree top, out of sight.

And the conversation turned to favorite trees, and Carol regaled stories of passing the *Shoe Tree* every Friday afternoon on her way into Town, and ten minutes before that, talking to the immense, craggy sycamore along the County Road, just south of the little hamlet of Hope, the one she chatted with every week….her not-so-secret Halloween tree. She told Ji and C that she had read online the sycamore was over four hundred years old, and that George Washington, in 1787, dismounted his horse and sat beneath its branches, on some jaunt from Philadelphia to upstate New York, the same branches she drove beneath every week, so the story went. The locals called it the *George Washington Sycamore Tree*, or so she learned years after eyeing it on that first, serendipitous jaunt to Belvidere. She hoped the story was true, she really did. But regardless, it would always be *her Halloween Tree*, and it was still one of the most beautiful trees she had ever laid eyes upon. It never ceased to conjure visions of the angry apple trees in the *Wizard of Oz* in her mind. The two watched her smile, retelling the story.

Carol kept the floor, talking of lying under an immense, pencil-straight, tulip tree atop Lemon Hill, in Fairmount Park, in Philly, beside some long-gone, dopey boyfriend, one of countless dopes she wasted time with over the years; she took a moment to recall his name....it took some thought. She remembered much quicker, much clearer, the upside-down nuthatch, hopping about that majestic tulip tree; she never forgot that, even though she long forgot the dopey boyfriend.

And Ji-Sue told, as best she could in broken English, lying with her favorite cousin under a magnificent magnolia, in Nash Square, downtown Raleigh, where her cousin lived. The Square and the magnolia were overrun with the cutest red squirrels, chasing one another endlessly, darting about the grounds. She described the two of them lying still, smiling and giggling quiet under a mesh of branches high overhead, legs and arms spread like snow-angels, waiting for the next big white flower petal to silently drop off the tree all around them, oversized snowflakes. She said the best part was the lick of breeze that made its way through the button holes on her blouse and tickled her stomach, and the birds, all the singing birds, and she couldn't see a *single* one, all hidden in the greenery. But they sang and sang all afternoon. It was one of her best memories, ever.

And they all agreed, there's nothing much better than lying under a tree.

"I haven't seen *him* for awhile."

Carol said, somewhat disgusted at the interruption, looking out over the Park. And there was Stinky-Steve, heading toward them, coming across one of the diagonal gravel paths in the Green, head down, typical sneaker-shuffle, carrying two, overstuffed plastic bags, contents unknown.

"Where he live?"

Ji-Sue asked.

"No one knows, just around; saint or beggar?"

C said.

"What?"

Carol sat up.

"Saint or beggar, which is he?"

Carol just looked at him and barked snarky.

"He's a bum."

"How do you know? Ever talk to him?"

"*No.*"

Carol said with disgust.

"Hey, after you wasted all that time laying under the tulip tree with that dopey guy whose name you couldn't remember, did you ever wander over to that *real* big building, down the road from Lemon Hill, you know, with the *Rocky* steps? Can't miss it."

Carol was annoyed.

"I know what building you're talking about, jerk, and yes, I've been in *that* museum."

"Well, some artists, one in particular, used to sketch guys like Stinky-Steve. You know, poor guys with hats and walking sticks, bent at the waist, peasants, at least that's what he sketched. Ugly, down on their luck. But this guy, this artist, he wasn't so sure if you could really tell the good guys, from the not-so-good guys. He wasn't sure if these sorry, sad-ass souls weren't really saints in disguise, you know, biblical, as opposed to contemptible, although my vote is they're one and the same."

"What's your point? Besides bragging, again."

"I'm not *bragging*, I'm making an observation about a guy walking across the Park, a guy you find contemptible, without knowing him, without ever even speaking to him, and wondering who he really is. Maybe he is a bum; maybe not. You talked about trees, and Philly, and then you saw Steve, and it brought to mind an artist I like, and now we're talking about that. Don't you go to museums and bring anything home with you? In your head? *Anything?*"

"Whatever."

Carol scoffed, annoyed at the condescending critique.

"I like what you said."

Ji-Sue added, to Cord's delight.

"Oh brother, keep your pants on Ji."

Carol snipped under her breath.

And Cord heard her, and stirred the pot. He seductively leaned over and whispered long in Ji-Sue's ear; she started giggling, not so much at what he said, but more from the stubble on his face tickling her cheek. She was embarrassed at the attention, yet ate it.

"Stop whispering; that's rude!"

Carol leered at C.

"Really? That his name? Wow, how you say it again?"

Ji giggled as she whispered to Cord, savoring her own little secret conversation with Ay. C just looked at Carol, smiled, and leaned over and whispered again, this time burying his head into Ji's neck, just for effect. And Ji giggled louder, and squirmed a bit.

Carol kicked C hard in the shin.

"Hey, cut it out, not on *my* porch! And I know who the artist is *anyway*."

C sat up, shit-grin, along with Ji, reveling in her little tidbit, hidden from the boss.

"Are you two having fun?"

And they both shook their heads yes, smiling.

"Really? Who's the artist? Impress me."

C said to Carol, matter-of-fact, knowing full well she was bluffing.

"I'm not telling you! I don't need to *impress* you."

Carol sniped.

"Uh-huh, that's what I thought."

C said deadpan.

Ji-Sue rose and turned, kneeling on the love seat, watching Stinky-Steve shuffle his way down the Third Street sidewalk beside the house; she leaned over the rail and wondered where he was off to. She already forgot the artist's name.

And that's when the red flag caught her eye, on the sidewalk, in full view.

"Hey, Mr. C....look!"

Cord turned around, his eyes widened, and he threw his Southside down, yelling:

Holy shit!

CHAPTER 200 – GET READY; TWO AND ONE SECOND AND I'M GONE

She froze.

She wanted to run, as she saw C round the corner of the porch, heading toward her, a freight train off the tracks. But her feet didn't move; instead, her mouth did.

"What?!"

She yelled in his direction, annoyed on steroids.

"Come on Lilly, what the fuck; do you think this is a game? Do you think I *want* to be a fucking babysitter?"

"Then *don't be*, asshole; I'm moving back home today anyway."

"No you're not, your brother won't allow it."

"Really? How about you? Will you *allow* it?"

"No."

"Well how 'bout me? How 'bout I don't **give a shit** what either of you two say."

"Wow, you're tough now aren't you?"

"Shut up asshole! I'm tired of being cooped up here, **here** of all places, Christ, watched, like a fucking child. Why don't you just move back downtown with me and Earl? Earl will stay with me, and you go upstairs, just like old times, and you both can keep an eye on me there; what's wrong with that?"

C just looked at her; he didn't have a quick answer. On the face, that option actually made sense, so there had to be some sort of catch. He wasn't even thinking that Carol would carve his heart out, by giving in to her and moving back, and more importantly, taking Earl back with him. She liked the set-up, sans Lillian, of course; that would be a tough pry-back.

"Uh...."

Was all he came up with, as his mind raced.

"Yeah, I thought so. Listen, last time he was gone for *three years*; it could be another three, it could be forever, and I'm not staying *here* another day, another fucking minute longer than I have to."

"Are you kidding me? Come on! He's coming back Lilly, you said so yourself, you said it...."

She cut him off.

"Whatever, I'm done; thanks for everything, thank the bitch, but I'm done."

"What are you doing?"

C said, looking at her running outfit, consisting of tiny blue spandex running shorts and a white jog bra. Her stomach was flat and tan, like the rest of her; the outline of her nipples shadowed the white cotton, and of course, he had to avoid staring at them, lest he endure her wrath for yet one more thing. And it was hard to avoid them, when all you were supposed to do was simply avoid them, and all you really wanted to do was stare at them.

"Are you an idiot? What's it look like I'm doing? I'm going for a run, then I'm packing; do you mind? And stop staring, perv!"

"I'm not staring! And you haven't run since high school, and now you just decided to go for a jog? Really?"

"Listen, I don't have to explain *anything* to you; why don't you go down and see Margery, and stare at hers?"

"Where'd *that* come from?"

C said, exasperated.

"Last thing I heard, she's a good squatter; why don't you go.....*squat* with her, because sure as shit you're not getting any *here*."

"You know, you're such an asshole; all I've done for you, after all the stuff you did with Button, after *that* night."

"Hey, I already said I was sorry, that's old news."

Lilly barked indignant.

"Really? That's it? That's all it takes? Well, I'm sorry about Margery too, you know, old news. There....done."

"No you're not, and I don't care anyway."

"Really, sure seems like you don't care."

"Whatever."

Lilly said, dismissive. C stared at her, mouth agape, incredulous.

"Lilly, wait a minute, you said you were happy I did it with her! You said...."

"I ***never*** said that!"

Lilly snapped back, venomous.

 "Oh, here we go; I *knew* I should have taped it!"

"Whatever."

"And have I even tried a *single thing* with you, **anything**, this week, to take advantage? I've tried to be supportive, and good, which for me is a big deal, and *this* is what I get?"

C pleaded, with an equal mix of disbelief and general annoyance. Lilly just glared at him, irritated at even having this conversation. She was in rare form, a foul mood made worse by C's handcuffs, and thoughts of Margery, and Carol, and Button and….everything.

"And now *I* get the annoyed look to boot? Are you kidding me?"

C said, in utter disbelief.

"I'm going."

"You're such a fucking asshole, you really are."

Cord spat angry on the sidewalk.

"You already said that."

"Well fuck you, how about that? I'm going with you, too fucking bad, and…."

Lilly cut him off.

"No you're not."

But he kept talking over her.

"….and when your brother gets back, you can tell him all about your *new* plans, and then I'm done with you, fucking done with all your bullshit….*just done!*"

C said, in disgust.

"You don't own me!"

"I know, no one owns you, except *Button*."

"Fuck you!"

Lilly screamed, and as she started to walk away, Cord grabbed her wrist, hard, and he could see that it hurt her, so he immediately let go, horrified that he did that, to her.

She rubbed her wrist, looking at the ground, and her eyes got red, like she was about to cry.

"What, you too?"

C's heart dropped, being compared to him, in that way. He quickly changed his tone to conciliatory.

"I'm sorry, I'm sorry I did that; I just don't want you to go, and get hurt. I'm worried about you; I thought I was your best friend."

"Best friends get treated like shit sometimes; best friends *understand* that, and best friends *are* best friends, *stay* best friends, good times and not....they're never ***just done!***"

Cord sighed, tired that he could never seem to get it right with Lilly, or keep it right, never. But the glimmers of good always kept him coming back, like a moth banging endless against a light. He knew he had no choice, he cared about her that much, he loved her that much. Fuck, he hated that.

"Lilly, I'm sorry. Please, just let me run with you, just this once. If I let you go, and something ever happened to you..../[C shook his head]. Look, I told your brother I'd keep an eye on you when he was at Sam's; either wait to run till he gets back, and he's okay with it, or let me go, and then do whatever you want, and I'll do what *you* want, stay in it, or stay out of it, promise, whatever you want. I *am* your best friend....I am."

And C reached out and gently touched her wrist with a single finger, the same one he just hurt.

Lilly kept her head down, staring at the ground in silence. She never moved her wrist toward him, or away; she just let it hang limp. And he stared at her, in silence, his single finger keeping contact with her wrist, just barely. And they stayed that way, it seemed like forever, one waiting for the other to act. Him thinking about her….and Button; her thinking about him….and Margery.

And both thinking about best friends.

She finally broke the ice, with a short, barely audible snort through her nose, followed by a slow head shake. Still looking down at her sneakers, rubbing her shoe forward and back on the slate sidewalk, she spoke in a low, emotionless tone. It was her best attempt at reconciliation.

"You've got two minutes to get ready; two and one second and I'm gone."

CHAPTER 201 – SHE FLEW STRAIGHT. *SHIT*

"There are two rules, are you listening?"

C was still out of breath from the quick change and sprint up and down the second-floor steps. He frowned at the lecture, but didn't say a word.

"Rule Number One, there's no talking."

C just stared at her, silent, as Lilly raised her finger and pointed accusatory, right at his mouth. Then she continued.

"And Rule Number Two...."

And Lilly abruptly stopped speaking and bent down to touch her toes in a slow stretch, in silence. C just looked at her. Finally, tired of waiting, he took the bait.

"And?"

Lilly stood up, looked at him plainly, and finished Rule Number Two.

"There's no talking."

And with that, she turned and, for the first time in twenty-five years, began a run.

Lilly kept a slow pace, about a ten-minute mile pace, maybe slower, good for him, but it was almost too slow. Maybe she was testing her forty-one year old legs.

They started their run down Third, heading west, past the Hardwick intersection; C didn't dare look back, knowing he'd see Carol on the porch, fuming. Hopefully, she and Ji weren't still there, but that was wishful thinking.

"Bye Mr. C; good luck on your run!"

Ji-Sue yelled at him down the street.

Busted, thanks Ji. He turned around, and saw her leaned over the porch waving wildly; Carol was behind her, head buried behind the open newspaper; he could see that was yet another batch of trouble from thirty yards. Too late now.

They ran the Park sidewalk, Third Street, the one he had run a hundred times with Earl, but it felt so different now, running alongside Lilly, like he had never traversed it before. He found himself unable to regulate his breath, bit of a hyperventilation, and he felt butterflies in his stomach....butterflies! What was that about?

Quick enough they were past the Third Street Elementary School, hooked a left on Greenwich Street, and were headed out of Town, he suspected. Since he couldn't talk, he couldn't ask, and he knew that's what she was waiting for, just so she could pounce on him for breaking *both* her rules.

So he kept quiet, and just followed her, trying to breathe even, like it was easy. In fact, now that he got into a rhythm, it kinda was; she wasn't going too fast, and he could hear her breathing more than himself.

They ran a slow, steady pace up the little knoll over the Pophandusing Creek, the little rivulet he saw that first day on that Belvidere sign heading into Town; it must dead-end into the Delaware, just south of the boat ramp.

Atop the hill, which wasn't all that big, he could hear her breathing more pronounced, like a smoker, but she still led the way, and didn't change her pace. He just kept the same distance, about five feet, watching her tight little butt, wrapped in that sky-blue spandex, roll up and down with each stride, like kneading dough. He wanted so bad to rip off that nylon, and that little jog bra, to see the nipples he wasn't allowed to stare at. He wondered how quickly those fucking clothes would have been off if she were running with Button behind her? The run would probably already be over and they'd be heading into the corn field just ahead, on the left.

Now his breathing was heavy; he was hyperventilating, getting mad at her cheating, mind-fuck with Button.

She heard him and turned her head to the right, just enough to see him, peripheral, and shot him an annoyed look with that one eye, the kind that means stop breathing so loud, or maybe just stop breathing, altogether.

"Hey, I never noticed, that's called *Foul Rift Road*."

C said, breaking both rules, just to annoy her. He was looking to his right, at the side road that ran toward the river, just past the sewer treatment plant.

"Hey!"

Was all Lilly said; the intent was clear in a single bark: *shut-the-fuck-up*.

C called her an asshole, in his head. She might be a best friend, and he might love her – most of the time, but she still could be such an asshole. Then he looked again at that cute, little kick-boxing spandex butt bouncing in front of him, not that he could look at anything else, and he smiled wry. And he knew he could never stay mad at her, never. It was a blessing, and a curse, and he wouldn't trade either for the world.

He wondered what would ever happen to Lilly, a year from now, two, ten….long after he left this place, which he knew he would; he always did. And that got him sad, and it reminded him of Kristine, fumbling her books on the school bus.

He hoped he would remember Lilly, hopefully forever; maybe she would remember him too, for awhile, anyway. He hoped she would; for some reason, to him, for once, it made a difference.

And they ran on in silence, for a good mile or so; Greenwich Street became Route 620 outside of Town, past a rundown laundromat and a string of corn fields, head-high already, rustling in the scant summer breeze. An immense fenced field, it must have been ten football fields deep, stretching toward the Delaware River, spread before them along the right shoulder. In it were two dozen cattle huddled close along a far stone row, under the shade of a stand of towering maples and oaks between pastures, lazily passing the day, chewing cud, an idyllic scene, until it was time to load them up in the cattle-car for the one-way to the livestock auction in Hackettstown, and then on to the slaughterhouse, butchered for next month's hamburgers. C shook his head; he should have enjoyed the bucolic scene, but couldn't shake the end-game slaughter-thoughts.

In the distance, well beyond the gathering of cattle, rose two, huge concrete cooling towers, hourglasses the color of Portlandt, offset by two pencil-shaped smokestacks. Everyone, when they first saw them, thought for sure it was a Jersey nuclear power plant, ominously growing out of the distant greenery, beyond the farm.

It had that look.

Truth was, it was simply a coal-fired power plant, and the hourglasses bellowed water vapor….cloud-makers. And the plant wasn't even in New Jersey; it was on the Pennsylvania shore of the Delaware, just downstream of Foul Rift, but you couldn't see the river from where C and Lilly were running, so it simply appeared as if an industrial monstrosity was plucked down beyond the dairy farm stone-row, in the middle of nowhere.

Over time, most locals came to ignore the stacks set amongst the greenery; some even grew to like them. And the builders of the power plant, for the industrial inconvenience to the native folk, built and provided public access to an extensive system of nature trails around the cooling towers, a buffer, so to speak, to be forever known as the *Tekening Hiking Trails*, culled from the local Lenni Lenapi Indian language, meaning *in the wood*. And those trails ran for miles, weaving the weald hugging the western shore of the Delaware, and they included Earl's infamous Blue Trail, with its secret access to the one, and only, *Couch Rock*, set idyllic in a thick, wooded bluff, high above the river.

As Cord and Lilly ran in column on the shoulder, traffic whizzed by steady, too fast, exceeding the speed limit, kicking dust and grit as they passed. Every third or fourth car would beep, invariably for Lilly; either they knew her, or wanted to, and she summarily ignored them all, never even proffering a glance their way.

Neither did Cord, which is why he never saw the metallic blue Mini-Cooper, top-down, drive by. That driver didn't beep. C was lucky that driver didn't mow him down.

The sun was hot, and the breeze not nearly strong enough to sweep the heat, and although he felt okay, from months of running, he could sense Lilly was starting to struggle, and knowing her, would never, ever admit it. This was going to be interesting; a gifted runner, a phenom in her youth, who really couldn't run that well anymore, just another thing for her to be pissed about, which would certainly manifest itself in some poison directed at him.

Great, he thought to himself.

"Stop staring at my butt! I can *feel* it; I can feel your eyes!"

"Jesus Lilly, what am I supposed to do, run with my eyes closed? Your butt is right in front of me. Sorry, it kinda takes up the whole field of view, like looking at the sky, wrapped in spandex."

"Hey fuck-nut, I got a small butt, *and stop looking*!"

And with that she quick-ducked behind him, letting Cord take the lead.

"Fine, look at my butt all you want!"

And C swung it side to side.

"Yuck."

Was all she said, even though she always thought C had a cute butt, a product of all that squatting, although she'd never admit it.

And they stayed that way, same pace, until they were fifty yards from the Route 620/Route 519 intersection, about a mile and a half outside Town.

Then Lilly, without warning, sped up and retook the lead.

Cord's mind was racing, doing the math. They had gone about a mile and a half; that was a three mile jaunt, plus or minus, if they turned around *right now,* which would be a decent run for Cord, especially since he had just started running a three mile loop Earl showed him out of Town, and could do it without stopping. But regardless, he still wouldn't characterize a three mile run as *easy.* Cord was starting to breath hard, just thinking about the alternatives. None of them bode well.

If they *didn't* turn around real soon, which he hoped they would, and instead took a left onto Route 519 North, they could head back into Town via the blinking red light at Hazen, which would take him past the main entrance to Brookfield, where he hopefully would not see Mae. A left at the light would wind him past the

High School and the Cemetery; that had to be closer to a five mile loop, maybe more, which was new territory for Cord, and very scary to his lungs and legs. He wasn't sure he could go that far without stopping, which he simply couldn't do with her; if he stopped because he was tired, she'd never let him live it down. *Never.* He started to hyperventilate at the thought; *please* don't take a left! *Just turn around!*

Christ, taking a left wasn't even the worst of it. She could keep going *straight*, on Route 519 South, heading toward Easton, which was a good fifteen miles away, with nothing but endless cornfields, dairy farms, woods and scattered houses along the way. And if that was the choice, God knows how long Lilly intended to run that endless ribbon of road. *Shit!*

He knew whatever the choice, it was meant to punish him, just for fun. Of that he was pretty certain, unless, of course, she was tired herself, and she seemed tired.

Please turn around, don't turn left, and for God's sake, don't go straight; *please turn the fuck around.* The plea circled in C's head as Lilly, five feet ahead of him, approached the fateful intersection. He tried to read her body language, where was she going; she was breathing a bit heavier now too, so she certainly wasn't going straight.

Thank God.

But taking a left was still a possibility, even if she was tired, just because of her stubborn streak, and her desire, her hope, that she could break him. God, he prayed for the about-face and a march right back into Town, past the same sorry cows; oh, how he wanted to see those cows.

Just then, without warning, she let up her pace, turned around and ran backwards, facing him, not saying a word, as if she was studying him, his *condition.* Her face wasn't red, and she wasn't sweating, but she *was* breathing heavy, through an open mouth.

But he was breathing louder.

"Stop breathing so loud!"

She barked in his face.

"I thought there was a no talking rule! You keep breaking it…."

He spit out, between gulps of air.

"I can talk, *you can't*!"

She said, continuing to run backwards.

"Your face is all sweaty and red; want to go back?"

She teased.

My God, he wanted to say **yes! Please, please, please, yes!** He could taste it, he wanted to say it so bad. But it would be a bitter pill, knowing the satisfaction she would get in him quitting, before her.

So he didn't.

In fact, he didn't say anything, not a single word; he just stared at her and kept running, picking up the pace and closing the five foot gap between them, till he was almost nose-to-nose with her, his own taunt. Her face turned to stone, showing no emotion; she simply stared into his eyes for a moment, as if giving him one last chance to submit.

Nothing doing.

To which Lilly spun around, just as they came upon the fateful intersection. Without a word, without a warning, she flew straight.

Shit.

1753

CHAPTER 202 – DISGUSTED, DUMBFOUNDED, SANDBAGGED

Lilly tried to increase the gap between them, but C got a shot of adrenaline, and a second wind, and wouldn't let her break away. In fact *he* pushed the pace, and could hear her breathing heavier ahead of him.

They passed some apartment complex called Colby Court, the Warren County Road and Bridge Department and the adjoining Department of Corrections, off to the right. He cracked the faintest hint of a smile at seeing the lock-up; why not just call it the County Jail, or Prison. Does anyone really get *corrected*?

Windtryst Way slipped by on the left, with tall cornfields to the right; by this point, they were about another mile out, two-and-a-half miles from home, in toto. He was keeping pace with her, pushing her, and he could feel her will begin to wilt. It was here Cord decided to make his move, to end this game, and bury her once and for all.

In a short burst, without warning, he passed her, by just a few steps. She didn't say a word, except she put her head down when he passed, as if in defeat. He felt a rush of exhilaration from the act, but as he looked back, and saw her head down, and her panting, it quickly faded to feeling like a piece of shit. He slowed down, to let her pass him again.

The pity was transparent.

"Don't fucking slow down! Keep going asshole, keep going; let's see how much you got!"

She yelled at him, her own burst of adrenaline.

And just like that, he got pissed again, and shot ahead of her, a good ten yards, which expanded to twenty yards, her lagging further behind. He was feeling pretty damn good, and didn't feel a bit bad about dusting her. To rub it in, he turned around and ran backwards, taunting her with his running prowess, watching her struggle.

Then, with that twenty yard spread, and him showing off, she suddenly stopped, and just stood there, on the shoulder of the road. She was done, winded....defeated. She had a face which said another step, just one more step, was one step too many.

He won! He beat her ass, but good. Served her right, taunting him.

So Ay stopped, waiting for her to speak, to concede defeat, so they could finally turn around and go back home.   C's chest was heaving, trying to catch his breath from that mini-sprint that put the final dagger in her.

But Lilly didn't concede; in fact, she didn't speak, she just stood there, hands on her hips, staring at him, with an expression he couldn't assign, but defeat, it certainly wasn't. And he noticed she was breathing lightly.

In fact, she was hardly breathing at all.

The two stood in the shoulder of the road, facing each other, staring at one another, dead silent, C still gulping air, her not, as the cars continued to rocket by, kicking up swirls of dust.

Just then, he happened to look across the street from where she stopped, at a bent signpost, marking a lonely side road that ribboned and disappeared between two tall corn fields. It said:

Foul Rift Road

He puzzled for a bit, and then yelled to her, between breaths.

"How's that Foul Rift Road too? That doesn't make sense, unless it's one big...."

And as he looked at Lilly, while he spoke, she yawned, a gaping, cartoon yawn, like she was bored. Then, seemingly pulled from thin air, Lilly turned and galloped in a full sprint across Route 519, and started to tear up that side road, Foul Rift Road, and she was running faster than Cord could *ever* run. Even in a full-out sprint, for only twenty yards, he would never be able to keep up with her. It was like a bolt of lightning, like she was running a hundred yard dash, a competitive, all-out sprint.

That's how fast she ran, and ran....and ran.

His mouth was open in awe, as he saw her quickly disappear up Foul Rift Road, cut between the head-high corn, swaying gently in the summer sun.

"....loop?"

Was all he said, finishing his sentence to himself, as the cars continued to fly by, kicking grit against his legs.

Lilly was quickly a speck, a jack-rabbit about to disappear over a crest in that narrow farm road; she had to be a quarter-mile away already, still sprinting full-out, and he hadn't moved, his hands on his hips, still sucking oxygen. And just like that, she disappeared from sight, swallowed by the corn.

He shook his head in silence, and spat on the pavement.

Disgusted, dumbfounded, sandbagged.

CHAPTER 203 – KNEE-DEEP IN A NOSE KISS AND NECK RUB

It was amazing how quickly his legs turned to lead.

He crossed the road, and lumbered up Foul Rift, although Lilly was long-since out of sight. His breathing was labored, and he might as well have already run twenty miles. He suddenly felt like an old man, a stupid, gullible old man, with very bad knees.

He plodded along, up the gently, rolling road, a long, undulating incline, with the power plant hourglass towers looming large, dead ahead, like the road was meant to meet them. That's when he felt the stitch in his right side, the first cramp he had gotten running in months.

"Fuck; fuck you Lilly!"

He cursed aloud and spat, although most of the thick cotton-mouth saliva stuck to his lips and swung onto his cheek, a disgusting, viscous glob, adding insult to injury, which riled him more than he already was. He couldn't even spit right, he thought, shaking his head, as he slow-motioned past row upon row of ripening corn….the fucking fields never seemed to end. He didn't even wipe off the spittle, he left it on his cheek, feeling it stick there, like glue, which pissed him off even more.

Maybe she just ducked in the corn field and was hiding, waiting for him to catch up, you know, kind of a joke. Yeah right, nice try; *he* was the joke.

A large white barn stood quiet, hugging the right shoulder, large swaths of peeled paint clung, just barely, to the clapboards. Beside it, three rusted grain silos stood sentry, like three fingers, big, bigger and biggest.

The din of traffic from County Road 519, at his back, had faded, only the sound of rustling cornstalks, scattered crickets and stray birds broke the lonely silence. Loose gravel swept to the white line crunched under his worn sneakers, ripped, full of holes and forever falling apart. He had glued them back together as best he could time and again; this pair dated back at least twenty years, and had traveled the world with him, the only companions that survived that long, the only ones that would tolerate him, and him them.

He crested the hill and the heavy summer sky suddenly smelled rank; he couldn't figure why. It wasn't field manure, and there was no road kill to be seen, but the scene smelled of rot, and he couldn't shake it, filling his nostrils with a bad breeze. Then, off to the right, he saw a recycling center sign, set beside a gravel road that curved and disappeared over the crest of a lazy hay field.

Compost, that's what it was, a hidden graveyard of rotting wood and leaves, piled to the sky. He tried to speed up, get upwind, side wind, some wind away from the heavy stench, but his legs wouldn't cooperate, and he was resigned to suffer the stink. Fucking Lilly, she probably had this whole charade planned, right down to the stench.

The compost plant eventually gave way to a gravel pit along this long, desolate stretch of country lane; not a car had passed him. The August sun baked the blacktop, cooking beneath his sneakers, bubbling the tar like gum. He could feel waves of heat buffet his shins. He was sweating profusely, drenched; at least it wasn't heat stroke....not yet, anyway.

The power plant seemed to grow, an *Alice in Wonderland* before him, the cooling towers and smokestacks looming ever-larger; he had to be close to the river, he *had* to be. He needed to know he was past half-way, on his way *back* to the house. Forget about catching Lilly, this was a matter of getting back without having to walk, to limp, to crawl, home.

He ran, more of a fast-walk, down a small incline, corn fields to both sides, as the sun-baked pavement curved slight to the right, and he soon found himself at a decision to be made.

Door number one: *Foul Rift Road* continued straight, through a narrow, one-lane, stone-arched tunnel, which snuck under a railroad trestle, with the blue of the Delaware River, *finally*, just beyond. He spied the water, tranquil, through the eight-foot high, half-round tunnel opening, picture framed, a hundred yards ahead. It was a welcome sight.

Door number two: to the left, *South Foul Rift,* another ribbon of pavement, stretched endless to the south, hugging the elevated rail bed, to points unknown. Another empty road, disparting tall green fields of summer corn.

No way was he going left; that was nothing but further from home, and he would never find Lilly on foot anyway – he'd end up road kill, cooked on the bitumen where he dropped from the heat stroke that was sure to come, fodder for the turkey and black vultures, unless the crows got him first. Best to limp home, get a car, someone's car, anyone's car, and go find her.

Best to get home was the operative phrase; those were his legs talking, and they made the most sense.

So he continued straight, through the tunnel and came upon the River, running calm, directly in front of the power plant, in full view, planted off the far western shoreline. There must have been a hundred mallard and white geese floating lazily in the river; he wondered if the mallard with the broken bill ever made it, he wondered if she was out there, somewhere, floating around, safe.

He liked to hope she was. But he knew she likely wasn't, so he stopped thinking about it.

The road dog-legged to the right, north, and ran along the river, painted in dappled shade, a welcome respite from the searing heat. He slowly shuffled along, passing cluttered river shacks along the way, hobo alley. It was quiet….and there was no Lilly to be found.

A not-so-small hill approached in about fifty yards.

"Shit."

He whispered aloud. Fucking hill; anything but level road was a fucking hill at this point, but this one was real, and it was *steep*.

C put his head down; don't look up, *don't look up,* and plodded the ascent. It took him from river level up over the rail line, the apex was a deeply worn, wood-plank, single-lane bridge, now about seventy-five to a hundred feet above the river; thirty feet above the rail track. For some reason, he half-expected Lilly to be sitting on the bridge trestle, legs hanging over the edge, smiling, waiting for him; it seemed the perfect place to rest a spell.

He half-laughed at his own delirium; of course there was no Lilly.

As much as he wanted to stop and rest, and drink the river scene below him, he didn't. He was determined not to stop, not that she would ever believe him anyway, but for his own sake, his own pride, he just couldn't. So, although his legs were screaming, and he was sucking wind, the mostly-shade along this stretch of road seemed to help a bit, and he kept moving. Soon, the rail bridge faded far behind; he never turned back to look.

A flat stretch of pavement brought him through a heavily wooded section, and more welcome shade. The river had bent out of sight; he could hear the faint beginnings of the up-river rapids, the very downstream end of Foul

Rift in the distance, beyond scattered river houses and the thick, woodland fringe.

This stretch had a backwoods Cajun feel, and not in a good way. Abandoned, crumpled cars were left to die in overgrown, weed-filled clearings; the lots slowly being reclaimed by the forest, bushy along the wood edge. A lone gray cat, feral and wary, crouched low atop the hood of a dark blue junker, grass growing coarse through the engine block. The mouser caught his eye and scurried, disappearing into the tall weeds.

He never saw it again.

Not a soul was present; the houses looked abandoned, silent markers along a darkened road, but they weren't. And he felt eyes on him; eyes on an intruder.

Creepy.

Up ahead, off the right shoulder, at the edge of a scraggly section of trees and understory, hung a black rubber sphere, about the size of a small volleyball, tethered by a thin string to a tree branch, dangling face-high. There was nothing around it, just woods, and this lone marker amongst it, hung there for some unknown reason, by someone unknown.

The hung ball displayed an automaton face, fashioned from bits of ripped yellow-tape; the mouth was set in the shape of a slight frown, and a pair of ski goggles were slipped over the sphere, covering yellow trapezoid-eyes, which seemed to follow him as he passed. It was strung-up and silent, as if watching and waiting for something to happen along the edge of the road, the edge of the ragged woods. He swore he saw it swing a bit, ever-so-slightly, left to right as it eyed him, although the air was dead-still.

Creepier.

He found the strength to pick up the pace and exit this wooded stretch, finding himself back along a reach of open, sunny road, along with ever-more corn fields and decrepit farms buildings.

Even though the searing heat returned with the open sun, he welcomed the change, as the hanging ball faded behind him, and with it, the back-woods skin-creep.

He could clearly hear the sound of rushing water, rapids off to the left, beyond the tree-line, out of sight. And he knew it was the Foul Rift. *Couch Rock* was somewhere across the river, close by, and he knew he must be getting near home.

He must be....*please*.

A little dirt driveway ducked off to the left, threaded through a half-moon under the same railroad line that paralleled the road, appearing and disappearing in pieces as it weaved through the forest. C could barely see the ridge-line of a few houses in the distance, beyond the raised tracks, closer to the river, figuring they must be the destination of the shared driveway. He passed it by, sticking to the main road.

The pavement lazily bent right ahead, and for a moment, he fancied this the homestretch, curving back up to that gritty laundromat he ran past first leaving Town; Christ, that seemed to be a week ago.

But the hope was false; beyond the curve, the road stretched filiform-straight for a much longer distance than he wanted to run. And he started to think how bad an idea this really was. His knees throbbed with each stride hitting the hard pavement.

At the end of the long straight-away, yet another gradient awaited, and he cursed Lilly again. He still hadn't stopped, but his will was wilting. The incline wasn't very big, but, again, at this point, anything less than flat was formidable, and he began to obsess about it….that upcoming hill.

The sun beat hard on his shoulders and scalp as he found himself at the base of the rise. Head down, he bulled his way up, running maybe a half-step faster than an old-man's shuffle, trying not to focus on the acid in his thighs. He really didn't think he would make it, but somehow he did.

And as he crested the hillock, gasping for air, he raised his head, hoping to see something, anything resembling the end of this odyssey.

And he did.

Stretched before him stood yet another farm, but this one was different, with compartmentalized, fenced paddocks filling both sides of the street, and a dozen horses, maybe more, lazily grazing to his left, and to his right.

In the closest paddock, on the right, a mere fifty yards ahead of him, was a chocolate-colored stallion, with a tall, broad chest, standing at a bend in the fence-row, abutting the road shoulder. Ay knew it was a stallion because he clearly showed it, half of it, anyway, a rock-hard, black and pink baton.

The steed was stunning, and he paid absolutely no attention to Cord, shuffling closer in what could be best described as a half-jog.

The summer air was still, broken only by the almost indecipherable background sound of the passed rapids and the low, throaty nicker of the mustang, one vibration after another, as he shook his massive mane side-to-side. He was clearly a happy boy, and why wouldn't he be. It was a beautiful sunny day, and there he stood, with Lillian, knee-deep in a nose kiss and neck rub.

CHAPTER 204 – HEAD DOWN, HE JUST KEPT PLUGGING AWAY

"Hey!"

Was all Cord came up with at the sight of her, more of a reflex than anything, as if stumbling onto something you never really expected to find.

Lillian raised her head off the stallion's nose, opened her eyes and frowned, reluctantly returning to the real world. She hugged his neck and gave him one last long kiss, turned, and sprinted away, once again leaving Cord in the dust.

Fuck he whispered to himself, exasperated; the short burst of adrenaline sapped.

He lumbered by the paddock, and the stallion stared hard and snorted long and loud through flared nostrils, stomping his front hooves, frustrated the nose-kisser left, and this bow-legger was the cause.

"Yeah, yeah."

C said aloud as he went by, knowing he broke up the tango.

"Get used to it."

He said in parting, as the stallion snorted behind him.

The road ahead took a sharp turn to the right and he prayed the sewer plant and laundromat lay ahead.....*they had to*.

Lilly was, once again, long gone, and only the ribbon of asphalt lay before him, corn to the shoulder on his right, and barking dogs on his left; the river sounds had disappeared.....he must be north of the Rift rapids. He rounded the bend and held his breath.

Thank God, the sewer plant *did* lay ahead; never was anyone as happy as he to see a sewer plant.

He made his way back up to County Road 620, and the seedy laundromat across the street, a slow slog. He hooked a left, over the bridge spanning the Pophandusing, and soon found himself back in Town, dodging root heaves in the mix of concrete and bluestone sidewalk slabs, five long blocks back to *Boreas*.

He got to the Square, and neither Ji nor Carol were on the porch; there was no sign of Lilly – he thought she may be on Earl's bench in the Park.

His legs were dead, he was dead; he hadn't run that long for God knows how many years, but for some reason, now, he wasn't ready to stop. So he looped the Park, once, and again found himself in front of *L'antre du Lion*.

But C didn't want to go in there and deal with the lashing he knew was coming, not now, not yet. So he ran past Carol's, down Third Street, to *Boreas*, but he figured Lilly was probably inside, packing, unless she continued to run to points unknown; the Cemetery - likely not….the boat ramp - definitely not.

As he passed *Boreas*, pondering, his question was answered. He saw her, briefly, walk past the second-floor window in the front bedroom, Earl's room. And he certainly didn't want to go there either, not now, not yet; and she certainly made it clear she didn't want to be with him.

So he kept running, and soon found his way down Third Street, heading toward the Cemetery, out of Town, on Earl's regular three mile loop. His legs hurt, and he was tired, but he didn't care, and he wasn't going to stop.

Head down, he just kept plugging away.

CHAPTER 205 – SHE MEANDERED IN FIELDS OF GOLD

Martin, sporting a carefully groomed butch-wax flat-top, was embarrassed by the attention, by the toast, and the needling, yet so proud he couldn't wipe the grin off his face. Rarely was he the center of attention, rarely the topic of group conversation, any conversation, in fact. He was more peripheral, that seemed to be his lot in life.

But he had worked hard his whole career for this, the culmination of drive, dedication, and time, lots of time; the crown for being a decent, respected man in this little, nugatory corner of the world.

"Seriously...."

C said, his glass raised high, facing Martin.

"....all joking aside, congratulations, Police Chief Martin Brewer!"

And a unison of cheers erupted and crystal clinked on the front porch from the usual suspects; Earl, Cord, Ji-Sue, Carol and Buck.

Carol gave him a peck on the cheek, Buck patted him on the back and called him *Marty,* which he now could get away with, without fanfare, having been admitted to the exclusive club. Cord shook his hand and Earl gave him a great big bear-hug, which lifted him off the deck and squeezed the air from Marty's lungs.

Ji-Sue just smiled, but what a smile. Marty seemed to like that one the best, and he stared at Ji and smiled back. And stared and smiled some more.

"Well, it's not *official*, official yet, I'm officially *interim* until the Council votes next Tuesday, but until then, I'm in charge; the Chief's on a plane to Florida, a one-way ticket. Sorry I didn't tell you guys earlier, but I didn't wanna, you know….jinx it."

"Who's on the plane?"

Cord asked.

"The Chief."

Martin said, innocent.

And C smiled wry.

"You mean the *ex-Chief;* the new *big dog* in Town is standing right here!"

And with that everyone roused and lifted their glasses again, smiling and laughing.

It was a grand time.

Lilly was on the second floor, all alone, still sitting statue in the bathtub since her slow undress from the run, two hours prior. She heard the ruckus next door, on Carol's front porch, through the open windows; she didn't know what was going on, but she knew she wasn't part of it, couldn't be….never would be.

She pulled her knees up to her chest and cracked the faucet again, introducing more hot water to what was tepid in the tub. After a few minutes of staring blankly at the wall, she shut it again with her toes.

She was sore and exhausted; dead-tired, as much from emotion than anything else. Her calves twitched, little cramp-spasms. She pulled her achy legs closer, tight to her chest, and rested her right cheek on her knee, closed her eyes, and listened to the almost-closed faucet drip. She had assumed the pose before, many times, but this was the first time she felt old on the outside, not just the inside, like the sketch, the only art she remembered from high school, the only art she felt she really knew, that talked to her, that understood the inside of her head.

She remembered it was called *Sorrow;* that word was written in script in the lower right corner. She didn't remember the artist; it was somebody famous, but she really didn't care about all that. The first time she laid eyes upon it, at her desk, in her textbook, she simply stared at the page, for what seemed like forever, without saying a word, as it slowly absorbed.

It was an old, wrinkled woman, but not nearly as old as she looked, completely naked, with rough worker's hands and straggly long black hair, falling down her back. She was slight, yet she had an old-woman's bulbous belly and sagging breasts, her face unseen, buried in folded arms, which rested on her knees; she was sitting on a rock, or a log....something like that.

Nothing connected with Lillian more than that small, crude pencil sketch; it haunted her.

That woman seemed forever lost; she was the utter pain, despair and loneliness that Lilly felt her whole life; she was ugly and helpless and hopeless.

She was Lilly, and Lilly her.

She raised her foot slowly and cracked the tub drain. Eyes closed, she leaned forward and grabbed her ankles. After that, she didn't move, a statue in stone, as she felt the line of water drop along her thigh, like a river gauge. The only sound she heard was her own breathing and the quiet gurgle of water down the drain. And with it, she relived all the years of abuse, and the excuses, and the shame. And she felt it, and Button, slip away, a last let-go, sad, necessary, and final; it finally felt final. Her mouth made an expression, but it couldn't be called a smile; it was a shape that didn't have a name - maybe melancholy, whatever shape that looks like - a life's emotions wasted, ending here, in a tub owned by a woman she despised.

How did she end up here? A life so full of promise, so wasted. A part of her wanted to quickly slip below the receding water line, while it was still deep enough, before it was too late....maybe then she could finally ask the questions, and hear the answers, she had waited a lifetime for from the woman who meant the world to her, the woman who abandoned her. She needed those answers to have any sort of life, even if she had to die to hear them.

The ruckus next door had disappeared; and she noticed the rasp of cicadas had filled the room, the void. That sound, the chatter, always soothed her; to her, it was the sound of summer.

The last of the water trickled away from her crotch, from around her rear-cheeks, down the tub drain; for some reason, inexplicably, she started to cry, and just as quickly, she stopped, and with it, so went Button. He was finally gone, he was finally done; she was finally done.

And she couldn't describe the feeling.

She rose slowly from the tub, still wet, walked down the short hall, and laid on Earl's bed, naked, and stretched long, laying on her side. As she slowly dried in the summer air, she thought only of her mom, of her childhood; she wanted to remember the good times, good thoughts about the two of them, best friends, for the first time in years. They existed, just in a drawer she rarely opened.

And the faintest of smiles creased her lips as she meandered in fields of gold.

CHAPTER 206 – HE WOULD HAVE BEEN UP FOR A NICE HOG-TIE

"How are we going to make this work?"

"Easy."

Marty answered Cord.

"Carol, Earl and Buck go in one car, and Cord, Lilly, Ji-Sue and me in the squad car."

"Lilly will never go for it."

C said, shaking his head in the negative; then he continued.

"She won't go with me, no way; she's still mad at me."

"For what *now*?!"

Carol said with an exaggerated sigh.

Carol had already *forgiven* Cord for the run with Lilly, feeling bad, but not so, after learning he got sandbagged and dusted by the bitch, and had to hobble his way back. And although it certainly was bad, and he was hurting on that long run, Cord played it up, self-deprecating, when he told the tale, to pile it on. And it worked; Carol, unlike Lilly, was much easier when it came to forgiveness.

Of course C couldn't tell Carol the real reason why Lillian was incensed with him; it was for the Margery-fuck, which C would never admit to in this crowd, and it was also because Lillian thought Carol was a stifling bitch, which he certainly couldn't say either.

So he lied.

"Who knows, it's always something with her when it comes to me; I gave up trying to figure it out. Besides, she'll have a fucking cow if Earl and Carol go together; it's got to be me, Carol and Buck, and Lilly, Earl, Marty and Ji."

"No way! Why does she always get Earl?!"

"For Christ sake Carol, be the better person."

C said, annoyed that his plan wasn't a gimme.

"Are you kidding with that statement? *Really*? As she's in *my* house next door? Does that mean I can't spend any time with Earl at the Fair? Can't look at him, can't talk to him? Are they any other rules I need to know about?"

C just sighed; this was way too complicated for the fucking Farmers' Fair, where cow-chip tossing, for Christ sake, was a highlight.

"I'll go talk to her, I'll do it! She'll listen to me; Bibby never misses the Fair, *never!* And tonight's the last night; she *has* to go!"

Earl yelped the last part.

"She'll find a way to mess it up."

Carol huffed.

"When are we gonna go? When? When!?"

Earl was rubbing his hands together excited, throwing the question out there.

"You *just* said you were gonna talk to….Lilly….remember?"

C reminded Earl, who was much too excited about the Fair to stay focused.

"Yeah, that's right! I'll go talk to Bibby! I'll do it!"

"Do you need me to come too? To hog-tie her?"

But Cord guessed the answer was no, as Earl had already hopped off the front porch and disappeared around the corner, heading next door.

What a shame, C thought, he would have been up for a nice hog-tie.

CHAPTER 207 – BEST FRIENDS DO TREAT BEST FRIENDS LIKE SHIT….SOMETIMES

Earl brokered the deal.

The two-car procession passed through the Fair entry gate like a funeral queue, Marty's squad car in the lead, followed by Ji-Sue in her sport utility, which was really Carol's, bought for Ji to use and run errands. The twosome traversed the sloping grass field, trampled flat by hundreds of cars and thousands of feet, guided by the motioning hands of bored parking attendants.

The two vehicles saddled side-by-side, and the occupants spilled out, Lilly and Carol instinctively assuming opposite ends of the queue. It was strange having the two, voluntarily, so physically close to one another.

The disembark had the look of a prisoner exchange, darting eyes, kept distances, stolen glances stiffened backs and pursed lips. Welcome to a barrel of fun at the *69th Annual Warren County Farmers' Fair.*

"We shoulda brought Chicken, C; we could have put her in the Sherpa!"

"Can't Earl, she'd be too scared, like I am right now."

C said.

"Yeah, but wait till you see all the pet animals here! She would've liked to see the rabbits and horses and cows! There's even ducks and goats and little chicks….*real chicks!*"

"Trust me, she's *much* happier sleeping at home, than being part of this….*fun.*"

"Hey! Look! Carol and Bibby are both wearing the same clothes!"

Earl blurted.

And to their joint horror, they were; both with ecru chino-style shorts, sandal flats and white cotton tops, short-sleeve. It looked like they were twins, dressed together. It was actually the first time either looked at the other, although no eye contact was actually made.

And now, seeing the other, both wanted to crawl out of their skin, neither believing the other bitch had the gall to steal her outfit. But not a word was spoken, by them, nor anyone else. Earl's bomb landed hard on the grass and was quickly ignored by all. It was safer that way.

The death-march crossed in silence over a small footbridge, spanning a creek; it was, in order: Earl, Lilly, Cord, Buck, Marty, Ji-Sue and Carol, bringing up the rear. The din of the carnival rides, game-barkers and the general mob of Fair-goers grew louder as they approached. The footbridge dumped them into the middle of a stifling crowd, three-quarters teenagers of every shape and size, with one thing in common….loud.

The line of them soon dissolved and absorbed into the mass of humanity; there were really no central plans for the group discussed beforehand, and within moments, Cord saw Marty grab Ji by the arm and head to the left, Carol did a quick end-around, hooked Earl's arm and disappeared to the right. Cord never saw what happened to Buck….he simply disappeared.

And he found himself alone; well, almost alone.

"Great, I'm stuck with you?"

The disgust was thick.

"Wow, and I was so looking forward to spending quality time with you too, since that run today was so delightful."

"You insisted on coming; I didn't twist your arm."

"Can't you ever be nice to me, just once? Or how about just not sarcastic?"

"I've *never* been nice to you?"

"Forget it Lilly, just forget it; go enjoy yourself."

"Why, hoping to find Margery?"

C just shook his head in the negative; tired of having Margery thrown in his face.

"You know, I don't get it; I have one mistake, one slip, and all I get is shit from you. But you can fuck that guy, what ten times a day, throw it in my face, and that's a-okay? You get a hundred fucking passes and I get none? I think I'm way behind, that's what I think."

"Really? That's what you think? You don't see a difference?"

Lilly said in an even, distasteful tone.

"Nope; there's no difference. Not really."

"*Not really*? If I don't suck his cock, I get choked; if I don't fuck him, I get punched in the face. And when I *do* fuck him, to avoid getting choked or punched, it's just humiliation, violence, rape; I thought I already explained this, but maybe you have a short memory. And, by the way, he *was* my boyfriend, on and off, long before you ever showed up; and I don't care whether I was stupid or not to have him as a boyfriend, *he was,* ever since I was a teenager. You have *no* relationship with her, *none;* you don't even *know* her! And I told you *specifically* not to do anything with her, nobody else, just her, because it would upset me, and hurt me, but you go and do it anyway, and even *brag* to me, right in my face, when I was really down, about how great a *fuck* she is, just to be vindictive, and spiteful, and hurtful….and it worked, like a charm, just like you knew it would. You hurt me, *bad*, and you **still** don't get it. I fuck Button because I get punched in the face if I don't; you fuck her, and talk about *squatting* with her again, just to be hurtful, to me. So you win….congratulations, asshole. Have you ever even talked to her again? Even once? Huh?"

C just stared at her, blank; there really was nothing he could say to that; what Lilly said was the truth, every single bit of it….every single word.

"Oh, so *now* you get it? The light bulb finally went off? Makes a little sense now, does it? Yeah, thought so; just a *tiny bit* different, I'd say."

Lilly shook her head in absolute disgust.

"You think hurting me, emotionally, makes you better than him because it doesn't leave a bruise? That you're somehow the better person? You know what I figured out today, at forty-one fucking years old? That I'm *done* with people hurting me; you're just the second coming of Button, in different clothes."

Cord immediately got belligerent.

"Are you kidding me? You're comparing me to him? Me?!"

"*You* said you're two sides of the same coin; **YOU** said that, not me *[Lilly angrily pointing at C]*. And you said, how many times, I can't even count, that you're bad, and that you hurt people, let people down, and that I'd be better off without you, and to stay away. Well, you know what, for once, I *am* gonna listen to you….and stay away. Far away! Why would I want to be with someone like you? I just decided, today, to finally, for forever, get rid of the person who has hurt me, over and over and over my *whole* life; so why would I just go and do it all over again, *with you?*"

And C knew she was right. He put his head down, and whispered, more like a plea; he was surprised he was even saying it.

"Your mom thinks I'm good, or can be, and that I'm worth it....worth something."

"Maybe. But maybe my mom's wrong, maybe she just made a mistake about you; trust me, she's made them before, *big ones;* maybe you're just another big mistake....another one of her big, fucking mistakes."

C raised his head and frowned at her, with a beat-down look on his face....not very different from the face staring back at him.

"You know, you're right Lilly, best friends do treat best friends like shit....sometimes."

CHAPTER 208 – ALL ALONE IN A SEA OF UGLY FACES

The two simply stared at each other, in silence, all alone amidst a dense thicket of people, churning and knocking into them as they passed.

Cord finally spoke.

"Lilly, why don't you just go out with Marty then? He's a good guy; he'd treat you like a princess, put you on a pedestal. He's loved you all his life; you can't get better than him."

Lilly just sighed.

"Please, I'm not that hard-up; plus, it looks like he's got a new *friend*. Marty's nice, but he's not for me; never was, and never will be. I'm not going out with anyone anymore, not for awhile, anyway; I'm done with men, I don't need 'em....I don't need anybody."

But she lied about that; she needed Earl, most of all, she needed him. But he had a new *friend* too, probably for life – he was wrapped, but tight, around her finger, and she could feel her brother slowly slipping away, a bit more each day. And she felt powerless to stop it.

"....maybe I'll find myself a girlfriend."

After a delay, she finished her sentence. C didn't answer.

"Listen, I just want to have some fun at the Fair tonight, like I did when I was a little kid, with my mom, and Earl; those were some of my best memories of my mom, right here, with her, and I want to kinda remember that, *alone*....okay?"

That was the final nail in this depressing coffin. C was about as low as you could be; he would much rather have Lilly yell and bitch at him than this - a heartfelt, quiet and complete blow-off - a complete *I-don't-even-want-you-near-me* send-off.

He didn't even have time to answer; not that he really could think of anything to say to that.

"*OH MY GOD!*"

Came the screech in unison from two forty-somethings: one thin and mousy, with glasses and a loose, little paunch for a belly; the other middle-aged, post-kids thick all over, double-chin and slovenly dressed. Both had hands over their mouths in a mix of exclamation and excitement, then six arms extended and wrapped in a raucous group hug amongst the duo and Lilly. And Cord saw a genuine smile on Lilly's face, the kind of smile he hadn't seen on her face in a long time, if ever.

"We haven't seen you since, my God....*graduation!* You haven't changed a bit!"

The two talked over one another, as Lilly soaked it in. The three then busily and loudly prattled on, talking of high school and moving away, and husbands and kids and their first time back and....whatever else came out in a non-stop stream of palaver.

And it was like Cord became invisible, *was* invisible; Lilly never even stopped to introduce him. And he felt the fool.

A mixed group of thirty-somethings Cord had never seen waved to Lillian, followed by a pack of twenty-something guys ogling her, followed by more greetings from an older couple, all while Lilly was surrounded by her two new-found old friends. Lilly gave half waves, and half-smiles to them all; C didn't know any of them, not a one. And no one noticed, or even acknowledged C standing there, alone, on the periphery of the chatty trio.

Cord slowly backed away from the scene in embarrassment, like he was intruding on someone else's party, and didn't want to be seen as a sad-sack, standing solo, with no one to talk to....with no one to even acknowledge his existence.

C turned and began to walk away. After ten steps or so, he turned to take one last look, but Lillian and her friends, were gone, absorbed into the crowd.

And C had a pang in his chest, a strong desire to simply go home, finding himself all alone in a sea of ugly faces.

CHAPTER 209 – PLEADING NOT TO BE MADE, YET AGAIN, THE FOOL

Cord wandered slowly, in no particular direction, with no particular plan, feeling sorry for himself.

Past wafts of grease from funnel cake kiosks, stands stuffed with oversized pretzels, the reptile tent and the football team's dunk tank – lured with jail-bait cheerleaders in skimpy tee-shirts. He elbowed his way through the jammed queue near an opening in the rickety cyclone fence, which served as the entrance to the demolition derby. According to the chatter about him, the main event was set to start in fifteen minutes in the open-air *arena*, which was nothing more than a crude oval of mud, ringed with recycled aluminum football bleachers. It was *the* main event on the last day of the Fair, and C found himself wanting to be as far away from *that* as he could.

He wasn't sure how long he walked, or what else he actually passed along the way, lost in sulky thought and surrounded by flashing lights, bells, whistles and the general din of people talking, screaming and laughing amongst themselves, all blurred into one.

He heard none of it. He was only brought to, startled, by the relative quiet of where his feet landed.

Before him was a large open air barn, hanging heavy with the aroma of hay and manure, away from the maddening crowd. He thought of Earl; he'd be in heaven smelling all this cow shit. A low, staccato mix of tired grunts, bleats and snorts emanated from a long line of cages and chicken-wire pens lining each side of the barn, with a wide straw path down the center. Goats, alpacas, rabbits, pigs and turkeys spread like the sea before him, a motley crew, all with some sort of ribbon hanging on the wire....blues, whites and reds: *First In Class, Third In Division, Best Show, Special Honors;* it seemed everyone was a winner, except the sorry animals stuck in small cages.

Depressing for them, and him. He felt like opening all the cages, en masse, and letting them go; anywhere had to be better than here, except, he guessed, the slaughterhouse. Actually, maybe that was better; at least it would get it over with, and be an end to *this*.

He walked over and read a handwritten sign on the chicken-wire enclosure of a large pig, with a satiny, clean coat of white hair, and an oversized pale-pink nose, wet, giving his name and details about his breed, his age and other arcane facts only other pig-growers cared about. Maybe he was the next *Fred*; soon to be abandoned when he got too big, ate too much, or simply became a bother. Then he too would be cast aside, scared and hungry, hunted in a fish bowl by peasant parents and their ignorant offspring, or maybe just butchered for breakfast bacon. He looked at the winner's ribbon stuck to the pig's pen, grabbed the polyester and rubbed it between his fingers, and shook his head in disgust. Somehow, he didn't think that pig felt much like a winner.

His thoughts turned to Mae, and her determination to beat some other old lady in Brookfield with flowers in some cryptic division; he couldn't remember the flowers, or the lady, or the division. What a crock of shit he remembered thinking it all was when Mae first told him the story, him half-listening and pretending to care just so he could tag that pussy, hard. Christ, that seemed forever ago. He wondered if she ever won, or even competed at all. He wondered more about that busy, little pussy of hers, and if his cock was that last one to punch it. He was sure it was. He started to obsess about fucking her; it sure would be nice to have a taste of that again, right about now. He had such a good, easy gig; she would serve it up whenever he wanted it, and, in hindsight, she set the expectations bar just about ground level. C shook his head at the blown chance for such low-hanging fruit; such was his lot.

And for some reason, his mind wandered to thoughts of Kristine.

Well, it really wasn't just for *some* reason; whenever he was sad, or lonely, or melancholy, or simply wished to taste, to feel, the innocence before the mess that became his life, before the puppet, cricket and flies, he would think of Kristine. In times like this, she was, without fail, his go-to, a security blanket – the one thing in his life seemingly immune to corruption. He thought of her like this maybe once a week, maybe once a month, or a quarter, but it was a constant; for thirty-plus years, it stayed with him, one of the few good things that did. Nah, it was the *only* good thing that did.

To him, she was what life could have been had he not climbed that fence. And, usually, failing all else, it made him smile. Kristine always had the ability to make him smile.

He hoped she was still alive; over the last few years, for some reason, he had a sinking feeling that she had died....he didn't know why he started to think that way, it just happened, and he was usually right about such things. He hoped he was wrong. He hoped, at this very moment, as he stared down the main alley in this God-forsaken barn, at the alpacas and rabbits and goats and the white pig who all wished they too were somewhere else, anywhere but here, that she was alive and well, wandering somewhere on this same planet.   And he hoped that she was happy, that her life turned out *happy*. And wouldn't it be cool if she somehow still remembered him, and thought about him, even just once. He wondered....

"Pretty stupid huh?"

He let go of the pig's ribbon, slowly spun and saw her standing behind him, holding a blue ribbon, as if she was embarrassed. And he felt his heart sink into his shoes.

"I know that's what you were thinking, probably thinking that about me, a ridiculous ribbon for nothing; that's if you ever even think about me? Do you?"

He just stared at her; she looked thinner than the last time he saw her, her face a bit sunken, her body a bit slumped, as if the weight of the world rest on her shoulders.

"What, not gonna talk to me?"

"Not sure what to say."

C said quietly.

"Don't say anything; safer for you that way."

C just shook his head and turned to walk away.

"You're just gonna walk away....*again*?"

"What do you want me to do, apologize? As if that would help; as if you'd even believe it anyway."

"How about say....no forget it."

Mae quietly reached into her pocketbook.

"Just do me a favor, a small one, nothing much; it won't take too much of your time. Just read something, that's all, that's it....one and done, and then you can be on your way."

And with that, Mae pulled out a white envelope, sealed, with his first name neatly written on the front. He glanced at the envelope in her hand, and it appeared to be trembling, but maybe he just imagined it. C sat on a hay bale, just outside the pig pen; she sat on another, beside his, but not too close, a respectable distance kept, as strangers do.

"I wrote this the day….well, you know the day, more to myself than anything, cathartic. Never really thought I'd ever see you again to give it to you, not that I wanted to see you. And certainly wouldn't mail it, so I figured I'd hold onto it, carry it around with me, till the day I finally felt like throwing it away, throwing you away. But, now, maybe, you can read it instead."

The cavernous barn was empty, except for the two of them, the low clicks, grunts, nickers and murmurs of the caged animals and the overlying aroma of hay, mixed with manure. Life at the carnival continued somewhere out there, beyond the barn.

C just stared empty at the crisp, white envelope; he didn't want to open it.

"Go ahead, I'm sure you can guess what it says."

"Then why read it?"

He said, deflated.

"Because you owe me that, at least that, don't you think?"

C stared at her, and he saw a hurt, broken, old woman, trying her best not to look old, broken and hurt.

He sliced open the white envelope with his pointer.

"I want you to read it aloud. I wrote it and then sealed the envelope; I'd like to hear what I had to say three weeks ago, which was a lifetime ago when it comes to the subject of you; my words, from your mouth."

Cord didn't argue; he simply did as he was told, in a low monotone.

Dear Cord:

I'll be surprised if you ever read this; it's more for me than you.

I wanted to address it to Mr. Brin, or C, but couldn't do either; neither one felt right.

I'm an old woman, I know that. And I guess I have to accept that; that's the hard part.

And I've had my fair share of disappointments and sorrow and heartache, like most do, over the years. And being in the business I chose, I have been surrounded my whole adult life by phony people; liars, cheats, and suck-ups.

I guess I'm one too.

But, given that, I can honestly say I have never met a man as hurtful, selfish and uncaring as you, never; yet wrapped in a package that, on the surface, seems so promising.

Utter indifference…it's far worse than any other feeling you can have toward someone. And in that category, you are the champion.

You have succeeded in making me feel old and worthless….something I had never really felt before, until I met you.

I wonder if you'll ever think of me? I wonder if you'll ever call me, or come see me, or apologize, or explain, or anything? I doubt it.

You'll just disappear, and move on, as if I never existed; something to fuck, till you couldn't anymore.

That's my guess; I bet I'm right.

And your endless proclamations that you will eventually disappoint do not absolve you; it doesn't give you permission to treat people badly. It's simply not that easy, although for you, maybe it is.

I should have never allowed myself to have feelings for you. But true feelings have a life of their own; it's not something you can turn on and off, not if you really care. And I really cared.

My biggest mistake.

As hurtful as it sounds, I truly wish I had never met you that day at Sam's; in many ways, it was the worst day of my life. And I hope I never meet someone like you again; I can only take this feeling once.

Believe it or not, I hope you someday find the happiness that eludes you. And please, don't treat anyone ever again the way you treated me....utter indifference.

Mae Edna Bastet

He finished, folded the single sheet and hit the paper lightly against his thigh, just once, without saying a word. He carefully placed it in the envelope, handing it back to her with a blank face. Her eyes were a bit red, but she wasn't crying.

"If I said I was sorry, you wouldn't believe me anyway, even if it was the truth."

She stared at him, and as much as she tried to prevent it, the first tear dropped from her left eye, and slowly tracked her cheek. She was mad that he got to see her cry.

"Mae, I'm sorry; I had no idea that was your daughter."

"It didn't matter that she was my daughter, you weren't supposed to…."

"I know, I know. I'm….I was mad at Lilly for what she just did to me, and Margery was mad at her boyfriend, and it just happened. It wasn't planned, it wasn't….anything. I just went there to be by myself, to lift, honest; I've never even spoken to her, or seen her, since."

"I know, she told me."

Mae said blank, as she stared at Cord, sitting so close, yet a world away.

"Well, in a strange way, you did me a favor; I'm actually talking to my daughter again, thanks to you *[Mae snorted a bit, and shook her head negative at the irony]*. And she told me it was her, not you, that started it, and you were both feeling lousy, and it just happened. She thinks you're a nice guy, and I should give you a break, forgive you. Guess she really *doesn't* know you."

C just frowned in agreement.

"Guess not."

Cord gently pulled the blue ribbon from Mae's grasp.

"So, you beat that woman you told me about?"

"Yeah, I did. Proud of me?"

C smiled small at her.

"Yeah, I am."

Mae didn't smile in return.

"She didn't even place, no ribbon at all. Her name was Arlene Schelling, by the way; I know you don't remember that. I won for my roses – *Class 16* – they're the only ones I entered. Just wasn't much in the mood, you know, but I would've won for my gladiolas too, easy, and probably my zinnias. Anyway, it's all stupid; it's what old ladies do, when they have nothing else to do. It doesn't really matter much; it doesn't matter at all.

"Did you come alone, or with Margery?"

C asked, to which Mae snorted a quasi-laugh.

"Were talking, a bit, but not quite up to hanging out together, you know, ideal mother/daughter thing….not yet anyway. But hopefully, maybe, some day; that would be nice. Maybe, at least, I'll thank you some day for that.   I came with Ms. Klein and a couple other women, but they're over looking at the quilts, or something, and I just wandered away; don't know how I ended up in the animal barn, not really my area. Maybe it was fate *[Mae said sarcastically];* what do you think?"

"Maybe."

C said, monotone, looking her in the eyes.

"Never expected to see you here; are you alone?   Fat chance."

Mae answered herself.

"Well, yes and no; I came with Lilly and Earl, Marty, Carol, Buck and Ji-Sue, but they all scattered and left me standing, you know, ditched me. So, yeah, I'm alone, I guess."

"Are you dating?"

Mae winced a bit at asking the question.

"No, I wasn't before, and still not; better that way, for everyone."

Mae shook her head in silent agreement.

"Well, I guess I should be going, find the girls. It was nice seeing you, it was. Please keep the letter."

Mae handed it to him, and he took it without argument, folded it twice, and slipped it in his pocket. She smiled forlorn and walked away. And he didn't think before he spoke.

"I know it doesn't mean much, but, if you'd like, maybe we can just, kinda, walk around together."

He knew that was the perfect set-up for her to say no, and make herself feel better. And he was willing to fall on that little sword.

Mae stopped about ten feet from him, but didn't turn around. She didn't make a sound, but she didn't have to, he could see her shoulders heaving, just barely. He got up and gently hugged her from behind, and could feel the hurt. He spun her around, and her cheeks were wet. He hugged her again, warmer, but her arms were limp by his sides.

"Listen, I know what I am; you were right, and could've been a lot harder on me. I deserve it, all of it. Why don't we just hang out together for awhile and enjoy each other's company, okay, like we used to. For all the bad, I was, sometimes, fun to be around, right?"

She frowned, knowing he already knew the answer was yes. He kissed her gently on the cheek.

"Come on, let's make some memories, good ones for once, for us, at this goofy County Fair, just you and me.

Forget about all the crummy stuff I did, for awhile anyway; you know, let's enjoy that *promising package* I pretend to be....deal?"

"Deal."

Was all she said, looking up at him with a face pleading not to be made, yet again, the fool.

CHAPTER 210 – A WHORE HE *DEFINITELY* WAS

"I like it, it's good, but it's nothing special."

"*Nothing special?* I think they're the best! And I can't believe they're here! I haven't seen them for years….*years*! Not the real ones, anyway. How funny is that, to find them here, in a farm field. You know, I had one for the first time on my very first date; well, the first date I ever kissed a boy. Funny, his name was Mike, and we went to a movie called *Three Guys Named Mike;* don't remember much about the movie, but wow, what a date….we held hands the whole movie!"

C smiled at how excited Mae was, retelling the story.

"When was that?"

Mae looked at him, like she was letting on a big secret.

"1951! Jesus, can you believe it? I just turned eleven; it was in the Spring and I wore my favorite dress….it was yellow, all frilly."

Mae popped another *almond roca* candy in her mouth. Then switched gears.

"You know, I passed you when you were running, with Lillian, the other day."

"Oh yeah, must have been before she dusted me."

"You were just leaving Town."

"Yeah, that would be before."

C said, shaking his head. Then he added a thought.

"Surprised you didn't run me over."

"I thought about it."

Mae said, with a wry smile.

"If you'd run me over, it would have been better than how that run felt, bad, after that God-awful run. But thanks anyway, for not running me over."

C playfully squeezed her shoulder. And Mae found herself smiling, happy again, for the first time in three long weeks.

"You know, I just decided, just now, we're gonna be good friends again, you and me."

She declared unilateral.

"Oh yeah?"

C said, half-believing the broadcast, like the doomed declarations on the first day of a diet.

"Yeah, just without the fringe benefits."

That got his attention.

"What do you mean?"

It was a whine, more than anything else.

"I mean I like you too much, and I'm getting old, and I've decided time spent with you is better than time without you; and if this is how is has to be, for it to work, then so be it....deal?"

C looked like a lost dog.

"You mean I'm gonna have to be sexually responsible?"

He whimpered, with a mock incredulous look.

"Yep."

"I'm not sure if I've ever been responsible, sexually; it already doesn't feel right."

She smiled at him.

"*The greatest test of courage is to bear defeat without losing heart;* ever hear that saying?"

Mae asked, sprite.

"No, and I don't particularly like it."

C answered, short.

"Well how about this one: *suck it up, sister!*"

Mae playfully taunted; she liked being in control again, for once, for now, at least for a little while.

"Well, now that I know I can't have it, that's gonna be all I want; now I'm gonna obsess about it!   This is a problem."

"Good; it would be nice for you to obsess a bit, about me."

She squeezed his butt.

"I bet you miss that butt, now don't ya? Could show it to ya, if you want? Right here, right now; wanna see?"

"No thanks, I'm enjoying the candy."

Mae said, strutting beside him, popping another *roca.*

"You're a little bitch, Mae, but you know I like that, and I like a challenge. Okay, you got a deal, because I don't want to give you up either, I really don't; I missed you."

C gently cupped her cheek with his hand.

"Really?"

She said, her face aglow.

"Of course. Can we fool around now?"

She pulled away, and he laughed.

"Seriously, I *love* hanging with you; it's not *all* about the sex, I'm not that much of a whore….please!"

C said, matter-of-fact, but couldn't keep a straight face for long. And they both laughed at that one.

A whore he *definitely* was.